Hillstation

Hillstation

ROBIN MUKHERJEE

Oldcastle Books

First published in 2016 by
Oldcastle Books Ltd,
PO Box 394, Harpenden,
Herts, AL5 1XJ
oldcastlebooks.com

Editor: Kesh Naidoo

ISBNs
978-1-84344-742-9 (print)
978-1-84344-743-6 (epub)
978-1-84344-744-3 (kindle)
978-1-84344-745-0 (pdf)

2 4 6 8 10 9 7 5 3 1

Typeset by Avocet Typeset, Somerton, Somerset TA11 6RT
in 12pt Garamond MT
Printed in Great Britain by Clays Ltd, St Ives plc

Thanks are due to many for the genesis and fruition of this book. So, a bow to Ion Mills, Claire Watts and Clare Quinlivan at Oldcastle Books, and to Kesh Naidoo my editor – without you this wouldn't be. I must also thank Tony Dinner who taught me about writing, and Harry Quinton who taught me about life. Thanks also to Neil Taylor who believed in *Hillstation* from the start, and to my family here for all their support. Finally, my thanks to all the great souls from Charu Rekha, and their families, who gave me sweets, hugs, and a place to call home. This book is for all of you.

1

IN THE VILLAGE WHERE I grew up everybody was either a god or a goddess. Rama, The Omnipotent Face of Cosmic Consciousness, ran the tobacco kiosk. Across the road, Brahma, The Supreme Creator Of All Beings, shoes peppered with crimson spittle, did a roaring trade in betel leaves. Saraswati, The Goddess of Wisdom, swept the dust of our houses from one room to the other, while Divine Lakshmi, Consort of the Heavens, made yak's wool hats that itched your head and never quite lost the smell of yak however much you beat them. But the greatest of all deities was Mahadev, meaning 'The Greatest Of All Deities'. He was a Doctor and had been to England. I called him Dev, an omission of syllables for which our father used to clip my ear over supper. Dev himself never seemed to mind. And me? Well, I was Rabindra, the Sun-god. Rabin for short. I blazed in the heavens and did as I was told.

Mahadev was the pride of our family since there's not a lot in this world to be more proud of than having a son who has been to England and is a Doctor. Although Father never missed an opportunity to mention it, Dev was a little more diffident, shrugging modestly whenever so introduced.Still, he practised his art with an assiduousness that did credit to his training. His white coat, freshly ironed by my sisters at the beginning of each day, would come back crumpled and stained by the end of it, sometimes from the various liquids used for his private research into the application of alcohol for sterilisation purposes, and sometimes by the practice, which he assured me was a peculiarly English affectation, of wiping his nose on his sleeve.

I must admit that sometimes I wished it had been me who'd gone to England and become a Doctor, except that a family like ours could only afford the one ticket, plus I was too stupid. And so, however much I might have dreamed of personal glories in that little bit of the heart where personal glories are dreamed of, Dev was the Number One Son and the Number One Son goes to England. The Number Two Son cleans up after him and speaks when he's spoken to.

Pol used to laugh at me. Pol was my closest friend in the sense that I didn't have any others. He'd catch me sometimes wondering how it might have been if I'd been the Number One Son or if Dev had simply never existed.

'What sort of a universe would it be,' he'd tease, 'without The Greatest Of All Gods? A directionless potage of meaningless nonsense jostling about for no good purpose.'

'But at least I'd have gone to England.'

'This is mere fancy!' he'd retort. 'For the very existence of a universe implies the pre-existence of its impelling cause, in the absence of which there would be no England for you to go to, even if you existed which you wouldn't, at least in a tangibly manifest form.'

'Sometimes,' I said once, 'we can take our names too seriously.' And he had stopped laughing for a while.

Pol was among the very few in our village who wasn't named after a god, the others being his two brothers and four – or was it five? – sisters. Pol's father was not only low-born but a self-declared atheist, which made him even lower than low-born. He was also the richest man in the village, a fact regarded as further proof, if it were needed, of his spiritual degeneracy.

Sometimes the snow-capped mountains glistening in the afternoon sun felt like a prison. Even their lilting streams trickling down the green foothills seemed to laugh at me as I kicked at their stones. In the winter, with its cold fog seeping through the clammy hollowness of my heart, they felt like a grave.

Pol and I would often sneak up to the pastures after work. We had long agreed that leaving home was the only way to find ultimate happiness if, indeed, it was ultimate happiness that we sought. I thought an aeroplane would do the trick. We could see their silver beads circling the sky above us, a trail of pale feathers thinning in the blue air behind them. And though we knew there was an airstrip somewhere on the plains below, we also knew we could never muster the bus fare, never mind a ticket to England. Pol thought a credible alternative was to spiritually transcend our personal identifications and unite with the Absolute Being that was both nowhere and everywhere. It annoyed me sometimes that he tried to resolve any discomfort, mental or physical, with metaphysics. I kept telling him that as a low-born he had no business with all that. He'd reply that he was making a start and, in a thousand lives or so, would have earned his thread, the sacred symbol of Brahminical purity that tickled my chest, and which I used to get told off for sucking. He'd poke at mine and say if I wasn't careful, in a thousand lives or so I'd end up like him or worse. 'What could be worse?' I'd say. 'My father,' he'd answer. And we'd both laugh

On other days those daunting peaks, each a reminder that our little twitch of life was hardly a snow-flake on the timeless folds of their mighty flanks, offered a kind of solace. We'd gaze from scented banks of wild flowers at a sky that could have been anywhere. Then we'd chase each other round the trees, our laughter bouncing across the mountains in fading jolts like the final arguments of a dying advocate. And perhaps that is what Pol meant by transcendence. Forgetting who you are and to whom you belong; a momentary ease of the sweet, sharp ache for a life you would never live.

In winter it was harder to get up there. Even our seasoned wood collectors could stray in the fog, their weeping families waiting for Spring when they could shoo the crows from an eyeless face gazing darkly back at a scuff mark on some precipitous ledge.

So far as my father was concerned, Pol was forbidden company. He would rail over supper sometimes if he suspected I'd met him somehow. I was never sure what gave me away, a smile on my face perhaps. Even Dev, though he was incapable of being cross for very long, felt obliged to chide me when I crept in late.

'Pol is not of our caste,' he'd intone, solemnly. 'And if you consort with him again I shall be obliged to inform our revered Pater.'

To be honest, I quite liked it when Dev told me off, his already-polished accent growing so sharp you could slice a mango with it, while his voice, deepened after the English manner, would plummet another five keys, breathy vowels pouncing softly on the trembling air.

'Talk to me of England,' I would say sometimes, lounging on his bed, at the end of a long day, Dev glancing round from the text-books on his desk.

His room, I thought, must be the grandest bedroom in all of Pushkara. Not only was it the largest room in our house but Dev had made it a shrine to all things English, with fabulous posters of red buses, policemen with blue temples on their heads and the secret underground city, connected with coloured tunnels, that lies beneath the London most people know. Sometimes I'd pick through his display of Limited Edition Kings and Queens of England Egg Cups or his Isle of Sheppey Summer Festival Souvenir Mugs. Most striking was the great flag pinned over his door with its dizzy stripes flashing in all directions like an accidental sniff of Entonox. This was the gaudy emblem of the United Kingdom, also known as Great Britain, The British Isles, The Yookay, or simply 'England, Scotland, Wales and Northern Ireland'. He tried to explain it all to me once but I could never make sense of it.

'Rabin,' he'd sigh, 'have I not already told you all there is to tell?'

'Tell me again,' I'd plead, 'about the University of Oxford Street and the River Thames on foggy mornings, of Sherlock Holmes who knew a Lemon Tree when he saw one, the bridge that splits in half, the market where cockneys flog their petticoats half to death, and the rhyming slang you learnt from an orphaned pick-pocket in the back-alleys of a rat-infested slum.'

And he would smile wistfully, eyes turned to the distant rhapsody of remembered lands.

And once I said, 'Tell me about English girls.'

Over supper that evening, Father's mood seemed especially severe. Had I seen Pol that day, yesterday or, for that matter, any other day within the past twelve months? When? Where? And what did we get up to?

I told him we'd met by chance after clinic and wandered up to the hills to chase rabbits.

'And your chores?' he demanded. 'Neglected, obviously, or you wouldn't have time to associate with untouchables while your sisters toil their finger to its bone and your beloved brother, bless his sacred name, keeps the village alive with unyielding diligence.'

'They were done,' I replied.

'Sloppily, no doubt,' grunted Father. 'I know your sort. Idly doing as little as you can, wishing you'd done what you had to do when you had the chance to do it, but too late, you did that which you should not have done and now you pay the price!'

'Please, Father,' I said, mopping water from the table where he'd thumped it, 'I can assure you that everything is clean and tidy for tomorrow.'

Father looked at Dev for confirmation but Dev was picking his teeth, brows furrowed with concentration.

'I know what is meant by "clean and tidy",' Father growled. 'Everything heaped into drawers after a cursory wipe from some grubby cloth you washed the floors with. Has no instruction dawned in that obstinate darkness you call a brain? Microbes and filth. That is the enemy.' Father stared at me. 'Or are you a friend now to microbes and filth? Do you run off to frolic in the hills with microbes and filth? Well?'

My sisters gazed at their plates.

'Dev has often explained to me the importance of clinical hygiene,' I said.

'*Maha*dev,' said Father, lifting his hand.

'If the tools are not properly sterilised…' I continued.

'Instruments,' sighed Dev, looking up now. 'Really, Rabindra, they are more properly called instruments. Carpenters use tools. Doctors use instruments.'

'Anyway,' said Father, impatiently now, 'never mind tools and instruments. What's this about girls?'

My sisters gasped.

'Girls?' I said.

Father laid his fishbone beside his plate with a deliberation that rarely signalled impending levity. 'You asked Mahadev about girls,' he said.

One of my sisters started sobbing so loudly she had to leave the table.

'Um, I don't know,' I said. 'We were talking about various things, anything really, and the question sort of popped out.'

'Sort of?' he spluttered. 'What is this "sort of"? Is it a word? A phrase? Does it have anything to do with even the minimum standards of linguistic dignity expected in this household? Hnn?'

It was probably something I'd heard Pol use. Pol would have got it from his father who might have heard it on the plains where he went to do business. But you didn't mention the city on the plains in good company, certainly not over supper and never in the same breath as any reference, whatever the context, to Pol's father, so I said nothing.

'If you are interested in girls,' said Father, 'we shall find you one. After all, you are twenty now. That's almost a man.'

'Twenty two,' I corrected.

'It is more than years that maketh us', he snarled, quoting, I supposed, some ancient phrase the context of which was long forgotten.

Mother didn't say anything because she was dead. But I wondered what she might have said if she hadn't been. Once, in her last year, she had gripped my hand, whispering in the breathless voice she had towards the end, 'Rabin my sweet, if you do one sensible thing in your life, marry the person you love, not some insufferable idiot who farts at night.' And I'd noticed a tear in her eye, which I brushed away because she no longer had the strength to do it herself.

I don't know why Dev had told Father that I'd asked about girls. I expect he was just trying to do the right thing, although Father might have instructed him to mention it the moment I gave any indication of a readiness for matrimony. It was village wisdom that marrying too early could result in the failure to procreate while marrying too late bred only resentment. Just a few years ago, one of the Gupta sons had been wedded before he'd properly understood why men and women get together at night. She became a regular visitor to the clinic where Dev performed every test he could think of but still couldn't fathom why she hadn't conceived. I personally took her temperature once a week for three months, carefully noting the results which Dev would cross-reference with fluctuations in her blood pressure. Nothing was out of the ordinary. A couple of times he asked me to measure her ankles just in case. I remember the embarrassment as she lifted her sari.

'I am so sorry,' I said, trying to apply the tape-measure without touching her, 'but this is a critical and most instructive test by which, I am sure, my brother will finally establish the cause of your failure to reproduce.'

At which she cried pitifully.

Her husband was furious when he found out that Dev had let me perform the tests, turning up with his mother, father, brother, sisters, uncles, aunts and other assorted members of the family who huffed indignantly behind him on the doorstep while he declared that he'd paid for a Doctor not the Clinic Skivvy and had therefore been swindled. Dev pointed out that under his expert tutelage I was now qualified to carry out a wide variety of examinations and that he alone had been responsible for their interpretation.

In fact Dev was allowing me to do more and more in the clinic these days, my duties extending to lancing boils, ear-examinations, eye-examinations, skin-scrapes and the holding of urine samples up to the light to see if there was anything odd about them. He even allowed me to choose the medication if I thought someone looked pale, sweaty or not quite themselves today. It made me a lot busier but allowed him to use his time more profitably, as he put it, furthering his important research.

In the end, it was that year's holy man who had sorted the Guptas out. We'd get holy men turning up every few years after a sign-post on the plains had fallen over and been incorrectly resurrected. They'd arrive in search of some hallowed shrine on the other side of the hills, demanding their promised abode by the sacred well. When their mistake was pointed out they usually declared that destiny had led them here until, after a month or so, they'd realise that it hadn't.

But that year's holy man had been quite helpful. The young Guptas offered him alms of various kinds before asking if he could bless them with progeny. He recited a few prayers, lit a fire, and sprinkled them with flowers. The results, however, had been disappointing. They offered him sweets, jewels and money. He blessed them, their families, their ancestors and, more to the point, their descendants. But not a sausage emerged from the dubious fertility of their respective loins. At last, the young Mr Gupta marched up to the holy man's cave and denounced him as a fraud. The holy man took a well-aimed swing at Mr Gupta and knocked him off his feet. Mr Gupta jumped up and threw a punch at the holy man who dodged it nimbly, spinning round to deliver another fearsome thump. Mrs Gupta, shrieking by now, grabbed the holy man's hair, yanking out a couple of tufts, any attachment to which he promptly renounced. Mr Gupta, bruised and dispirited, sat down to weep. Mrs Gupta, shocked by this display of unmanliness, hit him over the head saying what sort of a husband is it who can't even get his wife pregnant. Mr Gupta wailed that the gods must have cursed him for some ugly secret in her family undeclared in the matrimonial preliminaries. She said any ugly secrets were more likely to be in his stinking, rotten family than hers. In a moment of divine insight the holy man said do you have sex? They stared at him.

Nine months later she had a baby.

How he knew about sex, being a holy man, is a mystery. But perhaps holy men have knowledge even of things they aren't allowed to do. At any rate, she was a lot more cheerful after that and so was her husband.

The fact is, even without my prompting, Dev had often raised the subject of English girls, especially on those evenings when the effects of his research were most apparent. He would flick a toy taxi across his desk, rambling variously about the sharp sticks attached to their shoes which made them wobble as they walk, or skirts that come so far above the knee that their knee is no longer the most interesting thing about them. He talked of their soft voices, how they look you in the eyes, and how many of them become educated and even get proper jobs. Above all, he'd say, zooming a little aeroplane around his lampshade, they were ridiculously beautiful with long limbs and pale skin, a bit thin by Indian standards but ravishing nevertheless. And once, after a particularly rigorous research session, he said that English girls didn't require marriage as a prerequisite for sexual congress.

It might have been this thought which triggered off a seismic shift in my consciousness, or it might have happened anyway.

Pol and I could never decide which, but over the span of a single summer, what might have been a blur in the farthest reaches of our peripheral vision suddenly had the effect of jerking our heads round so forcibly that our necks hurt. An afternoon breeze, tugging playfully at the slender hem of an embroidered sari walking in front of us, would become the only visible thing in the universe. Whereas before it might have seemed effortless to nod and say good morning to the baker's daughter or the weaver's sister, suddenly it was all we could do to breathe. If any of these feminine apparitions actually spoke to us, the rushing noise in our ears rendered us incapable of hearing, while a gelatinous paralysis of our mouths left any sort of reply out of the question. And even when there wasn't a girl in sight, idle thoughts that might have wandered aimlessly over any old thing began to swerve violently towards the single, throbbing, oddly uncomfortable and entirely imaginary conjuration, based largely on guess-work with a little help from Dev's anatomy books, of a girl with no clothes on.

And so our talks, as we strolled up to the meadows or sat in the caves, changed inexorably from the best way to sneak up on a rabbit to whether Jasminda or Chocha provided the greater level of sensory intoxication. Uncomfortable as it was, we accepted the unsolicited arrival of carnal desire as something that eventually happens to everyone, even girls. And it wasn't too hard to work out that if you had the same effect on a particular girl as she had on you, then you were in trouble. Unless your respective parents approved, in which case it was marigolds all round.

Although I wasn't entirely ineligible, such prospects as I had were largely derived from my proximity to Dev. As a Doctor who had been to England he was the apogee of matrimonial desirability, the coveted prize of every high-born family, though he had thus far resisted their many propositions. As his brother, I might have satisfied most second sisters, but such were the aspirations of all sisters that I had either to wait until he'd made his decision, or settle for one whose resentments at the implicit failure would tarnish any hope of marital accord. Dev's argument was that a man of his stature required a properly educated wife, which is to say, from the plains. That no sensible family from the plains would consign their daughter, however ugly, to the hills meant a celibacy for Dev to which he seemed placidly resolved.

Pol stood by the cave-mouth picking stones from the wall. The bats had started to fly in and out, speckling the light with fidgeting silhouettes. For me, the sudden uprush of hormonal disquiet was merely another source of frustration. For Pol it was a catastrophic obstacle to his quest for spiritual perfection.

'All I wanted,' he moaned, 'was to meditate, do my *pujas* and not become like my father. But now the mind, like a tempestuous horse, races off in all directions to wallow in lascivious images of ankles, bangles and the hair over Kula Nabwar's shoulders.'

'Her skin!' I sighed, imagining its smooth undulations under my fumbling fingers.

Pol looked round, a liquid shape against the sky. 'It was in some previous life,' he said, 'that we turned our thoughts to the transient pleasures of the material world. A moment, that's all it took. Some footling thing. And now we must pine for liberty while our souls thrash helplessly in lurid chains of insidious discontent.'

'Yes,' I said, shifting the moss under my head. 'I expect that's it.'

Pol was dark-skinned as befitted his birth. He had a thin moustache which his father would have liked him to grow thicker though I'm not sure that was an option at this time. How can you be taken seriously in business, Malek Bister would say, without a decent moustache? His hair was another battle-ground, Pol preferring it tidy while Malek insisted he tussle it like a movie star. The fact that Pol cared at all about his inner being was a major source of irritation to his father who took great pleasure in declaring, preferably with elders in earshot, that there was no such thing.

Pol slumped back against the wall. 'We just have to accept,' he sighed, 'that we have becomes slaves to lust and the heinous consequences thereof.'

'Which is quite spiritual, isn't it?' I offered.

'What is?'

'Accepting the consequences.'

'If we have the strength,' he said after a while. 'Think about it. Marriage, family, the years of unremitting toil. To climb from the stained shame of a conjugal bed, slouching to work for a few meagre rupees, staggering home again to rage at nothing, the supper late, our slippers cold, and then, as night falls, to squirm before our demons, not least among which is the dream of how it might have been. Once a week we shall satisfy our wives. And once a month we shall become so inebriated that she beats us with a broom. And in this manner shall the days of our lives unfold as youth, joy and the tender aspirations of our early years bleed to nothing and we die.'

'I wouldn't object to marrying Jasminda Biswas,' I said, 'but the only reason her parents even talk to me is because they half-suspect that Dev fancies her so, really, I don't stand a chance.'

Pol turned slowly back to the sky.

'And as for you,' I said. 'Who's desperate enough to marry a Bister? You'd be lucky to get the squinty one with bad breath.'

'Your remarks,' he said, lifting a spider from the wall, 'are sometimes less constructive than you think.' He let the spider crawl back. 'It is true that our prospects are not high, but don't you see?' He looked at me earnestly. 'The uglier she is, the more stupid and unpleasant, the more useless and ungrateful, the greater our chances of spiritual transcendence. For what do the scriptures, and just about every holy man who ever came here looking for somewhere else, say? Through suffering alone is liberation possible. So let us agree, Rabindra, to find the worst possible wives, to spawn the worst possible children, to live the worst possible lives so that our spirits have no choice but to flap like free birds to the great beyond!'

As I've said, in my opinion merely metaphysical solutions are no solutions at all.

'You suffer if you want to,' I said, 'but I've got other plans.' He moved to speak but I carried on. 'You know Mr Dat? Of course you do. And we all know his wife, Mrs Dat. You can hear them shouting when he gets home at night. And how does he walk? Eyes to the ground. And why's that? I'll tell you: suffering. Is that spiritual?' Pol shook his head. 'And what about your mother?' I demanded. 'Completely mad. Everyone knows that. But why did she go mad? Assuming she wasn't mad to begin with. Because of your father. Because of her marriage. So how does that help her transcend the world of mortal delusion? She's more deluded than anyone I know. And what's the cause of that? I'll tell you again. Suffering.'

Pol studied his shoes in the half-light, then straightened his back. 'I shall marry as the gods decree,' he said. 'The least appealing she is, the more conducive to my inner calm, for there shall be no danger of me ever enjoying a single moment with her, carnal or otherwise. That is my vow.' He jutted his chin out like an ascetic deciding on some terrible penance. 'As the gods will,' he intoned, 'so we act. There is no choice in these things.'

'But are they not,' I said, 'open to persuasion?'

He stared at me.

'And is it not customary,' I continued, 'for people with a particular wish to perform such oblations as may be necessary for the gods to grant it?'

Pol looked out again, stroking the frail strands on his upper lip. 'Only if the wish is lawful,' he said. 'But can it ever be lawful to wish for personal happiness at the expense of one's spiritual prospects?'

'Maybe,' I said, 'maybe not. All I know is that my wish is to marry an English girl.'

He moved his mouth for a moment. 'A what?' he said at last.

'An English girl.'

'But why?' he said.

'Because they are effortlessly beautiful. Because they are elegant, mysterious, and wear peculiar shoes. But most importantly, because they live in England which is where I wish to live, with an English wife, in my English house, doing nothing but English things on a daily English basis.'

'Your father would never send you to England,' said Pol.

'Then she will have to come here. We'll meet by chance and fall in love. Father will be impressed, my brother delighted. They'll sit around discussing whether The Charge of the Lightbulb Brigade was heroic disaster or just plain stupid. And then, once the formalities have been completed, she'll take me home with her.'

He ran his hand through his hair, inadvertently ruffling it. 'How?' he said. 'No English person has ever come here, never mind two English girls looking for husbands. Not in living memory, not in dead memory, never!'

'Exactly,' I said.

He stared at me again.

'Well, think about it. The longer it hasn't happened, the greater the chance of it happening now.'

'That is not the proper application of the laws of probability,' he said, looking at his shoes again. 'Alright,' he said after a while. 'I accept that your wish is an appealing one. But let me tell you, there is no wish less lawful than for what can never be. For if it were the slightest bit lawful the gods would not have made it impossible.'

'Perhaps it is up to us to make it possible.'

'How?' he barked suddenly, his eyes, a little bulgy anyway, threatening to pop out at me.

'In the traditional manner, through sacrifice and austerities,' I said calmly. 'We'll light fires, burn some butter, recite a few prayers and, if it please the gods, they'll grant our wish.'

Pol began to walk in circles. 'And if this desire is not lawful?' he asked. 'I mean, inherently sinful, devious or malicious.'

'Then they won't grant it.'

'They will punish us.'

'What could be worse,' I said, 'than staying here for the rest of our lives?'

He twined his fingers nervously. A bird called from outside. Then he took a breath and sat down. 'No,' he said. 'I am resolved. God willing, I shall marry some local harridan nobody else in their right mind could possibly want. If we cannot find one here, then my father will make enquiries in the city on the plains. Those with a shortage of decorative features, brains and modesty are in plentiful supply down there, by all accounts, and generally available. The dowry will not concern us. But if I marry an English girl...' A vein on his temple began to throb. 'I shall never be free of the bad Sanskara that has rendered me an outcast. Happy yes, but never free.' He folded his arms with the finality of one so flattered by the sound of his own argument he no longer cares if it's right.

'No-one doubts,' I said, 'that you must have done some pretty dreadful things in a previous embodiment to earn such a bad one this time around. But if you really want to make up for it, what greater sacrifice could there be than to imperil your soul for the sake of a friend?'

'Perhaps,' he retorted, 'to imperil a friend for the sake of his soul.'

'Well, good luck,' I said a little tartly. 'No doubt you'll be happy to come back as a temple monkey.'

'It was not my intention,' he answered quietly, 'to aim so high.'

'The fact is,' I said, 'you've read the Vedas, you've studied the rites. If I tried reciting prayers, the gods would send me back to school. I'm asking you, for my own personal happiness, even at the expense of my future embodiments, please.'

He remained motionless.

'I'll invite you to my wedding,' I said.

'I would not be allowed at your wedding,' he replied

'The reception?'

'We'd still need a Brahmin,' he said, 'even if I performed the rites.'

'I'm a Brahmin.'

He stared at the sky, stared at the floor, took a deep breath and said. 'Very well, if that is your wish.'

And so we began.

Over the next few weeks Pol devoted himself with all the zeal characteristic of those for whom the road to enlightenment runs via discomfort. He took to wearing the itchiest clothes he could find, eating nothing but vegetables and drinking only water. He spent hours at night reciting the *Mahabharata*, the *Ramayana* and even verses from the *Vivekachumadi*. His Father stopped me in the streets one morning.

'What have you done to my son?' he said, jabbing at me with a cigar. 'Poisoning his mind with all this Brahminical shit. I caught him in the bathroom yesterday trying to stick his leg round his neck.'

'Your shadow is on my foot,' I said.

'Huh?'

'It is not proper for a low-born shadow to cross a high-born foot.'

At which he marched off, muttering.

My contribution was to wash more thoroughly and to bow each morning to the little effigy of Ganesh, the elephant-headed god, on our mantelpiece. It is Ganesh, after all, who imposes and removes obstacles and, since the obstacles to my finding an English wife included, among other things, an eight-hour drive from a city foreigners rarely visit, plus the many thousands of miles she'd have to cross even to get that far, I reckoned he was worth a few nods.

I also refrained from eating meat which worried my father who was of the opinion that red meat enhances virility and if I was to get married it wouldn't do to be non-virile at the very moment when such things are most called for. He consulted Dev about this. Dev consulted his text-books and, after a few days' research, advised my father that vegetarianism was not inconsistent with Hindu practice which had done the Indian people well enough over the centuries. Father asked if 'well enough' included getting our arses thrashed by the British who ate nothing but meat all day and invented guns. This rather upset Dev who didn't like to hear ill spoken of the people who'd taught him to be a Doctor. After which Father, feeling contrite, expunged the remainder of his rage in my direction by telling me that every family he'd approached on my behalf had slammed the door in his face.

Each evening, after sweeping the floor and putting the instruments in a tub of hot water to soak, I would close up the large front doors of the clinic and head off towards the mountains. The clinic was at the lowest end of the village, near the bus stop. The mountain road, with its teasing glimpses of a world beyond, ran from the other side, along the high street, past the shops and houses from which people would call me over sometimes, asking for a little more of whatever it was I'd given them last time. Perhaps their rash had returned or their grandmother's disposition was still cantankerous. More recently some of them had taken to making fatuous remarks along the lines of 'no daughter of mine would be seen dead marrying a Clinic Skivvy', and I would make a mental note to give them something for constipation, whether they had it or not. But at last, leaving the houses behind, my breath would catch a little as the road turned sharply upwards, hard stone giving way to dusty dirt, the sides growing precipitous, as the distant slopes across the valley stretched into haze, veiled in the silver shrouds of early evening.

Pol would be waiting for me with a crackling fire and some tasty samosas from his mother's kitchen. Just as I worked for my brother, as a menial in the clinic, so Pol worked in his father's various business ventures. Although Malek Bister had started out with a simple scooter repair shop, he had soon expanded to saris, foodstuffs, jewellery and domestic accessories, taking advantage of his frequent visits to the plains to buy in bulk and undercut the competition. The collective fury this provoked in the village was not, however, merely the result of failed shops, bankruptcy and destitution. Although Brahmins are genetically obliged to look down on merchants, it is the privilege of merchants to look down on everyone else. That a low-born outcast should have engaged in commercial activities was seen by many as imperilling the spiritual equilibrium of the entire village. For proof, they pointed to the growing divisions among them since, while many vowed never to buy a single item from the tainted shelves of a Bister retail outlet, others found the prices a bit too tempting.

But what caused the most outrage was his 'cynical attempt to emulate the natural philanthropy of his betters', as it was put one evening at an angry village meeting, with the construction of a new village hall, 'on his own land, from his own design and with his own bloody money' as he riposted at the very same meeting. Thereafter, The Sri Malek Bister Memorial Hall had continued to be a source of acrimony, particularly between the musicians who would have liked to play there and the elders who forbade it. Eventually after several hikes in the price of petrol that Malek was forced to institute 'in order to recover the costs of his civic munificence', it was agreed that a concert would be held. To Malek's delight, the first recital, a classical performance on the Rudra Veena, had taken place to a sizeable audience though some of the elders refused to turn up and one or two walked out during his opening speech. For various reasons the concert itself had not been a success, and the hall, thereafter, had remained closed. At any rate, Pol was at liberty to exploit the diversity of his father's enterprise since nobody knew, at any time of day, which of the many premises he was in.

We had decided that, along with Ganesh, the principal deity to whom we should direct our sacrifice was Parvati, whose strenuous efforts to win the heart of a beloved would, we hoped, naturally dispose her towards a couple of mortals struggling to meet theirs. Pol kneaded an effigy from river mud, with a tuft of hair from his own head, a tubby belly and voluptuous breasts, which is how Indians like their goddesses. In the meantime, I made a simple shrine with stones gathered from around the cave on a little plateau by the entrance. Pol doubted that Parvati would be impressed with flowers collected from the meadows but the repetitive purchase of marigolds from the village shops might have aroused suspicions. I hoped that the sincerity of our offerings would compensate for the fact that we hadn't paid for them. Along with some ghee, rice and the earnestness of Pol's prayers, we reckoned we had everything necessary for even the most intransigent deity to take pity on us. Personally, I was a bit sceptical in spite of my early assurances. I had no doubt that gods existed, either as abstract representations of natural phenomena or as quasi-tangible beings in some heavenly abode, but either way I feared their reaction to our supplications might fall somewhere between ambivalence and scorn.

Pol's fervour reached its crescendo on what we had agreed would be the last evening of our penance. He even brought a knife suggesting we add some blood to the fire, but I thought that was going a bit far. His chanting had grown softer but more powerful over the weeks. Sometimes I could almost believe there was a point to all this as I watched him pray, eyes closed, swaying gently, a flare of burning ghee lighting his face with momentary incandescence. Untouchable or not, I thought, there was something about him in that moment that made the moment sacred. We walked home in silence, the first of the stars peeking out through the darkening sky, our rituals complete, penances done, mantras recited. All we could do now was wait.

The next day, a bank of clouds draped the peaks with plumes of ominous purple. Even Mr Dat glanced up briefly and shuddered. As night fell, a thick mist began to finger its way into our houses. Outside, the sky was darker than anyone could remember. Elders muttered. Children hid. And then the mountains flashed with spears of white. A moment later, the sky roared, the valleys shook, dogs barked, ornaments toppled over and people spontaneously expostulated Vedic aphorisms. After which it rained. For three torrential hours the heavens wept their rage over the sodden streets, washing a muddy river into living rooms as distracted wives dashed about their bobbing furniture exhorting husbands to do something about it. Father sloshed around with a bucket saying this was just typical, though of what he wouldn't elaborate. Dev retreated to his room. My sisters prostrated themselves in front of Ganesh promising to be good. I looked out from my bedroom window and wondered if this was the answer to our prayers or the sound of gods laughing.

By morning it was quiet again. And two days after that our English wives turned up. Which, I suppose, only goes to show.

2

THAT THE BUS HAD BEEN arriving once a month ever since I could remember made its arrival once a month no less exciting. Spluttering up the hill, it would cough to a halt beside the old Bodhi tree, bags and boxes lashed precariously to its roof as chickens and sheep peered from their rickety cages unaware that the man who greeted them so warmly was the restaurateur. Apart from ferrying people around the hamlets that speckled the hills beneath us, it would sometimes bring goods from the city ordered by some of our more enterprising retailers, and carry away small quantities of our village produce. Pushkara was known mainly for its yak's wool hats, reputedly among the least itchy in all of India, a special concoction of bats' droppings distributed to herbalists in the South, and a piquant tea, popular with the cognoscenti of the village but spat out, generally, by those who didn't know any better. More recently, Bister's Brocades had become a significant export, described by Malek as a speciality re-labelling service by which garments purchased from the city had their labels replaced with odd-sounding alternatives such as 'Gucci', 'Versace' or 'Pierre Cardin', and sold back for six times the original price. In spite of Pol's repeated attempts to explain it to me, I had concluded that retail would forever remain a pursuit that defied reason.

Once the doors had been wrenched open, visiting uncles

would brace themselves for the onrush of elated relatives, while the driver retired with a bidi, leaving the shopkeepers to scramble over his intractable knots. Scrawled across the side of the bus, in blue and yellow letters, was the phrase, which I always thought slightly paradoxical, 'Long Live Brahman The Immortal!'.

Pol's father was usually waiting with a clipboard and his clerk, Mr Chatterjee, to find out how much of his cargo had gone missing on the way. Mr Chatterjee enjoyed being out of the office since it gave him a chance to talk to people. In fact, Mr Chatterjee loved talking to anyone whether they were listening or not, the latter being more likely since his universal ex-communication on the grounds of working for Malek. Even at home, simple questions to his wife such as, 'what about these socks?' were met with a stony silence. He tried talking to himself for a while, but found the predictability of response frustrating. Now he only talked to himself with others present which was, at least, communication of a kind.

On this occasion he was trying to ascertain why a batch of saris had mysteriously, if not unexpectedly, failed to appear. The more vehement his inquisition, however, the more nonchalantly the driver, puffing on his stick, slipped into that blessed equilibrium wherein no amount of berating from Mr Chatterjee, or anyone else for that matter, held any meaning. Sometimes Malek would jump up and down shouting, 'I know what you're up to, you stinking bloody thief.' Which only made the driver smile more.

I had gone to collect some medicines I'd ordered from the Pharmaceutical Rep who came to the clinic from time to time. We'd run perilously low on fruit pastes after an especially virulent outbreak of foot fungus, while our re-useable mouth swabs had all but lost that essential fluffiness with which they came endowed. I was checking my list when something struck me as odd. Everything had gone suddenly quiet. Even the children, who had scampered through its plumes of blue smoke, stood in mute clusters staring at the bus. Malek Bister, hitherto in mid-tirade against all those thieving bastards along the road who were now the proud owners of premium saris they'd bloody well filched, had stopped abruptly, the cigar falling out of his mouth.

A man was standing by the steps, gazing round with a face like nothing I'd ever seen before. It had two eyes, obviously, and the mouth common to most human beings, and animals too I suppose, but there the similarity ended. His hair, neither black, henna nor any recognisable colour, was an indistinct shade of stale chapatti. His blotchy skin, where it hadn't peeled, was pink and wet. He was portly like a businessman, his crumpled white suit patched with darker shades under the armpits, a frayed blue shirt open at the collar. He mopped his forehead with a handkerchief, glanced back at the bus and said, 'Yeah, I think this is it.'

A gasp rippled round as a female face emerged through the doors, though one couldn't see much of it behind sunglasses so large she resembled a fly. Thick tresses of black hair cascaded over her shoulders, while the long fingers with which she clutched the hand-rail were tipped with nails of brilliant crimson. Her shoes were an ethereal matrix of white straps with, I noticed thrillingly, sticks on the underside, although they made negotiating the steps a careful process. Her dress billowed lightly, muscular calves undulating as her foot touched the dusty ground, so blessing the village, its denizens and the mountains around us for all eternity.

She stared at the first few houses that marked the outer tendrils of the village and pushed her glasses up. Faces flinched from the dazzle of her eyes. 'Mike?' she said in a rich, throaty voice.

'What?' said the man she'd called Mike.

'You've got to be joking.'

'Joke? Moi?' he said, dabbing at his cheeks.

'So where is this, exactly?' she asked, pulling a cigarette from her handbag.

'Push something. I don't know. Pushmepullyou.' But his attention had been taken by someone nearby. 'Hey,' he said, pointing.

People drew back nervously as his finger lanced a gap through the crowd leaving Malek Bister in the middle. Malek looked helplessly at the retreating villagers and said in a quavering voice, 'I don't know. Who is this man? I've never seen him before.'

'Malek,' said Mike, walking towards him, 'how are you? What's going on?'

'Yes,' said Malek, creasing his face into the imitation of a grin. 'Yes indeed. Ha ha.'

'So where's the hotel, I mean, you got a car for us? What's happening?'

'Ah...' said Malek, flapping at his pockets for a cigar. 'Yes. Indeed. Well, that's... that's very...'

'It was a crap drive,' said Mike. 'So we're all a bit knackered. We had people sitting on top of us. Fat gits and everything. Even the girls.'

Malek spotted the cigar he'd dropped and bent to pick it up.

As if to show how it could be done beautifully, the black-haired woman blew a silver stream of smoke into the air. 'So where's the rest of it?' she said.

'The rest of what?' said Mike.

'This place. Pushme whatsit.'

'Well, it's a mountain resort, isn't it?' said Mike. 'So I guess it's over that bit of mountain, round that bit of mountain, over the other side of that bloody great heap of mountains over there. This is the outskirts. Okay? What do you get on the outskirts? The bus station. What do you get in a bus station? Buses.'

'One bus,' she said.

'So they're out and about,' said Mike.

'And who's this?' she said, nodding at Malek.

'He's the bloke I told you about,' said Mike.

'Mr Bister,' said Malek trying to light his cigar with shaking hands. 'At your service.'

'You're kidding me,' she said, looking at Mike.

But before I had a chance to ponder why she continued to suppose jocularity in a man whose demeanour suggested anything but, another gasp rippled out from the rapidly gathering crowd of villagers. A second lady had emerged even more startling than the first with hair so fiery red that I wondered, for a moment, if it wasn't in fact on fire. It was pushed up in ragged tufts through a tattered band of yellow cloth. Large rings of jade and silver undulated from her ears. Her blue jeans were so tight that movement would have seemed impossible had she not descended in slow, graceful steps to the ground where she stood at last, smoothing her white blouse, jaws grinding. Several ladies put their hands over their eyes and some over those of their husbands.

'I don't know,' she said, 'I think it's cute.'

At that moment, two leaves, dislodged from the tree by no apparent means, fluttered down to my feet. And suddenly it was clear to me. Two leaves from the same tree. Separate and yet connected. A single being with separate and yet connected aspects of the one tree-ness, as we are all separate and yet connected leaves of the one tree. Actually that part wasn't entirely clear but what I did understand, with absolute certainty, was that Pol's wife had arrived with mine. In fact, she was either the flame-headed chewing one in tight trousers or a third lady who had just poked her head out scowling, her strong face wreathed in blonde hair, the wafting gauze of a petticoat shimmering over powerful thighs as she clambered down the steps. Several husbands were now being marched off to their respective homes as yet another pale hand groped its way towards the rail. I didn't see what apparition this presaged – except that it seemed to be large and hairy – since I was already hurtling up the road to share the news with Pol.

The downside of nobody ever quite knowing where Pol was at any given time was that neither did I. After waking everybody up in the scooter repair centre and bumping into the sales assistant from Bister's Boutique creeping out the back with a bundle in her hands, I eventually found him at home with his mother.

'It's under my bed!' she screamed as I ran in. 'Take the money. But leave my last child, I beg of you, that it may comfort me in the twilight of my lonely life. Oh sickness that steals the tender seed of joy leaving only the bitter crusts of desolation for us to weep, to weep!'

'We all died of cholera,' sighed Pol.

Vidya Bister was a pretty lady with a graceful face, much admired by the gentlemen of the village, but quite mad. Her family history, in reality perfectly normal, was variously reinvented to include evil step-parents, rapacious husbands and psychotic children. Sometimes Pol had been kidnapped by thieves and sometimes he had just attempted to strangle her, depending on the novel she happened to be reading at the time. Convinced that the nobility of any credible heroine was equivalent only to the depths of her melancholy, she would stroll the streets, sighing forlornly through the sweet delirium of inconsolable distress as she gazed at the mountains that alone held the secrets of her lost love, family tragedy or cruel twist of fate.

'Murderer!' she shouted, lunging at Pol. 'Flesh of my flesh! A dagger to my heart! What do I care of life when my children are dead, dead, dead…?' Her voice tailed off as she flopped back on the divan.

By this time I'd got my breath back and was able to say a bit more than, 'Pol! Pol!' in an over-excited manner. 'They're here,' I gasped.

'Who?' he said.

'Our wives. They came on the bus.'

'From where?' he said.

'From England,' I said, 'Where do you think?'

'How?'

'I've just told you. On the bus.'

When we got to the turning circle, however, they'd gone. For a moment Pol squinted at me, suspecting perhaps that I'd gone as mad as his mother. But they'd left a trail of animated villagers, some of whom had seen them arrive and others who wanted to know all about it. One or two retailers were trumpeting the first wave of an unprecedented tourist boom while several elders thought it the arrival of demons. One stall-holder said they could be the appendages of Ravana for all he cared, so long as their money was good. Which led to some heated discussions. I gave the driver a prod to see if he knew where they'd gone but he just waved at me irritably. Eventually we learned that a party of three English women, two English men and some large English boxes had been taken to the Hotel Nirvana, and that Malek

Bister was in some way connected so it had to be bad.

The Hotel Nirvana was a crumbling edifice of tilting windows and sloping walls on the corner of two streets that lurched steeply in different directions. Much of the back had fallen away in consecutive monsoons, leaving several doors opening vertiginously to a pile of rubble that used to be the en suite. It was run by a Tibetan lady called Mrs Dong, and her cook, a Buddhist monk, who prepared its food on the toilet floor. The clientele, such as it was, consisted of an occasional trader from the plains, gentlemen of the village temporarily exiled for some domestic infraction and, reputedly at any rate, the drinking den that didn't exist.

From time to time I'd book the 'Dalai Lama Suite' for the Pharmaceutical Rep which, being at the front, still had its bathroom intact. Dev refused to trifle with inventory, but I rather enjoyed picking medicines with a satisfying resonance such as 'Diazepam', 'Tryptophan' and my favourite, 'Naftidrofuryl'. I would also order one or two of the latest 'must-haves', usually new remedies for old complaints like warts and colitis or precautionary treatments for ailments not yet evident in the village though pandemic elsewhere, such as Epidermodysplasia Veruciformis, plus new socks for winter evenings when the clinic got a bit chilly. In exchange for our loyalty we'd sometimes get free gifts, the most recent being a valuable ashtray embossed with the company logo, which promptly disappeared from the waiting room after I'd put it there for all to see.

'This is my fault,' sobbed Pol, digging his heels in the ground as I dragged him down the street. 'I have desecrated the ancient rites and brought a plague upon us.'

'Just wait 'til you see them,' I chuckled. 'Listen, Pol,' I lowered my voice as a couple of elders glanced towards us.

'I can understand that you're feeling a bit nervous, especially as you're not exactly presentable at the moment having spent much of the morning, if my nose is correct, chasing cockroaches out of the spice bins. But if you don't want to meet them right now, at least you'll forgive me if I mention you.'

'Don't!' he shouted with a level of hysteria reminiscent of his mother. 'It is said that my father has something to do with this. The gods perhaps, but my father undoubtedly. We need to find out what he knows. After that, you have my word, I shall come with you.'

Malek was sitting in their spacious lounge with his head in his hands. Mrs Bister could be heard in the kitchen throwing pots around. They had long ago put anything breakable under lock and key, so the worst she could do was dent some pans or smash the occasional window.

A cigar curled threads of haze from an ashtray on the table.

'Father?' said Pol.

Malek didn't move. A smashing sound came from the kitchen.

'Father?' said Pol again, 'Whatever troubles we may have, they can be overcome with humility and trust.'

'I don't believe in karma,' said Malek, staring at the floor, 'And I don't believe in gods.'

Pol shrugged apologetically towards the ceiling.

'You know what I believe in?' said Malek leaving us a little space in which to decide that we didn't. 'Hard work and thinking straight. That's what. Hard work and thinking straight.' He savoured the words for a moment. 'And do you know what else? Do you?'

'Tell me, Father,' said Pol, quietly.

'Luck!' he said looking up with a grin, which quickly

disappeared when he saw me. 'Oh, what an honour,' he sneered. 'The Brahmin. So long as he doesn't mind the shadow of my low-born occasional table falling on his high-born bloody foot.'

'Please Father,' said Pol, drawing him back to the point, 'Tell me about luck.'

'Huh?' said Malek, 'Oh, yes, luck.' He stood up. 'I'll tell you about luck. Ha ha.' He circled the table, lighting a fresh cigar. 'You're on the plains, yes? On the plains doing some business. Some bloody business. I'll tell you about business. What do these bloody people with their stinking tea know about business? Huh?'

'I expect they know nothing,' said Pol, patiently.

'They don't even know that,' said Malek triumphantly. 'But I can make business,' he stubbed his cigar next to the ashtray, 'from nothing. From Nothing!'

'And a bit of luck,' said Pol.

'What are you talking about, luck?' Malek glared at his son, lighting another cigar. 'Luck has nothing to do with it. Everyone sits on their arse waiting for luck. But you have to get off that arse and make your luck. That's luck. That's business.' He breathed out heavily and sat down again.

'But on the plains,' prompted Pol, 'what happened there?'

Malek grunted. 'Ah, yes, the plains. Well, alright, there I was, doing my business, staying in that tatty shit-hole I inexpensively stay in when I'm on the plains doing my business! And what should happen? Hm? An Englishman. That's what happened. In the bar. Well, so what? I've seen Englishmen before. You think I haven't but I have. Your brother, Maha-la-di-da, drinking tea with the Queen, well I've met them all. English, Dutch, French... and... and all sorts.' He pulled on his cigar having, I suspected, run out of countries he knew the names of. 'Not that they talk to you. Obviously. They read their bloody guide-books and hope you'll go away. Well, I am not an idiot. I go away. They can have their mausoleums and colourful bloody markets and the railway timetables they'd cocked up big time or they wouldn't be there in the first place. But this man. Well, this man…' He blew some smoke out to join the rest of it above his head. 'He wanted to talk. Now, if somebody wants to talk, I'll talk. If they don't mind my low-born bloody shadow falling on their high-born bloody glass of English whisky, I'll talk 'til morning. Which we did.' He leaned round to adjust the pillows behind him.

'What did you talk about?' said Pol.

'Everything. Anything,' said Malek kicking his slippers off and settling back. Pol and I glanced at each other. If his father was beginning to feel a nap coming on we had to act fast.

'For instance?' I said.

'For instance what?' mumbled Malek.

'Did you talk of anything in particular?'

'History,' he said, resting his chin on his chest.

'The history of what?' asked Pol knocking a chair slightly to make a noise.

'India,' said Malek, straightening a little. 'Where else has any sort of history worth talking about? And do you know what he thinks?'

'I have never met him,' said Pol, 'so I cannot.'

'I said he's English,' grunted Malek, 'so obviously he thinks we're a bunch of idiots. He said they did us a favour teaching us how to wear clothes and read. I told him they'd have done us a favour by shooting the bloody snobs like they did everywhere else.'

'Mr Bister,' I interrupted, 'what has this to do with him coming to Pushkara?'

'Did I say it was him who came to Pushkara?' said Malek. 'I said I met an Englishman in a brothel and then an Englishman comes here and what do you do, you put two and two together and make five!'

'A what?' said Pol.

Malek blinked for a moment. 'I didn't say that,' he shouted. 'Why would I say that? Clearly you have something wrong with your ears. Somebody says something and you hear something else entirely. It's ridiculous. I met him in that grubby little piss-pot I stay in because I do not wish to squander the inheritance of my progeny. But yes, he is the man who came here. You are right but for the wrong reasons. For no reasons. You just threw a wild fact into the air and hoped it would fall butter-side up. And you call that clever, you people, it's no wonder this country's such a bloody mess.'

'So it was him who came here?' I confirmed.

'Plus,' said Malek, 'once you receive a fact you can't help turning it over and over to see if it remains a fact however much you turn it, until it's hardly a fact at all, just a filthy, grubby thing in your sweaty little hands.'

'So why has he come here?' asked Pol.

'I was getting to that!' said Malek fishing his cigar from the ashtray. 'He was impressed, obviously.'

'By what?' said Pol.

'Well,' chortled Malek, 'it's not everyday you meet somebody famous.'

'Who?' said Pol.

'The founder of the Sri Malek Bister Memorial Entertainment Complex, of course,' said Malek. 'Who do you think?'

'You mean the village hall?' said Pol.

'To men of vision,' said Malek thumping the table and making us jump, 'a thing is not just what it is but what it might be. A hall, yes, for now. But in years to come, who knows? Of course I did not boast. Why should I boast? Do you suppose that I boasted?' He glared, challenging me to suppose it. I shook my head. 'I merely informed him of it. That is all. And he was impressed because he knows a man of vision when he sees one.'

'So you told him what, exactly?' asked Pol.

'They will see,' he said waving his hands to the world at large. 'You will see,' he said to me personally. 'Men of vision. Men of art. They get together and what happens? Art and vision. That's what. Rudra bloody Veena. I know your game. One note every ten minutes, everyone dying of boredom. But now we shall have it all. Music and dance. And why?' He chuckled again. 'Men of vision. That's why.' He picked up his empty whisky glass and drained it anyway, leaning back with hooded eyes.

'What sort of music' said Pol, a bit confused now, 'and who will be dancing?'

'Aha,' said Malek, smiling mysteriously as he drifted at last into a sleep from which nothing we said could rouse him.

'No, no, no,' said Pol as I grabbed his hand and pulled him through the door. 'It would not be appropriate. Rabindra, please, by the celestial deity after which you are named…'

'I am not a deity,' I said, recalling a recent comment by my father. 'I'm just a boiling cloud of hot gas.'

'Without which every plant would perish and every stray dog would die and what would become of us then with nothing to eat?' said Pol trying to get his other hand round my wrist.

'Since when do you eat stray dogs?' I said, gripping tighter.

'These are just figurative illustrations,' said Pol using his fingernails now to scratch at me. I let go and laughed.

'Come on,' I said. 'Our wives await us.'

'Of that I have no doubt,' he said breathing heavily. 'And for that very reason I ask only that we act with propriety. Think, please, Rabindra. You can't just rush in and sweep her off to your conjugal boudoir.'

'Why not?'

'Formalities,' he gasped. 'Your father must be informed of your intentions. Her father must be informed of your intentions. After which, via some carefully selected intermediary, she herself will have to be informed of your intentions.'

'If I swept her off to my conjugal boudoir,' I said, 'I don't think my intentions would be much in doubt.'

But I knew what he meant. The last thing we wanted was elders meddling on the grounds that we hadn't followed procedure. But I was also concerned that Father's response would more likely be, 'Why would she want to marry a Clinic Skivvy when there's a first-born Doctor who has been to England knocking about?' A question to which I had no answer. Why indeed would she opt for a life of drudge and vicarious derision when she could sit around all day being attended to by my sisters? The gods might have delivered our destiny but they hadn't changed human nature for all the millennia in which they'd tried.

Pol seemed to read my thoughts. 'I doubt your father will have heard of this yet,' he said.

'I should think everyone has.'

'Not so,' he countered. 'For we all know that Pushkarans are slow to accept that which they have not personally verified. Those who witnessed the arrival will therefore be unlikely to communicate it widely for fear of ridicule.'

'Except…' I said.

He looked at me.

A vision flashed through my head of all the people in Malek's enterprises who'd stared at me as I burst in shouting, 'Where's Pol? Our English wives have arrived on the bus!'

Pol put his hands to his temples, a gesture he'd developed to signify too many thoughts jostling in a limited space. 'Though you are named,' he said quietly, 'after the flaming orb of the day, and I am referred to as some daft nonsense that doesn't mean anything, please listen to what I have to say.'

'I'm listening,' I said.

'We have reached,' he continued, 'a critical juncture in our lives. On the one hand: our destiny, which is to say the ultimate glory to which our hearts aspire. On the other: fate, being the miserable unfolding of our past mistakes to their desultory conclusion.' He glanced round at a sudden noise, but it was only the mango-seller trundling his empty cart. 'So we need to stop and think, the purpose of which being, almost invariably, to work out which of the two anything happens to be.'

'But gifts are different,' I said. 'Especially from gods. You don't have to think about them. They're just there. So come on. Why are we haggling over the niceties of karma when our wives await us?'

He stared towards the Hotel.

'Alright,' I said. 'We'll go and see my brother. For, as they say, impetuosity is the thief of caution, not that I can think of anyone who's ever said that apart from me, but anyway. As a Doctor who has been to England, he can advise us on their courtship formalities along with the cosmic implications of whatever it is we decide to do. I shall explain that our brides have come here for the sole purpose of uniting with their beloveds. They are therefore not in search of Doctors or any other, let us say, more premium candidates. He will give us his blessings after which we'll be free to sweep them off to our respective boudoirs or wherever it is betrothed people sweep each other off to. How does that sound?'

I always found the waiting room a little strange when it was empty, as I did when it was full. The one desolate, the other seething as if there were two rooms in different universes that had nothing to do with each other. Even the framed picture of Her Majesty the Queen smiling at Dev, which was our proudest possession and, indeed, the pride of the village, seemed oddly futile with nobody around to be humbled. The various health notices, some of which had been removed on the grounds that there is no need to warn people of activities they would otherwise know nothing about, hung to no edifying purpose, though they covered some cracks in the wall which was their other principal function. I still missed the one about syphilis. My bulk purchase of condoms in advance of the expected rush had been among my least successful clinical acquisitions, although they came in handy for other things.

The seats had been arranged in strict rows after one of our patients, Mrs Mukapadhyay, had been rudely sniggered at by a group of workers from the plantation. That her husband's book on the conceptual basis of astrological forecast had failed to find a publisher was common knowledge, but it was the cruel remark that 'he'd failed to forecast that, hadn't he?' which drove her to flee in tears. The elders had decided that if the castes had to mix, we should at least prevent the baser ones from talking amongst themselves. Sniggering is, after all, a collective activity and therefore difficult to accomplish with your mouth shut facing the front. In spite of a notice to that effect, they gathered anyway, in the corners and by the door, sniggering to their heart's content, so potent is the urge, I suppose, for those discredited by birth to discredit others. It was something I had always thought vaguely understandable, though the term 'Clinic Skivvy' had been coined in just such a caucus.

'I think he's in there,' said Pol, indicating the door to Dev's office.

'How do you know?' I asked.

'I heard a bottle topple over, roll across the table, bump a glass out of the way and fall to the floor.' Years of living with his mother had made Pol an expert on the sound of breakages.

I pressed my ear to the door, but all I could hear was silence.

'He must be conducting experiments,' I said.

Pol snorted. 'Try knocking.'

'I can't,' I said. 'It is forbidden to disturb him in the middle of his research.'

'The pursuit of destiny,' said Pol, thumping on the door in spite of my attempts to restrain him, 'is to do that which, ordinarily, one cannot.'

After a moment we heard a low moan.

'Revered brother?' I called gently.

'Go away,' answered Dev.

I shrugged at Pol but he pushed my face to the door.

'Mahadev?' I said, mouth pressed to the keyhole, 'the clinic would seem to be closed.'

'Who cares?' said Dev.

'I think people who need a Doctor might care,' hissed Pol, pulling me aside. 'Mahadev, Doctor Sahib, this is Pol Bister.'

'Hello, Pol,' said Dev. 'How are you?'

'I'm fine, thank you very much.'

'Then you don't need a Doctor, do you? So piss off.'

Pol's face reddened slightly. I gently nudged him aside.

'My most noble brother,' I said, 'by virtue of diverse supplications to the gods, I'm happy to report that our English brides have arrived safely. There is also a third one, oddly, both numerically of course, but also in the sense that we hadn't asked for her. It may be that she has come to marry Pushkara's most eligible bachelor, which is to say my handsome and distinguished elder brother who has been to England and is a Doctor. You may wish to know that she is quite striking in appearance and would, I am certain, make for an agreeable wife.'

Something thudded against the door under which, after a moment, an amber puddle of sterilisation fluid began to seep.

Pol turned back to the entrance while I sat down in a 'Brahmins Only' chair.

'I have often said,' I said, though in truth I probably hadn't, 'that the gods are cruel.'

'Yes,' said Pol.

'That they toy with us as we toy with flies.'

'I didn't know you toyed with flies,' said Pol.

'Well, I don't. But then I'm not a god.'

'You are not cruel,' said Pol, picking at the frayed edge of a 'Do Not Expel Your Nasal Contents Onto The Floor' notice.

'Once the elders meet, it's all over for us,' I said. 'Dev gets first pick, obviously. Then Mr Bhota's son. After that it might go to Jaganath from the bakery or even Ramadev who's a bit old now but gets a decent salary.'

'Did they perform sacrifices?' said Pol. 'Did they endure penances? Did they go without food, sleep on the floor and hold their hands over an open flame?'

'Did we?' I said, slightly shocked.

'Didn't you?'

'Of course,' I mumbled.

He stared at the wall as if to some distant horizon. 'I have always believed,' he said, 'that there is good in all beings which, when confronted by The Good Itself must emerge from all that is bad to greet it.'

I looked at him, sceptically.

'That our wives have come is good,' he continued. 'That we shall speak to them must also be good. Your father, when he sees all this good sloshing around, must surely crawl in his good form through everything that isn't and embrace both the will of the gods, if that had anything to do with it, and the prospect of your happiness.'

'Well,' I said, 'I suppose anything's possible.'

My two sisters were huddled in the sitting room while Father put a tie on, shouting.

'That wretched Bister,' he roared, 'And his wretched hall. We should have burned the damn thing down, with him in it, and jumped on their stinking remains. What's he doing here?' he said, seeing the genetic extension of his nemesis leaning in the doorway.

'I think he lives here,' said Pol missing the point, I suspect, deliberately.

'Father,' I said, 'It is my belief that there is an element, be it ever so small, of what might be called the good in...'

'The only thing Bister's good for,' snorted Father, turning back to his tie, 'is the cheap batter stuffed with floor scrapings and rats droppings he dares to call a samosa.'

My sisters glanced nervously towards the kitchen from which I could smell cooking.

'That hall is closed for a reason,' added Father. 'And closed it will remain. Whether you will or no. It is an outrage, a wart, an architectural obscenity that will be destroyed.' He stared at the ends of his tie having forgotten which was which.

One of my sisters rose to help him. Father's hatred of the Hall had often erupted over supper when there was nothing else to erupt at. He had led both the campaign against its construction and, subsequently, for its demolition, toiling far into the night collecting precedents, *obiter dictums*, and biscuit crumbs under his chair as he ruminated on the downfall of his enemy. That it had remained closed was a source of much satisfaction, even if the reason for that had more to do with Malek Bister's decision to avoid further humiliation than Father's legal prowess.

Although he spent most of the time slouching around the house in a loose dhoti, when Father dressed up he could really look the part. And when he took his glasses off, carefully wiping them on his tie, you could almost believe that he had once been the scourge of the criminal classes in Allahabad. It was in Allahabad, up to his waist one morning in Ganges water, that he had realised two important things. The first was that his home village was in need of a lawyer. The second was that his eldest son, when he had one, would travel to England and come back a Doctor. In commemoration of this epiphany, a postcard from Allahabad was proudly displayed in the clinic waiting room wishing whomsoever beheld it to be there. My sisters helped him on with his coat.

'From now on, Rabindra,' he said, 'you are confined to the house and, in so far as your duties require it, your brother's clinic. Is that understood?'

'Not entirely,' I said.

'What is difficult about this?' he sighed. 'You are not to be seen anywhere else except this house and the clinic.

'But how am I to reach the clinic,' I said, 'except by means of the streets which must surely fall under the designation of "anywhere else"?'

He stamped his feet a little. 'Well, obviously you can walk there and back, you imbecile. But you must do so in such a way as to not be seen. Why is this so tortuous?'

The truth is that a cold sense of apprehension had begun to creep through my bones. If I was confined to the house and clinic, how was I to meet my beloved? Moreover, how many pretenders would queue up in the meantime to protest their superiority, or convince her that my absence was the result of indifference? The answer was probably half the eligible young men in Pushkara.

'But if, as I have heard, there are visitors from England,' I ventured, desperately, 'then surely our family, above all, should be among the first to greet them.'

'You are not to go near them,' he hissed through lips so tight they whitened slightly. 'And how many times,' he said, nodding towards Pol, 'have I told you not to go near him?'

And with that he was out of the door.

It is true that the inaugural concert held to celebrate the opening of the Sri Malek Bister Memorial Hall had been excruciating. Even some of the elders could be seen digging fingernails into their flesh. The performer was Sergeant Shrinivasan, our policeman, who was said to have played the instrument to great acclaim through numerous lifetimes, though less so in this one. In the hands of a lyrical artiste, the Rudra Veena is quite capable of producing lilting melodies. In the hands of Sergeant Shrinivasan this was never going to be the case. He preferred the traditional motif in which a single note, resonating slowly back to the silence from which it came, is followed by another note some time later. Allegros, which is to say two notes played within several minutes of each other, are rare. It is said that by following the drift, as it were, the listener too can melt back to the silence from which all things come. This is all very well if the people around you aren't coughing and snoring. Never has a clock on the wall so longingly been stared at. Never were the hands of time so earnestly beseeched. Never have buttocks been so numbed by the unforgiving rigours of a wooden seat.

Since the Sergeant's usual role conferred on him considerable powers, along with a stiff cane with which to exert them, nobody dared question his artistry. The elders meanwhile, having decreed a strictly classical programme, were obliged to grunt the more ecstatically the more agonising it became. Euphoric croaks of 'ba!' could be heard periodically as they plunged helplessly into the bliss of eternal nothingness. Since this only encouraged the Sergeant to play even more languidly, with every 'ba!' came a chorus of groans from the back row. At one point, I swear the second hand on the clock came to an actual stop. When I remarked on this to Pol, he said that I had evidently entered the blessed realm of undifferentiated timelessness, though I noticed that he too had teeth marks on the back of his hand.

The applause, when Sergeant Shrinivasan finally laid his Veena to one side, was thunderous. Overcome with relief that it was all over, some of the elders even chanced their luck with a traditional and, as it turned out, unfortunate call for an encore. Malek Bister who had persuaded himself, as benefactor, to sit ostentatiously at the front, unable to fidget never mind catch a snooze, vowed never again to let the elders dictate what he did in his own bloody hall built with his own bloody money. And from that day the place had remained closed.

Until now. For, as my sisters explained, a notice had appeared in the glazed box by the front door announcing that 'Coming Soon' would be a 'Renowned Troupe of International Dancers', along with the statement, underlined three times with an exclamation mark, that they were 'Direct From England!'.

My father had been furious for two reasons. The first was that three underlinings and an exclamation mark represented the sort of facile overstatement more characteristic of some backwoods peasant enclave than a village with its own mythology.

'What,' he demanded to know, later that evening, 'will people think of us?'

'That we are a backwoods peasant enclave?' ventured one of my sisters, anxious to further his argument.

'With a place in the scriptures?' he barked. 'With a history that dates back to before there was even history? Have you any idea how long this village, this abode of legends, has nestled here among these hallowed hills? Hmm?'

'Since a very long time, Baba?' suggested my other sister.

'Then why do you say this is just some backwoods peasant enclave?' he demanded.

'But I didn't,' she bleated.

'Then who did?' said Father, glaring at me in case I had. Fortunately he didn't wait too long before getting on to the second thing that annoyed him. The fact that Malek Bister had organised anything at all.

'How dare a man with not a jot, nor a particle, nor the tiniest, most microbial speck of learning presume to opine upon, never mind determine, the shape and substance of our widely respected, nay universally envied cultural programme?' Father took the long, slow breath of an advocate who has just delivered a point so weighty that the heaving of it has left him momentarily enfeebled. When he recovered, however, it was not to argue further but to pass judgment. 'It is clear to all right-minded, clear-thinking people,' he said in the sonorous tones of one whose words cannot be doubted, 'that these so-called "Artistes from England" are nothing but a fraudulent imposition to be dispensed with at the earliest opportunity. Meanwhile, let us remember that that which is not achieved by Proper Procedure is not achieved at all.'

That night I slept fitfully, Father's words circulating endlessly through twisting dreams of sunglasses, petticoats and crimson nails. What, exactly, had he meant by 'procedure'? If the gods had brought our brides to Pushkara, surely they would have arranged for the appropriate visas? Or perhaps this was just another round in the stand-off between Malek and the elders in which Malek never sought permission for anything because they wouldn't have granted it anyway. But where did that leave me? I had tried to explain to Pol that any delay on our part would leave us vulnerable to the exertions of our rivals, but he was in fatalistic mood declaiming the need to trust. There was much talk of karmic inevitability, surrender to universal Will and the unimportance of personal desire in the Grand Scheme of Things. At several junctures I had to work hard to suppress a personal desire to grab him by the scruff of the neck.

'What if the gods are toying with us,' I had said at one point, 'and all this is simply an attempt to make us look stupid?'

'If that is their intention,' he had muttered, 'they needn't have gone to so much trouble.'

Although I set off early the next day, keeping to the backstreets in order to remain unseen, I was constantly accosted with, 'Rabindranath, why do you skulk along the backstreets with a pillow-case over your head?' By the time I abandoned subterfuge and returned to the main road, all I heard was, 'Aha, so you've given up skulking along the backstreets with a pillow-case over your head!' I decided that if my father asked, I could at least say that I'd tried.

When I arrived, finally, it seemed that half the menfolk of Pushkara had fallen inexplicably sick. The queue snaked as far back as the notorious pot-hole, the scene of many a broken bicycle and responsible for much of my clinical endeavours. Several of them were stooping pitifully or holding their heads in pain.

'And what is wrong with you?' I asked Hanuman whose parents sold brass elephants. Normally, of course, I'd wait until I was behind my desk before seeking a diagnosis but, in matters epidemiological, not only is urgency of paramount importance but, conveniently, to ask of one is to prognosticate the many.

'My internal organs,' he groaned, 'are extremely sore.'

'Which organs specifically?' I pressed.

'How should I know?' he retorted. 'Do you want me to get them out so you can have a look?'

Next in the queue was Parasurama, a young man in the company of his wife.

'I have the most terrible nausea,' he winced, pressing his knees together.

'You said it was a headache,' shrilled his good lady. 'So which is it? Or perhaps it is neither. Perhaps it is some other bit of your body that makes you suddenly need to visit the clinic.'

'Please,' I said. 'It is my job to ascertain the whereabouts of his discomfort.'

'I'll tell you the whereabouts,' she hooted. 'It's in his mind. That's where.'

'Are you saying these symptoms are psychosomatic?' I said, hoping to baffle her with arcane scientific terminology.

'I'm saying he's a liar,' she shouted, jabbing him in the stomach.

'That is not quite the same,' I said as he bent forward groaning. 'What you are possibly referring to is "Munchausen Syndrome", a condition to which people of the Germanic continent are particularly susceptible.'

'And this... this syndrome is what?' she said, flailing at him as he tried to put an arm around her. 'Leering at that which should not be leered at? Lying to your family and skiving off work to satisfy one's carnal curiosities?'

'Well, no. It's mainly about staying indoors and eating too much in order to draw undue attention to oneself,' I said, though to be honest that particular page in the medical dictionary had been one of several abridged by mice.

'He is a married man. I didn't know he had carnal curiosities.' She wiped her nose on a fold of her shawl. 'Perhaps there is something you can give him for that?'

'There is usually something for everything,' I said cautiously. 'And what we don't have, I can order.'

'Well, whatever it is you give him,' she said, waving at the lengthening queue, 'you'll need plenty of it.'

When I managed to push my way through to the waiting room, the first thing I noticed was a widely contagious neurological disorder causing people to stare fixedly, their jaws locked open as they stretched their necks and waved from side to side. In a fleeting moment of clinical excitement, I wondered if we hadn't discovered a new disease. This was something I had often dreamed of as a just reward for Dev's medical explorations. To stand at last on a gilded podium and receive the Noble Prize was something, I knew, that he coveted above all accolades. He had mentioned it one evening after I'd expressed concern that too much research might be slurring his speech and making him clumsy.

'No prize without sacrifice,' he had laughed maniacally. 'If you want those yacht parties and Swedish women, then you've got to put the hours in. You've got to take those hours, every last one of them in your grubby, greasy hands and shove them right in as far as they'll go.'

On another occasion he told me about some of the prize-winners he most admired such as the eminent Dr Watson who had developed a crick in his neck from solving mysteries. 'Observation,' he had tried to explain, though we both knew I struggled a bit with the more rarified echelons of abstract science, 'is the you know of the something or other, which is that, the thing, which it is, you see.'

It struck me that our new discovery might forever be known as 'Dev Sharma Syndrome', or even 'Pushkara Disease'. Doctors would nod sagely at the stiff necks and rigid eyeballs in front of them and say, 'My good fellow, I fear that what you have got is a bad case of the Pushkaras.' Although I could see objections to this. While it was established practice to name ailments after the clinicians who discovered them, I wondered sometimes if it didn't pale after a while to find your name eternally cross-indexed with vomiting. How did the good Doctors Crohn, Elephantitis and Stool feel as yet another hotel receptionist tried not to smirk? Among blessings, scientific renown can be especially mixed.

It was only when I reached the central vortex around which the epidemic swirled that I too was struck by its contagion, my eyes locked open, my jaw hung slack and my limbs refusing to move.

She was sitting in the middle of the room, a simple blue

dress hanging lightly over her legs. Her shoes were black, flat and rather plain. A delicate chime of silver bangles slid back as she raised a hand to brush the hair from her eyes. Standing next to her was the man in the crumpled suit whose name, I remembered, was Mike.

'How much longer, do you reckon?' she said.

He shrugged.

'Bloody goldfish bowl,' she said, after a moment.

'Where?' said Mike.

'Not where. Us.'

'Oh,' he said. 'Yeah.'

The babble of voices hushed abruptly as I stepped forward. Eyes, in spite of their rigidity, swivelled to watch me. Breaths were held, limbs frozen. Even the flies seemed to hover silently in the sultry air. If it wasn't for clinical decorum I would have leapt over to her, laughing and crying, for here she was, my destiny, my beloved, the consummation of my heart's desire, the apogee of all my longings, waiting with a quiet grace and solemn humility I had never seen before in any human being, ever. In this moment hung the fecundity of generations. And I promised never again to doubt the powers of Pol to win celestial favours.

'What?' she said, noticing me.

'Perhaps you would like to come with me,' I said, indicating my office.

'Are you the Doctor?' said Mike.

'Not at all. I am merely the Clinic Skivvy. My brother, who has been to England, is the Doctor. But I can provide you with a preliminary consultation until he is ready to see you,' I thought. What I actually said was, 'Yes of course.'

'I'll see you at the hotel,' said the man.

'You're not waiting?' she said.

He looked around. 'I dunno, there's got to be a drink somewhere in this bloody town.'

'Mountain resort,' she said dryly.

'Yeah,' he said, 'whatever.'

I closed the door and gestured to the chair in front of my desk.

'It is my opinion,' I said, getting one or two matters out of the way, 'that we should not have sex before marriage.'

'Word gets around then,' she said, sitting down.

I opened my diagnosis pad and sharpened a pencil.

'Anyway,' she said, looking at her hands, 'it's not sex, it's acting.'

Dev had often told me that in love nothing makes sense, even things so simple, ordinarily, that they don't have to. Love, he had said, is a distress you never want to end. And though I had found that slightly paradoxical at the time, I was beginning to understand what he meant.

'Anyway,' she added, looking up, 'you've got your opinions and I've got mine. Right now I just need something for the runs.'

'And how long have you had these "Runs"?' I asked, making a note.

'About a week now,' she said. 'Well, it's got worse the last couple of days.'

'And where does it hurt?' I asked.

'It doesn't hurt. It's the runs.'

'Right,' I said, reaching for the medical dictionary with a calm professionalism that never failed to put my patients at their ease. A deft flick of my fingers opened it to the section marked 'R'. I nodded knowingly and began to wend my way through Rabies, Rickets and Rhinitis.

'What are you doing?' she said.

'Rubber Allergy,' I said. 'We're almost there. Oh.'

'What?'

'We've got to "S" without any mention of "The Runs", or even "Runs, The". Still,' I smiled at her, 'let us spare a thought for the good Doctor Rubinstein-Taybi and pray that the disorder to which he lends his name is not too unsightly.'

'What are you talking about?' she said.

Reading the dictionary had long been my favourite part of the consultation, the patients visibly relaxing as I intoned, 'Club Foot, Coccidioidomycosis, Coenuriasis' and finally, 'aha, it seems to me that what you have described is the Common Cold.' If, on this occasion, it only seemed to agitate her, I reminded myself that a little bewilderment in the presence of one's beloved is perfectly natural.

'Perhaps it's a new disease,' I smiled. 'If you like we could name it after you.'

'It's not new,' she said. 'I've had it before. Everyone's had it. Mike was laid up for three days in Bombay with it.'

'Right,' I said, my pencil poised. 'And would you say that your neck is unusually stiff at the moment?'

She stared at me. I made a note of the fact that it might be. 'When in doubt,' Dev had said to me once, 'make a note and gaze into space as if you're thinking of something far away.'

'You know,' she said insistently. 'The Squits.'

I was there in a flash. 'You have a squint?' I said.

'Do I look as if I've got a squint?' she said.

'You have been attacked by a squid?' I said, in a moment of clinical inspiration.

She shook her head.

'I'm sorry,' I said, 'but that is the nearest I can find to what you describe, and to be frank there is nothing in here about squids, that was just a guess. But I suggest that you try focusing your eyes on something in front of you until both of them are pointing in the same direction. Did your parents have a squint?'

'My Dad wore glasses,' she said.

'Then it's more than likely to do with the particularities of your Deoxyribonucleic Acid,' I said. Another thing Dev had impressed upon me was the use of long words that meant nothing to the patient but nevertheless made their condition sound important. 'It is nothing to worry about,' I said. 'We all have some Deoxyribonucleic Acid in us. Though too much of it can sometimes lead to an upset stomach.'

'That's it,' she said. 'It's an upset stomach.'

I leaned back in my chair and smiled. 'You see,' I said. 'Meticulous analysis leads invariably to the correct diagnosis.'

'So what can you give me?' she said.

'How bad is it?' I asked.

'Well, I can't keep anything down, diarrhoea, the usual. Probably ate something, or drank something. I don't know. I think Cindy's getting it, she was looking a bit off this morning.'

'Cindy?'

'Oh, sorry, one of the other dancers.'

'Pol's wife?' I said.

'No. She's not married.'

'Not yet,' I chuckled, 'but let's not get ahead of ourselves. What I suggest you do is eat lots of Chapatis which are excellent for binding.'

'You mean, like roughage?' she said.

'That's exactly the word,' I said, feeling that we had, by now, developed something of a rapport.

'Okay,' she said, 'but don't you have tablets or anything like that?'

'Tablets?' I smiled, waving my arm at the pill store. 'We have many tablets for all sorts of things. But we can't just give them out willy nilly for no reason.'

'My stomach?'

'Um, yes,' I said. 'That might qualify as a reason.'

I got up and walked to the shelves. Pharmacy is largely a science but also, to some extent, an art. Sometimes I arranged the medicines alphabetically and sometimes according to the anatomical regions with which they were concerned. Thus headache remedies were kept with dandruff ointments, verruca pads with corn plasters and so on. I had, quite recently, sorted them according to colour, which was visually harmonious if clinically a bit confusing. But if it is both a science and an art, then it is also, in some unquantifiable way, a matter of luck. There, among the white boxes with green lettering, was a small carton the text of which promised to 'Stop Diarrhoea Fast!'.

'It seems,' I said, 'that we have just the thing.'

I popped the package into a little bag and handed it to her.

'So, what's the dosage?' she said.

'In the box you will find a neatly folded piece of paper with extremely tiny writing. This will tell you what you need to know in as many languages as you need to know it in.'

'Thank you,' she said. 'Is that it?'

'For the moment,' I said. 'I'm sure we'll have a lot more than roughage and diarrhoea to talk about over the coming years.'

'I remember from school,' she said, standing up.

'Remember what?' I said.

'Roughage and all that. We had to draw a picture of a meal and write about vitamins.'

'Ah, yes,' I said, 'vitamins are very important.'

'Yeah, that's what they said.'

I pushed my chair back and stood up. She looked at me for a moment then rustled the bag.

'Well,' she said, 'thanks.'

'Making people better,' I said.

'I beg your pardon?'

'The clinic motto,' I explained. 'Or it would have been if the elders hadn't decided that it overstated our importance.' I shrugged, beginning to get the feeling that we were both, as they say, skirting around the subject.

'Right.' She rustled the bag again and moved to go.

'Do you know,' I said, 'that you have not told me your name?'

'Oh, yes' she said. 'Of course. Sorry. It's Martina. Martina Marvellous.'

'That is a marvellous name,' I quipped but the words had already sunk into the core of my soul, their warm vowels and lilting alliteration like a joyous gasp, a sunny morning waking up together.

'It used to be Norma Stopley,' she said, moving towards the door. 'But hey.'

'I think we ought to acknowledge,' I said, 'that because of your father's affliction there is a high probability that our children may have to wear glasses.'

She looked at me with an expression I couldn't fathom and was gone.

3

MY LITTLE OFFICE HAD NEVER felt so empty, nor so still. Even the hands of time had stopped, though the 'Twelve Things You Need To Know About Flatulence' wall clock had a tendency to do that anyway. I'd once asked a holy man about the feeling you get when a ceremonial elephant passes you on the High Street. 'It is not the parade,' he had answered, 'but the silence it leaves behind.' Which I didn't appreciate at the time, poking my tongue out thinking him too saintly either to throw his shoe or report me to my Father, in both of which I had been wrong. Lazy particles of light tumbled across the window. A cackle of crows rose and fell over the rubbish outside. A crunch of scooters gave way to the sound of raised voices. And yet nothing changed. As if all the movements of the world couldn't ruffle the silence beneath.

I wondered if my inaugural meeting with Martina had gone as well as it might have. Perhaps I'd been too anxious to show off my clinical expertise, like those young men strutting the market place, shirts unbuttoned to the first chest hairs. I thought of all the little spaces in which I should have flung myself across the desk to smother her in kisses. I recalled her look of quizzical bewilderment that seemed to say, 'My love, why are we talking about rectal inflammation when you know what brings me here?' But then again, what did I know of these things? My only romantic encounter thus far had been with an ephemeral woman who turned into a goat when I attempted to fondle her breasts. It wasn't a happy experience and I had woken up considerably embarrassed.

The waiting room was vacant again, everyone having melted to wherever people melt when the object of their fascination has elbowed its way out the door with a few choice words not listed in the Pushkara Lexicon of English Usage. A little thrill coursed through me, quite suddenly, as I wondered how long before I too would melt into the hot bliss of a thousand whispered endearments. Not long, I thought. But then, how long is not long? Today? Tomorrow? What if not long, in Pol's Grand Scheme of Things, is forever to a little fellow wanting only to be with his beloved? In so far as it was in my power to determine how long not long might be in this instance, I decided that I had to move fast.

As usual, however, Pol was impossible to find. His mother pointed to a pillow on the floor.

'That!' she screamed.

'I am sorry to trouble you, Mrs Bister,' I said, 'but I've looked everywhere and nobody seems to know where he is.'

'Oh, he's too clever for that,' she snickered, 'he'll be far away by now, gloating in the luxury of his crimes. That!' she said again pointing at the pillow.

'A pillow?' I said, getting drawn into one of her conversations, something I always vowed never to do again.

'Yes,' she said. 'That's exactly what it is. You're quite observant for someone a little bit dim if you don't mind me saying. To be precise, the pillow he tried to smother me with. My jewels!' She clutched her hair. 'They were all I had to remind me of my great grandfather, the Maharaja, whose lands and titles I would have inherited had it not been for the wickedness of my evil step-brother, may he rot in hell with his fast cars and swimming pools, the scheming bastard.'

'When did this happen?' I asked.

'When I was but a child,' she whispered. 'Innocent as the new-born day.'

'I mean Pol trying to smother you, not the evil step-brother business.'

'I'm not sure.' She fingered her throat. 'I think I may have passed out. Was it a moment ago? I can still feel his murderous hands, and those wicked eyes, devoid of remorse or compassion…' She leaned forward, lank hair flopping across her face. 'He is not my son. This is the truth. Listen to me…'

Sensing a tale epic even by Mrs Bister's standards, I began to edge towards the door.

'You see, I found him,' she glanced nervously towards the window. 'On the night of my lover's untimely demise at the hands of blood-hungry robbers.'

'That's very interesting,' I said, 'but if he turns up, could you tell him I've been looking for him?'

'A bundle of rags, mewling and wriggling by the side of the road. For a moment I thought it was a bundle of rags mewling and wriggling, but then I thought, rags on their own don't.'

'I'm sorry, Mrs Bister,' I said, easing myself into the hall, 'perhaps another time.'

'It was dark. Obviously. I know it gets dark at night, I'm not an idiot, but this was… a darkness beyond darkness.'

'It was nice to see you,' I said, carefully opening the front door.

'And from somewhere distantly a dog howled.'

I heard nothing more except the sound of a tea cup striking the door through which I had just left.

Mr Chatterjee was hurrying down the street with a box of lever-arch files.

'Mr Chatterjee,' I called in a genial but urgent way.

'Young Mr Sharma,' he said, stopping. 'You have correctly identified me on this beautiful morning. And with the early mist cleared by a soothing breeze, are the mountains not revealed in all their majesty? I have often wondered why the mornings are so misty, especially in the bathroom after a shower, unless one wakes up with a fuzzy face!'

I laughed politely.

'Of course,' he continued, 'it might get cloudy later. Or not. Who's to know? That is the thing about the weather. In the end, it will be exactly as it is and there's really nothing we can do about it, whether we want to or not. No pun intended.'

I chuckled again. 'Do you happen to know where Pol is?' I asked.

'Yes, that is a worry,' said Mr Chatterjee, shaking his head. 'I mean, he's a fine young man, don't misunderstand me, but he lacks a certain… I'm not sure what the word is…'

'Being easy to find?' I suggested.

'Indeed,' said Mr Chatterjee. 'Although that's a phrase, I'm afraid. The word itself like its subject proves elusive. You know how it is,' he continued, into his stride now, 'that exact sense you can't quite put your finger on, or at least not its verbal locution, so you go poking about under dusty piles of old clauses…'

I let him carry on as I turned to the mango-seller, Mr Premar, who was passing by with his empty cart.

'Excuse me,' I said, 'have you…?'

'If you're hoping to buy some mangos,' he interjected, 'you're out of luck.'

'Then why do you push that cart?' asked Mr Chatterjee.

'Why do you carry that box?' said Mr Premar, mysteriously, moving on.

'You see, a proper businessman is predictable,' said Mr Chatterjee. 'Take Mr Bister. One always knows where to find him. Sometimes, having found him, one wishes one hadn't but that is beside the point. I'm not saying he's perfect, of course. Who is? And though some people like to think unkindly of him, I have to say that he has always been fair to me. Firm but fair. And if I fall short in my duties from time to time, is it unfair of him to call me a fat-headed hoity toity?'

'I suppose not,' I said, wearily.

'And to administer a curt flick across the top of the aforesaid?'

'He does that?' I said.

'Sometimes with the application of his foot to my rear quarters as I am hurrying out to put a damp cloth over the smarting consequences of the heretofore.'

I stared at him.

'Hope is with the son,' sighed Mr Chatterjee. 'At least I hope so. For can one truly prosper in matters of commerce without kicking people in the bottom? I don't know. Perhaps he is too soft. For instance when I saw him at the Hotel Nirvana a few minutes ago, having gone to ask if I should sort the stock-inventories by traditional means or according to my new index system in spite of the chaos it caused last time, not to mention a sore head and rear end, he said, "Mr Chatterjee, whatever makes you happy". "Do you mean that, young sir?" I replied. "Please," he laughed, "You may call me Pol. It is too ridiculous for someone of an elevated birth to act deferentially towards one who has not only failed thus far to achieve a respectable embodiment but after last night is most unlikely to."'

'The Hotel Nirvana?' I said.

'Indeed. But what a young man of aspirational intent could possibly find there to occupy his attentions...'

The rest of which was lost to me as I hurried down the hill. The Hotel Nirvana was a place which good people were said to avoid. According to Father, its many windows were darker than even the morning sun could pierce. Elders would sometimes mutter about a drinking den though nobody could ever quite say who organised it or how. It was merely observed that some of the men, disappearing from time to time to 'discuss matters', would come back disoriented. One night a small but angry delegation of wives had descended on the hotel to 'catch them at it'. After an hour or so of running up and down the baffling labyrinth of staircases, many of which led to precipitous drops or simply nowhere, they eventually found the men sitting around with cups of tea discussing the difference between moral certainty and phenomenal chance. Some of the wives swore they'd searched that very room when they'd first arrived but the men just shrugged, pointed to their tea and carried on with the discussion. It was rumoured that one of the staircases led to a roof but nobody bar its initiates ever knew which.

Today, however, the two roads outside its main entrance were packed with villagers, mostly tradespeople. Even Mr Premar had arrived shouting, 'Mangos, mangos, tasty fresh mangos!' in spite of his empty cart.

'It's an outrage,' snorted Mrs Ghosh clutching a chicken under her arm. 'Bister's got the foreigners locked up with him so he can sell them his own produce.'

'But Mr Bister doesn't sell chickens,' I said.

'No, but he will,' she retorted, chasing the chicken as it broke free and flapped up the road.

I managed to squeeze between Mr Jalpur who was waving

one of his saucepans on the end of a stick and Mrs Knapp who was shaking an aubergine.

'I'll bet even now he's trying to buy moth-eaten, over-ripe aubergines from down the hill,' said Mrs Knapp thrusting one of hers under my nose. 'The Queen of vegetables,' she said. 'Peerless among foods for its fragrance and texture.'

'Personally,' I said, 'I have always found them somewhat inedible.'

'And if they want a saucepan?' said Mr Jalpur. 'You know he's gone into kitchenware now? "Kitchenware"!' he spat. 'Hammered-out bits of tin that don't last five meals. Look at this.' He lowered the stick. 'What do you see?'

'A saucepan?' I offered.

'No, no, you are not looking.'

'A most excellent saucepan?'

'Your face, you idiot! You can see your face in it. And after twenty meals you can still see your face. After twenty hundred meals, properly cared for, notwithstanding the terms of the warranty, please refer to the notice behind me, you will still see your face!'

'But why should our visitors wish to buy a saucepan?' I said.

He stared at it for a moment seeing his face, presumably, but no answer.

I pushed past the two chocolatiers who were ramming their wagons into each other while denouncing the quality of each other's nut bars. Closer to the steps, people were pushing forward while those at the top tumbled back, saris and chapatis flying over their heads. In front of the door stood the Buddhist Cook, his bald pate catching the sunlight, bare feet planted lightly, ready for the next assault.

'Salutations, holy one,' I said with a bow. 'I am looking for

Pol Bister who is, I believe, presently therein.'

His hooded eyes gazed somewhere above my shoulder.

'It's no use,' said Mrs Peerival who had dropped her tomatoes making everyone slip about. 'He's under instruction not to let anyone in.'

'But I am a friend of Pol,' I said opening my hands in the universal gesture of peace and harmony.

He tilted forward on his toes.

'Besides which,' added Mrs Peerival, 'you can't argue with followers of Zen since they don't accept that you exist.'

I crept round the back, clambering over the rubble to the rear windows, all of which seemed to be firmly shut.

'Pol!' I shouted. 'It's me, Rabindra!'

'Rabindra? Is that you?' said Pol appearing at one of the windows and pushing it open.

'Well, who else,' I said, dodging a shard of glass, 'would be shouting, "Pol, Pol, it's me, Rabindra"?'

He leaned out and offered his hand. After a little puffing from both of us, I finally hauled myself into the room.

'How many times have I dreamed of a lover?' said Pol, pacing anxiously about as I got my breath back. 'And how many times have I beaten myself up for it afterwards?'

I thought about mentioning the goat incident but decided not to.

'It was not my choice,' he continued. 'My father sent me to assist with preparations for the dance recital. Naturally I declined and naturally he insisted. Naturally I declined again and naturally he became irate.' Pol stopped for a moment, then stared at me helplessly. 'The fact is,' he said, 'my soul is on the precipice. The very perfection for which I have striven is in my hands, these hands. But they are failing. They have grown weak, Rabindra, with desire. All the books I've read, the verses chanted, the *pujas*, *japas* and austerities practised, the long hours spent in rapt contemplation of matters spiritually uplifting are wasted. Wasted. Oh, Rabindra! Do you recall the time my father ordered too many fig delicacies and told me to eat as many of them as I could before they went off?'

'Yes, I remember,' I said.

We had gorged ourselves for days until Pol began to fear they'd run out before we had gorged ourselves enough. He had stopped abruptly as we sat in his father's sweet shop and said, 'Rabindra, I am enjoying these so much that I have begun to grieve at the fact that one day there shall be no more.'

'But your father could always order another lot...?' I had said, chewing.

'That is not the point,' he had replied. 'I have become attached, and with attachment comes misery.'

After which he ate no more. For several weeks, whenever I went to see him, his sisters told me he was overcoming an attachment to fig-based confectionary and was too depressed to see anyone. He emerged, eventually, looking pale but redeemed.

'Well, that was just figs,' he said. 'A momentary excitation of the taste buds. But this is every sense at once. And not some fleeting anxiety that the object of my affection is finite, but a burning desire to possess her completely in every way imaginable for ever and ever. Rabindra,' he looked at me gravely, 'I have never been so happy nor so desolate at the same time.'

'You're in love,' I said, recalling some of the things Dev had said about it. 'Which is wonderful, surely.'

'Yes, perhaps. Who can say?' He giggled suddenly before looking miserable again.

'And what colour were her eyes?' I asked.

'I don't know.'

'Did you look into them?'

'Of course.'

'But you saw neither form, colour, nor even the eyes themselves. For there was only the infinity within.'

He stared into space, contemplating the wonders of that which cannot be described.

'Right,' I said. 'Now listen to me for a change. This morning, just about every young man in the village, not to mention plenty of older ones who ought to know better, came to the clinic to catch a glimpse of my beloved. How long, do you think, before they start sending letters of introduction, photographs, flowers, and family delegations to suggest alternatives to the Clinic Skivvy and his low-born friend?'

'But the gods...' said Pol.

'Yes, I know the gods sent them,' I said, waving him to silence, 'But there are more than gods in this world. There are also demons, devils, snakes and bits of mischief left over from previous universes to thwart even the best-intentioned acts of providence. Think about it. Is Pushkara not awash with handsome bachelors sporting athletic torsos and regular incomes who could point disparagingly to the mere food and board that I receive as recompense for my labours? Are there not high-caste families with first-borns, second borns, distant relatives in the city and other sundry familial adjuncts gagging for matrimony? Even as we speak, demons are whispering into the ears of our brides that they've inadvertently turned up at the behest of Pushkara's least eligible sons.'

'How can you be sure,' he interrupted morosely, 'that it was not demons who brought them here?'

'I cannot,' I said, walking to the door and turning to

face him. 'But there's only one way to find out.'

It took us several attempts to reach the lobby, during which we found ourselves back at the first room at least twice. But at last we heard the voices of Malek Bister and Mrs Dong from the end of a corridor.

'These my rates,' she was saying, 'always been.'

'That's not what it says on your bloody sign marked "Room Rates",' said Malek.

'Them local rates,' she said. 'These tourist rates.'

'You've never charged tourist rates,' he spluttered.

'Never had tourists. So noborry ask. These my rates. You like it or they go lumpy somewhere else.'

Pol led me past the lobby to the reception lounge.

'Oh, look,' said the lady with blonde hair. 'It's another one.'

'What does he want?' asked a man with hairy hands kneeling over a large box on the floor. He had a wispy grey beard covering much of his face, and hair drawn back over small patches of pink into a pony-tail.

'I don't know,' said the lady. 'Ask him.'

'You ask him,' said the man. 'I'm busy.'

'What if he don't speak English?'

'They all speak English,' said the man.

'Yeah,' she said. 'Bit weird that.'

'The Raj,' said the man.

'Oh hello, Raj,' she said to me.

'No, I mean it's cause of the Raj they all speak English.'

'So he's not Raj?'

'No. Well, he might be. I don't know.'

'I knew a Raj,' she said. 'From Oldham. Big bloke.'

'My name is Rabindranath,' I said. 'And I blaze eternally in the heavens.'

'That's nice for you,' she said, flicking a glance at the man.

'For your information, our prodigious facility in the English patois,' I said, showing it off a little, 'is consequent upon historical circumstances. Several generations ago, there came to reside among these fragrant peaks a gentleman in receipt of an education from a most illustrious establishment, far away from here, in which English was the prescribed means of linguistic intercourse. Being of a pedagogic inclination, he established our first school and decreed that the vocabulary and grammar would proceed henceforth according to the modus in which he was proficient. And so it came to be. His successor continued likewise, and then his. Now, not to be disingenuous, the usage of, let us say, more indigenous dialects is considered to be indicative of a somewhat vulgar predisposition even among the plantation workers. It is never to be encountered among the literati, cognoscenti or intelligentsia.'

'I thought you said they spoke English,' she said.

The man with hairy hands snorted and stood up. Across his stomach was the stretched image of a half-bearded face with curly hair and a headband, possibly him, I thought, in his younger days. Helpfully, his name was emblazoned beneath it.

'Mr Hendrix,' I said, 'it is a pleasure to meet you.'

'Huh?' he said.

'Pol! Pol!' A woman's voice trilled from the door making me jump and turning Pol suddenly rigid.

She wore khaki slacks and a light cotton top stitched with flowers of yellow and pink, her crimson hair knotted loosely in a white flannel turban. 'Where have you been?' she cried, 'leaving me all a-moody and a-broody without my little sugar pops? Shal, I borrowed your shampoo, is that okay?'

The blonde lady shrugged.

The red-haired lady hurried over to Pol in a way that made me think of the goat-woman shortly before she attacked me. 'You're not to leave me,' she said pinching his cheeks, 'ever again. I was all alone.' She turned to Hendrix. 'Isn't he just the cutest, wootest little spice-popsicle ever?'

'Whatever you say,' said Hendrix, coiling a roll of black cable over his arm.

'And who's this?' she said, nodding to me.

'Hang on,' said the blonde lady. 'He told us. What was it? Raj? No, it was…'

'Rumplestiltskin,' said Hendrix.

'Rabindranath Sharma,' I said. 'At your service.'

'Oh, they're all just so *sweeeeet*!' said the red-haired lady, squeezing Pol so hard he lifted off the floor.

'So, do we get tea or anything?' said the blonde lady, lighting a cigarette. 'You know? Cuppa tea?'

'I think Mrs Dong's talking to Mr Bister,' said the red-haired lady, breaking into giggles.

'This can't be real,' said the blonde lady, reaching for an ashtray.

'I see that you are not unfamiliar with the central precept of our philosophy,' I remarked, smiling.

They all stared at me for a moment.

'So what about that bald bloke with the orange kind've… whatsit,' said the blonde lady, 'I thought he did the tea and stuff.'

'He's out front,' said Hendrix, kicking at the box. 'Eight cables. I'm down to eight sodding cables.'

'Doing what?' said the blonde lady.

'I believe, he is keeping the crowds away from the door,' I said.

'Oh, I love it,' said the red-haired lady, clapping her hands.

'So what about Lazy Arse, where's he at?' said the blonde lady.

'Got the jips,' said Hendrix.

'Oh,' said the blonde lady. 'So what about Marty? Is she any better?'

'I think she got something at the Doctor's,' said the red-haired lady.

'Some daft twot in a crap-hole clinic gave her tablets,' sneered Hendrix. 'Didn't even know what they were. Said she hopes nobody gets seriously ill around here.'

The reason my head began to throb as the floor took on a sponge-like texture was not the result of his obvious misrepresentation of what Martina might have said about me, but the fact that she was there, in the doorway, draped in a long silk robe with purple dragons across the front, their fiery tails sweeping down the copious folds of her sleeves.

'Oh, hullo,' she said to me.

'You know him?' said the blonde lady.

'Yeah, he's the Doctor,' said Martina.

Hendrix rummaged noisily in his box.

'Them tablets helped,' said Martina.

'Oh, Doctor I'm in trouble,' sung the red-haired lady.

'Leave it out, Cin',' said the blonde lady.

'It pleases me that you are feeling better,' I said, with a little bow.

'Boom boody boom...' sung the red-haired lady.

'Cindy!' said the blonde-haired lady, sharply.

'Have you all introduced yourself?' said Martina. 'Yes? No? Is anyone talking?'

'I'm Cindy,' said the red-haired lady. 'You can call me Cin'. Everyone does. Cin' by name...'

'Moving on,' interrupted Martina. 'This is the Doctor. Like I said. Ah...'

'Rabindranut,' said the red-haired lady.

'Something like that,' said Martina. 'The old git with the toolbox...'

'As they say,' said the blonde lady.

'Goes by the name of Brendan.'

'Or Hendrix,' said Hendrix with a wink, smiling at me now.

'And I'm Sharon,' said the blonde lady, flatly, 'Sharon Shiver. You can call me Shal. Shall I, shan't I, blah blah.'

'Then you are indeed at home,' I said. 'For we have many among us who go by that name'.

'What, "Sharon"?' said Hendrix sceptically.

'Shiva,' I said. 'It is one of our most honourable nomenclatures. Generally, it is bestowed only upon first-borns and then only in the best families.'

'Well, fancy that,' said Sharon, stretching her legs out.

'Hey Pol,' said Hendrix. 'If you've got a minute, I reckon we could use a drink around here.'

'I'll ask Mrs Dong if she can prepare some tea,' said Pol, quietly.

'I was thinking, maybe, something a bit more... you know...' said Hendrix.

'God's sake, Bren,' said Sharon. 'It's not even lunchtime.'

'Yeah, but I been working my arse off.'

'We've all been working, honey,' said Cindy.

'Like washing your hair's working,' snorted Hendrix.

'Making myself beautiful,' she said, stroking it.

'You're right,' said Hendrix, 'that is a lot of work.'

'Alright,' said Martina, 'everyone's a bit tense but Mike's on his way. So any grouches, like he said, take them up with him.'

'And what could there possibly be to grouch about in this lovely, lovely place?' said a hoarse but somehow authoritative voice from the door. Mike strolled in with a commanding air, nodding to Hendrix, bowing to the ladies and frowning at me. He stopped in the centre of the room as one might upon whom lives hang.

'Which is where exactly?' said Sharon, holding up a guide book.

'Uh,' said Mike, 'I can explain that.'

'Go on then,' she said.

'It's um… well, you know…' he said, fumbling in his pocket and glancing towards the window. 'Some of these books and stuff, they… you get what you pay for.'

'It has long been the case,' I said, 'that we have lacked cartographical recognition. In fact, this has been a source of chagrin to many generations of elders.'

'It's just squiggles,' said Sharon, jabbing at a fold-out map at the back of the book.

'Which does not mean that we're not here,' I said.

'He's right,' said Mike. 'First rule of here, wherever it happens to be, is that it's got to be somewhere.'

'So how come it ain't mentioned?' said Sharon.

'A good question,' I said, glancing at Martina who was studying her fingernails. 'According to some historians, these hills were once occupied by violent Thugees. Anyone travelling through was therefore devoured, with the result that nobody ever returned home to speak of them. This included an unfortunate delegation from the British Royal Geographical Society. By the time the Raj had avenged their lost scholars, most of the maps had already been published with, as you say, just a squiggle of fanciful peaks in the area that is now Pushkara. Subsequently, anyone turning up on the plains clutching a theodolite was told only that there was nothing up here worth looking at. And thus a squiggle we forever remained.'

I recalled the zeal with which my father had rekindled the flames of an ancient campaign. Although some elders disputed the notion that our ancestors were venous cannibals, pointing instead to some fragments of poetry that spoke of a 'Princely Race among the snowy peaks', it was generally agreed that since it was in Pushkara that Shiva had slain the Demonic Turtle, we deserved at least some navigational acknowledgment if not inclusion in every school book in the land.

Father prepared and sent a lengthy dossier on the subject, along with extensive footnotes and appendices, to the All India Institute of Cartography, receiving an embossed reply shortly thereafter assuring us that they would deal with this 'as a matter of urgency'.

A year later, after some polite reminders, they sent another letter, similarly embossed to say that they were, regrettably, unable to accredit a place without visual verification of its existence. And though they would have liked to visit Pushkara to see for themselves, attempting to do so would tacitly acknowledge the very existence that was in question. The letter went on to say that while Cartographers enjoy nothing more than finding hitherto uncharted portions of the planet, the pay of a government clerk was not so great these days and there was the matter of expense, especially in a rather difficult year after the death of his brother whose voracious, and it had to be said, ungrateful children he had taken on along with a sick sister-in-law.

The village went to work. With the exception of Malek Bister who laughed that perhaps he should rename his hall

'The Nowhere Worth Bloody Mentioning Centre'. Collection tins for the 'Cartographical Relief Fund' bristled from every shop window, vending cart and go-down. School children paraded the streets dressed as Shivas and Turtles performing songs of their own composition to illustrate the spiritual hazards of not coughing up for the greater good. After some weeks a quantity of money was posted to New Delhi along with a selection of pastries from Mr Chowdhury's pastry shop and one of Mrs Dilip's yak's wool hats 'for the children'.

A month later we got another letter from a senior clerk at the All India Institute of Cartography saying that the official dealing with our claim had recently retired and the case had therefore been reassigned. He apologised for the delay in replying but he'd been somewhat preoccupied of late with his asthmatic wife and idle children who had, moreover, taken their toll on his own health not to mention the household finances which were, to put it crudely, a little bit tight at the moment. We didn't write again.

'Well, wherever we are,' said Mike, briskly, 'the good news is that we're in business, we're on the road, and we're rocking it.'

'So what's the bad news?' said Sharon.

He looked at her sourly. 'Okay, I know things went a bit tits up recently,' he said. 'But right now it's bish bosh sorted. We're back on track and the show, as they say, goes on!' He left a little space, looking around expectantly.

Sharon clapped her hands slowly.

'Mike,' said Hendrix, 'hey Mikey. Mike. You know... like, what we said. Hey? I could really use a little... a bit of something. Soon as.'

'Relax,' said Mike.

'That's what I'm talking about,' said Hendrix.

Mike lifted his hand for silence. 'You know Mr Bister,' he said. 'He's a good man. Cindy, stop giggling. Almost the first thing I asked him was, how do we get something for Brendan. Okay? And he says it grows wild here. It's all over the place. So chill. Yeah?'

Hendrix nodded.

'Okay,' said Mike, 'I've also talked to Mrs Dong. Cindy, please. She's going to make sure we get brekkies on time, yeah? Toast, coffee, all that.

'Marmalade?' said Cindy.

'Marmalade, jam, whatever. It's all in hand. The thing is, you're all still lovely. You know you are. And I mean all of you.' He nodded to each of the ladies in turn. 'And you know what?'

'What?' said Sharon, rolling her eyes.

'Out there,' said Mike, waving towards the window, 'they have gone mental.'

'I thought I heard a bit of a noise,' said Martina.

'You thought Bombay loved you? That was nothing.'

'Oo,' said Cindy, dancing in a little circle.

'So where's the venue?' said Martina, holding her hand to the light and squinting at it.

'Good question,' said Mike. 'Now, I've mentioned about the you know, Shri Malek Bister Pushkara Entertainment… Thing, okay? I've not been there yet but I can tell you this: we're talking state-of-the-art. The words "High" and "Spec" don't even cover it.'

'I'm down a few cables,' said Hendrix.

'They'll have cables,' Mike smiled. 'Like I said, chill.'

'When can we see it?' said Martina.

'You'll see it. Don't worry,' said Mike.

'This morning,' said Martina. 'With you.'

Mike nibbled on his lip for a moment. 'Yeah, okay,' he said.

'Me too,' said Cindy. 'With my little brown nut.' Pol gasped slightly as she pinched his bottom.

'Fine,' said Mike. 'We'll all go. Okay? Everyone happy?'

'How do we get there?' asked Martina.

'Malek's just sorting the limo.'

'It's got cabinets, right?' said Hendrix anxiously.

'You name it,' said Mike. 'In the meantime, there's a bit of merchandising gone AWOL I need to check out.'

'What do you mean AWOL?' said Martina.

'It is a military expression,' I explained, 'meaning, "To have developed an unexplained absence without the appropriate foliage".'

'Calendars,' said Mike, glancing at me briefly. 'But we got a few left. So no worries. Alright?'

'I want to go for a walk,' said Cindy. 'When can we go for a walk? Please, please, please can we go walkies?'

'You'll get your walk,' said Mike, moving off. 'I'll sort security, press, itinerary, cetera cetera. Just don't scratch your legs, okay, on like bushes and stuff.' He turned at the door to smile at everyone. I felt obliged to return a particularly amiable grin since nobody else smiled back. He looked at me again for a moment, and left.

'The hills above the village are most conducive to "walkies",' I said to Cindy. 'Not to mention family picnics, audiences with holy men and the performance of sacrifice.'

Pol coughed a little and glared at me.

'Holy men!' said Cindy. 'I just love holy men, with their fierce little eyes and spindly legs. I want to see a holy man. I want want to see holy man!'

'There are none to be found at this time,' I said. 'But soon, I am sure, one shall appear through the morning mist of the mountain pass offering wisdom and asking for directions.'

'Well, maybe after lunch,' said Martina. 'It might be nice to get out a bit.'

'What did Mike say?' said Sharon, lighting another cigarette, 'about travel and that? Exotic climes? See the world? Yeah? And what? What have we seen? Hotels, hotels and ah, what was it? Oh yeah, more sodding hotels.'

'A bus?' said Cindy. 'I'll never forget that bus.'

There was a little pause as all three of them never forgot the bus.

'I blame the restaurants,' said Sharon. ''Specially in Leicester. Flipping great pictures of shiny white palaces, blue sky, pink flowers. Little man comes over, brushing the crumbs up. Oops there's a crumb, we can't have that. That isn't like home. We don't have crumbs lying around. Just mangy dogs all over the street, heaps of garbage, cows every bloody where and total head-case drivers trying to kill you. But you won't see crumbs. Cause all the bloody beggars have eaten them up! That hotel, yeah? wherever it was, I go for a stroll, out jumps a monkey. I run for my bloody life, ants this big, fricking mosquitoes, like my leg's got acne.' She took a breath. 'Tandoori sodding Paradise!' she said finally, leaning back again.

'Yeah, but they love us,' said Martina, dryly, glancing at Cindy.

'They love me in Hamburg,' said Sharon. 'They love me in Hammersmith. I don't need the squits to be loved. I don't need to get eaten alive by a million crawly things to be loved. I don't need to get woken up at four in the bloody morning by some lunatic shouting down a megaphone...'

'That's the call to prayer,' interrupted Cindy. 'It's spiritual.'

'Well, you go pray, then,' said Sharon. 'While I shove the megaphone up his —'

'Okay, okay, girls, right, yeah, okay. We're all a bit you know,' said Hendrix, closing the box and straightening up. 'But that's how it is, alright, that's where we are in the end and... well, you know.'

'What?' said Sharon.

'Well, whatever. It is what it is. I lost half me cables, you don't hear me complaining.'

'That wasn't you, then?' said Sharon.

He grimaced slightly, smoothing his pony-tail with a hairy hand. 'So you're the Doc around here?' he said.

I glanced at Pol who looked as if he was about to say something.

'Why do you ask?' I said quickly.

'Well, only cause, ah, I mean, if there's any chance of a word some time...' said Hendrix, eyes darting at everything except Sharon who seemed to be staring fixedly at him.

'I shall be in the clinic tomorrow,' I said.

'Well, by "some time", I was thinking more like now,' said Hendrix,

Pol grabbed my arm. 'Perhaps I could have a word, first,' he said, dragging me into the corridor. 'What are you doing?' he hissed.

'It's not what I'm doing,' I said. 'It's what I'm not doing.'

'You mean not telling them who you really are?'

'Possibly similar to that,' I said. 'But don't worry. I have no intention of deceiving them. I will merely offer such advice as I can and if I can't, I'll refer them to Dev. That is precisely how we function on a daily basis. There is nothing unusual or untoward in this.'

'You think she won't marry you if she finds out you're a Clinic Skivvy,' he said.

'Clinical Assistant,' I mumbled.

'Then what faith do you have in her?' he asked.

'Infinite. Except for that.'

Hendrix came to the door. 'Only, I do get a bit of medication from time to time,' he said. 'All above board. You know. Bit of this. Bit of that. I was just wondering what you could, maybe, do for me.'

'Rabindra!' said Pol, shaking my shoulders.

'Please excuse my friend,' I said, trying to pull free. 'He is a little over-excited. But if you tell me the nature of your concern, I'm sure I can find the appropriate remedy.'

Pol moved off to clutch his head.

Hendrix leaned in close. 'Concern, you see, that's just it. Lots, in fact. And they, well, they concern me. I guess that's the thing about concerns. So maybe, you know, if you've got something just to tweak 'em down a bit...?'

'Perhaps it would help,' I said, wishing I'd brought my book, 'if you could tell me the precise name of the medication you're receiving...?'

'Prozac,' he said. 'That's good. Takes the edge off. I don't know if you do that. I mean, Mike's sorting a little weed for later but I lost my cables so I'm a bit... you know.'

'You have fish phobia?'

'Ah, no,' said Hendrix frowning. 'I don't think so.'

'But this Prozac,' I said, 'was designed specifically as a remedy for fish phobia.'

'Right,' said Hendrix. 'I didn't know that.'

'I do have some but it is reserved for this condition only. We had a patient once, brought in by his wife. He wouldn't eat fish, however she cooked it. Fried, boiled, she tried everything. Being a lady whose ancestors came from the coast, cooking fish was among her greatest pleasures. In fact that's all she could cook. So this was very problematic for them.

She even consulted my father over legal proceedings against her husband's family for not mentioning this impediment to their matrimonial compatibility. They said they'd counter-sue on the grounds of failure to reveal her culinary limitations.'

'Tricky,' said Hendrix.

'When I asked my brother...'

'Who?' said Hendrix.

'He is also versed in clinical matters,' I said, glancing round to see if Pol was listening.

''kay,' said Hendrix.

'He said it sounded like a classic case of fish phobia.'

'Sounds right to me,' said Hendrix, nodding thoughtfully.

'For which there is no cure.'

'Oh,' said Hendrix. 'That's a shame.'

'However, when I mentioned it to the Pharmaceutical Representative a few months later, he said that new research had achieved a major break-through for this very condition.'

'Prozac?' said Hendrix.

'The wonders of medical science,' I said, smiling.

'Well, that's exactly it,' said Hendrix. 'You know the last time I saw a fish I completely freaked.'

'I think we are beginning to narrow the possibilities,' I said.

'And the nightmares,' he said. 'Like, swarms of fish and... fish-type things all... swarming. I wake up sweating. You can ask Shal. I mean even the word, you know, "fish" brings me out, like, take a look at my forehead...'

'It appears that you are perspiring,' I said.

'Cause we're talking about fish,' he said.

'In that case,' I said, 'I have no hesitation in prescribing you the necessary medication.'

'You're a brick,' he said, patting my arm. 'Soon as you can, hey?'

'I'll pop over to the clinic today,' I said.

'Champion,' he smiled, turning back to the room. 'That patient,' he said, stopping by the door. 'he's okay now, is he?'

'Much happier,' I said. 'In fact he now eats anything his wife puts in front of him, though his mango business isn't doing so well.'

'Well, I guess that's... that's something,' said Hendrix sauntering back to his box.

Pol rushed over, flinging his hands about. 'Are you mad?' he said. 'What's she going to say when she finds out? Rabindra! Think about it! What are you doing?'

But Cindy was calling him now. 'Pol? Pol? Where's my little nut-brown buddy?'

'I believe your wife is looking for you,' I said.

Pol glared at me for a moment and went back to the lounge. I could hear him gasp as she squeezed him.

'My little pecan pie,' she said, 'if you keep running off, I shall have to tie you up. Now, that's a thought!'

I felt happy for Pol though the rebuke in his look continued to sting. It seemed to me that his dream was assured in spite of its metaphysical conundrums. For me it was different. The truth was that Martina had yet to give any real indication that she wanted to pinch my bottom. In fact, she had a tendency to yawn when I spoke to her which, try as I might, was hard to construe as infatuation. So, why had it all gone so right for Pol and so not right for me? The answer was obvious. Because I had lied to her. If love is the dissolution of barriers, what greater barrier could there be between two people than a conscious falsehood? In spite of my protestations to Pol, I had done more than merely fail to apprise her of my true position when I declined to wear my white coat with its name badge upon which were printed in stark letters: 'R.Sharma.

Clinical Assistant'. And even if she couldn't know the depths
to which my deception had plunged, she would have sensed,
surely, that something was amiss. It was beginning to strike
me that not only were my nuptial prospects in peril but also,
if you believe in such things, my innermost soul. For what is
karma but rough justice for the wicked? Had I been wicked?
Yes. Was I about to face justice? As I crept back through
the window to fetch Hendrix's medication, it seemed to me
that the gods were, ultimately, unfathomable. They give.
They take. They give while somehow making it feel like
they've taken something and, of course, vice versa. Most of
the village was now clamouring at the doors of the Hotel
Nirvana. What were they hoping to get? And what, in the
process would they lose? I decided to let Pol deal with the
philosophical dilemmas. Right now I had to concentrate on
winning the heart of my beloved. It was not, I thought as I
picked up speed to lose a couple of dogs who had started to
follow me, looking good.

4

'I JUST LOVE THIS BIT,' giggled Cindy, clapping her hands.

We had gathered in the lobby where Mrs Dong was nailing a notice over the reception desk headed, 'Rools!' Item One of which was, 'No Loitering', problematic, I thought, in an area designed principally for that purpose. Item Two was, 'No argue bout Rates!' Item Three was, 'No argue bout Rools', and so on. She had somehow persuaded Pol to hold it up while she hammered.

All the ladies, meanwhile, had changed. Martina was in knee-length cream shorts and a pale pink blouse. Cindy, whose fiery hair now tumbled playfully over her shoulders, wore a tight black dress that flowed in a single piece from her neck to her calves. Sharon, meanwhile, had a pair of faded jeans, long tan boots and a blue t-shirt stencilled with the words, 'Go Ahead Punk, Make My Day'. Mike had remained in his crumpled suit and was looking, as ever, overheated.

Cindy peeked through the shutters. 'Are the press here?' she said, excitedly. 'What about TV? I don't know, do they have TV? Is it autographs or straight to limo? Marty?'

Hendrix had snatched the medicine a little too hastily and was now chasing its contents across the floor. I was still out of breath from my sprint, though the journey had been relatively uneventful. The dogs who chased me had thudded against the clinic door as I slammed it behind me, whining and scratching as I headed for my office.

From Dev's room, I could hear Father shouting, 'Research, I'll give you research. Sit up when I'm talking to you.' However generous the offer to assist with Dev's work, Father had evidently failed to appreciate how prolonged study causes one's head to rest on the desk.

It took me a while to find the remedy for Hendrix's fish-phobia since I'd forgotten what colour the box was. Still, I thought it would give the dogs time to get bored and go away. In the event, they had merely camped in the shade opposite, leaping up when I reappeared. But I was ready for them, scattering Imodium pellets as I ran down the road, something they always lapped up enthusiastically, though it made them quiet for a few days afterwards.

Pol was ready to help me through the window, which was just as well since one or two tradespeople had, by now, made their way to the rubble at the back. I thought the mood less festive and a little more earnest than earlier, especially when Mr Briniwal, the upholsterer, rushed towards me brandishing a mallet.

Mike was in the middle of a speech when we finally reached the lobby. 'So let us remember,' he said glancing through the shutters, 'that we are not merely Entertainers, we are Ambassadors. And as Ambassadors, we bring to this country, to this land, to the good people of… ah, this place, a little touch of England, though, strictly speaking, touch and you're out, sonny.' He chortled.

'Can we get on with it?' said Martina.

'Just waiting for the nod, darling,' said Mike, glancing out again.

'You must let me know if the symptoms persist,' I said to Hendrix who was fishing behind a sofa.

'You're the dude,' he said.

'Seriously,' said Mike, 'a lot of people talk about The Brotherhood of Nations…'

'Like who?' said Sharon.

'Well, lots of people.'

'Name one,' said Sharon.

'Just take it from me,' said Mike, a little sharply, 'that people do. But how is that to be achieved? Through wars, conquest and exploitation?'

'You mean there's another way?' said Sharon playing, I suspected, the devil's advocate.

'There is only one thing that can truly forge new bonds, new chains…'

'Now you're talking!' said Cindy.

'And that is art. Paintings, music, all that. Stories and legends. For instance, they've got this thing about some… whatever, having its head chopped off. And we… well, we've got two thousand years of civilisation culminating in the invention of the Calendar.'

'Gregorian?' said Pol.

'Pirelli,' said Mike, straightening up. 'Okay ladies. We're on.'

'Yippee,' said Cindy, jumping up and down.

'Got anywhere for this?' said Sharon, holding out a wrinkled piece of gum.

'Find something,' said Mike. 'Brendan? You ready?'

'Huh?' said Hendrix from under a chaise longue.

'My people,' said Cindy, waving at the window, 'I love you all.'

'Okay,' said Mike gripping the door handle. 'Keep it loose, nice and relaxed. Marty, that's beautiful. Shal, maybe a smile.'

'I'm pouting,' said Sharon.

'Okay, but not too much. They'll think you're gonna to throw up.'

'They might be right,' said Sharon.

'Rock and Roll,' said Mike thrusting his chin forward, wrenching the doors open and marching out with his hands above his head.

For a moment the noise hushed to an eery silence. Somebody sniffed. A foot scraped. It seemed to me that I could hear the crowd breathing. Then a hundred voices erupted as one: 'Saucepans you can see your face in!' 'Handmade shoes in finest leather all styles considered!' 'The best samosas in Pushkara, don't listen to that lying bastard Bister!'

'You have waited a thousand years!' shouted Mike, arms outstretched.

'Somebody tell him the meaning of OTT,' muttered Martina.

'Remember when he said we was the best thing to happen here since Queen Victoria put her foot on it?' said Sharon.

'Lead balloon or what?' said Cindy primping her curls with brusque fingers.

'But wait no more!' shouted Mike.

'Yak's wool hats to keep your head toasty!' 'The only Aubergines in Pushkara worth stuffing!' 'Don't listen to her, she gets her produce out of my rejects.' 'Shut up.' 'No you shut up.' 'Your son isn't worthy of my daughter!' came the response.

'I bring you, direct from England,' Mike continued, sounding a bit hoarse now, 'a bevy of bouncing beauties, the gorgeous, the wonderful, the aptly-named Heaven's Blessings!'

'You know he used to call bingo?' said Sharon.

'You're kidding,' said Cindy.

'It's a great honour,' continued Mike lowering his voice, 'to introduce the star of show, representing Legend's Lingerie, the award-winning Queen of the Screen…'

'That's how he started. Up in Scarborough,' said Martina.

'Come a long way,' said Hendrix.

'You reckon?' scoffed Sharon.

'I mean this is a long way from Scarborough,' said Hendrix, wistfully.

Mike was glancing round, gesturing urgently with his hand. 'Voted Gorgeous Girl of the year in *Gorgeous Girl* Magazine not just once, not twice but three times, the unbelievable, the stupendous…'

'Go boogie,' said Cindy, giving Martina a quick kiss.

'Martina Marvellous!' shouted Mike.

Martina breathed in, lifted her head, pushed her shoulders back and stepped through the door.

The crowd surged forward. Mike jumped back. The Buddhist Cook sent Mr Bophal sideways with a clatter of enamelled coasters. Several traders attempted to retreat as others pushed their way up, but the porch was now so slippery with squashed vegetables that they all slid into each other and tumbled collectively down the steps. Tradespeople at the back, meanwhile, started flinging their goods at the door. Mike ducked as a watermelon thudded against the wall beside him. The chai seller threw tea over the people in front of him for which he received a finely made shoe in the face.

'Was that a watermelon?' said Hendrix.

'Makes a change from underpants,' said Sharon.

In all this commotion the only person, it seemed to me, who stood unruffled was Martina, her head slightly tilted, one hand resting delicately on her hip, the other caressing the nape of her neck as a number of men, tripping over the top step, prostrated themselves at her feet. As if gradually beginning to notice the mildly perplexing enigma of time and space, along with some of the people in it, she smiled down at them, a ripple of light streaming through the rich, brown tresses of her hair. The men stared upwards, like monks whose relentless austerities have finally yielded a glimpse of the divinity to which they had devoted their lives – in spite of the wives, aunties and grandmothers grabbing frantically at their feet in an effort to haul them back.

'And a big round of applause, ladies and gentlemen,' said Mike, keeping a wary eye out for more fruit. 'Give it up now, for the slinky, sexy, stunning, delectable, delicious Cindy Swish. Let's hear it for Cin by name, Sin by nature!'

'Wish me luck,' said Cindy giving Pol's hand a little squeeze before striding out, hips flicking, arms wide as if to hug the whole of Pushkara, mouthing the words 'I love you' to anyone who cared to lip-read.

Scuffles were beginning to break out. Some of the young men, while fending off their wives had accidentally struck the people around them who, searching for the culprit, lashed out randomly causing yet more victims to thrash around in search of an adversary.

'And last but not least...' said Mike.

'So if I'm not least,' said Sharon, 'how come I'm always last? Hey?'

But as it was unclear whom she was addressing, it was equally unclear who should reply.

'The fabulous, fantabulous, stupendous...'

'He's used that already,' said Sharon.

'The indescribably beautifluous Sharon Shiver!'

'Oh right,' said Sharon, 'they get a shopping list, and I get, what, four measly words.'

She smoothed her t-shirt, pressed her gum under the rim of Mrs Dong's Rools, licked her lips and glided forward, nudging Martina aside as she swept her hands across the crowd in holy benediction, pinching the Buddhist Cook on his bottom, turning elegantly on her toes and strolling back to Martina, smiling.

'You ever pull that again…' snarled Martina.

'Maybe we should go back inside,' said Mike picking tomato pips from his lapel and flinching as a sandalwood biro bounced off his shoulder.

'No, hang on,' said Sharon pointing at the far edge of the crowd. 'What's that?'

As in a miracle, or by some tidal phenomenon, the villagers were parting slowly down the middle as a long bamboo cane twirled in the air above them. After a moment I could make out the brightly-feathered parade hat of Sergeant Shrinivasan as he strode purposefully forward, thwacking at anyone who didn't move quickly enough and sometimes at those who did. At last the Sergeant, medals glistening, presented himself at the top of the stairs.

'The Pushkara Police Force at your service,' he said with a bow.

'Alright,' said Mike. 'Let's go. Where's Brendan?'

'Who?' said Hendrix.

'Jesus Christ,' said Mike. 'How much have you taken? Okay, everyone, stay close.'

Cindy looked round. 'Where's Pol?' she said. 'I'm not going anywhere without my little spice boy.'

Pol grabbed my hand and dragged me, protesting, through the door. The Sergeant was beating his way back through the villagers, Mike close behind him, stepping gingerly over lost shoes and broken merchandise. Cindy squealed when she saw

Pol, seizing his free hand and skipping daintily down the steps. I followed on, keeping my face down though I could hear the mutterings around me. Martina was smiling beneficently at the people while Sharon, it seemed to me, scowled, though she might have been pouting. Hendrix kept stopping to ask various villagers if there was any chance of 'scoring a little something around here' before Sharon pushed him brusquely on.

Malek was standing next to his car beckoning vigorously for the Sergeant to hurry up. But the Sergeant knew how to march and was taking his time, red feathers swaying to the rhythm of his gait. Next to Malek's car was a rusty blue jeep which, along with its original inscription of 'Pushkara Police Force' bore various slogans of the Sergeant's own invention such as, 'The Law is the Law and Don't you Forget it, Mister' and 'There is No Escape from my Very Long Arm'.

'What's he doing here?' said Malek, pointing at me.

'Tour Medic,' said Hendrix.

'Well, you'd better make sure your low-born shadow doesn't accidentally fall across his high-born bloody foot.'

'Where's the limos?' asked Sharon, looking around.

'Stuck in traffic,' said Mike glancing at his shoes. 'Guess we'll have to use these.'

Behind us, the villagers were regrouping. 'Please take your seats,' said Sergeant Shrinivasan, poking viciously at Mrs Geegli who had stepped forward with some hand-pressed funeral briquettes.

'I'm not getting in that thing,' said Sharon.

'Suit yourself,' said Mike sliding hastily into Malek's car and rolling up the window as Mrs Mahmoud hurried towards us with a trolley of coconuts.

Sergeant Shrinivasan opened the door for Martina, saluting

as she climbed in. Cindy blew a last kiss to the crowds and jumped in with Mike and Pol. I found myself sitting next to Martina as the Sergeant switched on his blue lights and tooted the horn. Hendrix clambered into the front, wiped his forehead and said, 'Hit it, Sarge!' in the tone of one who has always wanted to. The jeep jolted forwards with a squeal of tyres and cloud of smog, pressing us back into our seats.

'I must apologise for these ruffians,' said the Sergeant, swerving with a slight thud into Mrs Mahmoud. 'What a carry on! And have you ever heard such nonsense? The best saris in Pushkara! In fact, they are very poor quality. Mr Bister, on the other hand, has good saris but somewhat expensive. I can get you the same quality for half the price. Perhaps after you have seen the hall we can visit the police station to try some on.'

'I'm okay for the moment,' said Martina.

'When have you seen what you are missing, then you will not think that you are "okay",' chuckled the Sergeant.

'No offence, mate,' said Hendrix, 'but put a sock in it?'

The Sergeant chuckled again. 'You bargain well, my friend. I can indeed put a sock in it. And not just one sock but two, thus providing a complete pair.'

'Brendan,' said Martina, 'did Mike say anything about Bombay?'

'Like what?' said Hendrix.

'Those dicks,' said Martina.

'What dicks?' said Hendrix.

'Two pairs,' said the Sergeant, accelerating at a group of dogs.

'The sponsors,' said Martina.

'What about them?' said Hendrix.

'Did Mike say anything?'

'Um, I dunno,' said Hendrix. 'I don't think so.'

'Alright,' chuckled the Sergeant. 'You are clearly adept at the rumpty tumpty of retail discourse. So let us say, three pairs of socks and one set of lady's undergarments at no extra charge with two saris.'

When she had stood on the hotel steps I thought I had never seen a woman so adamantine, impermeable and resolute, as if the tumultuous crowds were an ephemera she could shrug off with a mere flick of her head. But she seemed fragile now, somehow vulnerable, and I wanted to seize the hand that lay so limp on the cracked leather seat between us.

'And what was that about something having its head chopped off?' she said. 'Do you think he's alright?'

'That's just Mike stuff,' said Hendrix.

'I expect he was referring to The Turtle,' I said. 'Perhaps he'd heard about it from Mrs Dong. It is our great legend. In fact, it is our only legend but it is very great and famous, therefore, throughout Pushkara, and possibly even some of the villages further down the mountain.'

'Oh, right,' she said.

'And it is in honour of the Turtle's demise,' remarked Sergeant Shrinivasan, 'that I am able, on this occasion only, to offer socks, undergarments, saris and necklaces, did I mention the necklaces, at such unbelievable prices.'

'I didn't think you get turtles up mountains,' said Hendrix, turning round from the front seat.

'How it came to be here,' I said, 'is part of the legend. You see, once upon a time...'

'Dig it,' said Hendrix.

'... there was a pious sage,' I continued, 'who lived in an ants' nest...'

'Respect,' interjected Hendrix.

'... eating nothing but dust, dried twigs and sometimes not even that. In winter he slept in the snow. In summer he wore heavy goat-skins and sat motionless in the noonday sun. There was no pain he would not endure, no suffering he could not enhance by ingenious means. All he wanted was for Shiva to reward his austerities with a visit. Some say he was also hoping to be raised heavenwards on a pillow of light, though scholars are divided on this point.'

'So what happened?' said Hendrix.

'Well, one day it seemed that his efforts had been recognised when Shiva appeared before him in all his glory. The Sage leapt out of the icy stream in which he was meditating and shouted, 'Great Lord, by my sufferings have I won your praise.'

'Whoa,' said Hendrix.

'However, to the Sage's disappointment, all Shiva said was, "Who are you?" To which the Sage replied, "Who am I? Who the hell do you think I am? I have roasted in summer, frozen in winter, lived in the company of biting insects resisting the urge to squash the buggers..."'

'He said that?' said Martina.

'According to some interpretations,' I mumbled, realising that I'd picked up this embellishment from Mr Bister whose reverence for the legend was notoriously fickle.

'And then?' asked Hendrix.

'The Sage fell to the ground, kissing Shiva's feet, and cried, "Blessed Lord, I am your most devoted supplicant."'

'Your biggest fan, yeah?' said Hendrix, smiling.

'Possibly he said that too. It would not surprise me.'

'I've seen a lot of Gods pissed off by that,' said Hendrix.

'Shiva was a little more phlegmatic. He said, "Thank you but I just happened to be passing through. Your presence here is incidental." And off he went.'

'Sage goes mental,' anticipated Hendrix.

'You are correct,' I said. 'He ran around like a crazed thing, stamping on ants, cursing the heavens, cursing the gods and vowing eternal vengeance on Shiva himself. It is said that he howled for three hundred years demanding that Shiva come down and fight him.'

'Gotta salute him for that,' said Hendrix. 'So what did Shiva do?'

'Shiva is not much perturbed by such things. He just carried on with his duties, keeping the universe in order, collecting the dead, that kind of thing. But the Sage was immutable, and for many lives thereafter contemplated only the destruction of Shiva by ever more horrible means. In time, so single-minded was he, that his back grew a crusty shell, his head became heavy with scales, his jaws sharpened into solid bones with two holes for a nose, while his arms and legs shrunk into the stubby limbs with which he scurried about in search of his enemy.'

'A turtle, right?' said Hendrix.

I smiled. 'He wandered the hills and valleys, the deserts and forests for several thousand years until, one day, he found himself back in Pushkara. He decided that if Shiva had happened by once, he might do so again. So The Sage Who Was Now A Turtle settled down to wait, which was not good news for the village, since The Sage Who Was Now A Turtle...'

'Just call him The Turtle,' said Hendrix.

'... ate the goats on the upper pasture, the yaks on the lower slopes, trampled the tea trees and sometimes tore the roofs off houses to consume the people inside. After several millennia, during which the villagers had grown accustomed to bolting their doors at night only to find their grandmothers devoured anyway, Shiva passed through once more on an errand for Rama. Weary from travelling, he stopped to rest among the sweet breezes and snowy peaks for which the village is so admired. He took off his armour, set down his weapons and laid back to enjoy a little sunshine when, with a blood-curdling scream, the Turtle jumped out from behind a rock and snapped at his head. Shiva leaped up, skipping nimbly away as the Sage rolled, turned and sprung again.

'Who are you?' said Shiva, batting him aside. 'You look like some kind of hideous turtle.'

'Who am I?' cried the sage. 'Ha, ha. Well, that's the question isn't it? Who the hell am I? Ha ha. Ha ha ha. Ha ha ha...'

'We get the laugh,' said Hendrix.

'Who else spends countless lives meditating on nothing but your demise? Who else is so fixated on vengeance that they mutate inexorably into what you call "some kind of hideous turtle"? I am the one you scorned. The one who deserved praise and didn't get it. I am your death.'

'I take it you're looking for a fight,' said Shiva.

'Yo!' said Hendrix.

'And with that they did battle. For days and nights they raged across the heavens. Their mighty steps carved out the craggy passes. The Turtle's tears of fury fell as snow. The sparks from Shiva's arrows, glancing off the Turtle's shell, became stars. The blood drawn from the Turtle's tail in one ferocious swoop of Shiva's lance turned the morning sky crimson, while a retaliatory slash to Shiva's arm so graced the dusk. The curses of the Turtle congealed into the black oozy stuff that comes out of the ground in certain places when you dig it, while the sweat from Shiva's brows fell as flowers. The breath from their exertions became the morning mist while

Shiva's resolve to fight and fight became the winter cold that chills our bones.'

'Is this out on video?' asked Hendrix.

'And then The Turtle did something terrible. He had requested a momentary truce in which to take refreshments, and Shiva had been kind enough to agree, setting aside his arms as The Turtle sipped from the mountain stream. But when Shiva knelt in turn to quench his thirst, The Turtle leapt at his back, jaws open for one terrible snap. Luckily Shiva saw him reflected in the cupped waters of his hands and stepped aside. The Turtle crashed into the stream where Shiva held him, choking and spluttering until he struggled no more. Then Shiva cut his head off and put it on a rock to remind the whole world of the day that Virtue conquered Spiritual Greed which, according to one of our visiting holy men, is the most heinous vice of all. And there it remains to this day, a welcome source of shade for penitents and picnickers.'

'Where?' asked Hendrix.

'On the far edge of the hills. We call it Shiva Rock.'

'Why not Turtle Rock?' asked Hendrix.

'Because that would honour The Turtle,' I said. 'Which is beside the point.'

'And that is why,' chipped in the Sergeant, 'our village is named "Pushkara" which is another name of Shiva, the Great Lord.'

'What did it used to be called?' asked Hendrix.

'This is now lost to us,' muttered the Sergeant. 'And, to be frank, is largely irrelevant. However, it is no co-incidence that the official musical instrument of this august domain is the Rudra Veena. Rudra being yet another name of Shiva, and the Veena his instrument of choice which, as I trust you will discover, I have performed to great acclaim through many lifetimes though less so in this one.'

'You play?' said Hendrix, looking impressed.

'Not at all. It is the god who plays. I merely wait for him to guide my fingers.'

'Man!' said Hendrix, shaking his head.

'It is the same with saris and socks,' said the Sergeant. 'I do not look for these things. But if the gods bring them to me at incredibly low prices then it is my duty to pass them on with only a small mark-up to cover overheads and expenses. This is not commerce. This is the sharing of gifts. To buy a sari or indeed two saris with matching socks and a beautifully crafted necklace, at prices that will make you laugh, from Sergeant Shrinivasan is to participate in the divinity of creation.'

'We've been here before,' said Martina.

'Not at all,' said the Sergeant. 'For hitherto I have waxed lyrically only about the saris. Now, permit me to speak of the necklaces.'

'I mean this road,' said Martina.

'These are not just any necklaces,' continued the Sergeant, 'with the beads all wonky and the clasp opening for no reason.'

'We passed that bloke jumping up and down with a three-legged ornamental table about two minutes ago,' said Martina.

'And as you sneeze, perhaps on the steps of a sacred temple or some hallowed tomb, the whole bloody thing falls to pieces...' continued the Sergeant.

'And that,' said Hendrix, pointing at the village rabbit.

'We did have a peacock,' I said. 'Until its escape necessitated a replacement. The rabbit is considerably less sacred, mythologically, but impressive in its relentless attempts to emulate the fortunes of its predecessor.'

'That's not the point,' said Martina. 'The point is we've seen it before.'

Behind us, Malek was leaning out of his car, shaking a fist and shouting.

'... or drops in your soup at an important dinner party, allowing everyone present to form the opinion that you have, if you will forgive me, bought cheap,' added the Sergeant.

'What's he playing at?' said Martina as Malek drew up beside us, gesticulating wildly.

The Sergeant accelerated.

'Steady on,' said Hendrix.

Mr Kapra was jumping up and down again, shaking a table as we passed by.

'In short, therefore,' said the Sergeant, 'I am prepared to offer you three pairs of socks and one necklace, handcrafted from only the finest materials, with the purchase of three saris. That is my final offer.'

We were now approaching the fork at the end of the High Street. One road led past the engine workshop to the Shri Malek Bister Memorial Hall, the other circled back to the village. This time, Malek had managed to get beside us trying, it would seem, to force the Sergeant towards the hall. The Sergeant switched his siren on but Malek persisted, swerving sharply into his path. The Sergeant braked noisily, swore out of the window but was compelled, finally, to take the lower road.

'Anything less,' he shouted above the siren, 'and I would be robbing myself. Meaning I would have to arrest myself, leading to unimaginably complex paperwork.'

Both cars screeched to a stop on the wide expanse of ground in front of the Hall. Malek slammed his door and marched over.

'What the hell do you think you're doing?' he demanded.

'I was obliged,' said the Sergeant defensively, 'to choose a route that would minimise the possibility of civil unrest.'

'I asked you to escort us to the Shri Malek Bister International Memorial Arts and Exhibition Complex not take us on a tour of the bloody village.'

'Do you not hear the siren?' shouted the Sergeant over it.

'Oh, is that what it is? I thought it was you on your bloody Veena.'

'It is against the law,' said the Sergeant, stiffening slightly, 'to obstruct a police vehicle when it is playing its siren.'

'So arrest me,' said Malek. 'Go on, arrest me.'

'I have a good mind to,' said the Sergeant. 'Not from any sense of personal affront but because it is my duty. You have terrorised a policeman going about his business, you have disregarded the warnings of a siren, you have obstructed justice, committed perjury by questioning my motives, and you have dared to insult the sacred music of Shiva himself.'

'I know what you're up to,' said Malek, turning back to his car. 'You think I don't, but I bloody well do.'

The Sergeant sat for a moment, breathing quietly. Then he straightened up and said, 'So what do you say?'

But Martina had already climbed out of the jeep and was staring at the hall alongside Hendrix. Cindy was twirling around with her arms outstretched while Pol looked on, chewing his lip. Mr Chatterjee hurried out from the entrance.

'Greetings,' he said. 'May I formally welcome you to the...'

'Never mind all that,' said Malek. 'Is everything ready?'

'Indeed it is, Bister Sahib,' said Mr Chatterjee as Malek followed him back to the hall. 'At least everything that I supposed ought to be. I must admit that when you told me earlier to "get everything ready" it crossed my mind to ask what you meant exactly by "everything". This is the point, really, not to labour it, but if one has a question, one should ask it for why else should one have a question? Of what use, in fact, is a question that one does not ask? It is not a question at all. It is the very poor relation of a question, a distant cousin or even a step-brother that possesses in some ways a secondary familial association but is nevertheless not related either directly through blood or historically through domestic...'

He stopped abruptly as Malek Bister, close behind, swung his foot sharply into the gloom of the open doorway.

'You're kidding me,' said Sharon.

'Huh?' said Mike, fishing for his hankie.

'The tour's off, the tour's on, the tour's just crawled up its own backside, I ask the Producer if he's taking the piss putting us on in this bloody shack and all he can say is, "Huh?".'

Cindy finished twirling and ran up to the entrance. 'I don't think it's so bad,' she said.

'Well maybe some people are lucky to be dancing anywhere,' said Sharon.

'Miaow,' said Cindy, giggling.

'Sorry to butt in,' said Hendrix. 'Only I get this buzzing now and then, in my ears, cause of the noise, you know, over the years. But I was just wondering, can anyone else hear that?'

Now that he mentioned it, there was a definite rumble coming from somewhere.

'Earthquake?' said Hendrix.

'Not here,' I said.

'Return of the Turtle?'

But I didn't think so. Sergeant Shrinivasan unhooked his cane from the back of the jeep. Sharon popped a piece of chewing gum into her mouth and marched towards the hall. Martina joined Mike who was mopping his forehead.

'Maybe you want to be straight for once,' she said, 'and tell us what's going on.'

'I thought you could work it out,' said Mike.

'You're not saying it had anything to do with Bombay?' said Martina.

'I don't know, what do you think?' said Mike.

'They didn't cancel for that, come on.'

Mike shrugged mysteriously and strolled towards the doors.

'Mike?' said Martina.

'Listen Marty,' he said, turning briefly. 'You made your choice. Okay? And that's no problem. It's your choice. Now you can tell the others or not but don't talk to me about straight.'

He had to raise his voice now over the rapidly growing noise of indeterminate rumbling.

'Everybody inside!' shouted Sergeant Shrinivasan as the first of the mob tumbled round the bend.

Mike stuffed the hankie back in his pocket. 'Marty, Brendan,' he said. 'Let's go.'

Sergeant Shrinivasan tapped the cane in his hand. I noticed that Mr Kapri was in the vanguard, in spite of the fact that he was now carrying three ornamental tables with an extra five strapped to his back.

'Please,' shouted the Sergeant. 'You must run for your lives!'

Martina turned towards the hall, took a few steps and tripped on her heels, crumbling like a broken kite, her foot twisting horribly. I knelt down, clutching her hand. Even without my book I could see that her ankle was badly fractured.

'Go,' she said.

'And leave you?' I said. 'But we have so much to talk about. There are the arrangements for one thing. I need to speak to your father, and you to mine, though in the latter instance I can foresee one or two complications.'

'There is no time,' she winced. 'Rabindra, you have to save yourself.'

I gently brushed the hair from her forehead.

'Oh my love,' she sobbed, looking towards the frenzied crowd hurtling towards us, 'I fear that we are lost.'

'No matter if we are together,' I said, as a sack of carrots landed beside me.

I stood up straight, buttons popping from the unexpected swell of my chest, one of them flicking into the eye of the first assailant who, temporarily blinded, sunk to his knees. With a mighty bound I leapt over his head, decapitating him on the way, and plunged into the melée, a blood-crazed thing of righteous destruction, thrusting here, slashing there, scrambling over the rapidly swelling pile of amputations, tracheotomies and even a couple of nifty circumcisions. But the more I slashed and skewered, the more they came at me: Pushkara's deadliest assassins, hungry for blood. And though the air was loud with the cries of dying, and the ground beneath me a slippery mire of severed limbs and slithering entrails, I knew it was hopeless. A chance blow knocked the breath out of me. I slew my adversary but the damage was done. I had faltered, they had flung themselves, and in that moment a thousand blades, cudgels and upholstery mallets rained upon me. I had only seconds to live, a few brief moments of glory before the darkness engulfed me forever. With the last shred of strength in my bones, I gazed once more into the eyes of my beloved.

'Are you alright?' said Martina.

'Sorry? Ah, yes, of course. Perfectly alright, thank you.' I looked round. Mr Kapri had stumbled, dropping some of his tables as the first ranks fell over him.

'I think we can leave them to the Sergeant,' said Martina.

It seemed to me that the scenario I had just imagined would have ended the day rather beautifully in spite of my absence from its epilogue. But what happened next was more testing, perhaps, than even the prospect of death. As I followed Martina towards the hall, I became aware of a gentle breeze rustling the leaves of a nearby tree. Normally, of course, I would have found that merely pleasurable but on this occasion it struck me as odd. The village had fallen silent once more and this, I knew by now, was never a good thing. Every sinew in my body wanted to carry on towards the hall except the one that turned my head to look back. A group of elders was pushing its way to the front. These included Mr Gingalarmakrshnamukpadawaya, in the black robes and mortar board which, at one time or another, had terrified most of the people in the village; Mrs Vasayabhni of the Pushkara Archaeological Institute complete with sun hat and spade; and Mr Ghosh from the Pushkara Civil Service who was always smartly presented in pin-striped suit and bowler hat though what he usefully did on a daily basis was anyone's guess. And finally, my Father, replete with gown and wig.

'Rabindranath!' he shouted. 'You will come here, now.'

Hendrix looked out from the hall. 'What's up?' he said.

I pointed to my father.

'Should I moon him?' said Hendrix.

'Would that be useful?' I asked.

'No!' said Martina.

'Rabindranath,' said my Father again, 'I do not expect to have to repeat myself and yet already I am doing so. What I have said before and what I am saying again is that you will come here now!'

I could hear the leaves tremble, Martina breathing softly beside me. The sun twirled diamonds on the ends of my lashes as the ground pressed up through the soles of my feet. The hall, with its sweet shade, beckoned my aching spirit. But Father's brows were knotted to a single throb of fury, his bulging eyes calling me back to my duty, my fear, my other self, the Clinic Skivvy, good only for lancing boils and mopping up, a penance for some ancient crime the memory of which, if not the consequences, had long since faded. And though I had gazed into the eyes of my betrothed in that earlier, imaginary battle, I could not look at them now.

5

DEV DELICATELY PLACED A TEA cup on the table beside him and leaned back in his armchair, rustling a copy of the *Pushkara Daily Gazette*. His body language, as ever, was inscrutable. After a moment, Father ushered in my sisters, waving them to the sofa where they sat, hugging each other.

'Malek Bister and his unspeakable son!' Father began, thumbs hooked into his waistcoat pockets. 'This you would expect of them. For what is their nature but to cheapen and soil, tarnish and despoil?' He paused to savour the resonance. 'But do not think that I am prejudiced.' He looked around, daring us. 'After all, is it my prerogative to decide who comes into being and with what nature they are graced or afflicted as the case may be?'

'Yes, Father,' said one of my sisters helpfully.

'Well, no it isn't,' said Father. 'That's the point. You see?'

She nodded nervously and glanced at my other sister.

'We all have our part to play in this glorious pageant of the universe,' continued Father. 'Which is the first point. The second is that, although some people are a disgrace to themselves and, if I may say,' he raised an eyebrow in my direction, 'to all with whom they come into contact, nevertheless their existence is a fact. The gods, whom we do not question, decided to create the Bisters. We must therefore learn to accept this, even if their reasons are

difficult to construe. It is the same with boils and bunions.'
He nodded to Dev. 'Nobody celebrates their existence. And,
given the occurrence of one or more of these, a visit might
be necessitated to my son who has been to England and is
a Doctor.' He smiled. 'But what we cannot do is berate the
heavens for our discomfort. Unsightly as they are and, as I
know from personal experience, painful at times, they are to
be endured with patience and equanimity even if, ultimately,
it is our intention to lance the little bastards until they afflict
us no more.' He took a breath. 'And so, what we have before
us are the ah... clear and cogent facts, unarguably assembled,
ladies and gentlemen, in such a way as to leave no... vestige of
a doubt as to the veracity of these deliberations nor of the...
constructive interpretation extrapolated from the ah...' He
flushed slightly, glancing down for notes he didn't have on a
table that wasn't there.

'But you wouldn't expect it from your own son?' I offered.

'Indeed, yes,' said Father, 'I am grateful to my learned...
don't interrupt me! This is obviously the proposition I am
coming to.'

My sisters scowled at me. Father cleared his throat.

'I would indeed not expect it from my own blood, my
progeny, the very fruits, as it were, of my loins.'

My sisters hid their faces.

'Behold your brother,' said Father, pointing at Dev. 'And
all that he has done with his life. His bearing, the fine brows
and aristocratic neck. That is not by luck. That is from hard
work over many lifetimes. Now, you may grumble to your
sisters about some cosmic oversight by which you were born
second...'

My sisters looked away guiltily.

'But you are wrong. And it is in your wrongness that you

are born second, that you are irrevocably stupid and that you consort with those who, though indisputably unsavoury, are nevertheless more akin to your sensibilities than the family to which you might otherwise belong.'

My sisters were glaring at me now with palpable pleasure. But I had heard it all before.

'I do not ask you to be like your brother.' He shook his head contemplating the futility of such a wish. 'But I do expect you to behave like a Sharma. A second-rate Sharma, but a Sharma for all that.'

'I am not aware, Father,' I said, 'how I might have displeased you.'

'Might have?' sighed Father with the tragic air of one struggling with unearned familial vicissitudes. 'Mahadev, show him.'

Dev put the paper down, reached behind the armchair and drew out a large flat book bound with a metal coil. He glanced at it, raised his eyebrows and tossed it across the table.

For a moment the breath stopped in my body. Even fixed in the static mirage of an image she was beautiful, her tanned body stretched languidly across a bed of crimson petals, one hand toying with a lock of hair, the other reaching back to the amber light that danced across her skin. By good fortune, a silken cloth had fallen across her breasts, while a posy of blossoms delicately sheltered that which no eyes but mine should see. She shifted slightly, smiling up at me. 'Rabindra,' she sighed, 'through forests and deserts have I journeyed in search of you, but we are together now, for I have found you at last.'

Father snatched it from me. 'That's enough,' he spluttered. 'Read the text. Go on. What does it say?' He shook it, blurring the letters. 'What was the first lesson hammered into your recalcitrant skull by the finest professor in all of Pushkara, Mr

Gingalarmakrshnamukpadawaya? Hmm? Or was he wasting his breath? Did you slouch in every morning, complaining under your satchel, for nothing?'

'Wash your hands before eating?' I offered.

'Well, yes, okay,' said Father. 'The second lesson.'

'Read the text before you look at the pictures,' said Dev.

'Exactly,' said Father, smiling at Dev. 'Once again your brother has demonstrated his impeccable retention of imparted knowledge.'

"Heaven's Blessings',' I read. 'World Tour, South East Asia. Official Calendar.'

'January,' grunted Father, flinging the front page back.

Martina was arm in arm with Cindy, her swimsuit an elaborate concoction of threads and triangles matching the delicate grey-blue of her eyes. Cindy's broad smile gave a whimsical hue to the coquettish pose of her lilac one-piece.

'Perhaps,' I said, 'we could hang this in the waiting room for all those people who don't seem to know what day of the week it is.'

Dev spat out his tea.

'February,' hissed Father, jabbing at it. 'Go on.'

I turned the page. Against a frozen background of gnarled trees Martina stood in a heavy trench-coat, one leg revealing the top edge of a black lace garter.

'March,' said Father.

Sharon pouted from a poolside sun-bed.

I reached for April but Father slammed his hand on the calendar. 'No child of mine is going to see what happened in April,' he said.

'Where does this come from?' I asked.

'From the bowels of iniquity,' intoned Father, making my sisters gasp.

'Sergeant Shrinivasan's selling them from the police station,' said Dev.

'So let me ask you a simple question,' said Father, puffing his chest and gazing at the ceiling. 'Did we talk yesterday?'

'Ah, yes, I think so.'

'Good. Very good. So your recollections extend to yesterday. Perhaps not a lot further but let's be grateful. Now, let me ask you another question. You might have to think about this but don't take too long. In the course of the aforesaid mentioned conversation, were you or were you not given an instruction?'

'Probably,' I said.

'Excellent. I must write to your teacher to say that his labours were not entirely wasted.' He smiled menacingly. 'The next question is a little more difficult. Can you tell me, to the best of your recollection, what was the nature of that instruction?'

'Ah... not to be seen...?'

'Is that a guess,' asked Father, 'Or something you actually recall?'

'A bit of both,' I said.

'Alright. That will serve. And can you suggest, perhaps, why you might have been given that instruction?'

'Um. No, sorry, I can't.'

'That is a good answer,' he said. 'You do not have to know why I do or do not give instructions. It matters only that you follow them.'

'Which is what I was attempting to do,' I said. 'Father, believe me.'

'So let me see if I understand this correctly.' He turned to the window, a classic trick of the advocate about to land the clincher. 'In your efforts not to be seen, you pranced like a buffoon on the steps of the Hotel Nirvana. You then transported yourself by means of a car with flashing lights and blaring sirens, in the interests of discretion, naturally, to the forecourt of that wretched so-called hall where you proceeded to parade yourself in the company of a lady who poses indelicately for everyone to ogle, waiting for the whole of Pushkara to turn up. Now, this is an extremely simple question but I suggest you answer it carefully.' He turned to me, blade raised, cloth rippling. 'How exactly did you think this would lead to you not being seen?'

'Perhaps it wasn't the best way to go about it,' I said, 'but...'

'No buts,' he said firmly. 'Either you are seen or you are not seen. So which do you think you were? Seen or not seen?'

'I'm not sure,' I said playing the stupidity card which, after all, was largely expected of me. 'It is possible that on one or two occasions during the period in question I might have been not unseen, as it were.'

My sisters began to sob.

'Alright,' said Father, pondering my response as a doctor might some liquid against the light. 'So when you say that you were "not unseen", are we to understand that, in your opinion, you were, as they say, "seen"?'

'Yes, possibly,' I said.

'In direct contravention of the instruction that you had been given?'

'Um. I suppose so.'

'You suppose so?'

'I know so.'

'Aha,' said Father. 'That's interesting. Very interesting indeed.' He began to stroll in circles chuckling to himself in a way that suggested he'd forgotten what he'd been driving at.

'The elders,' prompted Dev.

'Quite so,' said Father. 'Thank you. Now, let it be known

that, in the light of a general air of disobedience afflicting the least responsible among us, one of whom is, indeed, among us, the elders have met. And having met they have, of course, deliberated.'

'About what?' I said, feeling my blood slow. 'Me?'

'Don't be ridiculous,' Father scoffed. 'Do you think we have nothing better to talk about than the prurient misdemeanours of a Clinic Skivvy?'

'Pol?' I suggested.

'Well, yes in a way,' said Father. 'But look here, it's none of your business what was discussed. What matters is what we decided.' He smoothed the folds of the wig he wasn't wearing and lifted his chin to its most declamatory thrust. 'After proper consideration of the facts and full deliberation thereon, it has hereby been decreed by a Colloquy of the Elders of Pushkara, that there will be no performance of dance, international or otherwise, at this whatever it's called, this "hall" in the foreseeable future. Moreover, anyone who might have arrived for said purpose will be asked to leave with immediate effect if not sooner. All copies, meanwhile, of this… tawdry publication will be recovered from those who so inelegantly rushed over to the police station as soon as they heard about it, their respective parents determining individual punitive measures at their discretion. Moreover and in the meantime, all male citizens under the age of forty three are confined to their houses until such time as the Elders declare otherwise.'

'But Father,' I interjected, a bead of cold sweat tickling down from my armpit, 'are there not people from England who have arrived only recently for the very purpose of engaging in dancing activities?'

'No exceptions,' said Father with ominous finality.

'And do we not have a considerable fondness for people from England simply because they are from England?' I continued. 'In respect of which we could waive some of the terms of the edict to accommodate them. After all, do we not celebrate their cultural excellence in myriad ways? The flag in Dev's room...'

'Mahadev,' corrected Father.

'... The Heritage Edition British Rail place mats we get out for Diwali, the double-decker bus biscuit tin, my very own red pillar-box key-ring and the picture of my revered brother standing shoulder to shoulder with that nation's most illustrious monarch? How many times has he enthralled us with his tales? And how many times have we begged him for more? Of the great park where serpents hide from Peter's frying pan? Or the one-eyed fakir gazing down from his column on the battle of Trafalgar while pigeons nest on his head? Have we not marvelled at the Palace of Buckingham with a household so large they need horses to get from one end to the other? And was it not in England that my revered brother became the very Doctor whose efforts we all live on since your legal practice in Allahabad failed and you couldn't find any work?'

'Our decision is final,' roared Father. 'These so-called people from England are required to leave immediately on receipt of said declaration. If they refuse, they shall be driven out by force if necessary. They shall be lanced like a boil, sliced like a bunion, extracted like a septic tooth, amputated like a... a gangrenous limb, swabbed like some... sort of...'

Though he was obviously running thin on metaphors I felt no inclination to help.

'... whatever. Anyway. In the meantime, according to the edict and with respect to your age, it would seem that you are henceforth confined to the house,' he concluded, bending to collect his papers and straightening his trousers instead since there weren't any.

'But what about the clinic?' I said.

'Closed until further notice,' said Father looking at Dev who nodded back. 'That is my final word.'

Father's rage continued, however, to erupt intermittently over supper.

'Would you pass me another *roti*?' he'd say. 'The shame of it! My own son! And some chutney, please, if you wouldn't mind.'

My sisters had gone to bed early and Father was on curfew duty when I found Dev in his room reading the *Daily Gazette*. It was always an occasion for the village when its proprietor got around to printing an edition. In our house, by family custom, Dev would always get the first read.

'Revered brother,' I said, sitting at his feet, 'I am perplexed.'

'Join the club,' he said.

'All my life I have been told how admirable the English are...'

'There's a dog for sale,' he interrupted. 'But who'd buy a dog when you can chuck a bone out the window and five scraggy mutts jump to catch it?'

'At least culturally and administratively,' I continued, 'notwithstanding the occasional bombarding of Maharajas out of their palaces.'

'And these are dogs that don't even belong to anyone, just nameless bags of fluff and bone, I suppose. Do you think dogs who don't belong to anyone have names?' he asked.

'But now that we have actual English people among us, surely we should be welcoming them with open arms?'

'And if they don't have names,' he continued, 'what do you

think they call each other? Or maybe they don't. Maybe they just mooch around without bothering too much about who they are or why.'

'Is this not an ideal opportunity to celebrate our cultural similarities and even our differences; Indians never being much inclined to bombard anyone out of anything? You might even find that you have mutual acquaintances. I'm sure it's possible.'

'And here it says that Miss Gopal is now sixteen years old and available for marriage. But everyone knows her parents have been saying that for the last five years and she'll never get married unless they can do something about her vexatious disposition.'

'Perhaps they know the Queen and can pass on your regards.'

'Do you know she hit her last suitor over the head with a broom because he didn't take his shoes off at the door?'

'Noble brother,' I said, 'whose venerable feet I am not fit to touch, I implore you to discover what is irking Father. If it is the apprehension that Mr Bister is responsible for the arrival of our English visitors, then he is wrong in this.'

'Haven't you been to see Miss Gopal?' said Dev looking at me. 'Twice, wasn't it?'

'Three times.'

He chuckled, turning a page.

'Father still insists we would make a good match.'

'I don't suppose she attacked you, did she?'

'Yes, a little.'

'But you must have been warned about the shoes.'

'Indeed, but when I bent down to take them off, my shirt became un-tucked at the back. She said, how many times have I told you not to wander around like an over-dressed baboon with your shirt hanging out. I answered that, as she'd never mentioned it before, this could only be regarded as a first infringement.'

'And what did she say to that?' asked Dev.

'She attacked me with a broom.'

'Did she strike you?'

'No, I jumped aside. But the blow saw to some wooden nick nacks on the hall table, after which their pet dog, excited by all the commotion, attempted to seize the broom for himself. I left them struggling in the hall where, judging by her screams, I assumed he'd turned his attentions to something more accessible.'

'Well, that would explain why they are also advertising their dog,' said Dev.

'Mahadev,' I said, returning to the point. 'I have a confession to make. Or rather two. The first is of professional misconduct at the clinic this morning.'

'Oh, really,' he said, frowning into the vacant hollow of his empty cup.

'A patient came to see the Doctor but I attended to her instead.'

'So?' he said. 'You know I'm far too busy to footle about with every petty ailment that saunters in bleating for medical attention.'

'But I behaved as if I was the Doctor.'

'In what way?' he asked, tilting the cup and sucking at it.

'In the way that I ushered her into the consulting room with a vague air of pompous authority. By standing in front of the door so she couldn't read the words "Minor Ailments" on the plate. In not wearing my white coat so she couldn't see the name-badge pinned to my top pocket. On one occasion I allowed the sunlight to glint off my stethoscope knowing that nothing inspires confidence more than medical equipment the purpose of which is mysterious. When I sat at my desk it was with a proprietorial air, and when I gazed thoughtfully into space it was to convey the impression that I knew what I was talking about. And, worse than all of this, when she enquired obliquely as to my professional status I failed to refute the implicit suggestion that I might be medically qualified. All of which amounts, I fear, to the masquerading of myself as a person beyond his true credentials.'

'Did you kill her?' he said, squinting into the cup.

'I don't think so,' I said.

'Was she lying prostrate, mouth open, not breathing, with a glazed look in her eyes?'

'No.'

'Well, those are the usual symptoms,' he said. 'For future reference.'

'I am fairly certain,' I said, 'that she left the clinic alive.'

'No harm done, then.'

'However,' I said, faltering slightly, 'this transgression of clinical protocol pales beside the gravity of my other confession.'

'Do you think you could get one of our sisters to make me another cup of tea?' he said.

'They have gone to their room to entreat the gods to remove whatever blight in their souls caused them to have so reprehensible a brother,' I said. 'But I'll make you one, if you wish.'

As I watched the warm chai bubble in the saucepan, I couldn't help wondering if Dev's dismissal of my infractions amounted to an absolution or if I would still have to pay for them later. If the forced departure of my beloved was part of the bill, I was obviously paying big time, perhaps even for one or two past crimes. It was Sergeant Shrinivasan's view that a good thwack from his cane dealt not only with immediate misdemeanours but those from past lifetimes and even lifetimes to come. At least that's what he wrote in his deposition to the District Police Administration after some of the villagers had complained about his excessive use of force even in situations where no force had been required. His argument had been accepted and his use of the cane, thereafter, all the more enthusiastic.

Dev accepted the tea with a smile.

'Revered brother,' I said, 'If the arrival of these English persons has caused any upset in Pushkara, then I fear the blame is to be laid with me.'

'How's that, then?' he said, taking a sip and smiling. I knew just how he liked it.

'Because it was not under normal circumstances that they were brought here,' I said.

'Yes,' he said, picking up the paper. 'I know.'

'You know?' I said, startled.

'Their plane was struck by lightning which shorted out the electrical circuits forcing them to make an emergency landing in the city on the plains.'

'That is indeed how it might appear,' I said. 'But the lightning was no accident.'

'Lightning is always an accident,' chuckled Dev, 'it's hardly the sort of thing one can organise in advance.'

'But that's exactly the point,' I said. 'Pol and I made it happen, through our sacrifice and austerities, the storm, the rain, the aeronautically debilitating bolts of lightning, everything.'

'Well, that's very interesting,' said Dev. 'I didn't know you were in the habit of performing sacrifices.'

'I'm not,' I said. 'But I was desperate.'

'For what?'

'An English bride. Which the gods have now provided.'

He chuckled. Then he chuckled some more. Then he raised the tea to his lips and put it down again chuckling so much it spilt. I made a mental note to ask Mrs Pallabhi to mop it up in the morning.

'Rabindra,' he said. 'You might have wanted an English bride, but no amount of grovelling to abstract concepts is going to make one drop out of the skies.' He paused for a moment. 'Hmm, I see what you mean. But alright, obviously it can seem a bit like that sometimes. Things do. If you sit around long enough, sooner or later two completely separate things are going to happen in a way that seems connected. But the fact is it doesn't mean a thing, Rabindra. Really, it doesn't mean anything at all.'

'But didn't one of the holy men tell us that everything is connected to everything else and nothing happens without a reason?'

'Yes, he did,' said Dev. 'Until one of the goats attacked him on the upper slopes. You remember? The goatherd accused him of provoking the goat which the holy man denied. Well, either he had done something to provoke the goat or he hadn't. You see? Philosophy is just the loose assembly of whatever vague ideas happen to suit us at the time. You break a tea cup and say it wasn't your fault. It just happened to drop out of your hands. You might have carelessly let go of it, but are you responsible for gravity? Or maybe a breeze tipped it off the table, but that wasn't your fault either because somebody else opened the window. A plane is struck by lightning and you think it's because you chucked a spoonful of ghee on a fire. But let's look at it another way. The gods aren't concerned with our petty problems. They're too busy maintaining the balance of good and evil, right and wrong, justice and injustice, the great duality that is the weft of ignorance and stupidity commonly referred to as "the universe". So it's not that easy to catch their attention. You can't just trot along your whole life paying them scant regard until you want something and then come over all pious in the hope they'll be happy with a couple of marigolds. They want unremitting obsequiousness every day for years on end. And only then, if at all, will they even consider coughing up some grudging little boon.'

'It wasn't just a couple of marigolds. Really. It was... a whole load of penances. For instance, I washed every day, almost, well mostly...'

'And you prayed?' he interrupted. 'How often? Once? Twice? For a couple of weeks hoping they'll be impressed? Are you kidding? What about before then? You think they don't keep count? And I don't mean the daily requests for Mrs Pallabhi to cook something other than egg curry for once, or "please god, direct my shoe more accurately at that bloody cockroach." That's nothing. We still get egg curry and the shoe bounces harmlessly away as the cockroach scurries off laughing at our futile beliefs.' He leaned forward, earnestly now. 'When have you prayed, really prayed, with your entire being stretched out, flayed and sobbing, 'til it hurts?'

'When Mother was sick, I prayed for her to get better.'

'But she didn't,' said Dev quietly.

'And after she died, I prayed for her not to be dead.'

'Let it never be said,' he muttered, 'that you are undemanding.' He looked down for a moment. 'Well, there you are,' he said suddenly. 'It's just as I was saying. Things happen as they will and beyond the odd bit of tinkering with the few things we might be able to tinker with, there's nothing much we can do about anything. These holy men drone on about causality and connection but the truth is nothing means anything beyond this big, ugly, meaningless muddle we muddle along with until we muddle no more.'

His eyes had clouded now as they did sometimes after dinner, or when I needed him to advise on a diagnosis, or just because the day was warm, or cold, I could never quite determine the cause. In the days after Mother's death I had thought they would never sparkle again. It was during his first year back, newly qualified and the clinic thriving. They said he had the touch. Whatever that was. Until it came to Mother. He had tried every remedy at his disposal. Finally he was forced to pronounce her beyond the reach of medical intervention and we could only wait. Young Doctors, fired with the zeal of their new skills, often believe they can accomplish anything. That Dev's first disappointment should have concerned his own mother made the ineluctable rites of professional seasoning all the more bitter. Thereafter he had confined himself largely to research, leaving the humdrum ailments and clinical management to me. I was never quite sure if it was a misguided sense of guilt or the desire to find a cure for everything that made his devotions to the frontiers of medical science so earnest.

I left him to his contemplations, having long ago given up trying to lighten them, and went round to the *Puja* Room at the side of the house to talk to Mother. It was the quietest place I knew, with its soft lights and warm shadows, in spite of the busy streets outside. In the presence of love, they say, even the gods hold their breath.

My sisters had lit some oil lamps and sprinkled fresh rice over the altar. The centrepiece, as in every Pushkara household, was a figurine of Lord Shiva, God of The Dance, his four hands raised, one foot on the wriggling monstrosity of The Turtle. For generations these had been crafted by the same Pushkaran family, the Aptalcharys. Indeed, some said that every Shiva tended to look a bit like its maker, especially as their hair receded and the Great God began to sport a comb-over. When he'd grown a beard one year there was uproar. Later attempts to introduce a moustache met the same fate.

I knelt on the cushions, folded my hands into my lap and bowed reverently for a few minutes. When I looked up he was smiling back through his spectacles with the bemused squint characteristic of the present Mr Aptalchary. To his left was the newspaper cut-out of a guru, since no shrine was complete without the image of some venerable gent swathed in flowers. To his right was a picture of Mother in her twenties, long before I'd known her, though the slightly anxious eyes were familiar enough.

'Mother,' I said, 'I am confused.'

'You should try being a dead mother speaking through the imagination of her child,' she retorted.

'How are you?' I said.

'Dead,' she said. 'How do you think?'

'Silly question, I suppose.'

'When was the last time you gave your ears a good poke out?' she said. 'I'll bet you've got wax in there from two years ago.'

'That is no longer recommended,' I said. 'Scientifically speaking, it has now been established that cleaning your ears out only makes them dirtier.'

'What nonsense,' she said. 'You listen to these people rather than your own mother? And look at your hair, all ragged at the edges. You need a good trim and I don't mean by your sisters, go into the village and get it done properly.'

'Mother,' I said, 'if you are just in my imagination, how is it that you are still able to rebuke me?'

'I may be just in your imagination,' she said, archly, 'but I am still your mother.'

Which seemed like a fair point.

'So what are you confused about?' she said, her voice softening. 'I seem to remember, Rabindra, that you were always confused about something.'

'Well,' I said, 'you probably don't know this but some English people arrived yesterday.'

'Yes,' she said. 'And a fine lot they are too. Particularly that Martina. What a beauty. I hereby offer my unconditional blessings on your marriage.'

'Mother,' I said, 'are you just saying that because I'm imagining it or are you really saying it?'

She chuckled.

'The problem,' I said, 'is that I don't know what to do. If I cannot see Martina, I will be unable to pledge my troth, we will not get married and she will die, eventually, broken-hearted and alone. So either I disobey an edict of the elders or stand idly by to see the dreams of my beloved crushed. Could any lover worthy of the name do such a thing?'

'What exactly is preventing you from going to see her?' asked Mother.

'Father,' I said.

'You have not answered my question,' she said. 'What, exactly, is preventing you from going to see her?'

'Obedience,' I said. 'Duty.'

'Does this answer my question?'

I felt that somehow it didn't.

'You think that you do not know,' she said. 'But you know that you could know if only you knew how to know. Rabindra, there are many things unknown to you. Many of these are not worth knowing so I shouldn't worry about them, to be honest. But you will never learn anything until you learn to listen to your heart.'

'But what is it telling me?' I said. 'To obey my father as I have always obeyed him? More or less? To run helter-skelter to my beloved? If it is telling me both of these then it is asking me to cut myself in half, which is impossible.'

'Not impossible,' she said. 'For you have already been cut in half. And this is what causes you pain. There are two half-Rabindras running around, each desiring to be whole. But that can never be for they are running around in opposite directions.'

'Then how can they meet?' I asked.

'When you realise that you are neither of them,' she said.

'Help me, Mother, for I do not understand.'

'If your head stopped for just a moment, what would your heart do?'

'Fly to my beloved.'

'Then you know.'

'But what then?' I said. 'Father would beat me. The village would scorn me. I would be like Mr Chatterjee, trying to strike up a conversation while people walk past me humming loudly. I would be dismissed from the clinic. I would have to leave Pushkara and never be welcome back. And although I have dreamed of marrying an English wife and living in England, this is the only place I have ever known and I am afraid.'

But she said no more.

Was that all? I thought. The fear of going. The fear of

staying. Perhaps a fear of fear itself. How ridiculous we can seem if only we take the time to look. Shiva danced across the fold of my hands, cast by flickering candles, over the walls of the room, spectacles and all, his limbs a shifting serenade of shadows, creating and destroying in a single moment that was now and forever. I thought of Father patrolling the streets, and the young men pining for their confiscated calendars. I wondered what my beloved had indeed got up to in April. I thought of the Buddhist Cook, a thing of air and light on the hotel steps. I thought of smoke rising in a fine tendril from the fires we'd lit, of butter crackling over the charred wood. I thought of my socks in the corner of a drawer for some reason. And then I sat up.

Outside, the air was very still. Two elders on their respective patrols exchanged pleasantries and moved on. A dog was trying to squeeze through the railings to get at some rubbish while another sniffed at the front gate and, just for a moment, I felt as nameless and desolate as the nameless desolation of their grubby lives, furtively searching, incessantly sniffing and yet, with the open street and a vacant destiny to call their own, somehow free. I crept over to the shadows across the road and began to run.

6

THE HOTEL NIRVANA, FOREVER HAUNTED by the warnings and injunctions imprinted on my soul about its lurking venalities, loomed dark against the starry sky. Mother had finally told me about Mrs Dong, having initially refused, saying some things it were best not to know. But when an elder caught me resting in its shade one morning and declared that I had thus imperilled my future lives, and I had thereafter scrupulously avoided treading on worms and beetles in case I'd be accused of murdering relatives in a previous life during my next one, Mother had sighed, fearing that I might develop a permanent limp, and said perhaps it was time.

Fearsome as Mrs Dong now was, when she first came to the village she was merely Little Amchila, discovered on the upper slopes by a goatherd, a waif in rags fleeing the tyrannies of Tibet. We'd had a few in those years. Many, of course, never made it across the passes which were said to twinkle with the bones of fallen travellers. Of those who did, most moved on, but Little Amchila decided to stay. She was put up in the Hotel Nirvana which was very popular in those days. Its owners, Mr and Mrs Jafferjee ran an excellent kitchen, Mrs Jafferjee was often to be heard shouting at the cooks, and the food was first rate. Little Amchila, with her ragged hair and skinny arms, soon made herself useful clearing the tables and washing up. Mother said that Tibetans are often thought of as dreamers because they won't admit the existence of anything, but in her view they knew how to work. Mrs Jafferjee, who believed that a good beating now and then was an excellent tonic for staff morale, was especially severe with the scrawny wretch with no history, family, or name worth mentioning. But one day all that changed. The 'pitiful ragamuffin, who had climbed her way over the mountains to collapse at our feet', as Mother put it, had become a young lady, in fact, a rather striking one. She had stood by the kitchen doors, a plate of *shondish* in one hand, a tray of tea in the other, hips tilted slightly in one of Mrs Jafferjee's cast-off saris, gazing around at the suddenly silent room. After that there were many hushed conversations among the young men of Pushkara. Several boys of marriageable age even enquired about the possibilities, but of course it was out of the question.

In the meantime, Mrs Jafferjee became ever more vehement in the application of disciplinary measures, although she complained that the girl's quiet defiance in the face of a rebuke rendered the act of rebuking oddly unsatisfying. Mr Jafferjee, it has to be said, had never supported his wife's approach to staff supervision, though he lived well enough on its rewards. He preferred to smile and ask if they were having a nice day. With Little Amchila he would offer soothing words, dainties from the dessert trolley and, it was said, even the occasional hug. That is, until he died.

It came as no great shock. He'd already collapsed a few times clutching his chest and, since people who do that tend to drop dead sooner or later, there wasn't much anyone could do except wait. Unfortunately, Mr Chatterjee had joined him on the bench under the bhodi tree, so when he slumped forwards with a glazed look in his eye, everyone thought it a natural response to Mr Chatterjee's discourse. It was only when Mr Jafferjee failed to move as the bus arrived that his condition was fully appreciated. Some people, rather unkindly, accused Mr Chatterjee of boring him to death, but at any rate, that was the end of Mr Jafferjee who always said he'd like to come back as the owner of a Parisian Bistro. One hopes, said Mother, that he achieved this, assuming one comes back as anything at all.

For a while that also seemed to be the end of Little Amchila. The funeral smoke had hardly wafted away before her clothes were out on the pavement. She picked up what she could, left what she couldn't and walked off down the road. And that was the last anyone ever thought they'd see of our Tibetan waif.

Mrs Jafferjee mourned with characteristic extravagance. Most ladies like a bit of sympathy when their husbands die, but she turned it into a culinary art. 'The Mr Jafferjee Memorial Meringue' was especially successful, a sort of lemon mousse with a crusty top, and though the 'Widow's Lament' was a little too chocolaty for most tastes, it was edible enough with a dollop of cream. She hung a flag at half-mast, painted the front door white and even declared the anniversary of Mr Jafferjee's death a public holiday, though the elders felt this ought to be discussed.

As the village lawyer, Father had been asked to read the will at an occasion to which everyone was invited. Most people got a little something, though not necessarily what they'd expected. Some got recipes, others blessings or even advice, such as 'if you will steal napkins from the restaurant, kindly do so with more discretion, what do you think I am, a bloody idiot?'. Of course Mrs Jafferjee began to look increasingly pleased as Father read down the list. Until it got to her. Mr Jafferjee had much to say about his wife. Father had tried mumbling it but people at the back told him to speak up. Mrs Jafferjee stood up a few times and shook her fist but had to wait to the end to hear what she'd got: a room, a bed, some linen and 'enough food to maintain corporeal wellbeing', as he put it, to the end of her days. She accused Father of not reading it correctly and demanded he start again. So he did. 'To Mrs Gheenkal, a recipe for plum pudding.' At which she screamed that she'd only meant the last bit. But it was exactly the same the second time around.

'But what about the Hotel?' she shouted.

'I haven't got to that,' said Father.

'Ah,' she said, sitting down again. 'Why didn't you say? Go on then. Read it.'

'The Hotel Nirvana,' intoned Father. 'Founded by my great grandfather, cherished by generations of Jafferjees, no less by me, a testament to the goodwill and community spirit of my beloved Pushkara, I leave to…'

Father chose an unfortunate moment in which to clean his glasses. At last, however, he tucked his tie back under his pullover and straightened his collar before ruffling through the document in search of where he'd left off. Mrs Jafferjee looked as if she might spontaneously combust. When Father spoke it was to whisper, 'My Little Amchila.'

'What?' said Mrs Jafferjee, leaping at Father who had to beat her back with the will itself. 'What did you say? You leave the Hotel, my Hotel, to that filthy harlot, that whore? And you think that's funny, do you? You think that's clever?' Eventually, Sergeant Shrinivasan, who had been hoping for a bottle or two from the hotel cellars, managed to impress upon her the difference between message and messenger. After which she cancelled the tea and cleared everyone out, which a lot of people thought rather ungracious as they'd only stayed on for that reason.

A few months later Mrs Jafferjee found a legal adviser, which is to say someone rolling up in search of the sacred shrine who had been told that legal experience was a plus if he wished to stay at the Hotel Nirvana for nothing. For weeks thereafter huge bundles of documents tied with string would appear on our doorstep which, on inspection, turned out to be nothing more than pages torn from cheap novels. He might not have been a real lawyer, Mother had said, but he'd obviously understood the correlation between paper, time and money. He did raise one devastating point, however. Since Little Amchila no longer lived in Pushkara and nobody knew where she was, how could she contest a refutation of the will? Apparently it's an ancient legal principle that if there's nobody to fight with you can't fight at all. After that, the Hotel offered a whole new menu. The 'Law Is An Ass' coconut dessert didn't taste very nice, according to Mother, but the 'Victory Over Pompous Imbeciles' herbal infusion became extremely popular with the ladies. Her efforts to mark the event with an annual 'Good Riddance To Gold-Digging Whores Day', however, failed to gather support.

The legal adviser, meanwhile, proved to have rather more legal experience, and of a different sort, than he'd previously mentioned, when he was caught sneaking off with a bag of Mrs Jafferjee's brass ornaments. It subsequently transpired that he was wanted for a number of crimes in various states and has probably been adding to his legal experience ever since.

Nobody knows how she found out about the will, but one day the bus pulled up and out stepped Little Amchila and The Buddhist Cook. Of course she wasn't Little Amchila anymore, she was Mrs Dong. But whether she'd got married while she was away or had always been married but only now chose to reveal it, or whether she wasn't married at all but simply used the name for effect, remains a mystery. Some thought the Buddhist Cook might be her husband but monks don't marry, as a rule, unless he'd married her before he became a monk but really, said Mother, that would be far too confusing for everyone. 'You see,' she added, 'sometimes we know almost everything about a person and sometimes hardly anything at all. But whether we know almost everything or almost nothing there's always a little bit that nobody ever quite knows. Sometimes people don't even know it themselves. That's very much how it is in the business of knowing anything about anyone.'

To begin with, Mrs Jafferjee refused to let Mrs Dong, as she now was, into the hotel. But Father insisted that, pending a resolution of the dispute, they should both have equal access to the premises. Mrs Jafferjee grudgingly allowed Mrs Dong to sleep in a store cupboard, while the Buddhist Cook crept every night to the rubble at the back, where he'd sit perfectly motionless even when rats perched on his head, which a number of people claimed to have seen.

Mrs Jafferjee, meanwhile, got straight to business. She hired some lawyers from the plains who said she had a strong case and could be confident of an early hearing, possibly within the next twenty years. But shortly after she began to sicken. Some thought she was pining for her late husband, or regretting that she'd never had a kind word to say about him when he was alive. But the general opinion was that Mrs Dong was poisoning her. Sergeant Shrinivasan was asked to investigate but said he could find no evidence. The fact is, he didn't like Mrs Jafferjee very much, especially after she'd accused him of 'disappearing' supplies from the top of the bus. In any case, Mrs Dong was at pains to point out that if it wasn't for her, there would be no-one to look after Mrs Jafferjee at all. The Buddhist Cook moved in to the kitchen but his menus weren't a success. He refused to cook meat, fish or poultry and what he did cook was exactly the same whatever the names he gave it in the menu. On Sunday people would order the 'Himalayan Dish Of The Day' and get rice and Dahl. Then on Wednesday they'd ask for the 'All India Spice Supreme' and get what they'd eaten on Sunday. The puddings weren't much better, and some people were rather put off by the new names Mrs Dong had given them. 'So What Do You Think Of It Now You Bitch?' was just a lump of vanilla kulfi, while 'Ha Ha Ha! The Foot Is In The Other Boot!' was two lumps of vanilla kulfi.

When Mrs Jafferjee died at last, everyone felt a bit sorry and perhaps slightly guilty that they'd rather neglected her towards the end. Still, they put on a good show with flowers and incense, a big pyre on the lake, and the whole lot pushed out to smoulder while everybody wept and wailed. Mrs Dong asked for the privilege of lighting it but, as this traditionally goes to the holy man, her request was declined. The Buddhist Cook didn't attend, perhaps because he doesn't believe in birth and death, but more likely because he was too busy preparing for the reception. It was a disappointing feast, according to Mother, just the rice and Dahl, and not much to go round. Mrs Dong said if people didn't like it they could find somebody else's funeral to go to, preferably their own. Father wrote to the lawyers in the city telling them of Mrs Jafferjee's demise and that was the end of her case. To this day nobody knows if Mrs Dong was the rightful owner or whether, as Mrs Jafferjee had argued, the bequest was invalid on the grounds of insanity.

'Is noborry here!' shouted Mrs Dong from the lobby as I knocked on the door.

Behind me, the patter of slippered feet suggested the approach of a patrolling elder.

'But what about Pol?' I hissed through the letter box. 'What about the English people?'

'I said is noborry!' she yelled back. 'Why you talk like a snake?'

My shadow wobbled suddenly in front of me.

'Who's there?' called the elder, his balaclava dark against the shadows of the street. I dodged the torch beam as it swung after me, hoping it was one of the older elders, preferably deaf, mostly blind and unlikely to chase me round the back.

The rubble, hazardous even in daylight with its fragments of bathroom fittings and old wardrobes, was doubly treacherous in the dark. But I'd crossed it a couple of times already and quickly managed to find my way back to the windows.

'Identify yourself!' shouted the elder, panting from the effort of traversing a broken chest of drawers. I glanced round to see Mr Chatterjee who, far from deaf, could spot a conversation worth interrupting at five hundred paces. I lifted myself to the ledge, wedging my foot against a drain-pipe. Through a gap in the shutters I could see a dark room with a door at the end, slivered with light, which blotted out suddenly and reappeared. I tapped on the shutter.

'There you are!' said Mr Chatterjee. But he had only succeeded in grappling a tree at the edge of the precipice.

I tapped again, the stone ledge cutting into my fingers. Brick-dust trickled down from beneath my foot.

'A noise!' said Mr Chatterjee. 'I am sure of it. For I have

heard many noises in my life and consider myself, not to speak immodestly, more than qualified to know what is and what is not a noise when I hear it.'

Inside, the room flooded with light. A burly shadow moved tentatively towards the window.

'Hendrix?' I said, pressing my mouth to the shutters. 'It's me.'

'Well, that's a start,' said Mr Chatterjee, swinging his torch across the rubble. 'But you will need to be more specific. Who is you, exactly? An under-forty-three, I'll bet.'

'The Doc?' said Hendrix.

'That's right,' I said. 'Let me in.'

'Let me in?' scoffed Mr Chatterjee. 'That is hardly a credible response to my simple enquiry. A name. Your age. That is the sort of information you need to come up with if you wish to avoid a sharp rebuke from my umbrella.'

'Where are you?' said Hendrix. 'Is this some kind of yogic thing?'

'I'm outside,' I said. 'Right here.'

'I see,' said Mr Chatterjee. 'You are outside and wish to be let in. But how am I to let you in if I too am outside? This makes no sense whatsoever.'

The drain pipe creaked under my foot.

'How did you get there?' said Hendrix.

'Does it matter?' I squealed as the pipe broke free of its bolts and swung loose.

'Now, this is clearly a rhetorical question,' said Mr Chatterjee. 'Does it matter that you should be let in? But into what or where? This has not yet been established. I demand that you not only elucidate your meaning but reveal yourself, for I see nothing here but a lot of old junk and this tree. Unless it's the tree that speaks, of course,' he chuckled.

'Hang on,' said Hendrix.

'I'm trying,' I said, as my other foot began to lose its grip.

'Trying?' said Mr Chatterjee. 'Do you mean this in the colloquial sense of "effort" or the jurisprudential sense of establishing the truth, neither meaning being mutually exclusive since any effort tests the truth of ourselves while no truth is won without effort.'

Hendrix fiddled with the locks.

'Just open it, please,' I gasped.

'Open it?' queried Mr Chatterjee. 'What is there to open? What is it within my powers to open? My sensibilities? My senses?' His feet slipped on the scree, forcing him into a clumsy pirouette, umbrella flailing. He recovered his balance and stumbled to the edge of the chasm, knocking a bidet into oblivion.

'Stop!' I shouted. 'Right there.'

'You what?' said Hendrix.

'Not you,' I whispered. 'Yes!' I shouted. 'I am the tree that is speaking to you. Here I am. The tree that you embraced a few moments ago, the warmth of which still ah... warms me in an... an agreeable way.'

'Nonsense,' said Mr Chatterjee, stepping carefully towards it. 'Trees do not talk. And if they did, I am sure they would make more sense. No. I am certain of it. There is an under-forty three about the place making mischief, in fear, no doubt, of the sharp edge of my brolly. Not that it has a sharp edge, since it wasn't designed for that purpose, although, to be honest, it isn't much good for the purpose for which it was designed. It collapses in the slightest breeze and though I took it back to Bister's Bits and Bobs for a refund, all I received was the discovery, sharp edged or not, that it can deliver a most discomforting blow. What? Have you gone silent? Riddles, enigmas and then silence?'

'It's all rusted,' grunted Hendrix heaving at the lock.

'You have to understand,' I said, 'that I don't normally talk to people. So I'm a little bit shy. Usually I just chat with the other trees and some of the shrubs. You won't tell anyone, will you?'

'Even if I tried,' he murmured, 'I am not sure anyone would listen.'

The window jolted sharply upwards. 'There we go,' said Hendrix. 'Oh.'

'It's just the shutter,' I whispered. 'It's latched somehow.'

'Where?' said Hendrix.

I peered through the slats. 'On the left,' I said.

'The left?' said Mr Chatterjee. 'What do you mean? What is on the left?'

Hendrix forced the catch open, flakes of rust flicking against my face.

'Now the right,' I said.

'The right?' said Mr Chatterjee. 'You say it is now on the right? What is on the right?'

Hendrix snapped the catch. 'I think that's it,' he said pushing at the shutters.

'And above you,' I said. 'Look up. Just there.'

Mr Chatterjee stared at the night sky and shook his head. I pressed myself against the bricks.

'Come on, please,' I said.

'Yes, yes,' said Mr Chatterjee. 'If I only knew what you are referring to.'

The shutters opened suddenly, knocking me backwards. I grabbed one of them, my legs swinging helplessly in the air.

'Hey Doc,' said Hendrix, 'you're flying.'

'I am clinging,' I muttered. 'There is a difference.'

'Quite so,' said Mr Chatterjee as Hendrix reached out

and hauled me in. 'Clinging does rather describe one's predicament these days.'

'Who's that?' said Hendrix.

'One of the old ones,' I said, brushing the dust from my shirt.

'An elder?' asked Hendrix.

'No,' I said. 'There's a difference.'

'Like clinging and flying,' grinned Hendrix.

Outside, Mr Chatterjee was staring at the tree. 'You have beguiled me with conundrums,' he was saying. 'And yet I think I understand what you are trying to tell me. Your secrets are the mysteries I have been seeking as I cling, if I may use your terminology, to the treacherous ledge of hopes and dreams. And when I say treacherous, believe me, it's all gone frightfully horrid quite recently.'

'Can you though?' said Hendrix, ushering me towards the corridor.

'Can I what?'

'Fly?'

'No. I don't think so.'

'Have you tried?' he asked.

'I'm sorry, I can't say that I have.'

'So you don't know. I mean, for sure.'

'I am pretty sure,' I said, 'that I can't.'

As Hendrix closed the door behind us I could hear Mr Chatterjee saying, 'You see, I've never told this to anyone but for many years now I've rather admired the wife of my second cousin. And I don't mean intellectually.'

'This way,' said Hendrix, trotting downstairs. 'We're on the roof. War council.'

'War?' The word surprised me.

'They've shut us down.' He turned left, setting a brisk

pace along the corridor. 'Padlocked the venue, took the gear, posters, memorabilia, the lot.' We turned up some stairs. 'The Sergeant went nuts. Mike's happy as a buggered bunny. Nearly there,' he said. 'It's just a passage off the passage, down a couple of steps, across a landing and *voilà*!'

'But how do you know this?' I said. 'Even people who come here regularly can wander about for hours, stumbling into Mrs Dong at last and getting shouted at.'

He shrugged. 'It's what I do. Corridor-Man. Stairs and alleyways. Fag butts and spider crap. Carnegie, Sydney, I've done Earls Court more times than I've paid for a shag, Hammersmith's my second home, Blackpool, Hamburg, Bognor bloody Regis and the arse end of just about everywhere else. Here we go.'

He waved me to a door so small I had to crawl through.

'Is Pol here?' I asked.

'Doubt it,' said Hendrix with a smile.

'On your knees, you worms!' shouted Malek, paradoxically, as I stepped onto the roof. 'For the gods are among us or at least the nearest thing you'll find to one that doesn't fart stardust.' He waved a glass, slopping whisky over his lap.

Sergeant Shrinivasan, perched on a wall at the edge of the terrace, slapped his thigh and laughed.

I began to notice other figures on the roof. Sharon's face flared briefly as she lit a cigarette. The hunched tumble of a shadow in the far corner I took to be Mike, his crumpled jacket folded over him, snoring gently. I looked round hopefully, a little anxiously perhaps, but every hope and anxiety that had ever kept me awake at night or made me stare into space while a patient explained their symptoms melted suddenly into a cool, quiet ocean of peace. For there she was, the object of my adorations, sitting in a low seat, slim legs in blue denim, a bottle of beer poised on her lap. The soft moonlight cast a pale shadow of her profile over the broken slabs and in that moment I could have knelt and kissed them, sufficient merely in the joy of her silhouette for all eternity.

'So what do you want?' said Malek. 'Or have you come to gloat?'

'Oh, leave him alone,' said Hendrix sticking a glass in my hand. 'Poor little chap.'

'No, no,' said Malek, 'They don't do that.'

'Really?' said Hendrix.

'Why don't you sit down?' said Martina.

Hendrix dragged a chair over.

I wondered why the gods had so rewarded my feeble efforts to win their grace. Perhaps I had inadvertently pleased them on some occasion of which I was unaware. Sauntering off to work one day, my head in a dream, I might have thought: 'That bloody Mrs Ginko is nothing but an irritating hypochondriac with bad breath and alopecia but come now, Rabindra, that's not a very nice thing to think about a fellow human being, is it'? Or maybe I'd avoided treading on a beetle that, unbeknownst to me, was an incarnation of Brahma popping down to the world of his making to test our merit. Or, in a previous life as a toad or a mouse, I might have declined to croak from the pond beside which a monk sat meditating or, having sneaked up to the biscuit of an ascetic, had elected not to nibble it. Who knows why or by what means our destinies are shaped? What if I'd stepped on that beetle in a moment of carelessness, or nibbled the biscuit behaving only as the mouse I was, for Brahma surely made mice to nibble? The gods, omnipotent but unkind, play to rules that we mortals, shuffling in the fleshy confines of our fleeting bodies, can hardly guess at.

'All my life…' I began.

'Quiet everyone!' interrupted Malek loudly. 'For lo, the Brahmin speaks. And even if he makes no bloody sense you'll have to nod meekly and agree with whatever he comes out with or you'll be reborn squirming in goat shit.'

'Go on,' said Hendrix gently.

'All my life,' I began again, 'I have felt oddly confused. About all sorts of things, really. Who I am, what I'm supposed to be and... and all that. And on days when I'm not confused, I'm confused about why I'm not confused. But at last everything is clear to me. As clear as the night sky and the glittering stars above us.'

'Dude,' murmured Hendrix.

'For now I know,' I continued, 'without a shadow of a doubt, that not croaking beside the pond, nibbling that biscuit, or squishing the originator of all things with a careless step, were blessings of which I am undeserving as I am undeserving of you, Martina.'

'I'm glad it's clear to you,' said Malek, clapping his hands. 'You see? That's just what I was saying. Now you listen to me.' He stood up. 'Hopefully this'll make sense, but do let me know if it doesn't. Tell your father, I'm not done yet. The show... what will the show do, Sergeant?'

'Go on!' said Sergeant Shrinivasan teetering precariously.

'He doesn't own this town,' said Malek. 'In fact, when you think about it, I do.' He waved his whisky. 'Where does this come from? I'll tell you. Bister's Beverages. And this...?' He blew smoke towards me. 'Bister's Baccy.'

'And these...' said Sergeant Shrinivasan rattling his medals.

'Bister's Baubles,' said Malek, 'best prices, everything genuine.'

'NASA Space Mission,' said the Sergeant gazing at his top pocket.

'Bister's Backsides,' chuckled Hendrix tapping his deckchair.

'Bister's Fine Furnishings,' muttered Malek, fixing him with a squint before jabbing his cigar back at me. 'So he doesn't tell me what I can and cannot do in my own town. You understand me? This is my town. Not his. Not yours. Not anymore.'

'Is at door,' said Mrs Dong sharply from the entrance to the stairs.

'Huh?' said Malek.

'Is at door, jumping red-faced,' she said.

'Wives!' shouted Sergeant Shrinivasan, scrambling to hide the whisky bottle.

'No, is man,' said Mrs Dong.

'What man?' said Malek.

'Angry man,' she shrugged.

'Well, tell him to clear off,' said Malek.

'Told him,' said Mrs Dong, 'Made more angry.'

A sound of thudding came from the front door below us. 'Bister?' shouted Father, 'You let me in or I'm calling the police.'

'I am sorry we are currently unavailable,' intoned the Sergeant. 'Please call during normal office hours, which are Mondays to Fridays, eleven to four, excluding lunch which can last from ah... eleven to four sometimes, though not always depending on ah...'

'You've kidnapped my son,' shouted Father in a tone that suggested clenched fists.

'No-one's kidnapped anyone,' said Malek. 'Unless he's kidnapped himself.'

'Rabindra?' said Father, darkly. 'Show yourself.'

Hendrix looked at me quizzically. I shook my head.

'He's a bit busy right now,' said Hendrix, peering over

the wall. 'But I can tell him you called.'

'You tell him nothing,' said Father, stamping his feet. 'I will tell him myself. Now let me in!'

'Might as well,' said Sharon. 'He'll never find us.'

'Stomp all over shouting,' said Mrs Dong. 'Is bad for guests.'

'Rabindra?' shouted Father jumping up and down, 'What is the meaning of this? What are you thinking? What are you thinking is the meaning of this? What is the meaning of your thinking? What is this?'

'He's deep, is your old man,' said Hendrix.

'Not deep,' I said. 'Just hysterical.'

'I know,' chuckled Hendrix. 'There's a difference. So what happens next, he goes up in flames?'

'Worse,' I said.

There was a pause from below. In the sudden quiet of the night I heard Father clearing his throat. I braced myself.

'Was it not unequivocally stated,' he said, lifting his chin, 'that the streets of Pushkara shall henceforth and until further notice be off-limits to all citizens under the age of forty three? Which is to say that as of noon today they will, forty three years ago in standard calendar terms, have not been born to the extent that the umbilical chord has been severed, that process being for the purpose of this edict to be taken as the definition of the term "been born"...'

'I see what you mean,' said Hendrix, quietly.

'... such limits as heretofore mentioned being within the sense of "avoidable concourse" and are to include all places public or private in which the aforesaid citizen is not normally domiciled...'

'Oh my God,' said Sharon, her face glowing orange as she sucked on the cigarette.

'... such exclusions, the legitimacy of which may at the discretion of a panel of elders, specially appointed for the purpose thereof, be reviewable under appeal, to include only the avoidance of such circumstances as might be deemed hazardous to life and limb, though not including hazard to such property as is usually deemed necessary for the maintenance of normal domestic subsistence such as bedding, cooking appliances unless they are the source of the hazard, specially acquired furniture, icons and inherited *objets de famille* for which there is a provable provenance...'

'I get Cook, kill him,' spluttered Mrs Dong.

'... "Emergency" to be understood as the imperilment, as aforementioned, of said parties, the embarkation of said parties into that area designated as beyond limits being thus unavoidable...'

'Why don't we just tell him I needed a Doctor?' suggested Martina.

I felt the blood drain from my head.

'Hey,' said Hendrix, leaning over the wall. 'We needed the Doc, so we called him. He'll be home soon, I expect. Soon as he's done.'

'The Doc?' said Father. 'You are referring to The Doctor? My son, who has a special exemption from the edict under clause sixty eight, is at home asleep.'

'You know,' I said, 'why don't I just...?'

But Hendrix hushed me with his hand. 'That's not what I see,' he chuckled. 'Must be some mistake. But everything's under control, he's doing a great job and, like I said, he'll be home in a jiffy.'

'But is that not Rabindra with you?' said Father, sounding a little confused.

'That's the one,' said Hendrix.

Malek was beginning to make strange wheezing noises.

'But Rabindra is not a Doctor,' said Father. 'He is merely the Clinical Assistant. My firstborn is the Doctor. Rabindra cleans up. And even this he does poorly. We are forever giving him duties in the hope that he may fulfil them, but each time he fails. In this alone is he consistent. He could not even remember to feed the clinic budgie. A perfectly healthy budgie. A happy, bouncing, beady-eyed little budgie. Are we saying that Doctors kill budgies?' he scoffed. 'Of course not. It is Clinical Assistants who kill budgies through neglect and stupidity.'

'Budgies can be quite delicate sometimes,' suggested Hendrix.

'There is no tougher bird than a budgie!' shouted Father. 'Everyone knows they are one tough bastard little bird. But still he killed it. One day chirruping merrily with a smile on its beak, the next on its back. And who did that? Who?'

Father had never forgiven me the demise of the waiting room budgie, though according to my diagnosis it had probably died of smoke inhalation.

'You said he was the Doc,' said Sharon to Martina. 'That's what he told you, wasn't it?'

Martina nodded, watching me now.

'Well, that's a crime, isn't it?' said Sharon. 'Or something. He could be struck off. Only I suppose you've got to be struck on before they can strike you off. But still, it's like impostering and I'm bloody sure that's a crime.'

'Priceless,' squeaked Malek.

'Actually, I didn't exactly say I was a Doctor,' I said, but my words fell limp, somehow, in the silent admonition of their gaze.

'Didn't say you weren't,' muttered Martina.

'Sergeant?' barked Malek.

Sergeant Shrinivasan stood up, unsteadily.

'Arrest him,' said Malek.

'Please call during normal opening hours,' mumbled the Sergeant, saluting, 'Which are eleven 'til... or earlier sometimes if I'm... otherwise indisposed or... not as the case may be.' He sat back down again.

'But it's a crime!' shouted Malek. 'And what the hell do you do if it isn't solve crimes? "Infractions Will Not Go Unpunished". "Criminals Beware My Very Long Arm". What's the bloody point if you can't arrest an impostor flagrantly impostering under your very nose?'

'Enforcing the law isn't just a sharp crack over the head,' retorted the Sergeant. 'It's about evidence, procedure, forensic analysis...'

'Since when have you needed evidence to arrest someone?' said Malek. 'When Mrs Armachary said her glasses had gone missing, which was odd because she'd had them on only a moment ago, did you need evidence to arrest that holy man and keep him incarcerated until her glasses had been found on the bedside table where she'd left them?'

'He was a major suspect. I couldn't allow him to escape,' muttered the Sergeant.

'Escape? He was blind.'

'It is my duty to explore all possibilities in the course of an investigation,' said the Sergeant.

'I'll give you a possibility,' said Malek. 'There's an impostor in the village. His name is Rabindranath Sharma. That person there is called Rabindranath Sharma. I'm no detective but I reckon it's more than bloody possible he's the impostor.'

'Yes,' said Sergeant Shrinivasan, 'but it might also be possible that he's only pretending to be Rabindranath Sharma.'

'So that's a double crime,' shouted Malek, jumping to his feet. 'Which means you've got two reasons to arrest him. Not only is he an impostor but he's deceiving us into thinking that he's an impostor. How many laws does he have to break before you drag him away?'

I turned to Hendrix. 'What should I do?' I asked.

'I'm not sure,' he said, looking away. 'Maybe just go home.'

'Can't I stay here?'

'Is awful,' said Mrs Dong.

'Oh, I don't know,' said Malek, 'it's not so bad.'

'Aw full,' repeated Mrs Dong. 'Is no room.'

But I knew what I had to do. Hendrix's quiet evasion had stung me. Of course I had lied, deny it as I might. And there is only one remedy for lies. Even if we can't undo the harm, we can offer ourselves to its truth. 'Beloved Martina,' I said. 'It was not my intention to deceive you although actually it was, I don't know why I just said that. But I hope that in time you will learn to forgive me. If it helps, I can promise you this: I will never lie to you again. And though it was, I know, inauspicious to our conjugal prospects, let us put it behind us as a momentary aberration in the all-dissolving nectar of our love.'

'What's he saying?' said Sharon.

My voice began to choke a little. 'The fact is, you came. That is the truth. That is the rock of truth to which I bind myself now and forever. Through forests, across the unforgiving brine of tempestuous oceans, up mountains and down the other side of them, you have searched, unwavering in your desire, for me. And now we are together. Nothing can take that away from us, nor lessen its implacable truth. Obviously there are one or two details to consider, such as permissions, establishing the propitious dates, the wedding itself which

150

could last several weeks done properly, travel arrangements and so forth, but let me assure you that my dead mother has offered her unequivocal blessings in so far as she would if she wasn't just an imaginary voice in my head.'

'What have you done to him?' shouted Father. 'He's gone mad.'

'I've done nothing,' said Malek. 'Your son is more than capable of going mad by himself.'

'Not mad,' I called back. 'Except that love be a kind of madness. Father, fond as I am of our illustrious village, nevertheless my destiny draws me elsewhere. But grieve not, for I shall write to you of my adventures in England with my English bride and, who knows, shall one day return with a little brood of white-brown babies for you to love and cherish.'

'He has been drinking!' said Father. 'This is an outrage.'

'Yes,' I laughed. 'But only from the cup of love. From this moment on, our feet in perfect step shall step from joy to joy onwards and forever. Martina, my answer is yes.'

'What was the question?' she said.

'Shall we get married?' I chuckled. 'Obviously.'

She stared at me.

'You what?' said Sharon.

'After all,' I said, 'Cindy and Pol are now betrothed.'

'She's shagging him witless,' said Sharon. 'But I wouldn't read too much into that.'

'Who's getting married?' said Mike stirring from under his jacket.

'It's okay,' said Hendrix. 'Go back to sleep.'

'Why don't you do what everybody else does who wants to have her?' sniggered Malek pouring himself another whisky. 'Buy the calendar and find a quiet place.'

'Special Offer,' said the Sergeant. 'Ends today.'

'But I am the reason she is here,' I said. 'Martina, tell them.'

'Tell them what?' she said.

'Why you came to Pushkara. Why you sought for me in the clinic yesterday.'

'I wanted something for the squits,' she said.

Malek laughed so hard he spilled his whisky and had to pour another one, most of which he spilled again. Sharon chuckled quietly into her cigarette and began to cough. Even Hendrix started to giggle.

'Rabindra!' said Father. 'You will come here now.'

'Then perhaps I am mistaken,' I said, looking at Sharon. 'And it is not Martina that I am destined to marry, but...'

'Hands off my bird,' growled Hendrix.

'Wife,' said Sharon. 'If I was your bird you'd have got me another drink.'

'I show you way,' said Mrs Dong.

'Thank you,' I said.

'Glad be rid of you,' said Mrs Dong. 'You come big fuss.'

As I leaned down through the little doorway, I could hear the Sergeant beginning to laugh, then Sharon, then Martina. It was the last that echoed in my ears long after I'd ceased to hear it, a bitter chorus under the heavy clump of my solemn feet. Down the stairs, along a corridor, up some stairs, along another corridor, a sharp left, a right, to be honest I can't remember how we got there but at last she opened the front door where Father waited for me as she had described, red faced and jumping.

It was a long walk home, Father's rage spontaneously expressing itself every few paces with a wild swipe at my head.

Along the High Street, a group of elders had stopped to spice their betel leaves.

'Shri Sharma!' said one of them, 'I see that you have apprehended a miscreant.'

'To my shame,' muttered Father. 'For it is my own son that you see, the flesh, the seed, the very spawn...' He swiped again. 'Of our lineage.'

The elders chewed thoughtfully.

'It might as well be known,' sighed Father, 'that he was found on the roof of the Hotel Nirvana.'

Several of them tutted.

'The very epicentre,' added Father, bleakly, 'of iniquity.'

'But your eldest,' offered one of them, clearing his sinus, 'is he not a blessing to us all?'

'And your daughters,' said another. 'With a piety, dignity and obedience rare to behold in girls of such years. They are a credit to your good name and shall one day make most cherishable wives.'

'We must speak of that,' said Father bowing politely. 'For your grandson, if I may say, would make for an excellent suitor.'

'Indeed, it would honour my family,' said the elder shifting uneasily. It was well known that the young men of Pushkara had declared themselves rather disembowelled than married to one of my scowling sisters.

'The honour would be mine,' said Father. 'And I have to say, it is indeed a mitigation of this one paternal sorrow that my other children are so manifestly graced with modesty, good sense and discretion.' He jabbed me in the shoulder. 'The roof, I tell you!'

'Mrs Dong!' chorused several elders, some of them spitting with more emphasis than was needed to clear their palates.

'China!' said one of them, inducing another round of phlegm to hit the pavement.

'Oh, miserable the day she came among us! And monstrous

the day she returned!' wailed Father as I braced myself for another slap. But one of the elders had offered him a betel leaf, which he was carefully accepting.

It struck me as slightly shameful, but oddly thrilling somehow, that I should have become one of the less reputable gentlemen of the village, not that I had much of a reputation to begin with.

'And these English people?' asked one of the elders. 'Were they also, as it were, "on the roof"?'

'English?' spluttered Father. 'English people do not cavort about in their underwear. For one thing, it's too cold. For another, it is unseemly. And, as we all know, what is seemly or unseemly forms the principal rumination of the English sensibility. No. Whoever these barbarians are, they are impostors. Could they be otherwise? For we all know by what means they arrived.'

'The bus?' said one of the elders.

'That is not the point,' growled Father. 'The point is that they were brought here by you know who.'

'Bister!' said one of the elders, catching on a little more quickly.

A round of spitting followed.

'Desecrating our sacred domain, belittling our provenance, soiling our… in fact our blessed soil… as it happens… and…' said Father with that look on his face which always registered a slight loss of rhetorical coherence. 'May he be reborn as a beetle!' he recovered, artfully.

'As an ant!' declaimed one of the elders.

'No, no,' said another. 'I think a beetle is right, since beetles are less intelligent than ants and would therefore occupy a lowlier status in that which is commonly known as The Great Scheme of Things.'

'How so?' said another elder. 'Ants have smaller heads and therefore less room for the containment of their brains.'

'But they make homes and grow food,' said another. 'Which beetles don't.'

'Ants are not more intelligent,' said yet another, chewing thoughtfully. 'They are just more organised.'

'Well, whatever,' said Father tersely. 'An ant or a beetle, frankly I'm not fussed so long as it fits under my foot.'

At which they all chuckled.

'I have heard it said,' said one of the elders, wiping dribble from his chin, 'that photographic materials of a chronometric nature have been circulating in some of the more salacious quarters of our blessed purlieu.'

'One cannot help pondering their choreographic intentions vis-à-vis this "performance",' said another, inadvertently spitting crimson over my father's shoe. 'I mean, as a matter of cultural curiosity, not that I care to find out for myself.'

'It was cultural curiosity that took my son to the roof of the Hotel Nirvana,' snarled Father. 'Frankly, if it wasn't for my three good children I would surmise the line corrupt.'

'An aberration,' consoled one of the elders. 'Nothing more.'

'By their exception are proved the rules,' offered another. 'And the very wretchedness of Rabindranath makes it abundantly clear that your lineage is in otherwise excellent fettle. More Paan?'

'Not just now, thank you,' said Father with a bow. 'I have domestic matters to attend to.'

I made some attempts, as we walked home, to explain that I was only acting, as I supposed, at the behest of the gods but only got as far as, 'Please, Father, I was only acting, as I supposed, at the...' before he gave me a resounding slap and told me not to answer back.

As we reached the front door I wondered what sort of Rabindra had sneaked from it only hours before. Could that have been me? The fleeting fantasy of a picture-book hero, a fluffy-haired magazine marvel in a carefully dishevelled shirt gazing melancholically at the destiny that he alone can see? It was ridiculous. I was ridiculous. And my father was right.

Once or twice, treading the cold pavements, I had been seized by a momentary spasm of defiance. I could run. I could thrust my head back and stare at some distant star as my legs flung me fearlessly to other lives. But what lives? And where? The hotel? Up the stairs, along the corridor, left, right, up some more stairs, probably getting lost for a bit, and out to the sweet serenity of a moonlit roof where my beloved cradled a bottle of beer, its shimmering refractions cascading the fabulous contours of her ludicrously beautiful face as she laughed at me?

'Where,' said Father, kicking his shoes off for my sisters to put away, 'in the entire history of our illustrious family has the son of a Sharma been found on a hotel roof consorting with foreigners?'

'But they are not foreigners,' I protested. 'They are from England.'

'With their ridiculous clothes and preposterous hair?' he snapped back. 'I know what English people look like. Is there not a photograph of your revered brother in the company of an English person? And is this person wearing a t-shirt and no brassiere, or a pink headband with "Kiss My Arse" embroidered in purple lettering?'

'Not at all,' I said. 'She is wearing a copious evening dress with a glittering tiara but...'

'There are no buts in matters of English haute couture,'

shouted Father stamping his foot and hopping around since he'd just removed his shoes.

'She is formally dressed for an important occasion,' I insisted. 'And even though she's the Queen whatever the occasion, I very much doubt she wears that sort of thing while eating breakfast or cleaning the car.'

'So when, exactly,' he roared, 'do you suppose she sports cut-away jeans the rear crease of which all but disappears? When she's walking the corgis? In the company of His Royal Highness The Prince of Whales thus insulting all aquatic mammals over which he has dominion? Hnn?'

My sisters sobbed as I passed them, but they often did that anyway.

Tucking into bed with the blankets around my chin, I tried to remember when my father's rages had begun. Which struck me as an interesting proposition. For a thing that has a beginning suggests a time when it was not. And if there is a time when it was not, then it is reasonable to assume that it has a cause. And if it has a cause, it is equally reasonable to assume that it will have an end, since its continuation is dependent on the continued interest of that cause. I chuckled to myself. Up to this point I had assumed that the rage had simply been the result of me being something to rage at. Which is to say that it existed because I did. But if there was a cause beyond the mere fact of my existence, what was it?

In my humble role as Clinical Assistant I had learned much about cause and effect. For instance, if somebody has a cough, generally speaking, it is because they have inhaled something detrimental to their lungs. If they have a swollen leg it might be that their shoes are too tight. Headaches are often associated with exposure to irritating people, and sleeplessness can be put down to diet. It was all very simple. I only had to observe a symptom to understand that somewhere lurked its provocation. Once discovered, it could be dealt with. And once dealt with, the symptoms desisted. If the symptoms remained, one had simply failed to find the true cause and had to look again. In life, the usual assumption is that a thing is there because it's there. Which would make for an odd sort of medicine, telling people they were coughing because they had a cough, or that their joints ached because they have aching joints. In medicine we look for causes. In life we shrug our shoulders, blame the gods and get on with it.

Of course, it's true enough that blaming the gods can provide us with a consolation of sorts. Our son's ugly nose can be elevated from the merely unfortunate fact of a bulbous hooter to some vast celestial plan. That powers charged with the maintenance of all the universes, known and unknown, could spare a thought for our son's nose makes the problem of its protrusiveness infinitely more tolerable. But if I were to inform a patient that their stomach upset was simply the will of the gods and there was nothing to be done about it, the will of the gods might very well be expressed by a slap to my face.

Across the flickering haze of my dreams, Sergeant Shrinivasan rattled his chest, Sharon raised a bottle to her lips, and Malek Bister waved his whisky about. Hendrix rolled a remarkably large cigarette, while Martina stared over the rooftops saying nothing. I opened my eyes and gazed at the shadows of my room. A couple of geckos crept gingerly out from behind a picture to feast on insects that otherwise might have feasted on me. Either it all makes sense, I thought, or none of it does. Outside, a dog howled mournfully. Then it yelped once and didn't howl again. At which point, I think, I fell asleep.

7

'RABINDRA,' WHISPERED A VOICE. 'IT's me. Wake up.'

'Shiva?' I answered, dopily.

'What? No. Don't be silly. Come on, if your father catches me...'

I scrambled out of bed and pulled the windows open. Pol climbed in, grinning.

'Bad dreams?' he chuckled.

'I was The Turtle again.'

He slumped on the floor. 'You don't even look like a turtle,' he said.

'My reflection did. When I cupped the waters.'

'You're all mixed up,' he said. 'It was Shiva who cupped the waters. So what was he carrying this time, an axe?'

I nodded glumly.

He smiled. 'I didn't sleep much either.'

'Were you the demon or the god?' I asked.

'To be honest, probably both.'

'Then that is the worst kind of dream,' I said. 'One moment purity personified, the next a fanged turtle, endlessly shifting position until you sink at last into the brittle comfort of oblivion.'

'That pretty much sums it up,' he chuckled.

By now I had begun to notice that he was looking oddly pleased with himself.

'My dear friend,' he said, 'I feel it is my duty to inform you that spending the night with one's English bride is a joy beyond measure.'

'As indeed,' I retorted, 'is its unlikelihood a grief beyond fathom.'

'What are you talking about?' he laughed. 'How can what has happened be unlikely to happen? It is now. It is here. Hasn't everything we dreamed of been granted, plus a couple of things we hadn't?' He grinned again. 'Alright,' he said, 'I'll admit I was a bit sceptical. And when they arrived I thought at any moment I'd wake up having nodded off in my father's workshop attempting to glue someone's engine back together. Was I deluded? Had we gone mad? Were these creatures but the product of our imagination conjured by some dark art that you and I had inadvertently stumbled upon in the fevered lust of our impious supplications? But could everyone be mad? Could every young man of the village, stricken with the hot fires of lascivious blood, and every old man craving the substance to match his whim, have also gone completely la la? No, dear friend. My wife is as real as a freshly spiced chapatti. However close you look, she is real. However hard you squeeze, she is real. Wherever you taste, she is more real than anything I have ever known. And what's more, my brave, loyal and most gentle friend, she loves me as ever woman loved a man, with a totality beyond the totality of all the spinning stars threshed together on a cloudless night above the mighty peaks of our mountain abode. And how do I know this? Partly because my own love is an answered song-bird calling from a forest grove. But mainly because she said so. Over and over. She has cried it, called it, even screamed it. And though it stings me to wear my shirt, with every jab of agony my thoughts fly back to the wonders of the night and the endless declarations of her love through body, soul and fingernails. Rabindra, such marvels await you as you have never dreamed of. Smile. Stand. Rejoice. For our lives have changed forever!'

'Yours might have,' I sniffed ungraciously. 'But mine remains exactly as it was. If anything, it's got worse.'

'Oh, phooey,' he said. 'I suppose your father told you they were leaving and you'd never see them again.'

I shrugged.

'Well, he's wrong,' said Pol. 'For they danced here on the wings of prayer. They shall dance away with their husbands beside them. And, in the meantime, they shall dance for the village in the Shri Malek Bister International Arts and Entertainments Complex, book early to bag a seat!'

'It is not just my father,' I said, morosely.

'The elders,' he snorted. 'Stalking the streets while young men fester in the lonely sweat of their grubby rooms. I say, let them publish their edicts. Let them punish the children. But they cannot tell us what happens in my father's hall, built on his own bloody land with his own bloody money.'

'You can say what you like, but it's a village edict. Which applies to everything. Me, you, everyone.'

'I think you will find,' smirked Pol, 'that a previous resolution of the Grand Colloquy of Elders declared that the hall was henceforth to be understood as existing beyond any formal description that might encompass that which is generally known, or may be construed, as being, blah blah, an attribute of village activities. It is beyond the bounds. I think your father drafted it.' He leaned back, smiling. 'Honestly, Rabindra, you don't think I'd defy an edict, do you?'

'Fine,' I said. 'So let them dance. They can dance all they like. But they won't have an audience.'

'That remains to be seen,' said Pol, darkly. 'There are some of us who aren't afraid to know what happened in April.'

'Now you have gone mad,' I said. 'Edicts aren't a matter of consent. That's why they're edicts. You can agree with them or not but you cannot disobey.'

'Possibly,' said Pol, wincing slightly as he adjusted his shoulders.

'No,' I said. 'Certainly. For this is what certainly is. An edict is the very essence of certainly, as impermeable as the ground beneath our feet, the sky over our heads, the mountains that encircle us...'

'Until they do so no longer,' said Pol.

'Pol!' I slammed my hand, albeit soundlessly, on the blankets of my bed. 'Are you to move the mountains now? Has momentary success inflated your ego to monstrous proportions? I'll concede that you summoned our wives, and that is, admittedly, impressive. Moreover, it confirms what I have always believed, that your present embodiment is a mere chastisement for some minor infraction in a series of otherwise unblemished lives. Perhaps you... I don't know, threw stones at a dog not realising it was Krishna, or looked out one day from your forest hermitage to see a beautiful doe and wished it would stay longer. It doesn't matter. The point is that the gods have not forgiven you, they are testing you. Don't you see? Your redemption hangs in the balance. You know how it is. They grant you a little wish and wait for you to feel pleased about it. That's the trick. And out comes the Turtle. Have you forgotten the words of our revered teacher as he marched between the desks chiding us for turtle-like tendencies? Did he not say on a daily basis that Shiva would do well to practise his decapitation skills on half the wretches in this stinking rat-hole? And did you not hear his favourite dictum, every syllable punctuated with a whack round somebody's head, that the greatest peril facing the aspirant to virtue is arrogance? Then listen to yourself. It is enough that you summoned lightning to strike an aeroplane. But to think that you can move these mountains that have circumscribed our sacred environs since the beginning of time is an arrogance too dark to contemplate. Strike it from your mind, my imperilled friend. Strike it now.' I leaned back, mopping my forehead with a pillow.

'I only meant,' said Pol, 'that when we leave Pushkara we shall no longer be surrounded by them, obviously.'

'Oh,' I said.

He chuckled. 'But aside from that, I'm really not sure I agree with anything you've just said. Oh, I know we performed austerities and yes, it kept us amused. But, frankly, I don't think they had much to do with an electrical short-out on an aeroplane.'

'But was it not struck by lightning?' I asked. 'And was this lightning not caused by a storm? And did this storm not follow the culmination of our solemnities?'

'True enough,' he said. 'But maybe it's my turn to ask if you learnt anything at school. Perhaps you weren't listening when our revered teacher explained how hot winds go this way and moisture that, whipping up thermal vortexes over the mountains. Seriously, Rabindra, are you really suggesting that a handful of wildflowers and a pot of butter somehow conjured two women out of nothing and deposited them here for our personal amusement? And you call me arrogant! But think about it. If they didn't exist until we invented them, of what use would they be? They wouldn't know what a tree was. Or a shoe. They wouldn't know how to eat. They wouldn't know who their parents were because you and I had spun them out of some ethereal mishmash of hope and devotion. But the fact is they know stuff, oh boy. Stuff we didn't even know was there to be known.'

'Pol,' I said, 'this doesn't sound like you.'

'You're wrong,' he hissed. 'For the first time in my life I have begun to sound like me. Who am I, Rabindra? The low-born progeny of an outcast brood? A malignant blight on the fragrant face of the social order? Well let me ask you another question. Who says? In whose gift is it to pronounce my place on this earth, this globe, this mighty orb of soil and water spinning endlessly in space? The gods? And in whose ear do they whisper? To whom did they send the memo? Is it carved on my brow, written on the winds, muttered from mountain to mountain? So let me ask you again: who says?'

I opened my mouth but couldn't speak.

'Oh, my friend,' he continued, 'do you remember, all those years ago, when I first came to school? My shabby desk with its broken legs at the back of the class? Of course they'd only let me in because of my father's substantial contribution to the "Most Desperately Required School Roof Appeal". And do you remember the elders shaking their heads in disbelief, saying the recent disappearance of roof tiles could not be explained by natural causes?

'For a long time I couldn't understand it. My father said all I had to do was sit up, pay attention and remind myself that if water wasn't cascading through a hole above my head it was thanks to him. But I was invisible, inaudible. "Please, please sir, I know!" My little hand waving, my desk far beyond the sedate orbit of his pedagogic circumlocutions as he strode the room, correcting here, admonishing there. Until I handed my work in. His red scrawl like a trail of blood. The vicious stab of exclamation marks down the margin of my dreams. Oh,

Rabindra! Two out of ten. One out of ten. Nought out of ten.
And the smug whispers that you can lead a horse to water but
you cannot teach it calculus.

'Except for one child that I met by chance, or not by chance,
up in the caves. And though we played that day as innocents
in the free space of the open pastures, I expected only scorn
when we returned to the schoolroom with its elbows and
whispers. But to my astonishment, on that drizzly Monday
morning, he sat next to me and even shared his snack-box.
And though I had food of my own, I accepted it as one
accepts a lotus petal falling from heaven. For though I had,
by this time, understood the derision of my peers, I could not
understand the one among them who showed mercy. Surely
he, above all, would have known how my presence imperilled
him, how my look would shrivel his merits, my shadow his
purity; how, by touching his books, I would rob them of the
wisdom therein. Looking back, of course, I can imagine your
thoughts drifting off as your father ranted, an affliction to
which you were prone even then.

'But one day, scampering up to the school gates, he suddenly
realised why the other children no longer played with him.
An overheard remark, or simple epiphany, but from that
moment on he made amends. From that moment on, there
was none so brutal or relentless. The sneers. The jibes. The
kick in the back of the legs as we filed in to class. But I do not
blame you, Rabindra, for children are as they are and, in any
case, it was too late. For by now you too were shunned. Your
homework, once adequate, became a burden of woe to those
tasked with your betterment. "Must try harder". "What do
you call this?" "No, no, NO!" Carved in flames of red. And
in the playground, how they shuffled away from your token
Bhaji, how they wouldn't let you kick their ball.

'And so, because we all crave company however repugnant, you found me one spring morning in a corner of the playing fields and offered me a bite of your samosa. That I accepted was, in part, my infinite capacity to forgive and, in part, the loneliness that necessitated it. And thus we became friends again. I am not saying that you have been kind to me all these years only because you couldn't find anyone else.' I moved to protest but he waved me down. 'You have been loyal. I believe that you have been true. And you have been more than generous with your karma. For even now as my shadow falls across your sacred bed, do you protest? No. You merely flinch.'

Again I moved to speak and again he shook his head.

'Listen, Rabindra, not to the friend of yesterday but to the Pol that I have become. Yesterday I was a low-born. Today, I am simply a born. Like you, I was conceived, like you, gestated and, like you, delivered screaming to the chafing brutality of this unforgiving world. Like everyone, I am a shambling sack of bones and meat. And my shadow? A momentary obstruction of sunlight. A dog or a saint without a sensible thought in their heads can do as much. You keep moving to interrupt, but tell me, Rabindra, honestly, when you look at me, what do you see?'

'My friend.'

'The low-born.'

'No no.' This time I ignored his shaking head. 'I confess that I was weak. That I betrayed you. Does it grieve me? Yes, of course. Have I struggled over the years to make amends for it? Not at all. Our friendship isn't based on guilt. It's based on us. The dreams we've shared, our hopes and fears. This is not the stuff of people who can't find anyone better to be with. Now you listen to me,' I insisted, waving him down. 'If I spurned you in the playground it wasn't because I detested you. It was because I was afraid not to. It was wrong of me, I know. But for all my reprehensible conduct, and the pain it put you through, I have never considered you as anything but my equal.'

'You are most gracious,' said Pol with a hint of sarcasm.

'Pol!' I said. 'You have put me into the position where to defend my position is to imperil it.'

'I would have thought the son of a barrister could wriggle his way out of that.'

'You are right,' I said, tears beginning to smart. 'I do not know this Pol.'

'Of course you don't. He talks too much, argues back and stands up for himself.'

'Against his friend?' I said.

'Against everyone. Friends included. Even the charitable ones who harbour thoughts of my spiritual inadequacy but are too kind to mention it. I have had enough, Rabindra, of your charity, your pity, this wretched village and its pompous buffoons. I shall marry an English bride, live in England and to hell with the lot of you.' He leaned back, specks of phlegm wetting his lips.

'But did I not pray for this too?' I asked. 'Did I not kneel beside you, blow on the embers and provide the presence of a Brahmin without which such efforts are futile?'

He looked down for a moment. 'Indeed you did,' he muttered. Then he shrugged. 'Anyway,' he said. 'We did what we did. And that it made no difference makes no difference. Our brides are here. My troth is pledged. She loves me and I love her. So join me or not, as you please, but I am out of here.'

'And yet...' I said.

'What?'

'Nothing. It doesn't matter.'

'And yet what?' said Pol, leaning forward again. 'What?'

'It's just that… on the roof last night it was suggested that Cindy's love might, at times, be offered somewhat… freely.'

His face creased into a snarl that I found unrecognisable. 'You have wilfully misunderstood them,' he spat, 'in order to belittle my expectations. But you of all people should know that to the English this word means different things. Why, on more than one occasion I have heard Michael say that he would "love a cup of tea". Well, surely that is ridiculous if we take "love" to mean a profound bond of eternal union. Agreeable as tea is, it hardly lasts ten minutes and is, in any case, unlikely to provide the level of spiritual companionship we ultimately desire from a mate. Then again, he once said that he "could murder a chip-butty right now". But how? How is it possible to "murder" sliced potato wedged between two slices of bread? Are you saying he's mad? Or should we report him to the Sergeant for premeditated foodicide?' He laughed. 'Believe me, Rabindra, though words are used freely among them, by their actions are they proved.'

'Then perhaps you can explain,' I said, 'what is signified by the term, "shagging him witless".'

He smiled. 'While the linguists of our blessed country have spent the millennia devising ever more fanciful names for the gods, in England they have spent the same amount of time on "sex". Don't look so shocked. Some of them we already know. Conjugal rights. Carnal exchange. Nuptial congress. Polite euphemisms that tip-toe delicately around the subject. But there is no limit to the words they have, nor the nuances they indicate, from the delicate to the brutal. For it can be either or both and, in the arms of one who loves truly, it can be both at the same time. Believe me, Rabindra, such knowledge as you Brahmins are so proud of is nothing to what the English know of love.'

'You had sex with her?' I said, sounding more stupid, perhaps, than I intended to.

'Of course,' he shrugged. 'What do you think? But listen, Rabindra, I didn't come here to discuss nocturnal escapades. Our brides are here. The time is now. Take what's yours. All this stuff about the past. Forget it. It's gone. Footprints in the snow. The ladies shall dance. And after they have danced, they shall dance away with us beside them. We're getting out, my friend. This is it.'

'But why should they dance?' I said. 'Surely we can just leave.'

'I like your thinking,' he said. 'Unfortunately it's a bit more complicated than that. You see, they've run out of money. Mrs Dong says the Cook is prepared to suspend his vegetarian principles in order to make a stew out of them unless they cough up for their rooms. My father, meanwhile, says they're contractually obliged to perform, and if they don't he owes them nothing. I'm afraid it was all a bit tense over breakfast. So dance they must, and dance they will.'

'But the elders have never revoked an edict. Do you really think your father can persuade them?'

'Nope,' said Pol smugly. 'Nope is how the English say no sometimes.'

'Yep,' I said. 'I knew that.'

'Of course you do,' said Pol. 'Your brother. But my father isn't concerned with arguing. He says the elders can issue all the edicts they like. If they didn't they'd probably have to do some work like other people. But this is how it's going to be: the box office will open at the appointed hour. Whoever buys a ticket will be able to attend. If they don't, they can't. If they don't want to, why should they? It is nothing remarkable. In fact, it is merely what, in show business, is technically referred to as "show business".'

'My dear Pol,' I said, frustrated now at his monumental obtuseness. 'It seems that a night in the company of your beloved has dishevelled your thinking. But consider this simple fact. There is not a single person in the whole village who would go. You can offer as many boxes of tickets as you like. Nobody will defy the edict.'

'What about you?' said Pol.

I stared at him.

'Why not?' he said. 'It's your choice.'

'The elders have a choice,' I said. 'My father has a choice. I have no choice but to do as they command.'

'Obey, disobey. That's a choice.' He seemed to be watching me closely. 'Oh save your shocked look. I'm not impressed. You made that choice when you skulked up to the caves in defiance of your father. You made it when you kept the company of a low-born. You made it when you asked the gods for an English wife so you could flee forever.'

'It wasn't defiance,' I said. 'I just didn't think about it.'

He scoffed.

'Anyway,' I said. 'That was just a game. You said so. It kept us amused. It gave us hope. Maybe it was nothing more than two boys playing at being somebody else and trying not to feel too foolish in the process.'

'Okay, obey them,' said Pol. 'You can listen from the unwashed stench of your miserable bed to the cackling merriment of people enjoying the show. Or you can be there with them. Your ticket's complimentary, by the way.'

'With who?' I said. 'Who is this "them"?'

'I have spoken to many as I speak to you,' he said. 'And

there are many who, in spite of their protestations, cannot get a vision of ladies dancing about with hardly anything on out of their minds.'

I blushed.

'It is not just a new Pol,' he said. 'It's a new Pushkara.'

'That's treason.'

'It's a fact.'

'So you are changing everything that Pushkara is and has always been,' I said.

He nodded.

'And what gives you the right?' I said.

'That I can.'

'Because you have the power?'

He smiled.

'And is the use of power for one's own advantage a noble or ignoble pursuit?'

'I don't care.'

'Because you don't know?'

'Because I don't care.'

'It is ignoble, Pol. Ignoble and unworthy and exactly how the elders expect the low-born to behave.'

'Then I won't be disappointing them,' he said grimly, a flush rising to his face.

'Indeed you won't,' I said. 'For no Brahmin would speak of rebellion. No high-born would skulk around persuading the gullible to confound their births. I'm even beginning to wonder if you're not, after all, everything they say you are.'

He stared at me, his knuckles white. For a moment I thought he might strike me. But the anger in his eyes was mixed with something else, an odd flicker like the ghost of some ancient pain.

'Rabindra!' The muffled tones of my father rebounded in

the short passage outside my room. 'Who have you got in there?'

'Tell him,' said Pol.

'You are talking to someone,' said Father, rattling the door handle. 'Who's that? Why is the door locked? Open it now!'

'Then I will,' whispered Pol.

'No,' I said. 'Please don't.'

'Hnn? What was that? What did you say?' said Father, banging on the door. 'Can you not hear me?'

'Yes, Father, I can hear you,' I said.

'Then why do you not do as I have asked?' he shouted. 'I have said open this door and yet it remains closed. I am beginning to wonder what sort of hearing this is of which you speak. Of course, hearing nothing at all is the forgivable affliction of deafness. But hearing something and doing nothing is damnable insolence, I say!'

Pol smiled grimly. 'You can open that door and touch his feet. Or you can leave. Come with me. Back to the hotel where your lover waits. Run with me and we shall raise the village in revolt.'

'I don't think Martina loves me,' I said. 'At least I didn't get that impression when I saw her.'

'So that's why you are so miserable,' he chuckled. 'The sweet agonies of impeded passion. But this is how they do it. She might have called you a scrawny piece of Indian junk after you left last night...'

'She did?'

'But it's just a test.'

'Rabindra!' thundered Father, banging on the door.

'You have to woo her,' said Pol. 'By charm, stealth and the fervent demonstrations of undying love. To the English, courtship is an art. It's not just an ad in the paper and a quick chat among the aunties. You have to win her. You have to fight for her. The more she resists, the more impassioned you have to become. When Cindy first said "no, no, no", I said "oh, I'm terribly sorry for being so presumptuous". To which she said, "you idiot I meant yes". You see?'

'Have you learnt so much,' I asked, 'in such a short time?'

'I have learnt,' said Pol, 'that there is always more to learn.'

'That is indeed, much,' I reflected.

'You will open this door now,' shouted Father.

'Coming,' I said.

No sooner had I lifted the catch than Father pushed his way in, hand raised, staring around the room. 'Who's here?' he demanded.

'Nobody,' I said, though the window still swung from Pol's escape.

'Then who were you talking to? Answer me!'

'I wasn't talking,' I said. 'I was reciting verses from the Rig Veda.'

Father stared at me for a moment. 'And why didn't you open the door when I demanded it?'

'I wanted to,' I said. 'But my leg had gone numb from sitting on it.'

'Then why didn't you move it earlier?'

'Because I didn't want to interrupt the recitation.'

'Like some idiot Kshatrya?' he barked. 'You're a Brahmin. Or at least you're supposed to be. What's that on your chest? Under your filthy pyjamas?'

I lifted my hand to the sacred thread that was already damp from the morning's perspiration.

'Yes, that,' said Father. 'Kshatryas endure pain in the pursuit of spiritual excellence. Brahmins use their brains. If your leg's numb, shift it. Anyway, get washed. You stink. And get dressed. After which, report to the clinic.'

'Are we opening today?' I asked.

'Yes we are. But not for medicine. Well, a stout enema, perhaps, for the good of the village. Now be quick about it.'

I asked for clarification but he said nothing further as he stomped out. In the bathroom, mixing hot and cold water in the jug, I contemplated the Brahminical chord, symbolic of my spiritual efforts over many lives now, presumably, wasted. The element fizzed as I scooped a little more. I liked to get it just right. Of course a Kshatrya wouldn't have fussed. But a Brahmin fusses. A Brahmin can ease a limb, wriggle a toe, reach for a towel and rub himself until he feels warm again. Not because we're soft, nor that Kshatryas aren't noble, but because we have intelligence. I thought of Pol and the choices he had made. By what intelligence had he done so? For if one can move a limb, surely one can change a life. Is it less intelligent to shift a limb or a life that aches? I tipped the warm water over my back, letting it run down my legs. And though it felt good, there was something in me colder still than the cold of the morning alone could answer for.

8

UNDER THE ZEALOUS SUPERVISION OF my two sisters, half the village seemed to be in the clinic, writing on cardboard, arranging pens, sorting wood, or nailing the pieces together. Even Dev, precariously perched on a heap of placards, had closed his eyes to bring a hammer smartly down on his thumb.

'No, no!' shrieked one of my sisters at an elderly gentleman. 'What did I tell you?'

'But is it not neatly written?' protested Mr Dimpas.

'Neat? It's microscopic. Look at it. I thought you'd squashed a fly.'

'I'll have you know that I was once highly regarded for my calligraphic accomplishments,' he sniffed.

'It has to be bold,' shouted my sister. 'It has to be big. It has to be legible from more than three inches away. Don't you get it? This is for Pushkara, for the mountains that surround us, the valleys that protect us and the world that shall heed our cry.' She took a breath, smoothing her bun with a trembling hand. 'This is for Shiva,' she hissed.

'I could add an exclamation mark,' said Mr Dimpas, squinting at the paper.

'What's the matter with you?' she yelled, snatching the pen and flinging it across the room. 'Do you think he's going to strain his eyes staring at your puny scribble? Do you think he'll reach for his glasses? This isn't a note to the baker. This isn't a polite suggestion. This is the voice of truth proclaiming its destiny, the spirit of Shiva wreaking vengeance upon the crooked back of The Turtle himself. I want big letters. Until the paper screams, until the mountains shudder and the very rocks beneath us crack with the onslaught of your convictions.'

'Big letters,' said Mr Dimpas, dabbing his eyes with a handkerchief.

'Big letters,' said my sister looking round. 'You!' she shouted. 'Why do you stand around gawping when there's work to be done?'

'Um ah, I ah…' I said.

'If you are not helping,' she intoned menacingly, 'you are hindering.' A number of villagers had stopped to watch as she jabbed at my chest. 'There are those who stand at the barricades,' she continued, 'proud and defiant. And those who fraternise with the enemy. Beware, Rabindra, of who you are, for we shall not permit fraternisers, malingerers, or saboteurs. Where are you going?'

'To my office,' I said.

'Why?' she said, her voice rising.

'Well, because it's my office.'

'Is that so?' sniggered Father who had just arrived in his gown and wig. 'And where is this door marked, "Rabindranath Sharma". Let me have a look. Hmm. No. All I can see is a small sign sporting the words, "Minor Ailments".'

My sister straightened her shawl, smiling. It was common knowledge that I'd once stuck my name to the door in a moment of youthful bravado only to be downgraded from Clinical Assistant to Hygiene Supervisor for three months as a punishment.

'I just thought if there's going to be a battle then we ought to be prepared, medically speaking,' I said. 'Amputations, for instance, require morphine, a selection of saws depending which bones need to be cut and rubber wedges for the patient to bite on while we hold them down.'

Several villagers glanced at each other nervously, while my sister scrutinised me for evidence of irony.

'We've already had one or two injuries,' I said. 'Mr Drambha, over there, seems to have a nasty splinter in his hand for which my tweezers would provide the ideal remedy. Mr Bhat, on the other hand, literally has a cut finger which might require a stitch or two before it is fit once more for the purpose of sawing wood. If nothing else, the need to continually suck it is considerably impeding his labours.'

Father frowned, observing ruefully that I might be right.

'And I very much suspect,' I continued, 'that Mrs Beem is using her left hand to hammer because her right hand is tired, resulting in a growing collection of bent nails and pieces of wood split in the middle.'

'And if she's left-handed?' bellowed Father, sensing a possible flaw in my argument.

'I have it on record,' I said, 'that she is naturally right-handed. Unlike Mrs Aujla there who actually is left-handed. In fact for a long time her family thought she was stupid because she kept dropping things. Of course she regrets not seeing me about this earlier since she ended up in a second-rate marriage, as she describes it, with an especially mediocre husband. Mr Jalpar, meanwhile, happens to be perfectly ambidextrous, which is why he can produce so many brass pots all at the same time, although his eyesight is rather poor which is why they tend to wobble. Mrs Poona, conversely, seemed for a long time to be the very opposite of ambidextrous, which is to say in the possession of two left hands. She was always knocking things over or stabbing herself with hairpins. After several consultations I finally concluded that she was merely distracted by haemorrhoids, which a little cream and steadier bowel movements cleared up in no time.' I looked at her for confirmation, but she was hurrying out with her face in her hands.

'Do you think?' sneered my other sister tugging stiffly at the hem of her plainest Kamise, 'that the valiant soldiers of Pushkara would quail at the petty discomfort of a few minor injuries?'

'Of course not,' I countered, wishing I could just dash into my room and slam the door. 'But the sooner they are healed, the sooner they can be injured again. For instance, I have noticed that my illustrious brother, who has been to England and is a Doctor, is now wary of the hammer with which he repeatedly hits his thumb. And wariness, as we all know, thanks to the efforts of our magnanimous teacher, with a little help from the Mahabharata, the Ramayana and one or two epics of his own composition, is the genesis of fear which, in battle, is the swiftest highway to death. So please, if you would allow me...'

'You can't!' blurted my sister as I reached for the door handle. 'He can't. Father, tell him he can't.'

'Well, I'm not sure,' said Father looking hesitant now. 'Rabindra's argument, albeit unusually, is not without merit.'

'Too right,' said an elderly lady holding up a blistered palm. 'This is beginning to sting like crikey.'

From time to time, by some odd conflux of radio waves across the snowy peaks, our domestic transistors, usually tuned with fading hope to 'All India Radio', would pick up an ebullient gentleman called 'Brian'. With a curious accent, neither quite English as we knew it, nor anything else that we understood, he would exhort us to 'loop our lugs to the latest cool grooves', at which point somebody would shout random words while banging on a dustbin. Some of our youths would get terribly excited before Brian and company switched abruptly to the crackling tones of a Tagore poem. At other times, equally unceremoniously, a nearby parent would simply pull the plug out. Over the years some of Brian's favourite phrases had seeped into the local patois, although an edict had been issued forbidding his least pleasing usages. Thus, 'crikey' was deemed acceptable in situations of duress, while any reference to women as 'Sheilas' was strictly prohibited. As an act of defiance, Malek Bister had named one of his daughters 'Sheila', though it was never something she was entirely comfortable with.

'And my finger is well-sore, matey,' said an elderly gentleman holding up the evidence.

'Which, of course, is unfortunate,' said my sister. 'But wounds will have to be borne with dignity for the time being since, by order of the Supreme Executive of The Pushkara Resistance Council, the office has been declared "out of bounds".'

'And who is this Supreme Executive?' I asked.

'We are,' said both of my sisters simultaneously.

'Well, can't you just give me permission?' I asked.

'It would be far too much trouble,' said one of them. 'We would have to convene a meeting, making sure both of us were present. An application would have to be submitted, an agenda drawn up, minutes taken...'

'We are wasting time,' said my sister, sweeping her shawl back. 'By means of futile discussions Rabindra is deliberately jeopardising the very edge without which our undertakings are doomed to fail.'

'We will not tolerate jeopardisers,' shrilled the other sister.

'Cavillers, obstructionists, or...' added the first one fixing me with a penetrating stare, 'infiltrators. For why else should he so harm our cause but that he sympathises with the enemy?'

'There has been more than a little evidence to that effect,' muttered Father darkly.

'What evidence do you need?' shrieked my sister. 'See how he stops us working, how he flouts our directives, impedes our progress and frustrates the very urgency of our mission. Are these not the acts of a traitor?'

I could see a number of people warming to her theme as they muttered to each other.

'Alright,' I said. 'I'm sorry.'

'Sorry is not enough,' declared my other sister. 'The penalty for treachery is death!'

'What about this?' announced Mr Dak from the other side of the room. I breathed out for a moment. The silence following my sister's last words had been disturbingly void of objections. He was holding up his placard with the words, 'No Show!' scrawled in large red letters.

'It is suitably emphatic, I grant you,' offered Mrs Poon, 'but lacking grammatical propriety. I would suggest, "No To The Show."'

'Or indeed, "No To The Show Here In Pushkara",' said Mr Goli, 'to be more precise.'

'Perhaps, "No To The Show of Ladies Dancing Around Scandalously Here In Pushkara",' suggested Mrs Knapp. 'For the avoidance of doubt.'

'I think we ought to add, "In Their Underwear",' said Mr Peerival. 'Since we are not against the perfectly respectable activity of dancing per se, just this sort of thing.'

'And then what?' said one of my sisters. 'We chant it? How? One of us calls out, "No to the show!" and everyone chimes in with, "of ladies dancing around scandalously in their underwear we're not against the perfectly respectable activity of dancing per se just this sort of thing"?'

'Well, it gets the message across,' said Mrs Peerival. 'Which I thought was the point.'

'That is not the point,' said my sister, clenching her fists. 'If we want to get our message across we could write them a letter. We could advertise in the *Daily Gazette*.' She stamped her feet losing control of her bun which unravelled wildly over her shoulders. 'The point is to stop it, to drive them out, to save the soul of this sacred enclave, this jewel of the mountains, this blessed domain of the Great God, or die in the attempt.' She paused, panting.

'Couldn't we put that on a placard?' said Mr Mahmoud. 'It's rather stirring, don't you think?'

'We'd have to use smaller writing,' said Mr Dimpas contemplating his latest effort.

'Who's going to die?' interjected Mrs Poon, nervously. 'I was asked to come here with a felt-tip pen, that's all I know.' A ripple of concern shuddered around the room.

'Nobody's going to die,' said Father. 'Honestly, you girls are getting far too emotional about it all. I think what we should do now is go to the hall. I heard the Sergeant has already arrived at the hotel, so they're probably on their way by now.'

'We must act!' shouted one of my sisters. 'Before it's too late!'

'More placards!' shouted the other sister.

'You've got plenty of placards,' said Father, wearily. 'And since most of Pushkara is already apprised of our intentions, it surely can't be necessary to declare it so repeatedly in a variety of colours. When all's said and done, we'll mostly be waving them at ourselves.'

'And the demons that lurk among us,' said one of my sisters, glaring in my direction.

'Yes, well, if you see a demon by all means wave your placard at it,' said Father. 'But I really think we ought to get going before everyone starts talking about tea and snacks.'

'Our revered pater is right,' said the other sister. 'The talking is over. The battle begins. Rise up, my friends, to the barricade!'

'Ah, yes about that,' said Father. 'As you know, I've just come from the hall where a number of those tasked with the construction…'

'Did you give them our designs?' interrupted my sister.

'Yes, of course,' said Father. 'Though, as Mahadev pointed out last night, some virtue of a barricade is lost in the absence of its spontaneity…'

'But they must be impervious and resolute,' interjected my other sister, 'as the people behind them. For it is at the barricades that we shall face the enemy, our heads high, sinews tight, breasts bared…'

Father opened his mouth to speak but my sister continued.

'… hearts bursting, voices crying the ineluctable vehemence of our demands.'

'No Show!' cried my other sister.

'No To The Show!' echoed a couple of elders adding one or two modifications.

'Of salacious dancing by people purporting to be from England and such-like,' added Mr Buliwal hopefully.

'As distinct from the performance of dance, per se, some of which is perfectly respectable and rather nice, actually,' chipped in Mr Parasurama.

'... our faces turned to the dying rays of the setting sun,' continued my sister with only the slightest flicker of irritation. 'As the fires rage and The Turtle begs: "Please, please, have mercy." But what mercy did he show when...'

'Yes, yes, we get the point,' interrupted Father. 'But listen to me. Construction met with one or two difficulties. I'm not saying insuperable but certainly there are difficulties. It's a question of materials.'

'But did we not say they should tear down their houses to furnish the wood?'

'Over this there was some discussion,' muttered Father.

'Earnest discussion?' asked my sister.

'I would say heated even,' answered Father.

'Impassioned?'

'Certainly it was moving in that direction.'

'Then there is hope,' said one of my sisters. 'For nothing can withstand the impassioned fire of the Pushkaran heart. To arms! To arms! Let us go, my comrades, for destiny or death awaits!'

After which Father stood to one side scratching his head while my sisters busily marshalled the villagers into groups and sent them off to the hall. I took advantage of the distraction to nip into my office where the first thing that struck me was the smell. It me took a while to find the source but eventually, behind one of the filing cabinets, I discovered a collection of jerry cans, ropes, back copies of the *Pushkara Daily Gazette* and a box of matches. The smell, I realised, was of petrol.

'Rabindra?' called my sister.

I glanced out quickly but she was only marching around looking for me. I closed the door quietly and joined the crowds with a nonchalant look on my face.

'And you can wipe that nonchalant look off your face,' she said when she saw me. 'There is nothing nonchalant about war. Now, choose a placard and get out there.'

'Which one?' I asked.

'Any, it doesn't matter,' she said.

'How about, "We Would Rather Not Have This Sort Of Thing In The Village Since It Is Not The Sort Of Thing That We Would Rather Have In The Village If You See What I Mean!"?'

'Except that one,' she growled.

I picked another, hoisting it over my head. 'I look forward to sacrificing my entrails in the service of Shiva,' I announced, possibly overdoing the rhetoric, waving it around and accidentally catching a light fitting which shattered over my head in a cloud of glass and plaster dust.

'Never mind that,' said my sister as I bent down to retrieve the pieces. 'Get another one.'

'I'm sorry,' I said, 'but I'm not very familiar with the methodology of placard-waving.'

'Well, for a start, you don't wave it until you are out of operational headquarters,' she said. 'I would have thought that was obvious. I mean, what is the point of waving it in here?'

'Practice?' I offered.

'What practice does it need?' she shouted. 'You take it out of here. Once you are out of here, you lift it up. You carry it to the demonstration area. When you arrive you stand and wave it. How simple does it get? There is no methodology, that's all there is to it.'

'Rabindra,' said Father. 'Stop winding your sisters up.'

'Perhaps you would like this one?' said Mr Dimpas handing me one of his masterpieces. 'I think I've got the hang of it now.'

'Yes, yes,' shrieked my sister. 'Just take it and go.'

Pushkara could be stunning sometimes, with its silent peaks, trails of cloud and a sky too blue for its own good. On days like this the very earth seemed to intimate a substance beyond itself, like some of those beggars who claim to be a secret prince as we hustle them back on the bus. Sometimes I used to wonder if they really were. But how would you know? Flaking paint on a shop-front threw shadows over itself in an ever-shifting carnival of light. That it continued to play, even unobserved, made me think of all the lives around me, of birds, beasts, microbes and vegetation that didn't give two hoots whether I acknowledged their existence or not (unless they were some kind of bacterial infection, of course, in which case they probably saw me as their nemesis).

I joined the slow procession of protesters making their way to the hall. Some had stopped to chat while others were checking their shops and stalls. A group of elders had gathered under a bodhi tree to debate the epistemological implications of their slogans which leaned, for the time being, against its knotty trunk.

'Brevity of its own is an intrinsically misleading phenomenon,' one of them proposed, 'for it is not in the summation but the detail of a thing that its most fundamental characteristics achieve their proper manifestation.'

'But is not a summation simply the delineation of the essence of a thing?' queried another, provocatively. 'The essence being that from which the manifested details emerge?'

'Then you would have it that a human being is but a collection of limbs and body parts,' retorted the first elder, smiling. 'But if that were the case, you need only cut up some pieces of wood into the shape of arms and legs and so forth, nail them together and hey presto, you've made a human being. And though it may look like a human being, and might even move like a human being, and certainly in the dark you could easily mistake it for one, would you allow your daughter to marry it?'

'This might explain my son-in-law,' said another, at which they all chuckled.

'Why are you idling around when there's a war on?' shouted one of my sisters passing them with several placards under her arms. 'May I remind you that Shiva does not look kindly upon deserters?'

I joined her as the elders scrambled to collect their placards.

'Have they no sense of the peril we're in?' she sighed.

'Perhaps you could enlighten me, beloved sister,' I said, 'as to what peril, exactly, we are in?'

'Can you not see?' she answered. 'Already some of the young are asking their parents what's wrong with a little entertainment at the Shri Malek Bister International Events Arena.'

'And what is wrong with that?' I said.

'That we should even ask,' she muttered, clutching the placards to her breast as she hurried away.

'Psst.'

I looked round to see a group of youths pressed into the shadow of a doorway.

'Master Dimpal,' I said, 'how are your arches?'

'Groovin, dude,' he said.

'You must keep me informed about the dough-balls and let me know if you need anymore.'

'Sweet, bro',' he answered.

His flat feet had been a major impediment, quite literally, to any marriage prospects evidenced by the giggling of girls

as he waddled down the street. It seemed a shame, as he was
otherwise well-constructed and of an amiable disposition.
My solution had been the insertion of dough-balls into his
shoes which had largely mitigated the affliction. I'd even
suggested that Dev write it up for the *'Lance It!'* but Dev had
said there was more to medicine than the pursuit of noble
prizes from the hands of svelte Scandinavian women who,
in spite of appearances, are tempestuous little hotties under
their tight hair and spectacles. When I enquired, he explained
that 'svelte' is a compound noun derived from 'swelter' and
'velvet', which I thought interesting, if difficult to construe
many circumstances to which it could be usefully applied.

'You know there are plenty more of these,' I said, indicating
my placard, 'should you feel so inclined.'

'Word on da street, bro',' said Mr Ghosh. 'Is you was over
da hotel innit.'

'Well, yes, it's true, I did pop over there,' I admitted.

'Respec',' said several of them, nodding.

'You've been listening to Brian's friends again, haven't
you?' I said.

'You dissin' me?' Mr Gupta confirmed. 'Cause we fought
you was, like, one of us, know what I mean? Now you is one
of dem.'

'And who is us, exactly?' I asked.

'Dude, you is getting the lingo!'

'No, I meant, if I'm "one of them", then who is the "us"
against whom the "them" are juxtaposed. And please answer
me normally. In any case it sounds better when someone's
banging a dustbin.'

'Um,' said Mr Gupta, looking a little chastened, 'I suppose
anyone who isn't a "them".'

'That's what Pol was saying,' said Mr Ghosh. 'You is either

an "us" or a "them", meaning you is either wiv us or against us.'

'But you despise him,' I said. 'In your father's bakery, you serve him last and give him the worst cakes. How is that suddenly changed?'

'We still despise him, obviously,' said Mr Ghosh defensively. 'But it's the show, innit.'

'You are referring to the show explicitly banned by the elders?'

'Yeah,' said Mr Dimpas as the others nodded. 'And like Pol was saying, you know, what gives them the right?'

'The right?' I said. 'Nobody gives them the right. What gives a mountain the right to be a mountain? Does it have to renew its application once a year? Does it require a consensus of opinion from the youth of Pushkara? Does it wait in an ante-room somewhere to learn the outcome of your deliberations? Do we say, "yes, we'll let you stand mountainously around today but we're not sure about tomorrow come back in the morning and we'll let you know"?'

'So what's with big letters?' said Mr Shoni nodding at my placard.

'My sisters are of the view that the bigger the letters, the louder the sound they make in your head,' I explained.

'But it just says "Big Letters",' said another youth.

I looked at the placard which indeed said merely, 'Big Letters' in big letters. 'Well,' I muttered, strolling off towards the hall, 'I suppose not everyone understands the finer points of polemic.'

To my surprise the barricade was considerably advanced when I arrived, though my sisters seemed to be in a state of distress.

'Of what use are vegetables?' one of them was screaming at Mrs Knapp.

'Aubergines, collectively assembled, are extremely difficult to surmount,' replied Mrs Knapp, tartly.

'So why are they decorated with flowers?' She turned to Mr Goli's ice-creams, neatly arranged in their respective flavours. 'And what's this?' she shrieked, indicating a Banana Sundae, 'Who is this supposed to stop?'

Mr Goli picked it up. 'Let me assure you,' he said, weighing it in his hands, 'this is not a pleasant thing to receive abruptly in the face.'

She snatched it from him. 'It makes a mockery of us to think you can throw ice-creams at the enemy.'

'But if they stop to enjoy a nutritious treat in a choice of delicious flavours, then surely our purpose will have been served,' he answered, cunningly.

She tore at her hair, the bun abandoned, lank tresses flopping raggedly in her face as she marched off, sobbing.

My other sister, meanwhile, was attempting to organise the placard-wavers into ranks according to height. 'It does not matter that you have blue writing and she has red. We are not putting the colours together. I am asking you to stand here. You, the yellows, what are you doing?'

'We are the yellows,' said one of them. 'And we yellows stick together.'

To which the oranges, similarly aligned, murmured agreement.

'Perhaps we should arrange ourselves according to the size of the writing?' offered a gentleman. 'It would make sense if the smaller writing was at the front and larger behind.'

'Are you all idiots?' said my sister, turning to the assembled villagers. 'Have you no sense of impending calamity? The Turtle is on its way and all you can do is display your produce and come up with lame excuses to be the ones standing in the shade.'

'Excellent,' said Father hurrying along the road, refreshed from what I guessed was a mid-day nap, his gown around him like a shroud of black feathers. 'They should be here soon. And this is looking splendid.' He put an arm around one of my sisters but she shrugged it off.

'They are simply not co-operating,' she wailed. 'Either they hold their placards upside down or the wrong way round, or they just lean on them.'

'They'll be ready,' soothed Father. 'Don't worry. The raging heart of Pushkara and all that. At least we've got a lovely barricade.'

'But it is mainly constructed from soft vegetables and fruit,' she retorted. 'How are we to set light to it?'

'And wooden culinary implements,' said my father. 'Look, there is even a beautifully arranged collection of ornamental tables. I'm sure they'd burn nicely.'

'Excuse me,' said Mr Jeenkal, 'but nobody said anything about burning.'

'This is meant only figuratively,' smiled Father. 'Perhaps a few boxes to one side for demonstrative purposes, but nothing likely to endanger anyone.'

'But how can we endanger the enemy without endangering ourselves?' said my sister. 'Father, even though you are my father, sometimes I wonder if you are truly committed.'

Before he could reply, the air was shattered by the screech of Sergeant Shrinivasan's siren, wafts of dust curling over the nearby rooftops indicating his rapid approach.

Mrs Batti and Mr Soumodip began to jostle for position in front of their contributions to the barricade: tinned prunes and bead necklaces respectively. Mr Vemuganti turned his

'No To The Show' placard to reveal, 'Why Not Enjoy A Refreshing Cold Drink Instead?'

I found Dev on a chaise longue, smoking a bidi. Next to him a notice read, 'Today Only: Special Discounts For Barbarians'.

'How are the sisters?' he asked, exhaling slowly.

'Father won't let them set fire to the barricade,' I said. 'And they went to all sorts of trouble collecting petrol and whatnot.'

'Well, I'm sure they'll do what they think is best,' he chuckled dreamily, closing his eyes.

I looked round to see one of my sisters in the entrance porch of the Hall carefully decanting liquid from a jerry can into an old commode. The smell of petroleum spirits made my stomach knot suddenly.

'Dev?' I said.

'Mahadev,' he murmured, beginning to breathe heavily.

At that moment, the Sergeant's car raced round the corner, swerving to avoid a sleeping dog. The villagers began to squabble. One of my sisters climbed to the top of the barricade shouting, 'The Turtle is here, fight as it is written!', while my other sister looked round from the porch, a grim smile on her face, as she raised the commode and began to empty it over her clothes.

9

THE JOSTLING WAS OUT OF control even before the Sergeant had skidded to a stop in front of the barricade. Mrs Knapp gave up trying to retrieve her aubergines which had quickly been trampled to mush, and drove a placard through Mr Innuganti's cucumbers instead, accusing him of sabotage. He responded by brandishing some of his produce in a manner that made her retreat hastily. Dev, meanwhile, refused to stir from his chaise longue in spite of my attempts to draw his attention to our sisters, one of whom was now marching across the barricade kicking off non-combustibles while indignant fruit-sellers tried to poke her down with sticks. The other was walking towards the commotion with a serene, if slightly wet, smile on her face clutching a box of matches.

'Jammie,' I said, hurrying over to her. 'Whatever you intend to do, I beg of you don't.'

'Do not call me Jammie,' she answered, curtly.

I stepped back a little.

'You recoil not from the smell of petroleum,' she continued, perceptively, 'but at the fortitude of my resolve. I have plenty of both if you'd care to join me.'

'And what would that achieve?' I asked. 'Beyond two charred siblings?'

'There comes a time...' she said enigmatically, pushing past me.

I grabbed her elbow. 'For what?' I demanded. 'For reducing your precious body to a stinking heap of bones?'

'That is all it is anyway,' she said, pulling free.

'But you have so much to live for,' I said, hoping she wouldn't ask me to enumerate.

'What lives is what we have chosen to die for,' she answered, lifting her face defiantly.

'No, no,' I said. 'What lives is my dear sister with that spark in her eyes and the slight twitch of facial muscles that used to be a smile before she forgot how to extend them to any semblance of meaningful expression. It's what remains of the sweet child who used to giggle at cows munching on mother's herb garden until we chased them away with a frying pan, although questions were raised about the propriety of this, given their divinity. It's the little girl who used to gaze at birds and sigh at nothing, my gentle-souled, good-natured, slightly-too-sincere at times but undoubtedly well-meaning little Jammie-pops.'

'You have always been inclined towards sentimentality,' she snorted. 'But there is no place for snivelling in the face of wickedness. There comes a time when the good must face their foe, and either send it back from whence it came or perish in the attempt. This is what is known as "The Crunch".'

'I have no idea what a burning body sounds like,' I said, 'but I'm pretty sure it isn't crunch.'

'Plus you have always been too literal,' she said. 'Evil knows nothing of half-measures and neither do we. The good must be prepared to make whatever sacrifice is necessary.'

'But all they want to do is dance,' I said.

'Look at them,' she snorted.

Sergeant Shrinivasan was fumbling desperately with the clips that secured his cane to the jeep. Inside, I could see Sharon primping her hair while Mike rummaged in his pockets.

'Not at them,' said my sister. 'Them.' She indicated the villagers who were variously displaying their wares or hurling them at each other. Two of our fruit-juice sellers had abandoned the concord of generations to squabble over which end of the village was which, one of them declaring his ancient prerogative to the North, and the other arguing that, as the earth was essentially spherical, it was absurd to think of anywhere as the end of anything.

'The enemy might be in that car,' muttered my sister, 'but the evil is among us.'

The Sergeant tapped twice on the roof. Three doors swung open. Hendrix stood up clutching a bottle of beer, followed by Mike dabbing his forehead, and Sharon sucking fiercely on a cigarette. A moment later Malek Bister crept out, flinching at nothing as he tucked himself between Hendrix and Mike.

'Behold The Turtle!' cried my other sister from the barricade.

'Hi everyone,' said Hendrix, raising his bottle.

'Stay close,' hissed the Sergeant. 'And follow me.'

'What did I tell you?' said Malek as they hurried behind the Sergeant, 'such enthusiasm for the arts!'

'Yeah, but no freebies,' muttered Mike. 'I don't care how venerated their knowledge of the bleeding universe is.'

'Of course,' said Malek. 'It is unequivocally stated in the terms and conditions that complimentary tickets are for close family only.'

'Like ten thousand aunties,' grunted Mike. 'I know your game.'

'I don't want a frickin' chess set,' said Sharon to Mr Nageswar. 'Even if they all fit snugly into little trays and the whole damn thing makes a handy carrying case. Have you got that?'

He evidently hadn't because he managed to say, 'See how they all fit snugly into little trays and the whole thing makes a handy carrying case,' before he was barged aside by equally fervent retailers waving string puppets, brass elephants and table mats. I last glimpsed him trying to retrieve his pieces from the ground, the handy carrying case, it would seem, of little use when propelled through the air.

Hendrix meanwhile was winking randomly at young ladies. 'Catch you later,' he said to one as Sharon elbowed him and the lady's father demanded an explanation.

'Stop!' shouted the sister covered in petrol. 'Stop right there.'

'Oh God, the sisters,' muttered Malek.

'Be informed,' she continued, 'that I have in my hands a box of matches.'

'Just the thing,' said Mike popping a cigar into his mouth.

'Be further informed,' said my sister, ignoring him, 'that I am prepared to set myself on fire unless you desist from your heinous intentions and leave the hallowed air of our sacred domain by the swiftest means possible, undertaking never to return for as long as the Universe remains an existent entity.'

'Don't be ridiculous,' laughed Malek. 'You'll be lucky to singe your shawl with those pathetic little sticks.'

'Uh… the smell,' said Hendrix. 'And I don't think she's been fixing motorcycles.'

'She has doused herself with petrol,' I explained.

'Is she serious?' said Mike.

'If you set yourself alight,' barked Sergeant Shrinivasan, 'I shall have you arrested for unauthorised conflagration in a public place.'

'She can't be serious,' said Mike.

'I am deadly serious,' said my sister.

'What's going on?' said Father, pushing through the crowd. 'Jammie, why are you soaking wet and smelling of petrol?'

'The stupid girl is threatening to set fire to herself,' chortled Malek.

'What gives you these ideas?' said Father, mopping his face with his wig. 'Certainly not your family. Have I ever set fire to myself? Have any of your relatives ever set fire to themselves? Have you ever come home early for some reason to catch me reclining *inconflagrante* in the sitting room?'

'Mrs Dong's cook has many relatives of whom nothing remains but ashes,' said my sister.

'How do you know this?' said Father, frowning.

'He spoke of it,' she whispered, a little wave of pain flickering across her face. 'But that doesn't matter anymore. Nothing matters except that sin is punished and the virtuous stand up for what's right.'

'It is perfectly possible to stand up for what's right without being on fire,' sighed Father. 'Can't you talk to her?' he asked my other sister.

'As one torch of righteousness to another,' she replied, 'what is there to say?'

'Listen, sweetie,' said Hendrix, 'we're just here for the run-through, tech stuff, that's all. So how about you chill out, grab a beer. I'll do my job. Sound and lights...'

My sister raised the box. Hendrix stepped back.

'Tell you what,' said Mike. 'Save that for now. We'll make you the grand *finale*.'

'You hear,' said my sister, 'how he mocks us?'

Mike snorted and marched off towards the hall accompanied

by the Sergeant who twitched his cane at a loitering bangle-maker.

'Keep her talking,' said Hendrix, taking Sharon's hand as they followed Mike and the Sergeant. 'That's the thing.'

'This is your doing!' shouted Father at Malek.

'My doing?' retorted Malek. 'My doing is a rare performance of Traditional English Dance at the Shri Malek Bister International Events of Supreme Cultural Importance Centre. Your daughters are your doing. At least I hope they are.' He smirked viciously, turning his back on Father who had thrown his wig to the ground and was stamping on it.

Although I doubted that my sister would actually do as she promised, the proximity of numerous candles, incense-sticks, and tradespeople stopping for a smoke gave me cause for concern. Hendrix waited for me in the porch.

'Don't worry about your sister,' he said. 'The longer she leaves it, the less chance she'll go up in flames.'

'You think her resolve will weaken over time?'

'Evaporation,' he smiled. 'Anyway, you coming in?'

I hesitated. Behind us the village had regrouped into a frantic wall of vegetables, fruit, fine furnishings and ornamental nick-nacks. Hendrix made the decision for me, pulling me in and slamming the door. 'This way,' he said.

We passed Mike and Malek in the ticket office. 'That might be what you charged in Bombay,' Malek was saying, 'but up here that's almost the price of an average family scooter.'

'Where are the others?' I asked Hendrix as he pushed through to the auditorium.

'Gone walkies,' said Sharon flexing her ankles on the edge of the stage.

'Cindy wanted to check out the hills,' explained Hendrix. 'I think she was hoping to see some rabbits or something.'

'Can you hear it now?' called the Sergeant from somewhere.

'Hear what?' said Sharon.

'What about now?' he said.

'Nope,' said Sharon. 'Not a sausage.'

'Not even a small sausage?' said the Sergeant emerging from behind the curtains with a transistor radio. 'It is perfectly audible in my kitchen.'

'Mr Bister,' said Hendrix as Malek came in looking flushed. 'When you built this place did you ever think to install a sound system?'

The Sergeant gave the radio a brisk shake, producing a momentary burst of Brian shouting, 'Wrap your head-flaps around this tootin' tune, my lovelies' followed by a haze of crackling.

'Of course I did,' said Malek, looking slightly affronted. 'People receive their tickets out there in the ticket office. They come through that door where their tickets are taken so they can be used next time and then they sit down to watch the performance.'

'Not a sound system,' sighed Hendrix. 'A sound system.'

Malek stared at him.

'Okay,' said Hendrix poking about in a crate. 'We provide the dancers, yeah? The design, props, the engineer... and these.'

'Coasters?' said Malek.

'CDs,' said Hendrix.

'Yes, I meant that,' said Malek. 'I have seen them before, obviously. They are clever devices for making music.'

'But not by themselves,' said Hendrix.

'Of course not,' said Malek. 'Do you think I am simple? In the first place you need artists to play some music and only then is it stuck to that thing.'

'Right,' said Hendrix. 'So how does it get out again?'

'Out?' said Malek.

'Through a sound system,' said Hendrix.

'Well, clearly this is so,' said Malek rolling his eyes. 'The thing itself makes almost no sound at all. Even dropped, the most you are likely to hear is a feeble plinking noise. Certainly this would be insufficient for recital purposes and hardly enough to dance to. What's needed is a device of some description. This is so obvious it is a wonder you even mention it.' He laughed awkwardly.

'So where is it?' asked Hendrix.

'It is on order,' murmured Malek, studying his shoes.

'So what am I gonna dance to?' said Sharon lighting another cigarette. 'The whine of mosquitoes?' She slapped her arm. 'That bloody thing up there?'

'That is the finest air con apparatus in the whole of Pushkara,' said Malek, looking hurt. 'Is it not cool and fragrant in here while outside it is hot and stinking? Let me remind you where you are. This is the Shri Malek Bister Centre for Cultural Astonishments. Behold the front seats, luxuriously upholstered, the specially appointed stage, the curtains made from all the velvet left over after we'd finished the seats. You give them a good fondle and tell me if you have ever fondled curtains like that before.' He wiped his chin, sweating in spite of the finest air con in the whole of Pushkara. 'Did Malek Bister's Events Management Incorporated scrimp on the slightest detail nor fail to cater for every eventuality?'

'I don't suppose you've got any acetates...?' said Hendrix gazing up at the lights.

'Huh?' said Malek.

Mike had wandered in by now, chewing rather than puffing on his cigar.

'Mike?' said Sharon.

'What?' said Mike spitting out a fleck of tobacco.

'I think we're stuffed.'

'Oh,' he said, slouching heavily into a seat at the back.

'Alright,' said Hendrix, dropping the CDs back in the box, 'looks like it's "No To The Show Of Ladies Dancing In A Way To Which We Are Unaccustomed Not To Say More Than Slightly Averse".'

'So what do we do?' asked Sharon. 'Mike?'

'Yeah?' said Mike.

'What do we do?'

'Ah...' said Mike. 'I guess we... you know... I don't know.'

Sharon sighed, bending her toes back.

'There is perhaps a way,' said Sergeant Shrinivasan. 'If I may be so bold.' He smiled worryingly. 'Not so very far from where we are gathered, there happens by chance, perhaps by grace, quite possibly by the will of Shiva himself, to be a person universally acclaimed in the musical arts. I speak of a maestro, a genius, a gifted embodiment of song itself, and one of the finest performers ever to waft sweet melodies into the honeyed air from the wooden carcass of a simple artefact. Moreover, so far as I know he is presently available and remarkably inexpensive.'

'And who might this be?' said Mike.

The Sergeant smiled again.

'Yes!' said Malek. 'Of course. The Sergeant. Why, he is famed throughout Pushkara, and... and possibly even elsewhere, for his proficiency on the Rudra Veena. To hear him play is to hear what can only be described as music. Without any doubts at all.' Malek nodded vigorously though I noticed that his fists had momentarily clenched.

'Please, Mr Bister, you flatter me,' said the Sergeant.

'Although everything that you say is, if anything, an understatement. From the stubborn bloody strings of this nevertheless exquisite instrument, I am able to cajole the most delightful of tunes. Why, during my last concert, many people were reduced to tears and one or two were so transported they even fell off their seats.'

'So where is this... this thing?' said Sharon, sceptically.

'In the dressing room,' chuckled the Sergeant, 'where I left it after my last, if I may say without immodesty, sell-out performance.'

'Okay,' said Mike. 'Let's have a listen.'

As the Sergeant sprinted off through a side door, Hendrix frowned at me. 'Alright, kid, something's bugging you,' he said.

'You mean apart from his sisters going up in smoke?' snorted Sharon.

'Maybe,' said Hendrix, sitting next to me. 'But I was thinking, like, somebody who isn't here you were hoping would be...?'

'Give him a break,' said Sharon. 'Poor little thing.'

He waved at her brusquely and looked at me. 'Last night,' he smiled gently, 'up on the roof, you stepped out, took a minute, adjusted your eyes, saw her. Then what?'

'I'm sorry,' I said, 'I'm not sure what you mean.'

'I'm asking what happened.'

'I don't think anything happened,' I said.

'Exactly,' said Hendrix. 'Nothing happened. The world stopped. There was no world. Cause the world, when you think about it, and I do sometimes, not often but occasionally, is nothing more than a bunch of happenings all tumbling over each other like a writhing heap of...'

Sharon coughed.

'Okay, listen,' he said. 'I'm no expert. Not on anything. Cept corridors and this.' He kicked the box. 'But you see, that's just it. You look at me and think, "I know what he does. He sticks cables into sockets and rigs up lights". And yeah, maybe that's all I do. But no. It isn't. I'll tell you what I do. I stop the world. How? Songs. Music. What's that about? Crowded room, bus-shelter, park bench, on a roof, eyes meet. Yeah? Different tune, same old story. Found her, love her, lost her. Welcome to my world.'

'With respect,' I said, 'I'm not sure I entirely follow you.'

Sharon snorted. 'Don't worry about it,' she said.

'First point,' said Hendrix, undeterred. 'You are not alone. Right now, there's a lot of guys out there who'd like to, shall we say, get a bit closer to Martina Marvellous.'

'But I alone am her destiny,' I said.

'I hear what you're saying, but stay with me. Okay? On the steps, yeah, the hotel steps, you saw that? Oh, boy. The demure smile, a little bit surprised, so many people. And then she saw you. And she couldn't believe how happy, and yet somehow a little bit sad, that made her. Why? Cause now is now. This moment, forever. You and her. At last. Meaning what? Hey?' He leaned forward. 'Meaning she had you. She had them all. By the nuts. And you know why? Every single one of you, in that moment, now and forever, was completely alone with Martina Marvellous. Now tell me this, okay? When you look at her, what do you think?'

'I am unable to think of anything.'

'And when she smiles, what does it mean?'

'That I have made her happy, which is all I have ever wanted to do, and all that I ever want to do for the rest of my life.'

'Funny thing is,' said Hendrix, leaning back again, 'the

older she gets the better she does it. You've seen the calendar?'

I blushed.

'Yeah, I know. The photographer was a coke-head. The stylist kept trying to pull me.'

'You didn't have to lamp him,' said Mike, brushing ash off his knees.

'Believe me, I did,' said Hendrix. 'Palm trees, perfect sand, blue skies. You know where it was? I'll tell you. Croydon. Mid-November, bloody freezing.'

'I think what he's trying to tell you,' said Mike, singeing threads from the end of his sleeve, 'is that basically it's bollocks.'

'Well it is and it isn't,' said Hendrix putting his hand on mine. 'You saw April?'

'I didn't get as far as April,' I said.

'Lucky you,' said Sharon.

'I'll grant you April was a bit much,' said Hendrix. 'But you saw January? And Marty was smiling, right? Just a little. Not a lot but enough to tell you... what?'

'That she was pleased to see me,' I said.

'And March? A bit more serious. A little more sultry. Not quite smiling. So what was that about?'

'She was thinking of all the years we hadn't been together,' I said. 'Of the wasted days and lonely nights. But she was also afraid, as I was, that this was merely a dream, a momentary delusion from which we would awake suddenly to find ourselves alone once more.'

'She was thinking what's the cost of a frigging fan-heater to keep Cindy from snivelling?' said Sharon.

'Not my fault it didn't turn up,' said Mike.

'But the truth is,' said Hendrix, 'they don't know you. They've never heard of you. They don't care about you. They just want to get it done, get home, get paid and hope you buy a ticket. Why?'

'Cause dancing beats the crap out of acting,' said Sharon.

Hendrix chuckled. 'It's a game,' he said. 'Arnie, the golf caddy, takes his trousers off in the empty clubhouse because he's spilled drink on them, when oops, in walks Sharon, the lonely wife of a rich but dull business mogul...'

'That was "Bonking Belinda",' said Sharon. 'Arnie was in "The Scaffolder".'

'Oh yeah,' said Hendrix. 'Ladders.'

'Pigeon shit.'

'Five hours tweezing splinters out of your bum. Not my fondest memory but... high up there. So what I'm saying is basically this: it's not real. It's not even meant to be. Sharon? Give him a smile.'

Sharon sighed.

'Just a little one,' said Hendrix. 'That Sharon Shiver. C'mon.'

Sharon looked away, shook her hair a little then turned back, smiling.

'I hadn't realised,' I said, taken aback, 'that you so admired me.'

'I don't,' she said.

'You see?' said Hendrix blowing her a kiss which she shrugged away.

'No,' I said. 'I don't.'

Any further explanation Hendrix might have offered was obliterated by Mike suddenly shouting, 'What the bloody hell's that? It's enormous.'

'Isn't that a line from "Sheila The Sheep Shearer"?' said Hendrix, looking round.

'Probably,' said Mike, 'but I meant that thing.'

The Sergeant was returning through the side door, gingerly

cradling his Rudra Veena. 'You have identified it correctly,' he said. 'For what you behold is merely a thing, which is to say, an outward form. The real instrument is the ear through which Shiva sings. Truly, my bouncing beach bunnies, you are in for a treat.'

Mike looked at Hendrix who shrugged.

'There's no way I'm dancing to that,' said Sharon. 'Mike, give us a cigarette.'

'Again you are correct,' said the Sergeant, kicking his shoes off and climbing onto the stage. 'For it is Shiva alone who dances. We ourselves are merely blobs of jelly ambling about with neither rhyme nor reason.'

'You've met my family?' said Sharon.

'Without Shiva,' said the Sergeant, settling down on the rug, 'there is no melody, no rhythm, nothing.'

'You want me to plug that in?' said Hendrix.

'It is already plugged in,' chuckled the Sergeant.

'I mean to an amp.'

'What amp does it need when everything is its amp?' said the Sergeant, dusting his hands with powder and rubbing them together. 'When you hear a bird sing, it is Shiva's amp. When a scooter backfires, that too is Shiva's amp. When you speak, you are merely Shiva's amp. But do not worry. Soon you will hear. And when you hear you will understand.'

He closed his eyes for a moment and muttered a little prayer.

'What's he doing?' asked Sharon.

'He's muttering a little prayer,' I said.

'Who to?'

'Well, not to anyone, really,' I said. 'It's more of an invocation. At the moment he's asking to be led to immortality.'

'That'll take a few albums,' grunted Mike.

The Sergeant plucked a string.

After a minute or two Sharon began to fidget. 'What now?' she said.

Ever responsive to his audience, the Sergeant plucked it again.

'He's just tuning it, right?' she said.

'No, no,' said Malek. 'I believe this is one of our more thoughtful Ragas. Possibly an evening piece, or perhaps late afternoon, probably mid-week, I would say a Tuesday or Wednesday, and most certainly spring-time, just after a little nap in the shade with a bird hopping about in the branches above you.'

'Boing?' said Sharon.

'If you knew anything about the Rudra Veena,' said Malek, a little breathlessly, 'you would know that this is an exceptionally accomplished boing.'

'Sorry,' said the Sergeant. 'Just tuning up.' He coughed, straightened his back and plucked a string. We waited.

'And?' said Sharon.

'Shh,' said The Sergeant, plucking another string.

Sharon snorted and stubbed her cigarette out.

'So what was plan B?' said Hendrix.

'This is plan B,' said Sharon. 'Plan A was a sell-out tour of South East Asia. Big venues, easy money. Plan B is stuck here forever cause we haven't got the cash to get our arses on a frigging bus.'

'I am sorry,' I said, 'but that was not my intention.'

They all looked at me.

'What are you saying, dude?' asked Hendrix.

'Do not listen to these people,' said Malek. 'My son listened to him and became quite insane, jabbering about previous misdemeanours in past lives, and throwing stones at incarnations of Krishna as a dog.'

'Okay, shh,' murmured Hendrix. 'Get your point. But the dude's got something on his mind. This is all about the roof, isn't it?'

And so, as Sergeant Shrinivasan plucked his notes in slow succession, sometimes bending them and sometimes not, I spoke of the Clinic Skivvy and his friend Pol, of ghee and marigolds and how the storms had gathered, not only across the peaks, but in my own forebodings. I told them of improper thoughts when my brother spoke of English women. I explained that when my beloved first arrived I had wondered if we'd toyed, perhaps too frivolously, with the divine order of how things are. I ruminated on the fact that if the gods didn't want something to happen it didn't happen, but sometimes they made things happen that you wanted to happen just so you'd learn not to have wanted it. At which Hendrix nodded solemnly. I explained the nature of sacrifice, the power of incantation, ritual, and hope. I covered one or two branches of the science of Dharma, without getting too complicated about it. I told him how I'd wavered from mortal apprehension to wilful recklessness and back again. I finished off by saying that I didn't know what to do next. If the show was cancelled and they left immediately, then how was I to complete the proper formalities with Martina? And if they were, as Sharon had said, stuck here forever, then how were Martina and I to live an English life in our English house raising English children under the fragrant beneficence of an English summer sky?

'That's quite a story,' said Hendrix after I'd finished.

'I'll tell you why we're here,' said Mike cutting off Malek's sniggering. 'I mean, what you've said's great. It's amazing. Your rituals and all that, getting married, gnomes in the garden, marmalade. But we're here because our plane got zapped.'

'Certainly, that's a factor,' said Malek, wiping his eyes. 'But essentially they are here because of the unparalleled entertainment facilities. But anyway, enough said. Shall we book the Sergeant, what do you think?'

'And after it got zapped,' continued Mike, 'we had to put down. I mean it was all a bit crazy. Heads in our knees kinda thing. Except for Sharon, cause of her hair. And then hoofed out, obviously. Nobody around from the airline. Not sure it even was an airline. Some bloke in a clapped out plane. Big city. Full of people. Somewhere.' He waved vaguely. 'Five bucks in my pocket. The girls knackered. Cindy freaking out.'

'Surely, not every detail is necessary,' chuckled Malek. 'In fact this entire exposition is less than necessary to the degree of not being necessary at all.'

'Bit of a low point,' said Mike, fumbling for a cigar. 'Hotel Something. Pretty crap. Cheap though. Marty not speaking. Cindy crying. I went out. Just for a stroll, you know, to clear my head.'

'You dirty bastard,' said Sharon.

'Found this place,' said Mike with a shrug.

'And ended up here,' said Malek. 'Well, that was a fine tale. I'm sure we all appreciate Mike sharing that with us. Now… '

But Mike ignored him again. 'So there I was in the lounge, waiting…'

'Ba!' said the Sergeant plucking a string. Mike looked round but the Sergeant's eyes were closed, head swaying as he waited for the next note.

'This is all very interesting,' spluttered Malek. 'But sometimes Mike has trouble distinguishing the real from his dreams. If he doesn't mind me saying so. Next he'll be saying he met me in this… this bar or whatever it was.' He laughed loudly. 'Have you ever heard such a thing?'

'There was a couple of punters,' said Mike. 'Everyone keeping to themselves. The usual, I guess. I had a whisky. Couple of smokes. Feeling a bit better. Then I got chatting to the owner, nice guy, big guy, turban. I asked him about the trains, the roads, all that. I said what's up there? He said, nothing. I said there's got to be something, but we looked in the book and he was right. Just hills. Then out comes this geezer, chirpy as a wombat in a soft toy shop…'

For some reason, Malek appeared to have developed respiratory problems, breathing in short gasps, hands flapping loosely at the ends of his arms.

'Well, straight away he was on to me. Saris, badges, designer clothing…'

'Of course,' said Malek. 'For this was my sole purpose, to ply my wares. And, as any good wares-plyer might, I had ventured into a business establishment seeking commercial opportunities.'

'With a flipping big grin on his face,' said Mike. 'But anyway, I said I didn't have any money and he asked why. So I told him and he mentioned he had a concert venue. I said, but there's nothing up there and he said, the proprietor's always been a dumbo.'

'Ba!' said the Sergeant.

Malek had gone pale again.

'So I thought it could work,' said Mike. 'I wasn't exactly rolling in options. We'd come here, flog some merchandise, sell some tickets. Get the cash. Book a plane. Get home.'

'This is creepy,' said Sharon, standing now. 'I mean… I don't know, the music…'

'It is a Shiva-Rag,' said the Sergeant. 'Not creepy, but awesome.'

'Well, whatever,' said Sharon. 'It's giving me the heebies.'

'But what clinched it,' said Mike studying Sharon for a moment, 'is that it doesn't exist. It's off the map. It's nowhere.'

'If this were not here,' chuckled Malek, sweating, 'how could we be asking if it was?'

'Stop it,' said Sharon quietly. 'The music, it's… '

'I cannot,' said the Sergeant. 'For it is your music. The music of Shiva. The music of Sharon.'

'Oh yeah,' said Sharon, giggling. 'Sharon Shiva. That's really funny.'

'Not funny,' said the Sergeant. 'But meant to be.'

'The fact is,' said Hendrix, 'we're hiding out. Laying low.'

'And what is meant by the hiding of out or even the laying of low?' I asked, puzzled.

'It's keeping your head down,' said Mike, 'so people can't find you.'

'By putting on a show?' I said. 'For all to see?'

'Depends who's seeing it,' said Mike.

'I could do this,' said Sharon. 'Mike? I got some moves.'

'Remember,' said the Sergeant, rippling off a series of notes, 'that it is only Shiva who moves.'

'So if you can play a tune, why the bloody hell didn't you play one for the inaugural concert?' said Malek.

'Tell me about him,' said Sharon. 'This Shiva, what's he like?'

'Search your heart and you will know,' said the Sergeant. 'He is the splendid and the terrible, the firmament of all and the dissolution of everything that lives. He is alone, solemn, without a second. He is playful, frivolous, toying with our little lives, the fearsome shadow in the fleeting span of us all.'

'I don't know what you're on about,' said Sharon. 'But I like it.'

'There is another way out,' said Mike, glancing at Hendrix. 'But that's not up to me.'

'Woah,' said Hendrix. 'If you're saying what I think you're saying, then all I can say is she said what she said and that's that.'

'That was then,' said Mike, turning to me. 'This is different. You fancy a walk? Up in the hills?'

'Perhaps,' I said.

'Well, if you bump into Marty,' said Mike. 'Tell her we're stuffed, that your sisters are gonna burn, and that it's up to her.'

'But how is it up to her?' I asked.

Hendrix sighed. 'She's a big girl. Go tell her.'

'You want to see her, don't you?' said Mike.

I nodded.

'Use the back door,' said Hendrix. 'Behind the curtain, turn left, follow the corridor, take a right, it's in front of you.'

Perhaps it was Shiva's music lilting from the cavernous bowels of Sergeant Shrinivasan's Veena. Perhaps it was the sight of Sharon's feet as they traced a pattern of colourless nerves in the dust of the stage. Perhaps it was knowing that I was about to face the boundaries of a world that could spring free or clamp shut forever. But in that moment I was afraid.

The back door needed a bit of a shove before it burst open to the dizzy sunlight of the street. A dozing dog lifted its head to look at me. A crow flapped noisily from a heap of vegetable peelings. A monkey scrambled up a tree, chattering angrily from between its trembling leaves. From the other side of the hall I could hear the villagers arguing. Somebody was shouting about ice-creams. Fish was mentioned. The road stretched upwards, both familiar and not. For me, it had always meant freedom of a sort, if only the freedom to dream. As I stumbled slightly over the roughening ground, I thought that nothing could stop us now. Not even the screams that had erupted, mysteriously, from the village behind me.

10

SOMETIMES THEY WELCOMED ME AS a cherished friend. And sometimes they crushed the soaring feathers of my fragile dreams against the brute fortress of their implacability. Today they simply waited. Which I suppose is pretty much all a mountain does in the end. As for the rest of us, frolicking about on its granite flanks, we never wait for anything. Flowers bloom and beetles crawl, goats leap and people amble around musing on its majesty or, putting a foot wrong, splatter themselves against it. But never so much as a twitch in the mossy hollows of its bleak indifference.

For what they wait, I do not know. Perhaps they don't even do that. Perhaps they do nothing at all. If that's possible. I wasn't sure that I'd ever done nothing at all. Even desisting from action is the act of not acting. Nothing, it seems, can divest our nature of its need to run around up to something. And thus we fidget away the short span of our busy lives, building nests and hunting food until we slip and fall and finish it all in a moment. Even asleep we invent actions of one sort or another, chasing sweets or fleeing tigers, which probably amounts to the same thing. And for what? By what means are we freed from the relentless pulse of our restless nature, flouncing ludicrously towards the inevitable, if not the inevitable itself? Which hardly seems fair recompense for all our efforts. Death or penance. I had always thought the latter smacking too much of the former and a taste for either unhealthy under any circumstances. It could only be love. There was no other bliss, in my experience, so profound, inclusive and complete. In the loving arms of its mother sleeps the child at ease. In the loving glance of a true friend, the young man feels happy. In the loving embrace of one for whom we are destined there is nothing else to be wished for. With the love of Martina, no mountain could slice my joyful horizons into silhouettes of pitiless rock, nor serrate the azure canopy of my yearning spirit. In the arms of Martina there was nothing to fear, nothing to want and nothing to do.

For all the times I'd taken that road in my short life, it still felt, sometimes, like a road from the life of another. As a child I had crept up to its forbidden places to play with butterflies, until Mother fetched me home to my father's wrath. Later, I had understood that so long as people thought they knew where I was I could wander undisturbed. But it was hard to hold the time in mind with bees hovering around my feet, the wide sky above me and a gentle sun sinking over the incandescent snows.

As the years went by and my absences became more easily explicable, so I ventured further. I learned that those first fields sprawling out from the end of the road were just the beginning. Over the rise, once I'd summoned the courage to cross it, for it seemed like the edge of the world, were rolling pastures, verdant groves and twinkling ponds. And beyond even these, fading to the distant haze of a late afternoon, were the first hard contours of the mountain range, sweeping off to impossible heights. There were the caves, of course, each with its own shape and smell. Some crouched over you like a hungry bear, dank and gloomy. Others teased you with their innermost shadows like the impenetrable thoughts of a girl whose smile makes your head spin. But every one of them shared a cool dark space and a mouth that opened to the dazzling sky.

I took a breath as I always did when my feet met the spongy turf beyond the last hard steps of track. This was partly because I was out of breath anyway, and partly to sniff the air, its heady smells a vivid carousel of sense that was never the same twice. In Spring, it was a drunken swoon of giddy blossom, in autumn, heavy with the softness of warm loam. When the sun was a blazing ball and the ground itself seemed to shrivel in protest, the shifting cocktail of scents changed with every step. Even the sprayed claims of myriad creatures brought their own tart pleasures to the perfume of a summer day. By the time I reached the caves I'd be drunk on fragrance. Sometimes I'd even forgotten to fret, my little worries of school, or the clinic, or Father's latest rages so very small and distant in the vast emptiness of all this.

Being so vast and empty, it didn't surprise me that I couldn't see Martina, Pol or Cindy anywhere in it. The animals had scurried off at the sound of my approach. Although they usually reappeared once they realised that neither Pol nor I were capable of catching them. The rabbits, for whom death was a particularly transitory apprehension, would hop out first. The deer, slightly more cautious, being a better reward for the efforts of chase, would keep their distance, watching us warily as they reached down to pluck the grasses. If we were all part of the hurly burly of busy creatures, I thought, then we were also a part of the emptiness. Even filled, as a jar might be filled with water but remain defined by its inner space, so the mountains, crowded with summer breezes and winter winds, floating eagles and spinning butterflies, remained in essence the nothingness their arms embraced. It was only up here that I no longer felt surrounded by my surroundings, where the dull fabric of mortal existence might, it seemed, be most easily rent. And it was here, at last, where I could declare my love, if only I could stumble upon my beloved. It struck me as entirely consistent with cosmic irony that I would be among the rocks when she was in the woods, and in the woods when she was among the rocks, and that we would miss each other by a casual glance not taken or taken by something else.

Set above the highest meadow, where the rolling grass bowed to kiss the first bleak toes of stone, was our special cave. It was larger than most though smaller than some, cajoling from its granite neighbours a view of the valley that felt like floating in space. It was here that I'd turned one day to see a little boy creeping out of the gloom to beg for mercy. Personally, I was so relieved not to be fiend food, having been warned by Mother, whose versions of reality I normally respected, that 'up there' was crawling with them, that I gave him a hug. We spent the rest of the morning playing together. As we grew older we began to ponder the imponderables. What was life and why was it mostly a pain? How can a man find freedom? And by what, in the end, are we confined? Our bodies, obviously, were a limit of sorts, shaped of clay and dependent on it. Our minds too, forged of dreams and longings, were a constant torment of restless passions, while our souls, if such things exist, were as indecipherable as a mash of trampled aubergines. Pol thought it was the remarkable ability of the human brain to get things completely wrong. Which struck me as a confine more crushing than the tiniest of caves. Once, I had lain on my back gazing in wonder at a soaring eagle only to have it land on my nose, a tiny fly. You can be lucky, of course, like whirling round to find that a low-born, casteless ragamuffin smelt no worse than anyone else. But otherwise we are condemned to believe what we believe. I had believed in Pol, in his trust, affections and, above all, his endearing, slightly foolish but infinitely well-meaning honesty. I had even defied my father, believing that solitude was all the more tranquil in the quiet presence of a friend. But had I got him completely wrong? The hard look this morning as he casually dismissed all that we held dear. The Pol spoken of with a wry smile by Hendrix on the roof. Cindy turning in circles, like the folds of a paper parachute, and the blush on Pol's face as he watched.

Our little shrine lay in pieces, the marigolds gone, the butter licked, and everywhere the small, grey indications of rabbit. But that was all part of the offering. The gods could hop around as little brown bunnies if they chose. It wasn't all fire-breathing omnipotence, though they did that too. Further in, as the air cooled, I could feel Pol's presence, the ghost of his longing, flicking shale at the entrance, Rabindra beside him, worrying at the audacity of our dreams. We had quickly agreed that only thoughts of spiritual transcendence were permitted here. Pol's theory was that if we made an effort never to think of worldly things in a particular place then, after a while, it became impossible to do so. And he was right, in a way, though in my experience they merely waited further down to pounce again. Still, if transcendence meant getting the hell out of Pushkara, preferably by aeroplane, then my thoughts were positively stratospheric, even if Pol's understanding of the term was a little more philosophical. I tended to assume, and often hoped, that the passion of his sanctity would make up for the frailty of mine.

'Oh, wow,' said Cindy. 'Does it echo?'

'Shh!' said Pol.

'Why?' she whispered.

'It's sacred ground.'

'Oh gosh, is it?'

'So would that be sacred goat shit?' said Martina.

'Watch your step,' chuckled Pol. 'It gets slippery.'

'I'm a dancer,' said Cindy. 'I never fall over.'

'I've seen you fall over,' said Martina.

'They spiked my drink.'

'Ah,' said Pol.

'What?' said Cindy.

'It's the Brahmin.'

Although I'd shielded my eyes, I couldn't see more than a vague blur melting out of the sky.

'Will he mind us?' said Cindy.

'Probably not. So long as your low-born shadow doesn't fall on his high-born foot,' snickered Pol.

'I thought he was your friend,' said Martina.

'Depends,' said Pol.

'On what?' said Cindy.

'The charts,' said Pol.

'He's a musician?' said Cindy.

'Astrology,' said Pol. 'Brahmins can't fart without checking the planets.'

'My Mum was like that,' said Cindy. 'First thing, every morning. Over breakfast. Fag, porridge, mystic monkey or something. Oh yeah, I can see him now.'

'Pol, you know that isn't true in my case,' I said.

'For a Brahmin, what's true is what he wants to be true,' retorted the nebulous haze I took to be Pol.

'So what's he doing up here?' asked Cindy.

'I don't know,' said Pol. 'Some ritual, probably. They build these little shrines and sprinkle marigolds on them.'

'Oh, how sweet,' said Cindy.

'Then they tell everyone if you don't pay them to do it, your daughters will be ugly and your husbands unfaithful.'

'Is that true?' said Cindy, looking alarmed. 'Will they?'

Pol snorted. 'Of course not. But after they've taken your money, they say because they talk to the gods they must be better than you. And since they're better than you, they have to get the best jobs. So forget about a comfy office flicking papers over a desk. You have to fix cars. You have to sell fruit. And if you ask how come, they say you must have done something terrible in a previous life to get such a crap deal in this one. Meaning you're soiled, polluted, unclean. So now you can't go near them in case you tarnish their celestial presence with your filthy soul. But guess what? They can sort that. A quick chat with upstairs and hey presto: in a thousand lives they might even ask you round for tea. Just hand over your cash.'

'Well, that's a swizz,' said Cindy, frowning at me. 'Do they really?'

'Of course they don't,' I said. 'Well, not all of them.'

'Why do you say "them" when you mean "us"?' said Pol.

'It is true,' I said, 'That I'm a Brahmin...'

'Well there you have it,' said Pol.

'But there is nothing to have,' I said. 'This is just a fact.'

Pol shook his head. 'You really don't get it,' he said. 'Show us your chest.'

'Steady on,' said Martina.

'Go on, Mr "We're not all like that",' insisted Pol. 'Show us your chest.'

'Pol, you know perfectly well that I wear the Brahminical thread. I do so for traditional purposes, plus my father would go berserk if I took it off or nibbled it to the point of destruction again.'

'But you wear it,' said Pol, 'because you're a Brahmin.'

'Well, yes, of course.'

'And is being a Brahmin just your opinion, or is it a fact?'

'As being a man is a fact for a man,' I said.

'I've got the bits to prove I'm a man,' said Pol.

'You certainly have,' giggled Cindy.

'What have you got to prove that you're a Brahmin?'

'My thread?' I offered, feebly.

'Your thread,' said Pol. 'So you wear a thread because you're a Brahmin, and you're a Brahmin because you wear a thread. And this gives you the right to strut around inflated by your own superiority presiding over meaningless rituals and ridiculous sacrifices.'

'Oh, really?' said Cindy. 'Can I watch?'

'Watch what?' said Pol.

'A sacrifice. Are there chickens involved though? I wouldn't want to see a chicken all twitchy and that, cause I'm a vegetarian, mostly.'

'There are no chickens involved,' I said. 'But anyway, I'm not here to perform a sacrifice.'

'Oh,' she said, a little disappointed.

'I came here to talk to…' I faltered. Martina was shrouded in half-shadows but she caught my glance.

'Oh, right,' she said. 'Yeah, I'm good. Thanks. It did the trick. Brendan might be after you for a bit more how's your father, but I'm okay. I'm walking anyway.'

I couldn't believe that she recalled nothing of our conversation from the previous night. Had my protestations of felicity fallen like fledglings between the warm nest of my loving heart and the yearned-for twig of her understanding? I thought of asking her but felt the metaphor in need of further refinement.

'Also,' I said, 'Mike asked me to give you a message.'

'Tell him I know my steps,' she said, kicking a stone.

'What about a little one?' said Cindy.

'A little what?' I said.

'Like a bug or something, maybe an ugly one, it's not so bad if they get squished. As long as it's quick. But I don't suppose it will be if you have to slit its throat.' She shuddered.

'How can you slit the throat of a bug?' said Martina. 'They don't have throats.'

'Everything's got a throat,' said Cindy. 'There's got to be something sticking its head on its body.'

Martina sighed.

'Anyway,' said Cindy, 'it's the thought that counts. Isn't it? Like Jesus and the old biddy with her crumbs and stuff. Oh.' She looked worried suddenly. 'You don't believe in Jesus, do you? Marty, do you think it's alright if I mention that kind of thing?'

'I don't know,' said Martina. 'Ask him.'

'Is it alright if I mention that kind of thing?' asked Cindy. 'Like Jesus and that? He's our god, see? Or the son of him. I think. Anyway, they're pretty close, him and his dad. And we've got loads of rituals. Like Christmas, which is his birthday, when you put a big tree up next to the telly. And prezzies from Santa. Well, they say it's from Santa but really it's your Mum. Oops, guess I've just blown that for you. But anyway, you sneak down and rattle them trying to see what you've got and Dad comes in and goes mental. Then you have people round and Uncle George and Auntie Betts end up fighting cause George had a grope of you in the hall and you told your Mum who told your Dad who beat the crap out of you again. So Mum starts screaming and he knocks her round a bit. And later on you watch a movie

221

and everyone pretty much falls asleep. But anyway, it's called Christmas cause Jesus's other name is Christ, not cause of Father Christmas who's other name's Santa. It all gets a bit confusing.' She giggled. 'You wait 'til they get onto the disciples. It's Simon This and Peter That, and Simon Peter and Peter Whoever. But the one everyone knows is Judas. People even say, like, "he's a real Judas". No-one ever says, "Oh, he's a real Simon Peter". I mean, I've never heard that. But Judas had a really thick beard and bulging eyes and he wore black, obviously, being the baddie, cause the baddies always wear black. Plus undertakers. And vicars, which is a bit odd, really, cause they're meant to be goodies. I mean, Jesus was about as goodie as it gets. He was, like, absolutely, the goodest bloke ever and I don't mean he hung out in clubs and stuff, I mean like if you slapped him he wouldn't slap you back. Kinda thing.'

'I feel a hymn coming on,' said Martina, dryly.

'I'm just explaining,' said Cindy. 'I think it's good for, like, different cultures to understand each other. Cause a lot of the problems in the world, I reckon, are cause they don't. And if we could all just hold hands and maybe sing each other's songs and make love not war and stuff, it would all be really happy everywhere.' She smiled at Martina who smiled back. 'So, if you're up for a bit of sacrifice or whatever,' she continued, 'I'll find an ant or something and you can do the business.'

'We don't really do that sort of sacrifice,' I said. 'But we do have festivals which everyone celebrates, especially the Shiva Puja. I suppose he's a bit like our Father Christmas.'

'Has he got a funny head?' she asked.

'It's just a regular head,' said Pol, looking irritated.

'Oh,' she said. 'It's not like an elephant or anything? I mean, what is it with that?'

'It's not,' I said. 'But he does have six arms.'

'Woah,' she said, perking up.

'And four legs,' I added.

'That's my kinda god,' she giggled. 'I'll bet he's taken, though. Or don't they get married? Ours don't. At least, I don't think they do. The Pope doesn't, anyway. Does he?' She turned to Martina.

'Not being married,' said Martina, 'is pretty much what being a Pope is all about.'

'Yes, they do.' I said. 'All of our gods have wives or husbands and many of them have children too.'

'So what does he do with all those arms and legs?' she said. 'I'll bet he's pretty nifty, thwarting villains and stuff.'

'He dances,' I said.

'No!' she said. 'So he's like the patron saint of us! See, we've got loads of saints, like for nurses and snorkelling. We do!' she insisted to Martina who was shaking her head. 'My swimming teacher told me.'

'Do you really want to hear this nonsense?' said Pol, tetchily. 'He'll be charging you next. What's the going rate for a Shiva-mention these days? Ten rupees? Twelve?'

'Pol,' I protested. 'I am not a priest. Only a Brahmin.'

'Only a Brahmin,' he echoed, looking away.

'It's a bit like that,' I said to Cindy, 'except he's not a Saint exactly nor even the patron of dance but the dance itself.'

She looked confused so I continued. 'The dance is this. Everything that you see. The hills, the sky, those little spores of pollen, the flies over that lump of goat poo, the goat poo itself and the goat who pooed it.'

'Right,' she said, uncertainly.

'Perhaps I didn't explain it very well,' I said. 'But you'll be glad to hear that he also, as you say, thwarts an occasional villain.'

'Oh, don't start on about the Turtle,' said Pol, derisively.

'Turtle? What turtle?' said Cindy. 'Oh, come on Pol,' she insisted. 'You're such a tease. Just tell me. I love turtles. I used to have one. Well, a terrapin. Uncle George trod on it.'

'It's just a legend,' said Pol. 'You know what a legend is?'

'Course I do,' said Cindy. 'Like Clapton or Hendrix.'

'Hendrix?' I said. 'Then it is true.'

'A legend,' said Pol while Cindy and Martina squinted at me, 'is a story for old people to tell when they've run out of anything useful to say.'

'I think someone's a teeny bit tense today,' said Cindy, giving his arm a squeeze. 'But what happened?'

'Well, according to this legend,' I said, 'Shiva slew a turtle that was ravaging the village.'

'When?' said Cindy.

'There is no "when",' said Pol, 'because it never happened.'

'Okay,' she said. 'So when didn't it happen?'

'There were many ages before this one,' I said. 'And it was in one of those. I'm not sure which, to be honest, possibly the silver age. But they fought for several days until, finally, Shiva cut his head off and stuck it on a rock where it remains for all to see.'

'Where?' said Cindy.

'It's just a rock,' said Pol. 'A geological phenomenon. It doesn't mean anything.'

'Just past the glade,' I said. 'That way.'

'I want to see it,' said Cindy. 'I do. I really do. I want to see it. Oh, Pol, please, pleasey weasey, please, please, pleeeeeease!'

Pol sighed.

'Thank you,' said Cindy clasping her hands together and

bowing towards me, 'for showing us your lovely cave.'

'You are most welcome,' I said.

She moved off, smiling. 'So this is all a dance?'

'In the heart of Shiva,' I said.

'Then I'm a beat in the heart of a dancer,' she giggled. 'Pol?'

But he didn't reply and after a while her laughter was lost in birdsong.

'So what was the message?' said Martina. 'From Mike?'

'He said you have the power to change his fortunes. But he didn't say how.'

A ripple of irritation crossed her face.

'He also said to point out that my sisters intend to set fire to themselves if the show proceeds as planned.'

'Oh,' she said. 'I'm sorry about that. I mean we've had protests before, but I guess that's kind've extreme. What do you think? You think they'd do it?'

'I don't know,' I said. 'They have petroleum spirits, and matches. And I suspect they've taken advice from the Buddhist Cook, some of whose relatives are quite proficient at setting fire to themselves.'

'I guess kitchens can be dangerous places,' she said.

'I believe, in their case, it was deliberate.'

'Why?'

'Tibet.'

'Oh.' She looked thoughtful. 'I heard about that. That's a shame.'

'I am sorry,' I said, 'if this discussion about people setting fire to themselves has upset you.'

'I can think of cheerier things to talk about,' she said.

'But it will not be very cheery if my sisters are burnt, as it were, to a crisp.'

She walked to the entrance of the cave. It thrilled me

suddenly to think that she was actually here where I had gazed so often, dreaming.

'I get the Tibetans,' she said. 'I mean, that's something to shout about. But we're just dancing. Okay, we take some kit off but not everything. You know? We're not like... like it's a club or something.'

'I have tried to explain this to them,' I said.

'So what's their problem?'

'I think they have always been largely their own problem.'

'I've got a sister like that,' she muttered.

'Is she also more beautiful than is comprehensible in a mortal being?'

She looked at me for a moment then stepped carefully to the edge of the plateau. 'It's like we're floating in space,' she said. Which made me smile.

A squeal of laughter drifted on the breeze.

'I don't think I've ever seen her so happy,' said Martina.

'She is a happy person.'

'Yeah,' said Martina. 'I guess.'

'The dilemma is this,' I said. 'My father has banned the show and demanded that you leave Pushkara. My sisters have become somewhat over-excited by it all and, as I have said, are hoping to set light to themselves. If you leave, then they will have no excuse. But if you leave immediately, as the elders are demanding, there will be no time for us to marry in accordance with the proper procedures and therefore I will not be allowed to accompany you. At the same time, Mike seems to think that if you cannot do the show, then you cannot leave at all, with or without me, and that somehow you have something to do with this.'

She glanced at me for a moment then turned back to the mountains.

'Tell him it's not my problem,' she said.

'I don't understand.'

She sighed. 'I know what we are,' she said, 'I'm not stupid. "Dancers"!' She snorted. 'Okay, it's not exactly ballet, but that's what it says in my passport. Plus, modelling, obviously, and some acting. A bit, not much. You get your time and you decide. Maybe this, maybe that. And then you do it. I'm not proud. But it doesn't bother me.' She squinted towards me, then back to the sky. 'My agent said I should act. A couple of films. I dunno. Three, four. They were decent scripts. I mean proper dialogue and everything. Characters, you know, with feelings.' She paused for a moment. 'I get letters. From all over.' She paused again. 'And it wasn't real,' she continued. 'You know what I'm saying? I'm not Sharon.'

I nodded, though I had no idea what she was talking about.

'So you come here to pray?' she said after a moment.

'Ah, yes, sort of. I like to think of it as importuning.'

'Begging favours?'

'Kind of.'

'Like "oh god, give us a break"?'

'Usually more specific,' I said. 'And it takes time. You can't just submit your requests willy-nilly. You have to go through all the rigmarole so they know you're serious.'

'Kiss arse,' she said. 'Same everywhere.'

'Yes,' I said. 'Though it's generally explained in more philosophical terms.'

'A rose by any other name,' she said.

'Is what?'

'The same.'

'That's very clever,' I said. 'And, indeed, most poetical.'

I had already noticed that elusive particle of the infinite in her eyes, but was shocked to see that she'd smiled. Fleeting but unmistakable. 'It was one of my films,' she said. 'The only difference is you suck up to...' She waved her hands at the air. 'While I have to suck up to Bombay Suits. Which might not be a philosophical term but it kinda gets the picture. So where's this glade?'

She turned abruptly down the narrow path, slipping slightly on the loose pebbles. I followed her, placing my hand over the fading imprint of her open palm where she'd steadied herself on a rock, its fingers finer than mine, built for spinning the air into elegant shapes or soothing the brows of our sleeping babies. Mine were made for swilling bowls and cleaning the floor. It was only right they should be less beautiful.

On good days, Pol and I would skip headlong down the steeper paths, casting our steps to chance, tumbling finally to a screaming heap among the grass and flowers. I thought of suggesting this to Martina but didn't think she was the recklessly jumping type, even if jumping, or an element thereof, pertains inherently to the art of dance.

I thought it ironic that a denizen of Pushkara knew so little about the aesthetic to which both were devoted. The Elders had always been suspicious of non-functional bodily pursuits, so dancing was never strong on the curriculum. An attempt to found 'The Pushkara Classical Dance Company' had descended into a melee of shouts and hair-pulling at the opening recital while our Chief Choreographer, Mr Ramsamooj, had been rebuked later for kicking some of the older gentlemen who had, after all, being doing their best, in the bottom.

'Is this it?' said Martina as the path spilled abruptly to an open space of rich greens and shimmering flowers. She walked forward, running her fingers through leaves. A butterfly frolicked briefly across her shoulders.

'Who else comes here?' she asked.

'Just me and Pol.'

In fact I'd never heard it spoken of by anyone. For one thing, it was hard to find until you were almost upon it. For another, Pushkarans weren't very good at picnics. By the time the food was packed, the itinerary decided, the elders consulted and the uncles out of the toilets, it was usually too late to set off. Many plans in Pushkara were routinely abandoned due to the exhaustion of making them.

'So what do you think of Mike?' she asked, kneeling beside the pool.

'I think his jacket needs ironing.'

'That's the look,' she chuckled. 'But you reckon he's okay? Amiable Mike, doing his best?'

'Yes, I think so.'

'He's a bastard,' she said. 'And he's not even a sorry bastard.' She dipped a finger into the water. 'He made promises. And he didn't tell me. And now he blames me for all this.'

A bird leaped from a tree above us, fluttering to the far shore.

'To whom did he make these promises?' I asked.

The bird watched us from a high branch, twitching its feathers like an affronted Aunt.

'The suits, businessmen, whatever they are, financiers.' She spat the word. 'Of course he says he didn't.'

'And what did he promise?'

The bird hopped to a lower branch and then to the ground, skipping tentatively to the water's edge.

'Me,' said Martina. 'And when I wouldn't, they shut the money off.'

'Wouldn't what?'

'Shag them.'

'You mean have sex?' I said, shocked.

'He called it a bit of bother.' She shrugged. 'A couple of hours. Maybe more if they wanted seconds.' She looked at the bird. 'Hendrix said they could have Sharon but they weren't interested. Mike offered them Cindy but they'd already had her. Basically, they said if they couldn't have me they'd blow his knees off.'

The bird took a long sip, then, for no apparent reason, flung itself back at the tree squawking noisily.

'This is not how we do business in Pushkara,' I remarked.

'Well, I've got family in Luton,' she shrugged. 'So, anyway, Mike said what's more important, his knee caps or my virtue?'

'But this is your jewel,' I said.

She looked at me for a moment. 'He said page three didn't leave me a lot of that in the bank. But I know what I am and I don't do it for money. Or knee caps. But anyway, he cashed a cheque and they came after us. We blagged some tickets on this crappy flight. I'm not surprised it came down. I'm surprised it bloody well got up.' She lifted her chin to the sunlight. 'So then he says he's booked a biggie. Massive venue, state of the art.' She snorted. 'I guess we'll get the bus fare if we're lucky.'

'But not if the show's cancelled.'

'They can't stop us,' she said.

'Then my sisters will burn.'

She flicked her sandals off. The bird was above us again, watching.

'So what do you want me to do,' she asked, 'shag the suits?'

'Of course not,' I said.

'You love your sisters that much?'

'I wouldn't like to see them burn,' I said. 'Nor have them run around while we try to put them out. I believe petroleum spirits rapidly consume whatever it is they've been poured over.'

'I don't know,' she said, closing her eyes. 'I've never really thought about it.'

'You have never thought about people on fire?'

'Now you're just making conversation,' she said. Which was true in a way. She brushed a fly from her face. 'Have you ever looked down off a bridge or a balcony, somewhere high up and thought, right now, just here, I could jump and that would be it? And you step back quickly cause you're not sure if you would?'

'Not really,' I said. 'I have always had hope.'

'For what?'

'That you would come at last.'

Her toes sent a ripple across the pool. 'You know, for a second there, I almost thought that might be true.' She smiled a little. 'It's so nutty. You're nutty. It's a nutty place. But you know what? I got real again. Cause there's one thing I've learned and that's to keep it real.' She lifted her foot, glistening in the sun. 'This is nice. Just here. But out there isn't.' She looked at me. 'You don't really know "out there", do you?'

'Only what my brother has told me,' I said.

A spiral of flies spun round a lily pad. She watched them for a moment.

'It's beautiful,' she said, taking a breath. 'The smell. Is it from them?' She looked round to some flowers. 'Do you know what they are?'

'You mean the name? I don't. I'm sorry.'

She shrugged. 'Well, I don't suppose they need one up here.'

I tried to remember Pol's advice about the protocols of English courtship. Were gifts involved? I assumed they had to be since the importuning of anything seemed to require a gift of some description. In any case it was no effort to stroll across, pick a flower and offer it to Martina with a coy smile on my face.

'What are you doing?' she shrieked.

'It's a gift,' I said.

'No, no.' She snatched it from me. 'It's not. It wasn't anything. It was just what it was. Now it's something to give or get or buy or sell or stick in the dressing room with a phone number.' She cradled it like an injured child. 'Don't you see?' she said. 'You didn't have to give it to me. It was already there.' She sighed. 'I don't know what I'm saying. It's this place. Like I said. It makes you nutty. I'm sorry. I didn't mean to upset you. But half the time you talk nutty and half the time you... don't. I don't know.'

'I know what you mean about real,' I said.

'Do you?'

'Yes.'

'So what do I mean?'

'I'm sorry,' I confessed. 'I was only bluffing. I have no idea. Would you like me to put the flower back?'

'You can't,' she said, rubbing her knees and standing up. 'But anyway, thanks.' She looked towards the slopes. 'Still, you know what they say.'

'Who is they?' I asked.

'There's always a "they".'

'And what do "they" say?'

'The show must go on,' she said. 'I'm sorry. But like I said, your sisters aren't my problem.'

She was right, of course. The goddess moves as she wills. Of what concern are two silly girls doused in petrol? But I was her destiny and this, if nothing else, made me her problem.

'I think I have a solution,' I said. 'If we announce our betrothal, then my sisters would be obliged to wait until after the wedding before they set light to themselves.'

She glanced back at me for a moment. 'I think I've made it pretty clear what I think about that idea,' she said.

'What is clear,' I said, 'is that nothing can stand in the way of what's meant to be.'

Pol's words were flooding back to me now. When they say no they mean yes. When they say stop they mean go. This was the English way, passionate, expressive, and requiring, above all, an overwhelming declaration of intent. I had often noticed birds flapping their wings during moments of amorous engagement. I had even seen rabbits kicking each other as the one attempted to appraise the other of its affections. The bee must sometimes break the petal to retrieve its nectar.

I caught up with her on the far side of the pool. 'My love,' I said, taking her hand.

'Don't be daft, Rabindra, come on.'

'You are the spirit by which I move, the light by which I shine.'

'Did you get this out of a book?' she said, wincing.

'From the book of your heart,' I said, although she was right. Pol used to bring over some of his mother's romantic novels when they had pictures. 'For there can be no better rhyme, nor metre, than the sweet perfection of your smile.'

'You're hurting me,' she said.

'Martina,' I said as she dug her nails into the back of my hand. 'Love is not two things coming together to make one thing but one thing together always.'

'So you can let me go then, can't you?' she said with incisive rationality.

'Never,' I said, pulling her towards me. 'For we are the sun shining in different pots, seeming as many but forever oof.' I had closed my eyes to receive her kiss but instead felt a sharp pain in my lower regions.

'Nobody grabs,' she said. 'You got that?'

I tried to nod as my body bent double and my legs collapsed.

'You'll be alright,' said Martina, scanning the horizon before making her way down one of the streams.

As I waited for my breathing to normalise, and the pain to subside, several flies began to explore the end of my nose. Since my hands refused to move, I tried snorting them away, which only made them take an aerial tour of my face before landing again. I shook my head vigorously, but they seemed to enjoy that and, after a few minutes, came back with their friends. When a large bee buzzed over to see what all the fuss was about, I managed to find my feet.

I heard Pol's laughter long before I reached Shiva Rock.

'You are so mean,' said Cindy.

Which only made him laugh louder. He stopped when I tripped over just behind the ridge.

'What was that?' said Cindy.

'Maybe a goat falling over,' said Pol.

'Goats don't fall over,' observed Martina.

'They spiked its drink,' said Pol, laughing again.

'Goats don't say "bloody hell",' said Cindy.

'Please believe,' I croaked, 'that my intentions are, have been, and will always remain honourable.'

'You could have fooled me,' said Martina.

'But I understood that to be the procedure,' I said, struggling upright. 'Unless, of course, your response is also part of the procedure in which case there is much to admire in the resilience of the English gentlemen.'

They were resting in the shade of the rock, Pol and Cindy's

legs entwined, Martina to one side, rubbing her feet.

'If the procedure requires it on subsequent occasions,' I said, 'I would appreciate some forewarning.'

'That would spoil the surprise,' said Martina.

'Then our married life shall be characterised by a perpetual state of tension,' I said.

'That is married life,' she chuckled. 'But seriously, Rabindra. Okay? We're not going to have a married life. Why? Because we're not getting married. Cindy can do what she likes and I wish them every happiness. But I came here single and I'm leaving that way.'

Pol and Cindy were nibbling each others necks.

'You have already proposed?' I said.

'Accepted,' said Cindy.

'And the other,' giggled Pol.

I have never thought myself prone to the darker reaches of human emotion, such as envy, jealousy, and spite. But in that moment I could have scraped the grin off Pol's face with a blunt surgical instrument unwashed from its previous task of removing warts from the underside of a dhobi-wallah's foot.

'And we're going to be very happy,' said Cindy stroking Pol's face. 'Among the mountains and flowers and all these lovely people. It's everything I've ever wanted. Except babies. But we'll have lots of those.' Pol squeezed her hand. 'We'll come here for picnics. And I'll tell them the names of all the mountains, once Pol's told them to me, and the flowers and every single buzzy bee, even if it's different bees, it doesn't matter, kids don't really notice that sort of thing. And we'll chase rabbits and lie on our backs looking up at the sky, until our babies have babies and we're old and crabby like all those crabby old people down there, but everyone'll treat us like we're wise just cause we've been stupid longer.' She gave Pol a hug that crushed the air out of him.

'Well, hopefully we'll visit,' he gasped.

'Every day,' said Cindy. 'Even when it's snowing. We'll make snowmen and have snowball fights and hot chocolate afterwards, round the fire singing.'

'I mean from England,' said Pol.

'Stuff England,' said Cindy. 'I'm staying here. I want to skip among the hills. I want to saunter down the high street like those elegant ladies in bright saris shouting at street vendors and ordering their cooks about. I want to dodge scooters crossing the road, and kick stray dogs off my doorstep. I want to smell dust, and sweat, and god knows what all day long. I want to stare out of my window and see this.' She spread her arms. 'All around me. Every day.'

'Yes, of course,' said Pol. 'Every day of our holiday.'

'Phooey,' said Cindy. 'Holidays are only as good as the shades you see them through. Sun-hats, blokes with tashes, and cheap tat you can't think why you bought. They're not life. Life is potatoes. Life is clipping your nails on the side of the bed. It's the smell of soup in the cupboard under the stairs. It's cat litter on the floor, cigarette burns in your new dress, the shoes you bought you wish you hadn't, the things you want you'll never have. It's being me, waking up with the same thought I went to sleep with. It's not two weeks pissed and back to worrying about a spot on my forehead, or if my legs are getting fat, or how come I didn't make the Christmas Page this year when she did.'

'Change your agent,' said Martina.

'But the whole point,' said Pol, 'was getting out of here.'

'The whole point,' said Cindy, 'is that we love each other.'

'Which has been stated and is understood,' said Pol,

sharply. 'But as a wife you should listen more and talk less.'

'I hope you are,' murmured Martina.

'Of course she is,' said Pol. 'Because her husband is talking. Now, you think that you are going to enjoy some sort of relaxed and privileged lifestyle in this silly little place in the hills. You are wrong. You will be the wife of a low-born. You will always be served last in the shops. You will not be invited to tea with any of the other wives, and if you try inviting them you will find them all quite suddenly engaged on other matters more pressing. Instead we will spend the evenings listening to my mother imagining that she's just escaped her kidnappers and is presently hiding in a forest hovel. It will be a futile, agonising life of daily torments.'

'But not if we're together,' protested Cindy.

'Then why not be together in England?' said Pol.

'My Dad lives in England. And that's a good enough bloody reason for not living there.'

'Then the entire plan comes to nothing,' spluttered Pol.

'I never had a plan,' said Cindy. 'I didn't plan to meet you. I didn't plan to have the sweetest, cuddliest night of my life. I didn't plan to fall in love with a little village, silly or otherwise, in the hills. But I have. Because love isn't a plan.'

'It is for you to love and me to plan,' retorted Pol.

'I'll tell you what a plan is,' said Cindy, standing up. 'It's an immigration visa. It's an entry permit. It's telling someone you love them so you'll get past the blokes at Heathrow. And I'll tell you what love is. Love is trust. Love is believing what you're told. Love is saying what you mean. I don't trust you anymore and I don't believe anything you say.'

'You are wilfully misinterpreting my words,' growled Pol, 'in order to confound my authority and get your own way.'

'No,' said Cindy, quietly. 'I'm just saying that all this talk of love and happiness is just so you can get a ticket. Well, I'm not a ticket. And you know why? Because I'm not going anywhere. From the minute I set foot in this place I knew where I belonged. It's the happy hideaway I've always dreamed of. And I'm staying here whether you like it or not, with or without you.'

'For this disobedience you should be beaten!' shouted Pol, raising his hand.

'I wouldn't do that if I were you,' said Martina, menacingly.

'Without me, then,' said Pol, sensibly dropping it again.

'Okay,' said Cindy. 'If that's what you want.'

'No, no,' spluttered Pol, 'That is not what I'm saying.'

'Too late,' said Martina. 'You just said it.'

Pol looked at me for help but I was too busy enjoying the departure of his smile, as clinically complete as anything I could have achieved with my imaginary scalpel.

'A lot of people say they love me,' said Cindy. 'Usually cause it's in the script. But this wasn't a script. This wasn't acting. Not for me.'

Pol reminded me of a deer we'd accidentally cornered once in the caves, breathing sharply, his bony shoulders twitching. 'What have I done?' he cried. 'Every blessing I have ever sought now stands before me and I am speaking like an idiot. Oh, this is justice! For I have mocked the gods and now they mock me. The pride! The folly! Rabindra, my friend, why didn't you strike me for speaking as I did? My beloved Cindy, why do you stand there sobbing when you could dash my brains to the ground with a suitably selected stone? Oh ye Gods, why sit there laughing when you have lightning at your disposal, one flash of which could resolve my arrogance into ashes? Forgive me Rabindra. Forgive me Cindy. Forgive me, you heavenly graces. All of whom I have horribly abused.'

He looked up at the rock. 'It is no accident that we are here. For this is where pride perishes, where arrogance dies, where turtles are slain.'

'Okay, you've had a tiff,' said Martina, as Pol began to climb the rock. 'Don't worry about it. Cindy, talk to him.'

But Cindy had turned away and I was momentarily speechless.

'I wished only to penetrate the veil of illusion,' said Pol, slipping a little. 'I didn't care about aeroplanes, wives or England. But she came anyway. And in her love there was no veil.' He slipped again. 'No pretence, delusion or purpose beyond the simple fact of being. It was there and I couldn't see it.'

'Pol,' I said at last. 'I forgive you. And if you look at me you will see that I am no longer sneering.'

'I am glad,' said Pol, scrabbling up to a ledge. 'But the gods demand their price.'

'Do you remember that sage, when we were children,' I asked, 'who declared that the only fitting home for a disciple of Shiva was the very top of his rock? And do you recall how a stray dog dropped a bone one morning in the playground? And how we played with that bone until we were called to lunch? And how our revered teacher fetched his anatomy book and contemplated it before taking a party of elders to pick up the rest of the bits?'

'The sage was right,' said Pol, peeking over the ledge. 'In the end we must throw everything to the gods.'

'He probably just dozed off for a moment,' I called as Pol disappeared again.

'I have amends to make,' replied Pol. 'In this life and the next. However long it takes. Even if I have to come back as a worm, life upon life, slithering blind, trodden on by careless feet or burned in the belly of a bird. We have often spoken of destiny,' he said. 'Well, this is mine.'

It seemed to me that in the interests of friendship I ought to go after him. 'It seems to me,' I said, 'that in the interests of friendship I ought to go after him.'

'Maybe,' said Martina, 'but you might want to check that out.' She pointed towards the village where a thin tendril of smoke was billowing upwards. 'It seems to me,' she said, 'like something's on fire.'

11

WHILE MY SISTERS ON FIRE would undoubtedly provoke a great deal of shouting, I thought them unlikely to produce quite so much smoke. As I reached the village, gasping for breath, the sounds had become deafening and the plumes of black fog almost impenetrable. I stopped, clutching my chest, to see that the fire was in fact coming from a large black car parked in front of the barricade. Perhaps even more astonishing was that somebody was dancing on top of it. For a moment I thought it might be one of my sisters but couldn't imagine them dancing so wantonly, even on fire.

Swearing profusely, Mike was sprawled across the bonnet of another car, struggling with two burly men in grey suits. Two other men, also in grey suits, were rocking on their heels as a fifth man, dressed in a black suit, white shirt and maroon cravat, exhorted them to 'shoot the bitch'.

Several villagers had fetched fire-extinguishers from their respective homes, bought the previous year from Bister's Domestic Emporium, only to squirt a feeble spit of congealed paste over their shoes and trousers. Malek was responding to complaints with a vehement discourse on the finer points of warranty agreements. As I pushed to the front of the barricade, a fleeting gap in the smoke revealed the dancer to be Sharon, bare feet spurning the flames, hair spinning as she turned.

'What happened?' I asked Dev who had remained

comfortably ensconced on his chaise longue, tucking into a packed lunch.

'Oh, I don't know,' he said through a mouthful of roti. 'The usual.'

'My revered brother, I would not describe an English woman dancing on the roof of a burning car as the usual.'

'Well, not here, I suppose. But in England it's perfectly normal. I'm not sure why, I don't think anybody does, but every second Sunday of the month, especially in the more fashionable quarters, ladies set light to cars and jump about on top of them. It's a bit startling at first, but you soon get used to it.'

He had that half-smile he sometimes wore when he teased me.

'But these men in grey suits,' I said, 'are surely no ordinary phenomenon. And while I can accept that such people are common in certain parts of India and possibly even elsewhere, nobody in this village, so far as I know, has ever worn lizard skin shoes.'

'Ah,' said Dev. 'That's where you're wrong. They're not lizard skin shoes. They're fake lizard skin, which are much more expensive because fake lizards are harder to catch.'

'Please,' I said, getting exasperated, 'that's enough cultural induction for one day. My burning question, no pun intended, is what are they doing here?'

He took a bite from a spinach bhaji and chewed thoughtfully. 'These are good,' he said.

'Dev!'

'Alright, let me think. Our beloved sisters, having poured petroleum spirits over themselves, were hugging each other, grim-faced and slightly hysterical. Father was shouting, obviously. In fact everyone was shouting, mostly asking them to move away from the stalls. Mr Chatterjee was trying to bore them into submission by rambling on about the all-too-often underestimated perils of setting light to yourself. At one point he seemed to be arguing that this was contrary to vegetarianism but frankly, I'd lost his thread by then. I must admit I started to get a bit irritated by the whole kerfuffle and seriously considered putting a bloody match to them myself.' I looked for the smile but couldn't find it. 'But then I had another thought which, I have to say, in that particular moment was marginally more compelling.'

'Which was?'

'Research.'

'Your devotion is an example to us all,' I muttered.

'Well, you know how it is,' he said, poking around in his box. 'Vocation isn't a question of personal whim. It's the innermost throb of our spiritual being. And, so far as my spiritual being was concerned, I can tell you, I was beginning to feel the distinct onset of a throb.'

'And how did you resolve this dilemma?' I asked.

'I wouldn't call it a dilemma,' he said. 'More of a choice.'

'But presumably you went to the clinic since our sisters, from what I can see, remain unconsumed by flames.'

'Really, Rabindra,' he said, fishing out the emerald hemisphere of a sliced lime, 'I took you for a better diagnostician. That one thing is the case doesn't necessarily mean the other is.'

'Then please tell me, my revered brother who is a Doctor and has been to England,' I entreated, 'who are these people, why did they come here, how has this car come to be on fire and why is Sharon dancing on top of it?'

'Questions, questions,' said Dev. 'You have always been too curious for your own good. But alright. There I was, on the

one hand summoned by vocational impulses. "Dev, Dev,"
they were saying, "I am waiting for you, carefully concealed
under some judiciously placed papers in the top drawer of
your desk". On the other, an opportunity to finally shut my
sisters up. But before I could decide, these black cars roared
in. For a moment I thought they would strike my sisters,' he
sighed. 'But the two girls, suddenly fearful for the lives they
had only moments before reduced to the hollow semantics
of an infantile gesture, screamed, dropped their cans of
petroleum spirits, and jumped to safety. The cars skidded to
a stop in front of the barricade. Then these men got out.' He
studied the lime, wistfully.

'And?' I prompted.

'You know what this needs?' he said. 'A couple of ice-
cubes and a bit of research. Boy, those bhajis dry your mouth
out.'

'Please, Dev,' I insisted. 'Before you go for more research,
enlighten me as to recent events.'

'Oh. Okay.' He shrugged. 'Well, everyone went berserk,
you know, waving their vegetables, scrambling over each
other. Then the chap in the cravat pulled out a gun and
fired into the air. So everyone stopped. Then he mumbled
something to the men in grey suits, one of whom ran into
the hall while two others dashed round the back. Shortly
afterwards, they all came out holding that fellow in the
crumply white jacket.'

'Mike,' I said.

'Well, yes, whatever. Anyway, this "Mike" was thrashing
around with considerable vehemence, but it didn't seem to
bother the men in grey suits who picked him up and threw
him onto the bonnet of the car. Then the man with the cravat
started shouting at him.' The lime made Dev's face pucker.

'Can you remember what he said?'

'That is so refreshing.'

'Dev?'

'I don't know. I wasn't really listening. Something about a deal, and where they might be able to obtain some tart. Mike said he didn't know. But all the bakers rushed forward until the man fired his gun again. Then he said a lit cigar in Mike's eyeballs might help him remember.'

I obviously looked startled because Dev smiled at me. 'Don't worry,' he said. 'I doubt he'd waste a good cigar on somebody's eyeballs. In any case, at that moment the hall doors flew open and out came this rather large man with a pony-tail, clutching Sergeant Shrinivasan's Rudra Veena, pursued by the Sergeant himself howling something about sacred instruments and family heirlooms. Then the man with the pony-tail hit the man with the cravat over the head with said sacred instrument. One of the men in grey suits jumped on the man with the pony-tail and for a while I couldn't see much because of the dust. You know, this definitely calls for further studies,' he added, nibbling at the peel.

'What happened then?' I prompted again.

'Well, they wrestled around for a bit. Dust, obviously. More shouting. A couple of dogs got involved, you know how it is. If you look closely, you'll notice that one of the men in grey suits is keeping his rear quarters towards the car.'

'Did nobody intervene?'

'Well, Sergeant Shrinivasan tried to arrest the man with the pony-tail for cultural vandalism but dropped his handcuffs in the frenzy and retreated sobbing. Father said the Sergeant ought to arrest the man with a cravat though he didn't say on what grounds, sartorial ostentation perhaps. By this time, however, two of the men in grey suits had managed to hold the man with the pony tail while the man with a cravat got to his feet and proceeded to thump him numerous times in the stomach and around the head.'

'And then what? Dev? What happened after that?'

He tossed the lime aside, and began to rummage in his lunchbox again. 'Oh, I don't know,' he said. 'The man with a cravat pointed his gun at the man with the pony-tail and asked him if he had any last requests. The man with the pony-tail stopped wriggling for a moment and said if the guy from the Clinic was around he wouldn't mind a little something for his fish phobia.' Dev shrugged. 'Then the man with a cravat hit the man with the pony-tail who fell to the ground.'

'Where is he now?' I said.

'Behind the car, you can't see him from here.'

'Was he hurt?'

'Hmm. Let me think. He was struck on the head with a hard implement as a consequence of which he remained motionless. Six years of medical studies, eighteen sets of exams, two years as a registrar, numerous academic papers and a professional life dedicated to clinical research would lead me to posit a strong possibility that, yes, he was hurt.'

'I suppose he must have been,' I concurred, feeling a bit foolish.

'Then the man with a cravat pointed his gun at the man with the pony-tail and said "eat lead, sucker".'

'He said that?'

'No, but it would have been elegant under the circumstances.'

I could feel my heart thumping. 'And then?' I squeaked. 'Did he shoot him? Is Hendrix dead? The man with the pony-tail, is he dead? What happened? Dev, please tell me!'

'Well, something quite funny. Although, when I say funny I mean it in the English sense of odd. The doors to the hall opened once more and out came this blonde, shapely and, I must say, rather attractive English woman.'

'His wife,' I said. 'That's his wife. She must have been distraught. Did she run towards him, screaming and shouting?'

'No, not at all,' said Dev. 'In fact, quite the opposite. She was very quiet and rather stately, twirling her arms in the air, shoulders back, flicking her hair from side to side as her bare feet touched the ground, soundlessly, with a kind of infinite grace.' He stopped for a moment.

'Dev?'

'Ah, yes, sorry. Well, she stopped over there, near the cars, with that dreamy look people have sometimes when they're about to die and you're filling in the forms. By which time everything had gone quiet. Even the dogs stopped barking, although one or two took advantage of the hiatus to sniff each other's bottoms, I guess that's dogs for you. Everyone stared at her. Not a bird flew. Not a fly buzzed. And although she wasn't looking at anything in particular, you had the feeling, somehow, that she was looking at you. Not even at you. Through you. Into you. Further than you could ever look yourself.

'She walked towards the man with a cravat who stepped slowly backwards, eventually coming to a stop. Everyone gathered round until she stood, quite still, in this curious circle of calm.

'Then she climbed up on the car. The cigar dropped from the mouth of the man with a cravat and a tiny lick of blue flame curled from its tip, spreading out like an ephemeral flower, a shimmering bouquet of incandescence. The woman began to stamp her feet as the flames gathered speed, sweeping towards the car. She lifted her arms in the air. Then whoosh. In a single ecstatic eruption, that no doubt reflected how most of the men were feeling at that moment, the car burst into flames. Everyone jumped back. Even the man with a cravat. But not the woman, who just gazed around with a serene smile on her face. And that's where she is now, turning unconcerned as the fire feeds its rage with rage, like Father at the non-appearance of an earlier-requested condiment. Though not for long, I suspect.'

'Why not?'

'Because the car's about to explode. Once the tank gets it, the whole thing goes up. Kaboom.' He nodded thoughtfully. 'Now that'll be something.'

I found Hendrix behind the car, smoke blustering in all directions. The heat made my face tighten. He was quite motionless.

'Hendrix?' I said. 'It's me, Rabindra.'

'Huh?' He opened an eye. 'Jeez, dude, don't hog the bong.'

'You're alive!' I said, my eyes smarting with joy or smoke, it didn't matter.

'Is that your professional opinion?'

'I could, if you wish, seek confirmation.'

'I'll go with yours,' he said. 'Where's the wife?'

'She's dancing on the roof of a burning car.'

'I've told her not to do that,' he said.

'Then it is true?' I said. 'In England this is a common practice?'

'Rabindra,' he smiled, 'I'd hate to see you change.'

A sudden loud bang made me flinch. Hendrix struggled to sit up.

'No, no,' I said, 'you mustn't move until we have assessed your injuries. If you have been unconscious it might be the case that you have concussion. Tell me, do you feel slightly nauseous, is your vision blurred, do you have a strange sensation that you might not be quite real, and is it difficult to remember the last few moments of your life?'

'Stoned again,' he sighed.

There was another loud bang. I stood up to see the man with a cravat aiming his pistol at Sharon who was laughing at him.

'Oh my goodness, he's trying to shoot her,' I said.

'Robby,' said Hendrix, coughing violently, 'do you mind if I call you Robby?'

'Under the circumstances you can call me anything you like.'

'Would you mind asking her to get off the car?'

The man with a cravat took another shot as I hurried round. He evidently missed since she remained where she was, fingers curling the smoke into ribbons, her feet drumming ferociously above the sound of screaming villagers.

'Mrs Shiver!' I called. 'I fear that remaining where you are may be to your ultimate disadvantage.'

I glanced across to Hendrix who was nodding at me encouragingly. 'Maybe a bit simpler,' he said.

'The Lord Shiva,' cried Mrs Dong unexpectedly, 'has returned!'

'The Lord Shiva!' cried various voices.

'To slay the Turtle,' continued Mrs Dong pointing at the man with a cravat.

Sharon turned her face to the sky. The man with a cravat cursed under his breath and took aim.

'Mrs Shiver!' I shouted. 'There is a man with a cravat pointing his gun at you.'

As the man with a cravat fired, Sharon leaped into the air. For a moment she seemed to hover there, suspended on pillows of smoke, before dropping behind the car.

'Bitch! Shit! Bloody Bitch!' said the man with a cravat, shooting wildly in her general direction. I noticed that Hendrix was resuming his struggle to stand, though without much success. Sharon, meanwhile, appeared briefly through the smoke, blonde hair flying as she twirled in frenzied circles. The man with a cravat fired again. The villagers flinched again. Hendrix managed to get to his feet albeit bent double. And then the car exploded.

Personally, I was only aware of a dull percussive thud after which everything went oddly quiet. At the same time, the ground beneath me seemed to evaporate as the sky, cars, smoke, flames and people spun into free-fall. I saw Hendrix staring up at me and wanted to say, 'Hey, look at me I'm flying', but my short trajectory ended rather abruptly in a bruised heap beside the other car.

Whether anybody else was shouting or screaming I had no idea. A flake of soft ash floated down in front of my face. Behind it, a dense swathe of black particles drifted to and fro giving the otherwise invisible air a kind of shape and seeming purpose. In its own way, I thought, it was really quite pretty.

'Are you okay?' said Hendrix, leaning over me.

'What happened?' I said.

'It exploded.'

'Sharon?' I said.

'No, the car,' said Hendrix.

'I mean, is she alright?'

'I know,' he chuckled. 'She's fine. Can you stand?'

'I think so.' It was only when I got to my feet that I realised Hendrix's bent posture was all he could manage for the moment.

'I'll be okay,' he said. 'It's just my ribs.'

'I have an ointment, used primarily by athletes, which has proved most efficacious in the treatment of numerous complaints especially those related to feet which are, of course, a crucial asset in the athlete's physiological repertoire.'

'Once you got it, you never get rid of it,' said Hendrix cryptically.

The ball of flame that had driven most of the village to its knees had dissipated to reveal a scene of pitiful devastation. The ground was scattered with smoking debris and sprawled villagers moaning softly as they clutched their heads. One of the men in grey suits was sitting, dazed. Two others were curled up, sobbing. The man with a cravat lay close to the remains of his car, mouth moving, a crimson stain weeping slowly through the white cotton of his shirt. Pale slivers of smoke curled from burning embers lodged in the barricade. The only cheerful note in all this was Sharon, sitting on the shoulders of the Buddhist Cook, propped up with a little help from Mrs Dong and some of the younger men, the propriety of whose hand-positions I thought questionable.

'The Turtle,' cried Mrs Dong, rapturously, 'is brung to heel and prepare for slaughter.'

Sharon laughed.

The man with a cravat moved a little, the pool of blood under his leg shimmering a flare from the burning car. I knelt beside him.

'Man with a cravat,' I said. 'You must try to keep still.'

'Urgh,' he answered, wiping feebly at the shard of metal protruding from his chest.

I would have preferred to inspect him in my little office with all of its resources. Still, one didn't have to look up 'bleeding', since bleeding is one of those happy ailments wherein cause and effect are the same, and the cure is simply to stop it.

'I'm afraid I shall need your cravat,' I said.

He nodded weakly as I removed it from his neck and tied it round his thigh. It seemed to do the trick. With the bleeding stemmed, I could examine his chest more thoroughly, tugging at the piece of metal until I'd worked it loose. It came out quite easily in the end, along with a good deal of blood. Fortunately, the injuries to his head were only superficial, though some nasty lumps were beginning to form. I took his pulse and told him that in my opinion he was a little too portly for comfort and ought to think about his heart, particularly in view of his stressful occupation. He said thank you.

'However, I'm still worried about your thigh,' I added. 'Especially if the femoral artery has been severed although, on the bright side, if that were the case you won't have time to develop coronary problems. I suggest you remain here while I call my brother who, you may rest assured, is a Doctor and has been to England.'

The chaise longue was upturned and smouldering. Nearby were the remains of Dev's lunchbox and a forlorn shred of nibbled lime. 'Dev?' I called, beginning to panic. 'Dev where are you?'

Mr Chatterjee staggered over, breathing through a fold of his shawl. 'You call for your brother in vain,' he said.

'What?' I said. 'He's dead? Please, tell me it isn't so.'

'No, no, it's alright, Rabindra, by this I do not mean that he has expired. On future occasions you may call him with a more satisfactory response. To the word "Dev", he will answer, "yes, Rabindra, I am here" or by some such means acknowledge your request for his attention. Although I should remind you, as your father quite properly and not infrequently does, that the correct appellation, considering your respective statuses, and the fact that he has been to

England and was honoured by the Queen, no less, God bless Her Majesty even though we kicked the thieving bastards out many years ago, still it has to be acknowledged they gave us the railways and sanitation, is "Mahadev".'

'You mean he's here?' I interrupted.

'Honestly, Rabindra,' chided Mr Chatterjee, 'if only you had the patience to listen you would be availed not only of the information you seek but its subject. Since you deal with patients every day, it's a wonder so little of that quality has rubbed off on you.' He chuckled.

'I know,' I said. 'Now please, tell me where he is.'

'Well, by chance I happened to be standing next to him just before the car exploded, but soon realised that he wasn't listening to a word I was saying. In fact he was rummaging around in his lunchbox. Then he glanced up with that far-away gaze characteristic of those who see perplexities beyond the grasp of ordinary mortals and muttered the word, "research". I then proceeded to impart my long-held opinion that without those prepared, like him, to embark upon the very frontiers of knowledge, to sail the boats of their understanding, as it were, over the uncharted waters of ignorance in search of that rare and precious jewel of enlightenment...'

'Then he's at the clinic?' I said. 'Is that right, Mr Chatterjee?'

But Mr Chatterjee was in full flow now, an island of understanding emerging from limpid waters of endeavour, verdant with unknown vegetation and possibly parrots, it was hard to hear above the noise. It worried me that by the time I reached the clinic, the man with a cravat, untended, might have expired. So I asked Mrs Jeenkal, who was nearby, if she would be so kind as to fetch my brother while I remained with the patient.

'Fetch him yourself,' she answered, to a chorus of malicious laughter. 'What do you think I am, the Clinic Skivvy?'

I noticed that Mrs Moodi, nearby, had set up an impressive display of sewing materials, along with cushions, curtain fabrics and men's underwear behind which a slender lick of flame was beginning to play.

'Mrs Moodi,' I said. 'Would it be possible to have the slimmest of your needles and a length of thread, preferably silk?'

'Show us your money,' she said.

I fiddled in my pockets.

'Ha!' she said, 'I knew it.'

'This is a medical emergency,' I said. 'If you let me have these items as discussed, I promise to pay you at the earliest opportunity.'

She tapped a notice above the display. 'What does this say?' she demanded.

'"Available In Other Colours",' I read.

'"No Credit",' she retorted.

'But Mrs Moodi, it distinctly says, "Available in other colours".'

'It says, "No Credit", plain as daylight. Which means if you want something you pay for it.'

I had long observed that the hardest people to argue with are those completely wrong. However, since Mr Vaisvarya barged me brusquely aside to inspect Mr Gupta's cutlery stall, I decided to leave it there. It seemed an odd time to go shopping, although one or two of the villagers were striking bargains along the barricade. I found the man with a cravat surrounded by a small crowd led by Mrs Dong in a chant of 'Turtle, Turtle'.

'Let me through,' I announced. 'I am a Clinic Skivvy.'

But when they parted it was only for Mr Vaisvarya, now in

possession of a large carving knife which he handed to Mrs Dong.

'Death to the Turtle!' she shouted.

'This ain't gonna be pretty,' said Hendrix hobbling up beside me.

'They seem to think that the man with a cravat is the Turtle of ancient mythology,' I explained.

'Wrong place, wrong time,' muttered Hendrix ominously.

'But why did he come here?' I asked. 'Surely there is no sensible reason to wave a gun around, strike people over the head, and shoot at Sharon.'

'Oh, I don't know,' said Hendrix. 'He's our Indian co-producer.'

'Then if you know this man,' I said, 'you know that he is not a Turtle, and are in a position to convey this information to those under the misapprehension that he is.'

'Maybe they're not so wrong,' said Hendrix.

I couldn't believe that Hendrix, a man of reason, albeit fish-phobic, would have succumbed to this hysteria.

'We all need a Turtle,' he shrugged.

'Why?'

'Someone to blame.'

'For what?' I asked.

'For us. For this. For it. Some people blame their parents. The Spanish lob goats off balconies. Americans drop bombs. Personally, I hate Arsenal supporters. I mean if it wasn't for Arsenal...'

'The world would be a better place?'

'I'd have to blame somebody else.'

The chants were growing more rhythmic.

'I think we ought to stop them before they do something foolish,' I said.

'He doesn't make a bad Turtle, though, does he?' said Hendrix.

'You are only saying this because your ribs hurt. But it is never wise to let your wounds dictate your actions.'

'Okay,' said Hendrix with a sigh. 'I guess you've got a point.' He walked forward. 'Listen up!' he shouted. 'I think this has gone far enough. Yeah, yeah, love, he's a bit like a turtle isn't he, but not really. Yeah? Take a look at him. What do you see? Shell and flippers? Snappy jaws? No, you don't. Madame, I can assure you that you don't. So come on, give us some space. Shift it. You. Out of the way.'

While Hendrix pushed through to the man with a cravat, Mike hurried over to tug at his elbow. 'You're not thinking,' he hissed. 'Is this something we actually have a problem with?'

'He's still got his goons,' said Hendrix.

'Not anymore,' said Mike. 'They think she's a god come down for revenge.'

'I am so sorry,' said Sergeant Shrinivasan, collecting bits of Veena from around people's feet. 'It was the music. She began to dance and then she became the dance and now she is Shiva. Perhaps I should have played something a bit lighter.'

'You mustn't blame yourself,' said Hendrix handing the Sergeant some brass inlays and a tuning knob. 'And I'm really sorry about your banjo. I leant a guitar to Pete Townshend once, next thing it's in pieces. Or was it Kurt Cobain? Or did I make that up?' Hendrix frowned in the manner of one searching his brain for something no longer there.

'But perhaps it was destined,' said the Sergeant mournfully. 'For why else were my fingers guided to play the Shivarag?'

'I'm with you there,' said Mike. 'Destiny. What else could it be? And, let's face it, a god's got to do what a god's gotta do.'

The god in question was now standing in the centre of a hushed circle, the man with a cravat wriggling at her feet. Mrs Dong handed her the carving knife, its jagged blade flashing the afternoon sun against her face.

'Sharon!' called Hendrix but even he recognised that she was no longer his wife. She was Shiva incarnate, wielding the sword of justice over the trembling Turtle who had come to ravage and met, instead, his doom.

'Help!' croaked the man with a cravat, struggling to reach his gun a few inches away.

Sharon was circling him in short, rhythmic steps, her feet lifting the dust, skirt swaying as she hummed the Sergeant's tune.

'I think we ought to get the gun,' said Mike.

But none of us were able to move.

Sharon stopped. The crowd shuffled nervously, glancing away from her searing gaze and its glimpse of the infinity that all our petty efforts in life are merely an attempt to deny. The man with a cravat curled his fingers round the gun and began to drag it towards himself. He glanced at Sharon as she smiled down at him and, just for a moment, he too lay transfixed by the terrible light of her eyes and the understanding that death and life were merely a thing and its shadow and the dance of his darkness was nearing its end. He pointed the gun at her and pulled the trigger.

Click.

'It's empty,' shouted Hendrix. 'And she knew it. Ha! Dirty Harry. Brilliant. That's our favourite bloody film, pot noodle anybody?'

'It does not fire because she wills it so,' said Sergeant Shrinivasan, quietly.

'Off with his head,' shouted Mrs Dong.

'Huh?' said the man with a cravat.

'Exactly,' said Mike, clapping his hands to a steady rhythm. 'Off with his head. Off with his head.'

Voices began to take up the chant although Mike looked less decisive, I thought, than he sounded.

'Quality kitchenware as used for the slaying of Demonic Turtles!' announced Mr Gupta, opportunistically but somehow inappropriate.

The man with a cravat twisted his head, while he still had one, to peer at the crowd. I suspected he was looking for some assistance from his colleagues and would have been disappointed to see them on their knees begging forgiveness from anyone who cared to listen.

Sharon stood over him now, the knife raised. The man with a cravat, sweating profusely, began to pull himself across the ground, but since both Sharon and the circle moved with him, after several minutes of prodigious effort he looked up to see that he'd apparently got nowhere.

'Do it!' shouted Mike.

Sharon smiled again. The man with a cravat lifted a hand to protect himself.

'Ah... excuse me...' said Mr Chatterjee, stepping gingerly into the circle. 'Before any summary decapitation occurs, I think you ought to hear what I have to say.'

One or two people groaned.

'No, really,' said Mr Chatterjee. 'This is most pertinent to the present circumstances, concerning as it does a conversation I had last night with a tree.'

Sharon lowered the knife and looked at him. The man with a cravat breathed out. The whole of Pushkara stood open-mouthed waiting for Mr Chatterjee to speak, a situation so contrary to his usual experience that, for once, he was unable to say anything.

'Ah... you see... it... um...' was all he could manage before blowing his nose and grinning. Sharon ran her finger over the edge of the blade, producing a thin metallic note. The man with a cravat tried to move but found her feet on either side of his head. She bent down, grabbed his hair, forcing his chin back, and placed the blade against his throat.

'Yes, Mr Chatterjee?' I urged. 'You had a conversation with a tree?'

Several villagers tutted with irritation.

'Preposterous,' said one of them.

'If you can explain how an English dancer is able to transform into the incarnation of Shiva,' I said, 'I'm sure Mr Chatterjee can tell us how vegetation might develop the facility of discourse.'

'Indeed,' said Mr Chatterjee, gaining a little confidence. 'For the one is as remarkable as the other, and today is indeed a remarkable day. Now, although I wouldn't go so far as to say that any tree, given the appropriate circumstances, would be able to strike up a conversation, though perhaps all they're waiting for is a simple "good morning, how are you today?", nevertheless...'

'Just tell us what it said,' said Mike impatiently.

'Well, after we'd introduced ourselves and exchanged a few pleasantries, I thought it an opportune moment to present one or two questions,' said Mr Chatterjee. 'Some of a philosophical nature and some, if I may say, of a more personal bent.' He blew his nose again, blushing slightly. 'After all, though lacking, perforce, in experiences of an ambulatory nature, it may well have learned much from the observation of ours.'

'Cut both their heads!' spluttered Mrs Dong.

'But what did it say?' I pressed.

Mr Chatterjee froze for a moment. I nodded encouragingly.

'It said that what we seek is before, behind, above and below us. There is nowhere that it is not,' said Mr Chatterjee.

'Is that all?' said Mr Vaisvarya. 'I wrote that fifty times once as a punishment.'

'Ah, yes,' said Mr Chatterjee, 'Clearly the tree was, in spite of its outwardly arboreal nature, well-versed in philosophical aphorisms. But when I questioned it on specifics, for instance what was meant by the slaying of the Turtle, it said "the conquest of greed". Pressed further for elucidation, it said that the slaying is not of an individual, per se, nor indeed of a turtle, but of such personality adjuncts as arrogance, pomposity and the sheer bloody rudeness that most of you condescending bastards exhibit most of the time.' There was a shocked silence in which Mr Chatterjee also participated.

'Shit,' said Mike. 'She won't do it.'

Sharon's demeanour was indeed changing as she listened to Mr Chatterjee, the rapturous glow from her eyes dissolving into something more puzzled.

'I think Shiva is leaving her,' whispered Sergeant Shrinivasan.

'Mrs Shiver,' said Mr Chatterjee with a bow. 'You have cupped the waters and shown us the image of ourselves: liars and cheats who would jostle their neighbours for the momentary advantage of a retail opportunity, or call wantonly for the decapitation of a stranger. All have been revealed for the selfish, conceited, pusillanimous little shits that they really are.'

'Pusi-what?' said Mike.

'And thus are they decapitated,' said Mr Chatterjee, blushing again, 'according to the true import of the legend. For their heads roll on the ground, ugly and ignominious for the ants to eat and feet to kick.' He gave a little kick to demonstrate how it might be done. 'And, as it was foretold, so the turtle of their vanity rolls dusty, kicked and ah... ant-eaten... on the ah... the ground, obviously...' I could see that he was running out of steam. 'Where it is not so much the ants that are kicking it, though ants have more feet and thus, perhaps, the cumulative effect...'

Hendrix tapped him on the shoulder. 'Thanks, that's great,' he said. 'Hi Sharon.'

She stared at him.

'Okay, not quite Sharon yet.' He looked at the man with a cravat. 'Well now, what have we here? One lucky bugger. Thanks to this bloke...' he nodded to Mr Chatterjee, 'you've won today's star prize: a chance to live. But don't get excited now, it's only a slim one.'

The man with a cravat snarled at him.

'You see,' said Hendrix, 'this lady isn't a lady at all. Of course, normally I'd smack anyone who says that, but what I mean is she's now the Lord Shiva. I know. That might raise a few questions tonight but we'll face that when we get to it. Now, we all know about Shiva, don't we? Well, I don't, to be honest, but I figure you would, being, as they say, of an Indian persuasion. Am I right or am I right?'

'I'll have you,' hissed the man with a cravat.

'You lose a point!' groaned Hendrix. 'And you didn't have many to start with. So let's give you a hint. It's Hint Time, everybody. And the hint is: "Yes, Mr Hendrix, I'll do whatever you want, just please, please, don't let her cut my head off".'

'Ravi!' called the man with a cravat.

'If you're looking for your boys,' said Hendrix, 'I think

you'll find they've worked out you don't mess with Shiva if you don't want her messing with you. Hey, Shiva, show him your knife.'

'What's going on?' said Shiva. 'Where am I?'

'That's not Shiva,' spat the man with a cravat, though mainly to get some dust out of his mouth. 'That's just a filthy tart.'

'Oops,' said Hendrix, kicking him in the chest. 'That twitch again. So let's put it another way. You're bleeding to death, and you won't last long. But the good news is: there is a Doctor, his name is Robby and, thanks to the wonders of modern medicine, he's here with us today!'

Among the indignant voices around us I could hear the words, 'Skivvy', 'Clinic' and 'merely the'.

'Now,' said Hendrix, 'Robby could stop that bleeding with just a couple of stitches. Isn't that right, Robby?'

'Well, yes,' I said. 'Given the appropriate instruments. Unfortunately...'

'We can sort that,' said Hendrix. 'One thing at a time. But the point is he won't. Cause he doesn't like you. And even though he could easily save your life, bish bosh, he ain't gonna start 'til you get a bit nicer.'

'That is not quite correct,' I said. 'If I only treated people I liked there'd hardly be anyone alive in Pushkara.'

Which provoked a storm of protest though it was true and they knew it.

Hendrix chuckled. 'Well, he might have his professional ethics, but I've got mine. And you just called my wife a tart.'

'Oof,' said the man with a cravat.

'But hey,' said Hendrix withdrawing his foot, 'tick tock, time's out and if she won't chop your head off, I will. Happily.'

'I cut it,' shrieked Mrs Dong. 'Gimme knife. I kill all men in suits.'

'What do you want?' said the man with a cravat.

'The contents of your wallet,' said Hendrix. 'Everything your boys are carrying and whatever's in the boot of your car.'

'There's nothing in the boot of my car,' said the man with a cravat.

'Oh, there's always something in the boot,' smiled Hendrix. 'And I want cash wired over to the bank here, which is to say every penny you owe us for the tour plus a little extra for the inconvenience. Or you can just hand over your head. What do you say?'

'Damn you,' said the man with a cravat.

'Mrs Dong?' said Hendrix.

Mrs Dong seized the knife from Sharon and knelt beside the man with a cravat. Hendrix grimaced, looking away.

'Alright,' said the man with a cravat. 'Alright. Stop her.'

'We got a bank here?' said Hendrix, prising the knife from Mrs Dong's fingers.

'Of course,' said Malek. 'The Shri Malek Bister Bank of International Deposits and Loans.'

Several voices murmured puzzlement.

'Although it doesn't have a branch in the village as such. I am telling you this!' said Malek tartly to his disbelievers. 'Its headquarters are in the city and you have not heard of it because it is uninterested in the puny sums you'd scrape together if you toiled your whole bloody life and saved every paise you ever earned.'

'Okay, let's wire it over,' said Hendrix.

'I'll need a phone,' said the man with a cravat.

'Where's the nearest phone?' asked Hendrix.

'There are no telephones here,' said Mr Chatterjee after a short silence. 'Since anybody wishing to talk to anyone else has only to walk a few yards to find them. If they're not at work or at home, they'll be in the shops or at the bus stop. In any case, by the time you've found them you'll have told any number of people on the way, so they would have most likely heard it from somebody else anyway.'

'That's if anyone's listening,' snickered someone unkindly.

'There is such a thing,' said Sergeant Shrinivasan, 'in my office in the police station. It is a device of a peculiar shape with the word "Telephone" written on it.'

'Does it work?' said Mr Aptalchary, slightly shocked.

'Extremely well,' said the Sergeant, 'in that its primary purpose is to stop piles of paper fluttering about when the window is open.'

'But what else does it do?' said Mike, perking up.

'I am not sure,' said the Sergeant. 'But once a year or so it produces a terrible jangling noise that makes me jump out of my seat. In fact, one afternoon I accidentally knocked the top bit from the bottom thing and a ghostly voice called out.' The Sergeant clutched his medals, a frequent symptom, for him, of remembered anxiety.

'What did it say?' asked Hendrix.

'Hello, hello, is anybody there?' recalled the Sergeant, shuddering.

'Excuse me,' said Mrs Ginko from the other car. 'There is an attaché case in the boot, as you predicted, with a large quantity of money in it.'

The man with a cravat sighed.

'Okay,' said Hendrix. 'What we need now is a lawyer so it's all done properly. I don't suppose...'

Father pushed forward in his wig and gown. 'I am such a one,' he said, grandly. 'As will be evident from my attire.'

'You're the man,' said Hendrix. 'So have a chat with this bloke here. Draw some papers up, nice and kosher. Mr Bister can sort the deposit. Then I reckon we're outta here.'

'But is there not something else?' I said, quietly.

'Oh yeah,' said Hendrix. 'Patch him up. I've got some gaffer tape if you're short of the what nots.'

'No, no, that's not what I meant,' I said. 'It is some other business. You know?'

'Oh yeah, how did that go?' whispered Hendrix.

'Her knee inflicted a severe pain to my lower quarters.'

'That's what they call an "Essex no",' chuckled Hendrix. 'Which kinda means what it does.'

'But how could it be no?' I said. 'For surely if our love is true, she would feel the same way about me as I do about her.'

'What is this nonsense?' said Father, gruffly. 'Not only do you make no sense as usual but you are interrupting a lawyer in the middle of earning a few bob... I mean providing invaluable counsel in matters of litigation.'

'And if not,' I persisted, 'what then is true? Are mountains true because they never move? Or the sky true because it never stops? What is true for one is untrue for another. And just because everyone thinks something is true, does that make it so?'

'Well, everyone thinks you're a simpleton,' said Father. 'And that's good enough for me. Now, to business.'

'But they came because of me,' I protested, more stridently than intended. 'Or at least because of the sacrificial rites performed by Pol and myself in order to summon our English wives. I must admit we didn't expect the Turtle and Shiva and all the rest of it, but the fact remains that our importunings brought them here, and whether everything, anything or nothing is true they cannot leave until our pledge is fulfilled.'

Although it was difficult to pin-point any single rebuke

among the shouting that followed, I did gather, in general terms, that I wasn't entirely popular with much of the village. However, I also began to pick up some discordant voices, mainly among the younger men, who seemed to be chanting the word, 'Rabindra!'

'No, I think that would be excessive,' muttered Father to one of my sisters who was holding a can of petroleum spirits and a box of matches.

'But he has divided young from old,' she said. 'High from low and, by his own confession, has invoked the demons of calumny and chaos. What greater crime could there be? And thus,' she glared at me, rattling the matches, 'what better punishment?'

Whether or not he might have been persuaded I never discovered, since I was hoisted abruptly onto various young shoulders, from where I could see Sharon, likewise aloft, parading elegantly around the remains of the burning car. I could also see, from my new vantage point, that the barricade, unattended by its distracted owners, was now very much on fire.

'The barricade!' I shouted.

'The barricade!' shouted some of the young men. 'To the barricade!'

'No, no,' I said. 'It's on fire.'

At which point, calls of 'fire fire' spread through the crowd very much, in fact, like fire itself. The response was fairly swift as the stall-holders ran to save their merchandise, though the flames were already hot enough in places to beat them back. Malek Bister, meanwhile, stood to one side laughing.

'So now we know,' he jeered. 'how detached you Brahmins are when your stalls catch light.' His smile vanished, however, when the mango-seller pushed his cart to safety, in spite of the fact that it was already burning, straight into the hall porch.

'You idiot,' shouted Malek, running towards him. 'Do you want the only cultural institution of any repute in this bloody village to go up in smoke?'

The mango-seller climbed out from under his cart. 'Mangos!' he coughed, beating the flames with his hat. 'Lovely mangos.'

'Stop that!' shouted Malek, snatching the hat. 'Don't you know anything about fires? Beating only enrages them further. Look at it.' The door had already begun to plume with yellow snakes of flame. 'Get me a fire extinguisher!'

Several extinguishers clattered around Malek's feet along with some rather smug smiles. Malek picked one up, pulled the pin, pressed the button, scowled and threw it into the flames. He tried another. 'Bloody things,' he said. 'Give me that.' He seized the mango-sellers hat and began to flap at the burning door. 'Will nobody help me?' he cried.

'Suddenly it isn't so funny,' said Father, grimly.

'Oh, you've come to gloat, have you?' snarled Malek.

'If it means the end of that ridiculous building, I think I can be forgiven a moment of quiet satisfaction.'

'I built this for the glory of Pushkara,' said Malek, coughing.

'You built it for your own.'

'And why not?' said Malek, stamping on embers. 'What's wrong with a little glory for me?'

'Because your glory,' said Father, angry enough to take a swipe at Malek with his wig, 'is the village in uproar, your hall on fire, my son completely mad and English women dancing on cars.'

'He was mad anyway,' said Malek, flailing back with the mango-seller's hat.

'He was stupid,' admitted Father. 'But it was your son that made him mad.'

'My son?' said Malek as the mango-seller dodged around him, trying to get his hat back. 'I told him to keep away from you lot, with your gods and goddesses and metaphysical codswallop. Of what bloody use is transcendental consciousness for selling scooters? Can you repair an engine with a philosophical axiom or cook samosas with a semantic paradox?'

The porch timbers were beginning to creak, roasted specks of ash spitting down over their heads.

'It was your son,' shouted Father, 'who infected my son's head with commerce, calumny and carnal predilections.'

'My son was a dutiful boy getting ready to take over his father's business,' said Malek. 'Now what is he?'

'I don't know,' sobbed a lady's voice, 'but it doesn't look good.'

It was then that I noticed, not for the first time in recent days, that everything around us had become eerily quiet. Cindy stood at the edge of the crowd, knees bruised, arms bloody, her rich hair a tangled mat across her forehead. She'd lost her shoes and torn her dress.

Malek and Father stared at her. Hendrix hobbled over. 'Take your time,' he said.

She gathered enough breath to say, 'It's Pol. He fell.'

'What do you mean, "fell"?' said Malek. 'Fell over? Fell off? Fell under? What are we talking about?'

'I don't know,' said Cindy. 'Perhaps he didn't.'

'Then if he didn't, there is no cause to fuss, is there?' said Malek, stepping briskly away from a shower of burning wood.

Cindy shook her head. 'He was on the rock. The big rock. The ah…'

'The Shiva Rock?' I said.

'Yes,' said Cindy. 'He climbed right to the top, saying all

sorts of stuff about... I don't know, the gods and not being grateful. We told him to come down. But he just laughed, you know like people do when they don't care anymore. And I was saying, like, "Pol, Pol, please, my little peanut, come down from there, I'm sorry, and I love you." And that's when...' She choked a little. 'He fell or... he jumped, I don't know.'

'I'm guessing that's serious,' said Hendrix.

'The rock is very high,' I said. 'And there is nothing between the top of it and the ground below.'

'What, is he hurt?' said Malek. 'Is he... is he... ?'

'Dead?' I finished the question for him.

'I don't know,' she sobbed. 'But he's so broken.'

I pictured Pol, who could prance over rocks nimble as a goat, gazing down to the hard earth from which he had always sought to escape. Did he step? Or did he slip? And, either way, was he, in that moment, just before the unforgiving stone crushed the life out of him, neither earth nor sky but a free thing falling? Or was he thinking, 'oops'?

Cindy clutched at my arm. 'Help him,' she pleaded. 'You're his only friend.'

But what sort of a friend, I wondered as I turned once more to the dusty track. For if Pol were dead, whose fault was it but mine?

12

I HAD SEEN BLOOD BEFORE, obviously, in vials, cuts, and the
occasional stool sample. But never so much, nor disgorged so
wantonly over rock. Pol was lodged between two boulders,
one arm sporting an additional elbow, his leg twisted into
hideous shapes. Blood flowed from his scalp, the stones
beneath him spattered like a paan-seller's shoes.

Our School Master had often reminded us that sacred
places demanded special duties. 'It is not me that you are
messing with,' he'd remark, hurling the board rubber at some
recalcitrant wretch who'd stuck his bogies under the desk,
'but the gods. You think when you're all grown up you'll
be able to do as you please. But you're wrong. Getting older
just means the board rubbers get bigger. In fact the whole
world is one big board rubber that slaps you about the head,
day after day, year after year, for what? Why do you think
everyone's so miserable? Because they are being punished.
Because they spend their whole lives trying to sneak bogies
under their desks. You think I'm tough? Hah! If you annoy
me, all you get is a kick up the arse and a clip round the ear.
If you so much as irritate them, you'll develop untreatable
haemorrhoids and headaches, though it probably amounts to
much the same in the end.'

'Has he moved?' said Cindy who had run ahead of me,
turning every so often to usher me onwards.

Martina shook her head. If Pol had been felled by a board rubber of his own making, so Martina's quick, dry glance in my direction felled me no less brutally.

'Oh my sweet poppadom,' sobbed Cindy. 'Forgive me, please.'

'No, no,' I gasped. 'Don't touch him. Let me see.'

I knelt beside Pol as best I could, planting my feet between rocks, the blood beneath him like a spreading shade. His wrist was cold and limp but, after an agonising wait during which I could feel only the pumping of my own heart, there it was: a pulse.

'He's alive,' I said.

'Pol!' whispered Cindy.

'Well, he can't stay here,' said Martina. 'And I don't suppose you've got Air Ambulance.'

'We must get him to the clinic,' I said. 'Cindy, would you please run back to the village? If you don't know where the clinic is, ask someone. In there you will find my brother. He is a Doctor and has been to England. Tell him that Pol Bister is badly injured, and to prepare whatever remedies may keep alight the flame of life in the shattered body of our gentle friend.'

'I'm not leaving him,' said Cindy. 'What if he dies, up here, all alone?'

'From the moment he met you,' I said, 'he forgot what it is to be lonely. Now, I think you are the fleetest of foot while Martina, I suspect, is the strongest. Yes?'

Cindy nodded.

'And get some people up here to help us,' added Martina.

Cindy blew Pol a kiss and turned back towards the village.

Pol's position was awkward, with a large boulder pinning his leg. If we tried to drag him clear, I thought, we'd probably tear him in half. I remembered him just a few weeks ago, skipping among these very hills, wild, free and slightly frantic, laughing at the sky. The sight of him now stung my eyes.

'He'll be alright,' said Martina softly.

'Is this something you know?'

'It's just something to say,' she shrugged, pulling her skirt up and kneeling beside me. 'In England if you don't know what to say, you say anything. It doesn't matter. Okay, we need to shift this rock.'

I put my weight to it and pushed until I thought my head would burst.

'Why don't we do it together?' said Martina after I'd collapsed panting. 'I'll count and then we push.'

'Alright,' I said bracing myself.

'One, two, three.' She pushed for a moment then looked at me. 'What's the problem?' she said.

'I'm sorry, I don't know what you're counting, nor indeed how many of whatever it is you are counting there might be.'

'Okay,' she said, wiping a smear of dust across her forehead. 'I should have said I'll count to three. We push on four.'

'But you do not count the fourth?'

'No. That's right. The fourth is the push.'

'Alright, I think I understand.'

'One, two, three…'

With a prodigious effort we managed to edge the rock forward a couple of inches. But it slipped back when I leaned on it to catch my breath. Pol moaned pitifully.

'Don't worry, Pol,' I murmured, 'you'll be alright.'

Martina looked at me. 'You're catching on,' she said. 'Okay, we need to clear some of this stuff from the front. I think that's where it's getting stuck.'

She leaned down, pulling at twigs and stones, while I began to claw at the ground with a vehemence that would leave her in no doubt as to my alacrity in the removal of debris.

'Maybe don't throw up so much dust?' she said.

'I'm sorry,' I said, coughing.

'You're having a go,' she said. 'That's the main thing.'

'But surely the outcome of one's go is the main thing,' I said, sitting back on my haunches. 'Without the outcome, "go" can hardly be described as bearing the attributes of a measurable entity, which is to say a definable "thing" as such.'

'Well, let's just shift some of this crap without chucking too much of it in the air. Okay?'

Which we did.

'Alright,' she said after a few minutes. 'Let's see how we're doing.' She pressed her shoulder to the rock. It wobbled.

'Nearly there,' she said.

We scraped some more.

'Okay,' she said, wiping her hands on her thighs. 'This is it.'

We positioned ourselves as before. She counted to three. And then we pushed until our limbs cried, our breath stung, and the sweat trickled into our eyes. The rock shuddered and began to topple, stones cracking under its abominable weight. Then it tipped forward, teetering for a moment before crashing down the slope, throwing rocks and dust and pieces of torn tree behind it, resting finally somewhere in the silence of the valley floor.

'Extremely good counting, if I may say so,' I said.

'You may,' she smiled.

I could now see Pol's other leg, ugly and twisted, the trouser torn, blood oozing through its rent fabric from a gaping wound in his thigh.

'How long before help gets here?' said Martina.

'That is difficult to say. Fetching an injured villager, even a low-born, demands proper supervision. Seniority will be of paramount importance, meaning the frail and infirm, some of whom take many hours just to reach the bathroom. The younger men, meanwhile, would not be so impolite as to run ahead. In any case, by the time they've settled the various protocols it may very well be time for tea.'

'It's down to us then,' said Martina. 'I'll take his legs, you take his arms. It won't be easy, but I don't suppose we've got much choice.'

'Few things worth doing are easy,' I said.

'Is that why you make everything so difficult?'

To which I had no answer.

Though slim-boned and gangly, Pol was heavier than I expected. Martina managed to get her hands under his thighs leaving me the upper torso. His head lolled worryingly but at least he was still breathing which was more than I could say for myself after only a few steps. The ground was treacherous beneath my feet, either tripping me up or slithering wickedly away. The further we got, the harder it was to grip Pol's sodden shirt. I noticed that Martina's arms and dress were also streaked with blood but she didn't seem to mind. We stopped only when she needed to shake a stone from her shoe.

'That wasn't your sisters on fire, was it?' she said, slipping it back on.

'How did you know?'

'I didn't think they'd do it.'

'But they were so determined,' I said as we lifted Pol again. 'And they'd gone to all sorts of trouble, with matches, old commodes and petroleum spirits.'

'Yeah, but when it comes to it, people don't necessarily do what they think they'll do. Sometimes you realise what you thought was important doesn't matter that much.'

'I thought it mattered to them.'

'A bunch of third rate tarts from England dancing in their knickers? How's that going to matter to anyone?'

'You are not a third rate tart,' I protested.

'Thanks,' she said.

'I have not met many tarts, but of this I am sure: you are not just first rate, you are without equal. I would go so far as to say,' I said smiling, 'that you are peerless among tarts. The Queen of Tarts. In fact...'

'Yeah, alright,' she said. 'You've made your point.'

We trudged on in silence. From time to time Pol groaned.

'It is an apposite figure of speech,' I said after a while. 'And I am glad to have learned it only today from the man with a cravat. For, like a tart, your dry exterior conceals a soft bed of warm fruit. And, as the word suggests, one's tongue recoils slightly at its excess before diving helplessly for more. Indeed, though I can hardly breathe for the weight of my broken friend, my helpless eyes are drawn to the sweet confection of your form again and again.'

'Just keep walking,' she growled.

When we reached the last slope that tumbled towards the flat meadows at the end of the track, she stopped suddenly. 'What man with a cravat?' she said.

'He was in the village,' I said, 'accompanied by others. A maroon cravat. It might have been his car that was on fire.'

'I said they'd find us. Jesus Christ.' We resumed our walk. 'Mike's an idiot. So who burnt the car? How did that happen?'

'I think he dropped his cigar on a trail of petroleum spirits left by my sisters. I'm told it went up very quickly. Then Sharon danced on top of it.'

'Yeah, she would.'

'You must one day explain to me the curious English practice of dancing on cars,' I said. But I was in pain now. 'Martina, we have to stop. Please. I am losing my grip.'

'Okay,' she said. 'A quick one. That's all.'

I lowered Pol to the ground. There is always something less brutal about traumatic injuries nestled among flowers. For a moment he seemed at peace. I felt his pulse again to make sure the peace wasn't excessive, and nodded to Martina who was obviously waiting for my verdict.

'Don't sit down,' she said.

'Just for a moment.'

'He doesn't have a moment.'

But when I stood up again my legs wouldn't hold me.

'You have to try,' said Martina. 'For your friend.'

'I would do anything for my friends,' I said. 'For Pol, that is. I'm not sure about my other friends. Actually, I'm not sure that I have any other friends, but right now I cannot move. Not a muscle. Not an inch.'

'Then do it for me.'

It might have been the look in her eyes, or the weariness around her shoulders, or the soft sway with which she eased the strain of her hips, but suddenly my legs were moving, my back upright, and my head as clear as a morning sky. Pol was lighter than he'd ever been, the road less arduous, and the goal more desirable. It is by this, I thought, that knights do battle and heroes prevail. I had never felt so strong.

We met the first of the villagers where the loamy meadows frayed into the beginnings of the track that meandered down the hill to home. Unfortunately, she was of no use at all.

'My baby!' shouted Mrs Bister, running towards us, feet unshod, a forgotten saucepan in her hand. 'What have they done to you?'

Martina insisted that we carry on walking while Mrs Bister ran hysterically back and forth, occasionally trying to slap Pol, saying, 'He but sleeps, yet who shall awaken him?' From time to time, little bits of dhal would fly from her saucepan as she swung it around. I had often seen her grieve but never without a slice of onion to precipitate the tears.

'He's stopped breathing!' she wailed at one point.

'No he hasn't,' I said reassuringly, although it was true that his breathing was getting dangerously irregular. I decided to look up 'Irregular Breathing' in my symptoms book as soon as I got back, but dreaded finding only, 'Prognosis: impending death. Action: notify relatives.'

As the village came into view, we saw Cindy, Mr Bister and a group of excited young men hurrying along the road.

'Perhaps you'd run a bit faster if you lifted your dress up,' said one of them.

'I'm outrunning you, you creep,' retorted Cindy trying, in fact, to pull it down, as some of them craned their necks to peek.

'What is this?' said Malek. 'This crushed and devastated creature? It cannot be my son, for my son is neither crushed nor devastated. My son is a healthy, happy boy who skips along singing, not this gaping wound, this broken heap of brittle flesh!'

'It's Pol,' said Martina, bluntly. 'So either get out of the way or help us. You lot!' she barked. 'What's that under your sleeves? Seaweed or muscle? Let's see what you're made of, come on.'

Eager to please, the young men gathered round, some taking his legs, some his arms, others sliding their hands under his body. Cindy took charge of his head, kissing it fervently. 'Cindy, there's a love,' said Martina. 'We have to move.'

'This is my fault,' said Cindy. 'Because I was so horrid to him. Honestly, Marty, I didn't mean what I said.'

'Don't worry,' I said. 'For in time Pol will come to understand how English ladies like to dance on cars and say things without meaning. And once he does, you may dance to your heart's content and speak meaninglessly for hours.'

'Thank you,' she said, frowning slightly. 'That's very sweet.'

Just outside the village we came across those elders, designated to supervise the collection of Pol, sitting down for a light picnic to restore their energies. A little further on we could feel the heat from the fire.

'That's not just a car,' said Martina.

'Oh, the hall went up,' said Cindy.

'It is ruined,' moaned Malek. 'Everything is ruined. My son is ruined. My life is ruined. I curse this place. I spit on it.'

'Let's just focus,' said Martina.

Having salvaged what they could from their merchandise, most of the stall-holders were now watching as the hall slowly crumbled, tongues of fire licking its hollowed remains while clouds of embers billowed out every time another piece of ceiling collapsed. The men in grey suits were sharing cigarettes with a few of the traders, accompanied by cups of chai from the chai seller who had a large, albeit surreally illuminated, smile on his face.

'I've got an occasional table, thanks,' said one of them to Mr Kapra. 'And I seriously don't need a chess set.'

Sharon, looking slightly bemused, was surrounded by mothers asking her to bless their children, and elders requesting elucidations on the finer points of Sanskrit etymology. Some of the younger girls wondered if she thought they were pretty enough to marry a film star, while men of various ages pressed her for an autograph. Sharon seemed to please them all somehow, blessing a baby, scribbling on pieces of paper, saying 'what movie-star in his right mind wouldn't marry a lass like you', and, 'what's Sanskrit when it's at home?'

'Indeed,' muttered the elders. 'What is Sanskrit when it's at home? What indeed is the home of Sanskrit? That is the question.'

'Home is the heart of being,' said another. 'For it is into homes that we are born, by our homes sustained, and at home, ultimately, that we find our final rest.'

'Then it is being that is the heart of language. Why have we not thought of this before? How can one even begin to explore the linguistic roots of a verb until this is known?'

'Which, once known, all roots are known.'

'True it is that Shiva returns to lead his beloved to *moksha*.'

'Could you make it out to Bou Bou?' said one of the young men.

At Martina's suggestion we laid Pol across an ice-cream wagon, in spite of Mrs Goli's protests that the sprawling of a low-born across her wares would render them inedible. Malek had run ahead to make sure that everything was ready in the clinic. However, since emotional fatigue forced him to stop every so often to re-light his cigar, we overtook him several times and arrived first. Mrs Bister, meanwhile, had taken to hitting herself with the saucepan, saying that it was all her fault, though I thought she was being a little harsh on herself.

'Which way?' said Martina as we lifted Pol from the ice-cream wagon into the waiting room.

'The surgery, 'I said. 'Opposite the picture of my brother with the Queen of England, from which you will gather,' I said encouragingly, 'that there is no finer physician in all of Pushkara.'

But Dev wasn't in the surgery.

'I expect he's scrubbing up,' I said as we laid Pol on the examination table.

'He's had time for that,' said Martina. 'Didn't he know we were coming?'

'Yes, of course,' said Cindy. 'I told him myself.'

'What did he say?' asked Martina.

'That he'd have to... I can't remember, read something or...'

'Research?' I said.

'Yeah, that was it.'

'I'll fetch him,' I said. 'In the meantime, prepare some swabs and antiseptic solutions. You will find them tidily arranged and neatly labelled on the shelf there. Also, you should remove as many of his clothes as won't compromise his modesty. And prepare hot water. There is a stove there and a tap. I see that Mrs Bister has kindly brought a saucepan, if you can wrestle it from her.'

'Rabindra,' said Mrs Bister, struggling with Martina. 'Please tell me this isn't happening.'

'For once, Mrs Bister,' I said, 'it is.'

Dev wouldn't respond to my knock although I could hear him inside: a light cough followed by the sound of plinking glass.

'Dev?' I said. 'You are needed in the surgery.'

'Surgery shmurgery,' he answered.

'Pol Bister is very badly injured and requires immediate medical attention.'

'Never heard of him.'

'He is the son of Malek Bister, founder of the Shri Malek Bister World-Renowned Arts and Entertainments Complex.'

'Ashes,' he muttered as something fell over, possibly Dev himself. 'Who gives a toss?'

'Pol is my friend,' I insisted. 'I would give several tosses for him.'

'He's nothing,' said Dev. 'A low-born piece of filth. Just don't tread on him or you'll soil your shoes.'

'He isn't nothing to me,' I said. 'But that's not the point. The point is, he's a person. And he has a life, whatever its status. In fact for that I wouldn't give half a toss. He's a sweet and gentle soul with whom I have shared many dreams. Please, Mahadev, my revered brother who is a Doctor and has been to England, unlock the door.'

'Who said it was locked?' said Dev.

He was wreathed in a cloud of cigarette smoke, struggling to get back on his chair. In his hand was a specimen jar filled with amber liquid.

'I am studying,' he said, perching the jar back on his desk, 'precisely how much one has to consume before one no longer gives a shit. Now that's got to be worth a prize.'

'It is surely yours,' I said. 'Even now svelte ladies with Scandinavian accents are preparing themselves for the ceremony. But right now you are needed by a patient. And, believe me, revered brother, when I say right now, I do so in order to impress upon you its unequivocal urgency.'

He slouched back in his chair, fishing for a cigarette on the floor. 'I don't know,' he said, 'I expect you'll think of something.'

'But this is why you mastered the arts of healing,' I insisted. 'It is for this that you became a Doctor.'

He laughed. 'Did you know that England is named after a medical phenomenon? The gland which produces the hormone "En", vital for the regulation of certain cerebral functions, in particular a sense of the ridiculous.'

'What's going on?' said Martina, elbowing past me into the

office. 'What the hell do you think you're doing?'

'Phwoar,' said Dev.

'I'll give you phwoar,' said Martina. 'I'll give you a rocket up the arse. Rabindra, get him some coffee. Do you have coffee?'

'The lady who usually makes it is at the protest,' I said.

'Well, you make it,' said Martina. 'You know how to make coffee?'

'Not really,' I said.

'What is it with you people? It's a cup of bloody coffee. I'll make it. Where's the stuff? The kettle? The coffee?'

I looked at her blankly.

'Okay, I'll find it. Walk him round a bit.'

She stepped behind him and pulled the chair away. Dev fell to the ground, giggling.

'On your feet,' she said. 'Come on. Look at you. Call yourself a Doctor?'

'I don't know,' he chuckled. 'Everybody else does.'

'Give us a hand,' said Martina.

We took a shoulder each and hoisted Dev upright.

'Research,' he said, lunging for the specimen jar.

Martina swept it to the floor where it shattered in a pool of twinkling glass.

'Oh,' said Dev, staring at it.

'Get him into the surgery,' said Martina. 'Slap him if you have to.'

'That would not be appropriate,' I said. 'He is older than me.'

'Well, whatever,' she said. 'Can you shake him?'

'As long as it's done respectfully.'

'Just get him in there.'

The surgery was now busy, mainly with elders who had gathered to provide a measure of supervision. Mrs Bister had relinquished the saucepan and was hugging Cindy. Malek, who now had the saucepan, was heating water on the stove.

'How do I know when it's boiled?' he asked.

'Put your finger in it,' answered Mrs Bister.

'Though by no means a medical expert,' said Mr Dalliwal, prodding at Pol's thigh, 'I would say this calls for amputation.'

'You leave that bloody leg where it is,' shouted Malek, jumping around with his hand in the air.

'I believe that Mrs Dong has an excellent knife ideally suited for the purpose,' remarked Mr Batti to Mr Dalliwal. 'Perhaps you would be kind enough to fetch it.'

'But this amputation business was my idea,' said Mr Dalliwal, 'and therefore my role is not to perform menial errands such as fetching the necessary implements but to oversee the act itself.'

Malek ran his finger under the cold tap, breathing deeply.

'But I suggested the knife,' retorted Mr Batti, 'which represents a significant development of the proposal and therefore my proper place within the proceedings is of an equivalent stature.'

'That looks horrible,' said Dev, clutching the instrument trolley for support. 'I think I'm going to be sick.'

'The Doctor is here,' announced Mrs Vemuganti. 'Make way for the Doctor.'

'Make way, make way' said Mr Choudhury, elbowing her aside.

'That is precisely what I am saying,' said Mrs Vemuganti, indignantly. 'You are now telling the person who first said "make way" to make way?'

'Please,' I said. 'Let my brother examine the patient.'

'Well, that's nice,' said Mrs Vemuganti. 'Being spoken to by the Clinic Skivvy. You might be a Brahmin, young man, but that doesn't give you the right to start bossing us about.'

'Too late,' said Dev. 'He's dead.'

'No!' wailed Mrs Bister. 'Mahadev, Shri Doctor Mahadev, please please please.'

Dev shook his head and pushed his way out of the room. I followed him.

'Dev, I am no clinician, but it seems to me that someone who groans when you poke him cannot be dead.'

'Near as damn it,' said Dev.

'But surely there is hope for him?'

"fraid not, old boy,' he said warmly.

'But could you not try?' I said. 'If only to console his relatives?'

Martina came out of the back room with a cup of what I presumed was coffee. 'Here,' she said. 'Drink this.'

But Dev knocked it out of her hand. 'Oops,' he said, giggling maliciously.

'I don't care if he's older than you,' she said, 'but if you don't slap him, I will.'

'I cannot,' I said. 'For it would be contrary to every protocol I have ever known. Even to look askance at an elder, or accidentally to brush one's foot...'

'Then do it for me.'

I slapped him across the face.

'That,' he said, 'was surprising.'

Martina nodded. I slapped him again.

'Is this going to be a long series of surprises,' said Dev, 'by the end of which it will be less surprising but a lot more painful?'

I lifted my hand again.

'What is this?' shouted Father from the entrance. 'Rabindra, you will go to your room and stay there until suitable punishments can be devised. Never have I seen such a thing in all my life.'

'I'm sorry, Father,' I said, 'but I was merely attempting to nudge my brother out of his reverie.'

'Then perhaps this will nudge you out of yours,' said Father, slapping me in the face. Although used to this form of rebuke, I had to agree with Dev that it stung horribly. 'Now do as I say and go to your room.'

'Of course, my illustrious Father,' I said. 'But first we must tend to Pol Bister who, as you know, is horribly injured and may very well already be dead.'

Father glared at me. 'You needn't worry about him. These low-borns are surprisingly robust. Considerably more robust than my patience, in fact. Do not compel me to repeat myself.'

Malek Bister came to the door, his finger wrapped in a damp cloth. 'Excuse me,' he said quietly, 'but is no-one going to help my son?'

'Of course, someone is going to help your son,' said Father. 'This is a clinic and clinics are places wherein people are helped, reputable parentage or otherwise, although in your case it certainly is otherwise. At the moment we are equipped to deal with most ailments, but once in receipt of the promised investment, there shall be no medical challenges we cannot meet in our modern, purpose-built facility boasting state of the art examination rooms, an operating theatre, pharmacy and telephone.'

'What investment?' said Malek.

'From our Bombay associates,' sneered Father, 'who signed over the money shortly before their departure. Such funds to be allocated at the discretion of the Pushkara Worthy Causes Due To The Receipt of Unexpected Funds Committee, of which I am the Honorary Co-Chairman.'

'Then what is my role on the committee?' asked Malek.

'Don't be absurd,' chuckled Father.

'But are we not going to rebuild the Hall?'

'I believe,' said Father, drawing himself to his full height, 'the operative term is "worthy".'

Malek looked round at the surgery where Mrs Bister was caressing Pol's head. 'Doctor Sharma,' he said, bowing solemnly to Dev, 'my son is shattered into a thousand pieces.'

'Make an appointment,' said Dev. 'We're busy.'

'You've had his answer,' snorted Father. 'There is nothing wrong with your son that a few stitches and a little sugar-water cannot address. This is not a task for the incumbent physician who has more important things to do. Rabindra, you may see to it.'

'But this is beyond my skills,' I said.

'And mine,' whispered Dev, looking at the floor.

'Right,' said Father, 'I think we've stood around nattering for long enough. Mahadev? The Committee would like to discuss plans for the refurbishment of the Professor Sharma Centre for Clinical Excellence, in particular the sign outside. I suggested inlaid wood but some of the committee favoured brass. What do you say?'

'Please,' said Malek, taking Dev's hand. 'He is not the best of boys, nor the brightest perhaps, but he is my son. My only son. And you see his mother? She has never been so quiet in all her life. I beseech you, Doctor.'

'I am not a Doctor,' said Dev.

'That's enough,' said Father. 'Professor Sharma requires some peace and quiet. Fatigue, brought on by his unfailing endeavours towards the public good, has rendered him unduly humble. Rabindra, after you have seen to the patient, remember to mop the floors.'

'Mahadev,' I said, 'your modesty only enhances your greatness. But greater still are the arts you spent six years perfecting in London's finest medical institutions, all for that moment when a life hangs in the balance. Revered brother, that moment is now.'

'London wouldn't have me,' said Dev. 'Delhi wouldn't have me. Nobody would bloody have me. I spent six years in Madras.'

'But Madras is a most reputable establishment,' said Father, beginning to sweat, 'with excellent facilities and world-famous teachers.'

'I was a ward porter,' said Dev. 'And I could have made Senior Porter only Father said it was time to come home.'

'All this excitement about the new clinic has made you delirious,' said Father. 'What's needed is a little research, of which I believe there is some in your desk. Prizes await, after all.' Father chuckled nervously, as he attempted to ease Dev towards his office.

'How can I save Pol?' said Dev, bitterly, 'when I could not even save my own mother?'

'She was beyond medical assistance,' spluttered Father. 'This was clear to anyone.'

'No,' said Dev. 'We could have sent her to the City. They could have helped. They could have tried. But you wouldn't allow it. Because everyone would know.'

'She agreed,' said Father. 'For your sake.'

'For yours,' said Dev.

'But the picture,' I said, 'of you with the Queen. She is smiling at you. And you are smiling at the camera. Dev, I would know you anywhere. That is your face, your smile.'

'Yes, it's my face,' said Dev, pushing through the villagers towards the far end of the waiting room.

'No!' said Father. 'You will not touch that picture. Nobody touches the sacred picture of my son with the Queen of England.'

'But the rest of it,' said Dev, ripping the frame off the wall, 'is the Turkish Ambassador. Look at him. Are my hands so pale, my belly so big? Is that my fat arse behind the bulging tails of a ceremonial suit? That's the arse of a professional diplomat and this,' he said, picking at the picture, 'is stuck on.' He held up a little cut-out of his face. 'Me at a friend's wedding. I don't think the Queen was invited.'

'Then who can save my son?' sighed Malek, shaking his head.

'I'm sorry,' said Dev. 'But if his injuries don't kill him, I probably would.'

'Then fetch a priest,' said Mrs Bister. 'To bless, at least, the life to come.'

'I'm not paying those charlatan bastards to prance around with their mumbo jumbo,' said Malek. 'That's what got him leaping off rocks in the first place.'

'I could take it out of housekeeping,' offered Mrs Bister.

'That is not the issue,' said Malek. 'They talk nothing but rubbish. That is the issue. Death means death. Not floating off in a silvery vapour to come back as a toad.'

'This is not the time for eschatological disquisitions,' said Mr Chatterjee who had wandered in with a new-found grandeur born of his notoriety for conversing with trees. 'The young man is likely to expire long before the rest of you have finished talking about it. Why, only recently, while conversing with a philosophical acquaintance of the arboreal variety, I put this very question: who is it that acts? To which it answered: Around here? You must be joking.'

Martina eased me into the surgery and closed the door.

'Rabindra,' she said quietly, 'I think it's down to you.'

'But I am only the Clinic Skivvy,' I said. 'I lance boils and guess medicines.'

'We don't have a choice,' she said.

'And if I should fail?'

'Try. For me.'

'For you,' I said, 'anything.'

'I know,' she said softly.

From outside I could hear raised voices, Father among them. Inside, it was quiet and clean, the instruments gleaming in their metal trays, the air crisp with antiseptic. Pol moved slightly, a string of blood trickling from his leg to the floor below.

'I shall need swabs,' I said. 'And we should wash our hands.'

Mrs Bister fetched the saucepan. Malek collected cloths. I looked at Pol.

'Had we so enraged the gods,' I murmured, 'that, scorning our stolen flowers, they have made an autumn rose of my friend?' Martina looked at me. 'One of Mrs Bister's novels,' I said, plunging my hands into the sink. 'Now, let's get to work.'

13

THE TRUE NAKEDNESS OF A man lies not beneath his clothes, for under the dappled membrane of our skin, that lure for lovers and comfort of aunties, throbs a crimson charybdis of wet flesh. It is the dark underside of our prancing grace, the pumping secret of its outward poise. Doctors alone have the privilege to fiddle here. And the burden. For they know that the sweetest smile of our most beloved is twitched by glistening sinews over grey bone, and that, beyond even these indecent truths, lie truths more terrible. Believe me, there is nothing comely about a kidney, spleen or the unravelled tube of a reeking bowel. Although, fortunately, I didn't have to go quite that far with Pol.

A brutal shard of bone protruded from the torn mesh of his ragged thigh. One ankle hung loose. His arm was a crazy zig zag of random joints. Blood oozed in a steady flow from his head, some of it creeping out his ear, some of it from under his hair. I slipped slightly on the wet floor leaving a ribboned streak of red across the white glaze.

'What would you like me to do?' said Martina.

'Fetch my books,' I said.

'There's no time for that,' she said.

'Right,' I said emphatically, hoping that by saying something emphatic further words would follow. 'While there are concerns about his legs and legs are important for walking, walking is ultimately not as important as the things we need our heads for. Heads, in fact, are so important that without one the rest of it is really not much use at all. Therefore our first priority must be the head.'

'Should I clean it up?' said Cindy.

She was standing by the top of the bed, fondling Pol's hair. Mrs Bister was boiling some more water. Malek stood by the door, puffing nervously on a cigar.

'I think that would be a good idea,' said Martina looking at me.

'Yes,' I said. 'It certainly would be. And we need to get a drip up. You'll find various appliances associated with getting drips up in the cupboard over there.'

'Where it says "Drip Stuff Etcetera"?' asked Martina

'Quite so,' I said, my hands on my hips, chin slightly up, looking as Doctor-like as I could manage. 'Mr Bister, if you would like to go to my office, you will find therein a refrigerator. On the second shelf, behind various remedies for Hypertrichosis, Epidermodysplasia Verruciformis, Spasmodic Dysphonia and the like, are several bags marked "saline solution". These were purchased a little sceptically, I have to say, salt water being easy enough to prepare in one's kitchen, but perhaps the salesman's persuasion was not, in retrospect, entirely misplaced. Can you fetch those?'

Malek hurried out to a momentary wash of angry voices.

'They would seem to be arguing,' I said.

'That's a surprise,' said Martina.

Although the bleeding from Pol's head had been copious, it seemed that his cranium remained intact. Which was a relief. Split skulls are notoriously difficult to treat since the brains, once interfered with, are almost impossible to get back in the right order, even with the help of text-books. As it was, he had only gashed himself badly.

'Swabs,' I said. 'Preferably soaked in antiseptic solution.'

'Sure,' said Martina, fetching a handful and tipping some antiseptic over them.

'Thank you,' I said, rather formally, hoping she'd understand how the protocols of medicine sometimes over-rode the endearments of romance. I dabbed at the wounds in Pol's scalp. 'And we'll need suture materials. The blue cupboard, third drawer down.'

'Where it says "lunch"?' said Martina.

'Yes,' I said.

I had often practised my suture techniques on ripe tomatoes, just to pass the time when the clinic was quiet. The pharmaceutical rep had given me a little pamphlet on how to get the perfect stitch and, though my efforts were probably less than professional, many a torn tomato had looked much healthier as a result of my labours. Stitching Pol was little different. As the wounds closed with a gentle tug, I even thought how nice he would look in my sandwich. Which only goes to show how the mind, once habituated to a pattern of thought, repeats it for no other reason than that it does.

'Very good,' said Martina.

'Possibly my best tomato yet,' I said.

'Right,' she murmured.

Malek returned with the saline solution while Martina laid out a cannula and various tubes on the surgical table. With a little help from Mrs Bister, I wheeled the drip-pole to the bed and, in no time, had a bag hooked up to a line in Pol's arm. I couldn't help a momentary smile of satisfaction.

'Now for the tricky bit,' I said. 'We have to set his leg and plaster it. This will involve getting the plaster materials ready, which you will find in the store room along with a bowl for that purpose. I will also need someone to pull on his hips and another to hold him down while I ease his bones back into place.'

There are some procedures you cannot practise on a tomato. I'd read a book about plastering so at least I had something to go on, though I have to admit I'd been rather more drawn to the pictures than the text. There is something visually compelling about a broken limb grappled by confident hands. I only hoped that something of the book's bravado had rubbed off on me as I wrapped my fingers around Pol's ankle and pulled. In fact the bones were surprisingly easy to separate though getting them to fit back was more difficult, taking several attempts during which Pol began to fidget.

'He's in pain,' sobbed Cindy. 'My poor sweet poppadom.'

'Let's give him a little more Novocaine,' I said. 'In the refrigerator. And there are syringes on the medicine shelf.'

While Malek nipped off to fetch them, I fished a plaster-cloth from the water bowl, prepared by Mrs Bister, and spread it carefully across Pol's leg.

'Nice job,' said Martina.

'Thank you,' I said, slapping another cloth into place as best I could with Pol suddenly thrashing about.

'That Novocaine would be useful,' I said with an edge of urgency. Cindy stroked Pol's cheeks while Martina restrained him. Malek hurried back in, hands shaking as he handed over the equipment and lit a cigar. It was a quick matter to administer some further anaesthetic and, after a moment or two, Pol calmed down a little. 'Next, I must attend to his other leg which is severely marred by a number of alarming lacerations,' I said, professionally.

Fortunately the artery that runs along the inner thigh was undamaged, though much of the flesh around it had been ripped to shreds.

'This is more than I can stitch,' I said. 'And there is too much debris in it. I fear that he is already developing an infection. It is quite possible that he may lose the leg altogether.'

'Lose it?' said Cindy, eyes wide.

'Yes, though not in the ordinary sense of putting it down somewhere and forgetting where he left it. I mean in the clinical sense of surgical removal.'

'Oh my poppet,' said Cindy, stroking Pol's face.

'But this is not something that I can make a judgement on,' I said. 'I lack the X-ray facilities and the anaesthetics. A little Novocaine isn't enough for this sort of procedure. And we'd need blood, lots of it, for transfusion. We've never collected blood around here and frankly, I wouldn't like to try.'

'So what do you suggest?' said Martina.

'Well, the best thing would be to get him to a hospital.'

'But we don't have a hospital,' said Mrs Bister.

'Not here,' said Malek. 'But I believe there's a large one somewhere in the city. In fact, I'm sure of it. They have many departments for all sorts of complaints. In fact, so many it's a bugger, quite frankly, trying to find anywhere, it's ology this and ology that, and all you want is a little something for...' He stopped quite suddenly.

'Could we get him there?' said Martina, turning to me. 'And would he survive the journey?'

'I don't know,' I said. 'But he won't if we don't.'

'We can ask the Sergeant to drive us,' said Malek. 'He can use his siren. You know what it's like in these little villages along the way.'

'I'm not sure I do,' I said. 'I have only known Pushkara.'

'Well, it's not so different. As soon as they see a car coming they jump out waving things. But he's the law, and therefore entitled to mow them down with impunity.'

'Very well,' I said. 'Please ask him to be ready as soon as possible.'

Malek hurried out.

'Hold still,' said Martina.

'I beg your pardon?' I said.

'This is what nurses do, isn't it?' she said, dabbing my forehead with a cloth.

'Oh yes,' I said. 'Thank you.' But when I looked at her she was looking away.

Malek came back to announce that the Sergeant was outside with his lights already flashing, though he'd been asked to switch the siren off while the car was stationary. I stepped into the waiting room to clear a way for Pol only to find the villagers swarming in all directions, most of them shouting, with Dev running around evading their grasp as he jumped up and down waving the little picture of his face.

'Piles?' he was saying. 'Of what? Corns? Isn't that something you eat? Headaches? I can tell you about headaches. Don't come snivelling to me about headaches.' Some of the elders attempted to strike him, others grabbed at his shirt. 'That itch in your armpit, that lump on your neck, those persistent nose-bleeds; I'd just scrawl random letters on a piece of paper and hand it to Rabindra who thought the illegibility of any prescription was in direct proportion to its urgency. Oh, hello,' he said, seeing me at the door.

The room hushed as horrified eyes flickered across my chest.

'Pol Bister has lost a lot of blood,' I said. 'Some of which you can no doubt see on me. It is essential that we get him to a hospital as quickly as we can. So would you mind stepping aside, please, so we can pass through with the bed?'

An aisle parted to the outside door.

'You see?' said Dev. 'He's your man.'

Several people gasped as Malek and Mrs Bister wheeled the bed out, less perhaps at the sight of Pol than at the Bisters acting in unison.

'Excuse me,' whispered Malek. 'Broken son coming through.'

Mrs Bister stifled a sniff. Cindy held the drip.

'Nice and high,' I said.

My father was red-faced but silent. I wondered if I should nod to him but couldn't determine if he'd see that as sarcasm or the impertinence of one who doesn't know how to say 'good day Father' in an appropriate tone. So I did nothing as his head turned slowly to follow my exit.

The Sergeant saluted as we stepped into the street. Mike was leaning against the car, smoking. Hendrix looked up from the open boot.

'Any chance of a lift?' said Mike.

'I'm not sure,' I said. 'Pol has to lie down in the back, where Cindy and Mrs Bister will care for him while Martina sits in the front holding the drip.'

'I'll sit with Marty,' said Mike, dropping his cigarette and grinding it out with his toe. 'She won't mind.'

'But I don't think there's room for Hendrix and Sharon,' I said.

'That's okay,' said Hendrix. 'We're sticking around for a bit.'

'What about you?' said Malek.

'Me?' I said.

'You have to stay with him. He needs you.'

'But there is no room for me,' I said.

'You can take my place,' said Mrs Bister. 'I would rather a living son miles from home than a dead one on my lap.'

'I am not sure that I could help him any more than anyone else,' I said.

'Why don't you discuss it on the way?' said Malek. 'You will have plenty of time to reach a conclusion before you arrive at your destination.'

'Alright, let's go,' said Martina, clapping her hands. 'In the car. Come on.'

Cindy squeezed my knee as I sat beside her. Malek and Hendrix carefully lifted Pol across our laps. I squeezed Martina's knee, in the English manner, as she sat down, making her jump slightly. Mike climbed into the front and nodded to Hendrix.

'I'll miss you,' he said.

'How?' said Hendrix. 'You don't have feelings.'

'I'll feel that I ought to miss you,' said Mike, with a shrug. 'Best I can do.'

Cindy reached out to squeeze Hendrix's hand. 'See ya,' she said. 'Oh, and tell Sharon she's a beat in the heart of a dancer.'

'I think she knows,' said Hendrix, smiling. 'Well, Robby, I guess this is it.'

'Is what?' I said.

'What you wanted. The open road. New life.'

'But that was only a dream,' I said, feeling suddenly nervous.

'Maybe it is,' said Hendrix, enigmatically. 'Maybe that's all it is.'

'Indeed,' said Mr Chatterjee who had managed to push through to the police car. 'This is a view confirmed by many theologians. The phenomenal world is apprehensible only within the realm of interpretation, which is to say the mind. Therefore what we experience is, in effect, a dream. The reality itself is indefinable just as the dream figure can never know the dreamer, even though without the dreamer no dream figure could exist.'

'And that's without dope,' said Hendrix. 'But listen kid, maybe we'll meet up some day. London, Berlin, wherever. Just listen out for the noise. I'm usually there, cranking it up.'

'What are you suggesting?' said Mrs Dak, groping forward. 'Does Rabindra propose not to come back? His father would never allow it.'

'I guess that don't matter too much if he ain't coming back,' said Hendrix.

'But what of us?' said Mr Dak. 'Who will run the clinic now that your brother has been exposed as a charlatan?'

'Best get going,' said Hendrix, tapping the side of the car.

'We can start?' said Sergeant Shrinivasan.

'Hit the gas,' said Mike. 'No, not the siren, the gas.'

But the Sergeant couldn't hear anything now and neither could we. The mouths of various villagers moved soundlessly at me. They seem to be anxious, I thought, some of them clawing at the car, most of them wide-eyed. Perhaps I could have prescribed some of that fish-phobia remedy, so efficacious with Hendrix and the mango-seller, but it was too late. I craned my head to see those who could manage it chasing after us. Father had emerged from the clinic, wringing the perspiration from his wig. Mr Chatterjee was talking to Mr Dak, gesticulating elaborately to convey, I presumed, some metaphysical nicety. Mr Dak's eyes had already glazed over.

In just a few moments we had passed the bus-stop and the last of the houses. From there the road spun sharply down to a bend beyond which I had never seen. Martina glanced at me and said something inaudible. Then she shrugged, smiled and looked back out the window.

It is different, I thought. As I knew it would be. The trees are different, the stones are different, even the air has a different taste. And the further we drove the more different it got. There is nothing inherently wrong with difference, of course. It's just a bit scary if you're not used to it.

Some of the villages we passed through were familiar as names. Our teacher had always been strict on geography, making us recite the key places of the world every Monday morning. 'You cannot know where you are, if you do not know where you are not,' he used to say. 'Pushkara. Nearby villages. Distant villages. Everywhere else,' he'd chant, picking them out from the vast map that covered much of the back wall.

'That map in the school room,' Dev had scoffed one evening after I'd confided my plan to walk to America, 'is ridiculous. Have you ever looked at it? Where it says, "Copyright Calcutta Museum of Antiquities. Pre-Jurassic Cartographical Representation of the Globe"?' Later on I'd found a more recent map and decided to walk to Australia instead.

Although the Sergeant's siren made conversation impractical, it at least ensured us uninterrupted passage through the numerous hamlets and villages that ribboned the mountain road. Cats, dogs and chickens would scatter in all directions, adults grabbing children to drag them to safety. The Sergeant would salute them as we passed and I thought it only polite to smile apologetically. Cindy took to waving her hand in a curious sawing motion until Martina said, 'Cut it out, Cin.'

Pol stirred a few times, usually when the Sergeant hit a pot-hole, or swerved to avoid a cow. Cindy would stroke his head while I checked his pulse. Once or twice he moaned pitifully. While there wasn't much I could do for him in the back of the police car, I felt I ought to be alert, at least, to his needs.

But the constant shriek of the siren and the interminable shuddering of the vehicle began to make my eyes heavy.

'You should take a rest,' said Martina. 'I'll wake you if anything happens.'

'It's alright,' I said. 'A doctor on duty never falls...'

I woke with a jolt. Something was wrong but it took me a moment to work out what. We had been travelling for some distance without going up or down. In Pushkara, all roads eventually lurched or plunged one way or the other. But this did neither. I blinked my eyes to see, on either side of us, nothing. Not a hill, or a mountain, not a shack, goat or clump of trees, just desolate plains rolling on to a distant haze beyond which, I assumed, was only more nothing.

Martina had also fallen asleep, her head resting on my shoulder. The drip was hooked up to a hand-hold over the door. Pol was quiet but alive. Sergeant Shrinivasan was nodding his head in time to the siren.

'The mountains,' I said. 'They've gone.'

'Not gone,' said Cindy. 'They're behind us.'

I managed to turn my head without dislodging Martina, but could see only a thin streak of grey across the level blandness of a dull horizon.

'Without mountains,' I said, 'my soul has no limits.'

'Pol talks like that,' she said, stroking his hand.

'But without limits it has no form, without form no substance, and without substance it is nothing.'

'And?'

'Therefore I am nothing.'

She pinched my leg.

'Ouch,' I said.

'There. You couldn't say that if you weren't something.'

I had to admit that I was possibly over-thinking, as

usual. But the sky felt wrong without peaks to poke it, the horizon naked without the skirts of a mountain to preserve its modesty. To where, I wondered, do the eagles fly? From where does the rain fall? Without snow, how can there be streams of sparkling water, ice cold in the sultry stillness of a summer's day? With every mile of nothing my heart sank a little lower. And then we hit the town.

Martina stirred, sat up and wiped her mouth. 'Sorry,' she said.

'Not at all,' I murmured.

'Looks like we're nearly there,' she said. 'Do we know where the hospital is?'

'Pardon?' said Sergeant Shrinivasan.

'Do we know where the hospital is?' she shouted.

'Huh?' said the Sergeant.

As if from a swamp or some hidden schism in the folds of circumstance, the city had risen from nowhere to envelope us. Shambling bungalows jostled with gated mansions, mouldering shacks clustered round vast edifices staring back from a hundred windows. Bustling shops, markets, and go-downs slipped by in a dizzying stream; not just one sari seller, or two sari sellers glaring at each other from across the road, but shop after shop, parade after parade, each as busy as the next.

The Sergeant was veering wildly now as cars, cows, scooters, auto-rickshaws, cycle-rickshaws and suicidal pedestrians threw themselves at our wheels. I had never seen so many people. I hadn't known so many existed. Wherever I looked I saw more in a single gaze than I'd beheld in my whole life, and all of them striding, shoving, shouting. Even with the siren we hardly drew a second glance.

'The city,' I said, 'is so busy.'

'This is nothing,' said Cindy. 'You wait 'til we get inside.'

'Then where is this, if it is not inside?'

'The "burbs,"' she said. 'The further you go, the crazier it gets.'

By the time the Sergeant pulled up under a sign saying, 'No Parking Under Any Circumstances', I was numb to the complexities of existence. Several times we had careened around the same roundabout, its myriad streams spinning us in circles as bicycles, taxis, dogs, cows and people, seemingly reconciled to the brevity of their existence, hurtled around each other in a random choreography of shouts and waving fists.

'I can park where I bloody well like,' the Sergeant was saying to someone dressed like him but without the medals. 'So hop it, sharpish, or I shall thwack you with my stick.'

I clambered out after Martina to see that we'd stopped in front of a double door marked, 'Accident and Emergency'.

'As you can see from my regalia,' continued the Sergeant, 'I am a fully augmented Sergeant of the First Rank, while you are a lowly constable, fortunately proximate to a number of head and fracture specialists whose services you are imminently in need of unless you desist from haranguing me over these petty regulations about parking and noise.'

'Excuse me,' I said to the constable. 'As you can see from this leg sticking out of the window, we have an extremely sick patient here in urgent need of medical attention. Could you please go inside and find someone to help us?'

The constable looked at the blood over my clothes and saluted, turning briskly through the doors.

'These municipal police!' spat the Sergeant. 'They have no respect. In Pushkara my constables wouldn't argue with me. They jump to attention when I speak. Why, sometimes they even stop breathing in my presence if only to hear me the better which has resulted, on more than one occasion in the need to administer revival tactics after collapse due to awe-induced asphyxiation.'

'You don't have any constables,' said Cindy.

'But if I had, they would,' replied the Sergeant archly. 'It takes more than a waxed moustache to make a policeman,' he added, shaking his head. 'I'll bet he doesn't even play a musical instrument.'

With Cindy and Martina's help, I carefully eased Pol from the back seat as Mike climbed out, stretching his neck, and the Sergeant leaned against the car, pulling a packet of bidis from his top pocket.

'I don't mind you having a rest,' said Cindy to Sergeant Shrinivasan. 'God knows, you deserve it, but would you mind turning the siren off?'

'Pardon?' said the Sergeant.

The constable, meanwhile, had returned with a man in a white coat, two ladies in blue dresses and a porter with a trolley.

'What happened?' said the man.

'He fell,' I said. 'And he's lost a lot of blood.'

'So what's he had?' said the man taking a quick look at Pol's leg as we laid him across the trolley. 'Are you his Doctor?'

'Yes,' said Martina. 'He is.'

'So what's he had?'

'Ah, Novocaine,' I said. 'And saline solution.'

'And you set his leg?'

'I'm sorry, I thought that was the right thing to do.'

'Now, now,' said the man, smiling. 'I'm just asking. Dr Gupta, by the way.' He offered me his hand which I shook. 'And you're Doctor...'

'Sharma,' said Martina.

'Nice to meet you. Okay, let's get him in. Who's got the drip?'

'I have,' said Martina.

'And you are...?'

'Just a friend.'

Inside, the wheels of the trolley squealed across the waxy floor like a rhythmic mouse. People in white coats or blue dresses moved confidently among nervous people clothed in any old thing, looking lost. The air hummed with murmurs, pattering feet and a thousand doors creaking open and shut.

'So where's he from?' said Dr Gupta.

'Pushkara,' I said.

'Where's that?'

'It's sort of that way,' I said, gesturing, though to be honest the roundabouts had left me confused. 'Along the main road, back to the hills.'

'Oh, I know, near Bradinashwaya. I've got a cousin there.'

'No, no,' I said. 'Much further. Right at the top where the mountains begin.'

'I didn't think there was anything up there,' he said. 'Is that where you work?'

'It is,' I said.

With an abrupt turn, the trolley clattered through a set of doors into what looked like an operating theatre. Two more ladies took the ends of the trolley and positioned it beside a bed. A silver-haired gentleman glanced round from the sink.

'Transfer him please,' he said. 'I'm glad to see saline. Let's call for some more. And I want bloods cross-matched. Quickly does it.'

One of the nurses prepared a syringe. The silver-haired gentleman walked over to Pol. 'Can we get the temporary plaster off, please?'

Two of the nurses fetched scissors and a bowl while he picked gingerly at my handywork.

'Who stitched his head?' he said.

'Dr Sharma,' said Dr Gupta, indicating me.

'Nice work, Dr Sharma.'

'This is Mr Shankar,' said Dr Gupta, quietly.

'Right,' said Mr Shankar deploying, I noticed, my own rhetorical device but with presumably less need. 'Clinical staff only. Friends and relatives outside. There's a nice little room you can use. Nurse Sujatee will show you the way. May I ask what the patient's name is?'

'Pol Bister,' said Cindy.

'Thank you,' said Mr Shankar. 'We'll let you know how he gets on. Now, let's have those bloods, please. Not you, Dr Sharma.'

I stopped at the door.

'I need a full history. And I'm sure you'd like to see how your patient shapes up. No?'

'Yes,' I said, glancing at Martina who nodded to me.

'Excuse me,' said Cindy. 'Can I ask…?'

'What his chances are?' said Mr Shankar. 'I don't believe in beating about the bush, so I'll be straight with you. I don't know. At this moment I'd say his chances aren't high. But a chance is a chance. As I said, we'll let you know.'

Cindy bit her lip and left.

While Mr Shankar, Dr Gupta and the various nurses fussed over Pol, I began to tell Mr Shankar everything I could about the cause of his injuries.

'We can skip the marigolds and butter,' said Mr Shankar. 'I just need to know how far he fell and onto what.'

It seemed like hours later, and probably was, that I stumbled back into the teeming concourse of the corridor. Mr Shankar, remarking on my pallor, had prescribed what he called a 'steaming mug of Doctor's tea', and asked Doctor Gupta to direct me to the staff canteen. When I said I'd rather see my friends, he smiled and said, 'Visitors Room. First stairs on the left, one flight up, through the door, turn right, it's third on the left, you can't miss it.' I wished I had Hendrix to help me but Mr Shankar said to follow the signs and ask if I got lost.

I found the stairs easily enough, lifting up through the building's many floors, each a bustling labyrinth of pain, despair and finality, its steps worn smooth by the solemn tread of heavy hearts. How many hands, I wondered, had gripped these banisters, and how much hope had tumbled down its spiralling river of stones? I stopped on the first landing. Tall windows, smeared with dust, refracted the day's hazy sun, while pigeons on a ledge outside cooed and strutted over the grey-white landscape of their other principal activity. Beyond were more buildings, more windows. I closed my eyes, listening to the horns and engines, voices and radios that tumbled up from the streets below.

I remembered the quiet glade, Pol sweeping a lazy hand through its cool waters, twisting the surface into swirling clouds of mud. And thus, I thought, is humanity swept by the hand of some great Pol, spinning helplessly in the eddies of his mischief, thinking all the while it is they that move.

'Is everything alright, Doctor?'

A nurse had stopped, one foot on the next step.

'I'm sorry?' I said.

'Are you alright?'

'Yes, thank you,' I said. 'I was just contemplating the hand that stirs all this into motion.'

'You've had a bad one?' she said, indicating blood on the white coat that Mr Shankar had ordered me to be issued with.

A nurse had helped me on with it while Mr Shankar glanced over and nodded.

'It wasn't easy,' I shrugged.

She smiled gently and moved on.

As promised, the door to the Visitor's Room was labelled 'Visitor's Room', along with 'No Spitting', 'Please Use The Toilet Facilities For Ablutionary Purposes' and 'No Begging At Any Time'.

Cindy jumped to her feet when I came in. Martina looked up warily.

'He will live,' I said.

'Oh, Robby!' said Cindy, hugging me. 'Thank you, thank you so much.'

I tried to speak but couldn't get the requisite air. Eventually I managed to say, 'Please, it wasn't me but the dedicated skill of a certain Mr Shankar along with his excellent team of clinical practitioners.'

'But you got him here,' she said, renewing the clench. 'And if you hadn't, oh, Robbie, he'd be dead.'

'What about the leg?' asked Martina.

'He might limp for a while,' I said, attempting to re-inflate my lungs. 'Possibly always. But it remains attached.'

'He can limp all he likes,' laughed Cindy, 'as long as we can dance together to the edge of time. Can I see him?'

'Yes,' I said. 'I think that will be alright. Where's Mike and the Sergeant?'

'That's something we have to talk about,' said Martina, standing up.

Cindy glanced at Martina with a quick signal of complicity. 'I'll catch you later,' she said, giving me a last little squeeze.

'You know where he is?' I gasped.

'Of course.'

'Sit down,' said Martina closing the door. 'You and I need to have a chat.'

I sat down. Martina paced the room a couple of times then took a breath. 'Mike's gone to the airport to sort out flights,' she said. 'He made some calls and apparently there's one tonight.'

My heart, possessed of a sudden gravity, sank to the floor, through the lino, and down to the next, tumbling onwards from room to room, slipping quietly past some grisly procedure, some weeping wife, and further still to the dingy basement with its groaning pipes, resting finally at the very centre of our spinning globe where all is iron and fire.

'If you want you can come with us,' she said.

I looked at her.

'There's immigration issues, obviously, so we'll have to see. I don't suppose you've got a passport?'

'Passport?'

'I'm sure we could sort something. I don't know. But I'll wait for you if you want to come. Of course we'll have to get married. They won't let you in otherwise. The Sergeant said he could find someone to do that. We've got the money. I don't think that's going to be a problem.'

'You will marry me?'

'Why not?' she shrugged.

'And this means you love me?'

'You seemed to think so,' she said.

'There were some indications to the contrary.'

'You asked for that,' she chuckled. 'Look, I've known a lot of men. You know what I mean. But I don't think anyone's ever known me. Or even wanted to. The whole me. They just want a bit of it. A picture. But a picture fades. And pages turn. And sooner or later you close the cover. But I've never met anyone who'd do anything for me. Who'd carry his friend for miles, and find the strength he didn't know he had to do wonderful things. Who'd find it in my eyes. Whatever's there. Something. I don't know. I'm not sure you know me at all. And I'm pretty sure I don't know you. But somehow I'm getting to know myself a little bit better. And I never thought I could do that.'

'You are a goddess,' I said.

'Don't say that. I'll only disappoint you.'

'But only a goddess has that power in her eyes.'

'Well,' she looked away for a moment. 'Nobody's ever said that and meant it the way you do.'

I stood up and walked to the window. The hand that moves all this had given me my wish.

'It won't be easy,' she said. 'And I don't think England's what you think it is. I mean, it's great sometimes. The Autumn. Kicking leaves. Frosty mornings. And Spring. Like you'd forgotten what green was. We could find a place. Maybe quiet, maybe not. The cities are big. Not half so busy but they're big. We could find a mountain but we don't have mountains like you do.'

'I miss them already,' I said.

'You'll miss a lot of things,' she said, softly. 'Most people I know just want to get away from where they are. But you can only ever be where you are. So you spend your whole life dreaming of somewhere that isn't anywhere, and I guess, if you're not careful, you can end up nowhere.'

'I felt this today when I saw no mountains.'

She smiled a little.

'And so many strangers,' I said.

'The world's full of them,' she said. 'Everywhere you look. People who don't see you. People who don't care.'

'I don't think they care for me in Pushkara.'

'They do. They just don't know it. Perhaps they do now. You saw them crying when you left. And didn't one of them jump on the bonnet?'

'I think he was trying to sell us a wooden snake.'

'Who's going to sort out their aches and pains and give them little pills to keep them quiet? Who's your father going to shout at?'

'I think deep down he is only shouting at himself,' I said.

'He's got some issues, that's for sure. You should talk to him.'

'How can one talk to him?'

'Then shout at him,' she said. 'I think you need to shout. At him. At anything. Shout at me.'

'I could never do that.'

'Then it won't be much of a marriage.'

But I could see that she was teasing me now.

'Rabindra,' she said. 'When you came into the room just now there was something in your eyes I hadn't seen before.'

'I was pleased about Pol.'

'It wasn't just that. Think about it.'

I thought about it.

'I met someone,' I said. 'On the stairs. A nurse.'

Martina smiled.

'And for some reason I cannot get her out of my head.' I walked over to the window. The world seemed so very large, suddenly, with so many rooms and corners and corridors and stairs that you could turn up or down, or not, or stop, or not, or never take, or take looking down or up, and so many people among whom was the one whose eyes now haunted me.

'And what matters,' said Martina, 'even more than seeing

her again is that she's there. Somewhere. You know that. And you didn't have to burn butter or whatever it is you did for me. She came because she did. And you don't need her for anything. She's what she is and who she is and that's enough. And it doesn't matter where you are or where you live, you'll always have that.'

'But it also hurts,' I said. 'In a slightly wonderful way.'

'Of course. Because, in another way, the only thing you can ever do now is find her again.'

'This is not contradictory?'

'Did I say I was an expert?'

The airport was even more bewildering than the city, with its glittering lights, jostling trolleys, and aeroplanes screaming overhead. I hadn't realised how big those frail beads, trailing feathers across the pale skies, were as they stood on the ground, panting with impatience, waiting to fly. The terminal, teeming with families, businessmen, and suitcases, echoed with the cacophony of a thousand voices. And, as I quickly discovered, you couldn't stand still without somebody elbowing you aside and cursing as they hurried off.

Mike was looking more comfortable than I'd ever seen him as he walked through a door marked 'Departures'. He glanced round to smile but was interrupted by an official telling him to put his cigarette out. Martina turned from the man who studied her passport, more closely than I thought necessary, to give me a sad, sweet smile that I wear in my heart to this day. I noticed that even the Sergeant had red eyes, though his chest stood out, its glistening medals gilding him with stoic dignity. The last I saw of Martina was the hem of her skirt as it swung round the corner, and the briefest flash of tanned ankle, perfect in form and movement, before she was gone.

The drive back was conducted without the siren though Sergeant Shrinivasan had argued its need for several miles. I was surprised to prevail in my views and wondered at the new deference he was showing towards me. Perhaps it had something to do with the badge presented to me by Mr Shankar before we left.

'You did a splendid job,' he had said. 'Quite superb. I wish my students could stitch like that, never mind plaster so beautifully. But you kept him alive, that's the thing. In spite of the odds. Frankly, I'd say it was little short of miraculous.'

'Only miraculous,' I'd said, 'in that I could recall a few rudimentary procedures from the medical dictionary.'

'There's plenty of Doctors who can do that,' he had replied. 'Too many if you ask me. If it's not in the book, they haven't a clue. But there's a few, just a few, mind, who've got that extra something. People feel better when they should be getting worse. People live when they might have died. Wounds heal when the book says they shouldn't. It's not what you know, it's what you are. And I think that's you. And that's worth incalculably more than all the clinical drones who've read every book backwards.'

'Perhaps they should try reading forwards,' I suggested.

He smiled. 'Look, I know what it's like in these places, these hillstations or what have you. Precious few medics, if any. And you can't send people away to study. So the right man steps up. Which is how it used to be. Never mind these gadgets and gizmos. Medicine men. That's how it started. With just the few. The few that have it. In recognition of which, if you would allow us, there's something we'd like to give you.'

He nodded to a little group of Doctors and nurses who shuffled aside to reveal the nurse I'd met on the stairs.

'Nurse Devi?' said Mr Shankar. 'If you would.'

'Devi?' I said. 'A goddess?'

'She is indeed,' said Mr Shankar.

Nurse Devi held out a small plastic badge with a safety pin through the back.

'This is for you,' she said. 'Please. Take it.'

As I did so, my fingers brushed hers. She blushed.

'You should wear this when you're working,' said Mr Shankar. 'Well, if you like. It's up to you. It's just a bit of protocol, I suppose, but there's a place for that in this peculiar profession of ours. And, of course, should any future business bring you here.'

He patted me on the shoulder, smiled and walked off followed by Doctor Gupta and the nurses.

The badge read, 'Rabindranath Sharma, Associate Physician, University Hospital'.

'Nurse?' said Mr Shankar, stopping at the door. Nurse Devi had remained by the trolley.

'Just a moment?' she said.

'Of course.'

She looked at me. 'Where did you say you were from?' she said, blushing again.

'Pushkara,' I said.

'Where's that?'

'In the mountains.'

'I love the mountains.'

'You know them?'

'No. But if I did I'm sure I'd love them.'

'You should visit us,' I said.

She smiled suddenly. 'I just might.' Then she turned, following Mr Shankar into the busy corridor, and was lost from sight.

I'm not sure that the mountains welcomed me back. As I've said, I'm not sure they do anything. But they were beautiful and magnificent and I was glad to see them again.

Pol and Cindy came up to say goodbye a few months later. The new Memorial Hall wasn't completed, in fact it hadn't even been started, so we held part of their wedding in the Nirvana Hotel and the rest of it under the Rock. Although some priests officiated according to procedure, the final blessing was delivered by Sharon with all the powers that, so far as we were concerned, she now embodied.

I managed to spend a little time with Pol, though we couldn't skip up to the caves for obvious reasons. We sat under the bodhi tree instead, watching the world go by, or at least the little bit of it we had always known.

'I'm glad you weren't a fiend,' he said.

'Perhaps I was, in some ways,' I replied.

'You know,' he said thoughtfully, 'the Turtle's just what we think about ourselves.'

Which I pondered for a long time, concluding eventually that you don't have to fall off a rock to become wise but it helps. I also managed to put a question to Cindy which had bothered me for some time. Was Martina serious about marrying me or had she only said that to make me think? Cindy fingered the curls around her ear for a moment. 'With Marty,' she said at last, 'you never know.'

The farewell had everyone in tears. Malek and Mrs Bister were speechless for once, smiling with pride at their handsome son and his beautiful bride. That he was to live in England was a piquant joy, for they were happy in his dream come true, but sad not to be more of a part of it. Children scattered flowers behind the bus as Pol and Cindy leaned out of the window waving.

When the Memorial Hall was finished, finally, there was much debate over what to call it. Malek no longer insisted that it bear his name, though he commissioned a bust of himself for the lobby. In the end I suggested we call it 'The Pushkara Official Leisure Centre' or 'The P.O.L. Centre' for short. This was both satisfactory to the Bisters, who delighted in the memory of their son, and acceptable to the elders who didn't register its significance for years.

A small part of the man with a cravat's money went towards the purchase of a beautiful new Rudra Veena for Sergeant Shrinivasan to play once a month to packed houses. That he was merely accompanying a dance recital performed, in person, by the Lord Shiva herself might have contributed to the popularity of these events. Some of the elders grumbled that she removed a little too much clothing at times but, after some discussion, it was decided that as she was a god no impropriety had occurred. Gods and goddesses can happily go naked where ordinary mortals would cause embarrassment. Although Sharon never went quite that far, she did remove enough to attract an audience of younger men whose passion for matters metaphysical grew to an enthusiasm bordering on frenzy.

My brother Dev, who wasn't really a Doctor and had never been to England, suggested we rename our place of work the 'Rabindranath Sharma Associate Physician Centre' but I said its existing name was more than adequate. He researched less and smiled more and seemed to take pleasure in opening the Pushkara Clinic every morning, standing at its threshold to greet the first patients who hurried in coughing, limping or scratching indecorously at some bodily adjunct. As Senior Porter, he provided valuable service though mostly I was just glad of his smile. At the end of the day, after we'd mopped the floors and scrubbed the instruments, he would regale me with stories of Madras as we walked home; his adventures, friends and the pretty nurses he had known.

Father remained rather quiet, spending many hours in the *Puja* Room talking to Mother. He took to eating without complaint, or at least complaints offered merely as suggestions. Both my sisters married the Buddhist Cook which caused a bit of a stir, although Mrs Dong assured us that it was perfectly proper according to the cultural protocols to which she subscribed. I was never entirely convinced by that, but they all seemed happy enough.

Although everyone enjoyed having Hendrix around, it was obvious after a few months that he was getting restless. He told me one evening that he'd known some dives in his day but nothing had prepared him for life in a cave. We were coming back from one of Mr Chatterjee's public discourses with the sacred tree. Hendrix had sighed and said that you haven't lived 'til you'd lived with a goddess but he 'kinda missed the rock and roll. He said he'd visit again, obviously, and we hugged. He also said, 'you guys need to keep quiet about that black goo down in the valley'.

'Why?' I had said.

'Trust me,' he said, patting my shoulder. 'I'm a roadie.'

Otherwise, everything in Pushkara was much the same as it had been and, I suppose, would always be. The elders grumbled about the youth of today as the youth of today became the elders of tomorrow and grumbled in their turn. Many Sharons were born in those years, several Mike's and even a couple of Hendrixes. Cravats, meanwhile, in spite of numerous promotions at Bister's Boutique, sometimes undercut by Sergeant Shrinivasan, failed to catch on. Mahadev, though more Dev than Maha to me, was still the greatest of all gods, at least to the young ladies who swooned in his presence. Brahma's shoes were as speckled as ever, while Rama's cigarette stall remained a popular gathering point. Saraswati continued to move the dust around with her bundle of twigs, while Lakshmi made hats, and Indra sold tea from the streets of Pushkara to every deity under the sun. As for me, perhaps I was that sun. Hendrix had once said, 'Nobody looks at the sun, cause it burns their eyes. But without the sun, nobody sees nothing. So, blaze on baby.' Which I suppose, in my humble way, I do.

And of Nurse Devi who had smiled at me on the stairs and blushed when our hands touched? Well, that's another story.

OTHER TITLES YOU MAY ENJOY

JITTERBUG PERFUME

Tom Robbins

'One of the wildest and most entertaining novelists in the world'
— *The Financial Times*

Jitterbug Perfume is an epic. Which is to say, it begins in the forests of ancient Bohemia and doesn't conclude until nine o'clock tonight [Paris time]. It is a saga, as well. A saga must have a hero, and the hero of this one is a janitor with a missing bottle. The bottle is blue, very, very old, and embossed with the image of a goat-horned god. If the liquid in the bottle is actually the secret essence of the universe, as some folks seem to think, it had better be discovered soon because it is leaking and there is only a drop of two left.

978-1-84243-035-4
£12.99
noexit.co.uk/jitterbugperfume

LAST BUS TO COFFEEVILLE

J. Paul Henderson

World Book Night 2016 title
Longlisted for the 2016 International Dublin Literary Award

Nancy Skidmore has Alzheimer's and her oldest friend Eugene Chaney III has once more a purpose in life – to end hers.

When the moment for Gene to take Nancy to her desired death in Coffeeville arrives, she is unexpectedly admitted to the secure unit of a nursing home and he has to call upon his two remaining friends to help break her out: one his godson, a disgraced weatherman in the throes of a midlife crisis, and the other an ex-army marksman officially dead for forty years.

On a tour bus once stolen from Paul McCartney, and joined by a young orphan boy searching for lost family, the band of misfits career towards Mississippi through a landscape of war, euthanasia, communism, religion and racism, and along the way discover the true meaning of love, family and – most important of all – friendship.

Charming, uplifting and profoundly moving, *Last Bus to Coffeeville* is a chronicle of lives that have jumped the tracks; a tale of endings and new beginnings; a funny story about sad things.

978-184344-265-3
£8.99
noexit.co.uk/lastbustocoffeeville

About Us

In addition to No Exit Press, Oldcastle Books has a number of other imprints, including Kamera Books, Creative Essentials, Pulp! The Classics, Pocket Essentials and High Stakes Publishing > oldcastlebooks.com

For more information about Crime Books go to > crimetime.co.uk

Check out the kamera film salon for independent, arthouse and world cinema > kamera.co.uk

For more information, media enquiries and review copies please contact > marketing@oldcastlebooks.com